"Nothing feels real."

Ford squeezed her tight against his chest. "I'm real. This is real." His lips pressed into her hair in a soft kiss.

She held on tighter, not ready to let him go and stand on her own. She needed him to remind her that there were good things in this world. Amazing things like the flush of warmth that swept through her body. The tingle of awareness and need that grew as her breasts crushed against his hard chest and his corded thighs pressed against hers.

He brushed his hands over her head. She managed to suck in a ragged breath and look up and into his sad and reverent hazel eyes.

"Ford. Hold on to me."

He granted her wish and wrapped his arms tight around her again, his hands clamped onto her sides, crushing her to his chest. It felt so good. So right. So familiar. Like home.

By Jennifer Ryan

HIS COWBOY HEART

A MONTANA MEN NOVEL

JENNIFER RYAN

AVONBOOKS

An Imprint of HarperCollinsPublishers

Excerpt from *Escape to Hope Ranch* copyright © 2017 by Jennifer Ryan.

First Avon Books mass market printing: March 2017

ISBN 978-0-06-243540-8

17 18 19 20 21 QGM 10 9 8 7 6 5 4 3 2 1

There are people we don't want to live without but have to let go. We hope love will bring them back. Sometimes, if we're lucky, it does.

"Love is too precious to waste, too good to let go, and too wonderful not to enjoy."

Grandpa Sammy

HIS COWBOY HEART

PROLOGUE

Eleven years ago . . .

Ford stared down at his listless grandfather in the hospital bed, trying to hold back the tears stinging his eyes. Granddad's pale face and sunken cheeks warned of his tenuous health. They didn't know what was wrong, only that he'd collapsed in the house and lay motionless on the floor for God knew how long before Ford walked in and found him several days ago.

The same fear and crushing pressure squeezed his chest tight just thinking about it.

He and his brothers, Rory and Colt, had been taking turns staying by his side since the doctors admitted him to the hospital. Ford needed to get back to the ranch to cover for Colt so he could have his turn.

"He's going to be fine," the nurse assured him. "The doctors said it's the concussion from hitting his head on the floor that's the worst of his ailments. They're working to get his blood pressure down and to make sure there isn't anything else wrong with his head or heart."

"When do we get the results of the echocardiogram and MRI?" Ford asked.

"The doctor should know in a couple of hours," the nurse answered, touching his arm in comfort before she left the room to check on another patient.

He didn't feel any better for it and worried more about what the results might tell them. He and his brothers feared the worst and didn't want to admit that this brought the death of their parents too close to the surface. If they lost their grandfather and the failing ranch, what would they have left?

"It's not your time to go." He patted his granddad's leg. With his heart in his throat, Ford left the room, hoping he got to see his grandfather again.

He drove home without remembering the drive at all, his thoughts on family, the ranch, and the decisions he had to make.

Some decisions had been made for him by circumstances and family obligations and love.

Jamie sat on the tailgate of her brother's truck, sun-kissed legs swinging her tiny feet back and forth. Her face lit up when she spotted him pulling into the yard. She hopped off the end of the truck and ran to him. His heart did that funny flutter thing it did every time he saw her.

Ford slipped out of his truck and stood before the most beautiful girl in the world, her golden-red hair luminous in the sunlight, soft green eyes squinting against the harsh light beating on her pale skin. He desperately wanted to hold on to her, but knew he had no choice but to break her heart. They stood in the middle of the yard on his family's ranch, horses roaming in the pastures, his brothers out chasing stray cattle they couldn't afford to lose past the river. His gut tied into knots of worry about his hospitalized grand-father, sagging cattle prices, and what it all meant for his future with Jamie.

They didn't have one.

The ache in his chest throbbed.

God, how he'd miss her pretty smile that lit up his world.

Her head tilted in that cute way it did when she studied him too closely and saw too much. "What's wrong?"

I miss you already.

Deflecting, he asked, "What are you doing here?"

"Escaping."

He read the hurt in her eyes too easily. "What did she do this time?"

"Same thing, different day." Jamie huffed out an expressive sigh. "She's impossible. And delusional. She accused me of throwing myself at my stepdad. Again." Jamie's lips scrunched into a sour pinch at the distasteful thought.

Her mother read into simple, innocent interactions with a twisted jealous eye, heart, and mind that had no basis on Jamie's part or whatever guy was in the picture before Jamie's mother drove him away. According to Jamie, it started when she was eleven after her real father left her mother for a much younger woman, never to be heard from or seen again.

"She kicked me out. Shoved me out the front door more accurately." Jamie pulled up her sleeve and showed him the red marks on her arm.

Things were getting worse if her mother was putting her hands on Jamie. Though she wished for her family to be loving and close, it would never be. Jamie had been left to her own devices practically her whole life and done well in school and taking care of her little brother.

She'd taken care of him for more than a year. No one cared about him the way Jamie did.

She only knew how to pull it together and forge on-ward even when her choices were limited and none of them particularly good. He liked the way she made the best out of everything.

"I think she actually meant it when she said, 'Don't come back.' " Fear and anger darkened her eyes.

He wanted to comfort her, but didn't because he was about to hurt her far worse than her mother ever had with her warped taunts, accusations, and empty threats. Some women weren't meant to be mothers. Too selfish and self-centered.

Jamie was sweet, kind, and sensitive. Her mother's disapproval sliced away at Jamie. One cut stung. A thousand made you bleed and ache and wish for it to end.

She needed it to end. Now. Before it made her as angry and bitter as her mother.

He didn't want that for her. Jamie didn't deserve such poor treatment. He wanted her to be happy. Always. He wanted to be the reason she was happy.

Never going to happen now.

He tried to keep her away from her mother as much as possible. He drove her into town and home from her job at the day care center. One less thing to ask of her mother. One less thing for her mother to use against her and demand she be grateful.

Jamie loved the job, playing with the children and rocking babies. Nothing made her happier than sharing all the love in her heart with those kids. She lavished that love on him, too.

She squirreled away her paychecks. She dreamed of leaving her mother's house and living the life she wanted—a life with a bright future without the storm cloud of her mother's negativity darkening her world.

A life that wouldn't include him. Damn, it hurt like hell. Deeper than the ache in his chest, it ripped a searing path to his soul.

He wanted to beg her to stay here, give up everything she wanted, but he couldn't do it and watch her happiness shrivel and die along with the love she felt for him.

Some things could only be fixed by doing the hard thing, even if it wasn't what you wanted to do.

She pressed her palm to his chest. "Let's do it, Ford. Let's leave this place behind and buy that house with the wraparound porch on the ranch you want. You'll run the cattle. I'll help you with the horses. We'll raise our own family." She smiled sweetly, no doubt thinking of the kids they'd never have now. "I'll plant a garden just like your mother and my grandmother did when we were kids. We'll pick tomatoes and zucchini, cook them up, and eat together on the porch and watch the sun set."

Her enthusiasm and the picture she painted sounded like everything he'd ever wanted, especially with her by his side. He saw her on the porch swing, a blonde baby in her arms, her smile so bright he wanted to join her rather than do anything else.

"I can't leave."

Her grin dimmed. "I know we talked about leaving in a couple of months, but I don't want to wait. I can't. I want to start my life with you. I don't have all the money I wanted to save, but I'm close, and you've got what you saved. We can do it. Together."

They'd talked about leaving. Him because he wanted her away from her mother and to start his own ranch one day. Something of his own. To take what his father taught him from birth and run his own business outside the one Rory ran on their parents' ranch. He thought to take her to Wyoming. Far enough away they'd have their own life, but not so far he couldn't come home to his family whenever he wanted. She could visit her brother, Zac.

He didn't even consider it, because he couldn't leave. But she needed to go.

She needed a guy who could go all in, hold nothing back. As much as he wanted to be, he couldn't be that guy right now.

"I can't go to Wyoming."

"It doesn't have to be there. We could visit my cousin in Georgia. Her husband is in the military. She said we could stay with them as long as we need. Her husband has a ton of friends. He can help us get jobs until we find the perfect place to settle down."

Georgia seemed a million miles away.

"I didn't know you were close with your cousin."

"I'm not really now, but when we were little girls, you'd have thought we were sisters." Excitement for her new plan filled her bright green eyes.

"Sounds like you found the perfect fresh start. I'm happy for you."

"You're happy for us," she corrected, narrowing her gaze. Confusion dimmed her enthusiasm.

He gave in to his need to touch her, knowing it may be the last time he ever did, and traced his fingers down her long blonde hair. The streaks of copper shimmered in the sunlight.

Her head tilted to the side, rubbing against his palm. "Let's leave today. I'll go home and pack. You pack and finally tell your brothers we're leaving." Her eyes pleaded with him to say all the things she wanted to hear.

He'd held off saying anything to Rory and Colt because it had been the three of them since their parents died. They did everything together, including keeping this ranch running and a roof over their heads. Yes, they had their grandfather, but this place had been left to them. Now they might lose their grandfather and their home. He couldn't walk out on them. Not when they needed him the most.

Rory would push on, working himself into an early grave. He'd take care of Grandpa Sammy and make sure he got the medical care he needed. Colt would step up, take his share of the load. But Ford couldn't add his burden to his brothers' shoulders and ask them to carry it for him so he could run off with his girl, no matter how much he wanted to make a life with her.

Some things just weren't meant to be. This wasn't meant to be right now. Maybe one day, he'd find a way to make it right.

"I'm sorry, Firefly, but I'm not going with you." He'd given her the nickname the first time he saw her. Glowing with golden energy, it was a wonder she didn't take off and fly.

He stuffed both hands in his pockets to keep from holding on to her.

Her brows drew together, crinkling her forehead. "What do you mean? What's changed?"

Ford sucked it up and said what he had to say. "You want to go. You need to go. I get that, but my place is here."

"I can wait."

No, she couldn't. She'd endured her mother's torment her whole life. She deserved every happiness, but she'd never find it here.

"It's not about when."

"You really don't want to go with me?" The crack in her voice tore open his heart and made it bleed.

He didn't know if he could endure the pain before he gave in and told her the truth.

"No." He nearly choked on the word, but he got it out. For her.

"Is that why you've been so distant this past week?"

Not really. Worries about the ranch and his grand-father's poor health crowded his mind, making it near impossible to think of anything else. All the late night talks with his brothers, poring over the dwindling accounts, sorting through which bills to pay now and which to hold off, arguing about selling off a piece of land or trying to get a loan to tide them over—all of it was one big headache after the next, leaving them with few options.

He didn't answer her question, because if he told her about his grandfather, she'd stay to help the only father figure she'd ever had in her life, but if things kept going the way they were, he'd lose the ranch and have nothing and no way to provide for her. The money he'd saved to go away with her, he had to put back into the ranch to keep it going. They'd have mounting hospital bills to overcome, too. No matter how he worked it out in his head, it was all too clear that he had to stay here and fight for his family's ranch and do whatever he had to do to make sure his grandfather got the care he needed.

Jamie stepped close and put her hand on his chest again. "I love you. I don't want to go without you."

His heart thrashed against his ribs. Sure she felt it, he didn't let his roiling emotions show on his face. He had to do this clean, so she'd go with no regrets and move on with her life.

"Like you said, you'll stay with your cousin. Find a job. Start a new life in a new place."

"I thought that life included you, the home we dreamed about, the family we both want."

I wish, but not anymore.

His chest went tight. He barely managed his next words. "You'll be fine on your own. You'll figure out what you really want once you're away from here. I'm a rancher. This is where I belong."

"You really don't want to go with me." The disbelief in her whispered statement tore another strip off his battered heart.

Ford didn't move a muscle. He didn't answer that statement by word or deed, because the honest to God truth was that he did want to go with her. Hell, he just wanted to be with her, here, there, anywhere.

"Did I do something? Say something? If I did, I'm sorry." Tears glistened in her eyes as she struggled to come to some kind of understanding of why he'd do this to her.

Her mother always made her feel like everything was her fault. He hated to do this to her. Hated it. Hated himself for putting her through this.

He choked back his emotions. Had to. For her. "We were great together, but now you need to go. I get it. I'm sorry to see you leave, but I guess this was always the way it ended."

Someone should shoot him. Put him out of his misery. Avenge her for his making this seem like it was her fault. He didn't know if he had the resolve to keep this up much longer. She needed to go before he took her in his arms and begged her to forgive him for being an asshole. Before he begged her to stay with him even though she needed out.

He wouldn't trap his Firefly in a cage and watch her beautiful spirit and light dim and die.

He loved his family, the ranch his parents left to them, but sometimes it was a heavy burden, despite it being his heart and soul.

She opened her mouth to say something, but he cut her off. "Pack your bags. Leave today like you wanted. Get away from her, this place, all the bad memories, and start *your* life."

Jamie shook her head, golden-red hair swishing across her back and shoulders. Tears glistened in her eyes. "Why are you doing this?" Her voice cracked with the plea in that complicated question.

"You want to go. I need to stay." That's as close as he'd come to telling her the truth. "Go, Firefly. Fly away."

CHAPTER 1

Eleven years later—Fourth of July . . .

I'm flying. Nope. Arms out wide, a bullet slammed into her chest and sent her falling backward off the side of the armored vehicle. Another bullet ripped through her side. One more through her left thigh like a blazing lightning bolt. She hit the ground on her shoulders before her ass smacked the pavement and her head bounced, ripping off her helmet as she slid across the ground on her burned back. She gasped for a breath that felt like sucking in fire that seared its way through every cell in her body.

She stared up at the dark figure who had sprayed bullets everywhere, staring down at her with the automatic weapon pointed at her heart. The need to stop him and a deep sense of failure overwhelmed the pain.

She sat bolt upright, gun in hand pointed at the closed bedroom door in her grandparents' old house, breathing hard, sweat rolling down the side of her face, and cussing herself out for blurring her present reality and the past again.

This was good ol' Montana, not some insurgent infested town in Afghanistan.

Fucking nightmares.

She dropped her hand and smacked the gun on her knee. The small pain helped to fade the last of the nightmare, the echo of pain that mixed with the real pain throbbing through her body, and settled her in reality. She focused on the door again and the three bullet holes she'd put in it the last week she'd been living here after her family kicked her out of their house, because they couldn't deal with her erratic behavior, short temper, and potentially lethal insanity.

"At least I didn't shoot this time."

Small victory, but her shrink said those small victories would build until she found herself firmly rooted in the here and now, with the war and what happened a distant memory. Yeah, well, she didn't know what happened to her. Not all of it. Despite the scars on her body that told the story, the details were still missing from her black mind.

Her phone trilled with a text. She grabbed it off the nightstand and swiped the screen, noting the three missed calls from her old friend and the accompanying voice mails waiting along with the text he'd sent.

TOBIN: Call me. I miss you.

Yeah, I miss me, too.

She tossed the phone back on the table next to the crispy dead fern. Tobin sent it to cheer her up. It didn't. She didn't feel bad for neglecting to water it.

She tried not to feel much of anything these days.

If she let herself feel one thing, she'd have to feel everything, and that felt like drowning.

So she turned up the numb and shut down her heart.

Light filled the room through the slit in the curtains she kept shut. She squinted and raised her hand to her forehead and rubbed the headache pounding behind her eyes, not from a bad night of sleep but another night drinking herself into oblivion, hoping to keep the nightmares away. It didn't work. Never did. She needed to stop dulling the pain and find a way to make it stop.

She fell back onto her pillow, hoping to relax and figure out how to make it all go away, then it hit her all at once and she sat bolt upright again. Shit. She checked the clock. Overslept, again.

How that always happened when she barely slept at all eluded her.

She rolled out of bed with a loud groan for the pain in her whole aching body, grabbed the uniform she hoped to never wear again, and put it on anyway. She'd promised she'd do this. A few pain pills would help her get through it. She only hoped she didn't make a complete fool of herself in public, in front of the whole town, and hopefully not in front of the one man nothing and no one could erase from her screwed-up mind—or her broken heart it seemed.

After four tours of duty, Jamie didn't rattle easily, but the drive down Main Street sitting in the back of a convertible waving at all the Fourth of July parade onlookers set off all the bells and whistles in her gut. The urge to roll her eyes at herself didn't override her brain's unreasonable belief that she was in danger. She tried desperately to command her mind not to think every rooftop concealed a potential enemy sniper. That every backpack, tote, and garbage can along the route concealed a deadly IED. That any second someone would appear in the crowd with a rocket propelled grenade launcher on his shoulder aimed straight at her.

Been there, done that, had the scars to prove it.

And the messed-up mental state that went with it. That black hole in her memory haunted her day and night.

Why the hell did I agree to do this? Put myself on display with the crowd here to witness my total meltdown.

Suck it up. Get it done.

Seemed she lived her whole life by that motto.

She held her hands fisted in her lap. Her nails bit into her palms, but she didn't let loose. Couldn't really. The sting gave her something to focus on even as she desperately tried to keep the plastic smile plastered on her face. Her gaze swept the crowd again and again. No enemies. No escape, despite how she tried to find the easiest, safest way out of here. The urge to leap from the vehicle and run for cover nearly overrode her rational mind's command to stay put, endure, get this done. If only her rational mind prevailed more often. She feared the crazy part that slowly but effectively took over like a black ooze coating and concealing that part of her that held a glimmer of hope that she had a shot at a normal life here in Montana—far away from the war.

What was I thinking coming back here?

The war still played out in vivid detail in her mind. Well, most of it anyway. That deep, dark, scary black hole—vital time lost—remained a mystery to her. The investigation into the incident remained open. The Army wanted answers about the attack on her supply convoy she couldn't give. But they kept asking anyway, hoping her memory would return now that she'd come home.

She couldn't go back. She feared going back. She feared remembering what happened, but it nagged at her. Not knowing how she ended up in the field hospital, a guy ripping open her shirt, her fighting to get away, and him yelling at her that he was only trying to help, she'd been shot. Memories collided and muddied up reality.

Her life felt like one big mud puddle right now. She looked into it hoping to see her clear reflection, but found she saw nothing but a mess she needed to clean up.

If only I knew how.

There in the gathering of onlookers lining the street just ahead stood her family. Her mother glaring up at her second stepfather in ten years as he cheered and smiled at Jamie. She appreciated his support, but knew that any kindness from him meant a backlash from her jealous mother. Her brother smiled and bounced his nine-month-old son in his arms. She hadn't even known about her nephew until she arrived home a month ago. Even now, she had no idea how Zac ended up a single father, raising little Corey on his own with no mother in sight. No one wanted to speak about it. Zac refused to say a word about the woman he knocked up but never married.

Of course, no one in the family really wanted to talk to Jamie. The first few days home went well. Everyone was happy to see her and asked her a million questions about her life overseas and living on military bases these last ten plus years. At first, it had been easy enough to answer and talk about the routine she loved so much about military life, the places she'd been, the different people she'd met. But the inevitable questions came about the scars she couldn't hide, the way she acted, the changes in her personality, and what happened that sent her running home after staying away so long.

She wanted to come back to something normal. Something familiar.

The reasons she left had dulled over time, but came back into sharp reality the longer she spent under her mother's roof. While everyone else remained the same, she'd changed—and not necessarily for the better, judging by the fact her family asked her to move out after a month living back home. She'd been all too happy to leave again because she couldn't go back to being the girl she was before she left them all behind, or be the confident, purpose-driven woman she'd become in the military.

That bomb blew up more than her supply truck; it blew up her life.

The faces in the crowd went by in a blur despite the five mile an hour speed they took down the street. They neared the end of the parade route with one last blast of applause. She sucked it up, notched up the fake smile a few degrees, and waved to the crowd with her good arm. Thanks to the bullet to the chest, she still had trouble raising her other arm without it hurting like hell.

A strange sense of being watched swept through her. Ridiculous since everyone along the parade route stared at her, but one man stood out among the crowd. Stinging tears pricked the backs of her eyes. The smile dropped from her lips. Time fell away and she was that young woman sitting across from a man in the local diner she couldn't believe had asked her out, feeling in her gut one simple truth. That's the guy.

She'd wished for him every day since the day she left.

Ford Kendrick stood with his two brothers, Rory and Colt. They stared at her as she passed. Both of Ford's brothers held women at their sides. Rory had his arm around a pretty and pregnant blonde, a thick gold band on his left hand. Colt held a beautiful dark haired woman with striking blue eyes close, a ring on his hand, too. Wow, both of them married. She wondered if Ford had a wife, kids, the happy life he'd once wanted with her. The thought pinged her heart, sending ripples of pain through her soul.

He'd wanted those things with her until she told him she was ready to leave and learned he wanted to stay. She left for reasons that seemed important at the time, but felt very petty and inconsequential now, because her heart remained here with him—but her mind told her she was no good for him.

And where was Grandpa Sammy? She missed their talks, the way he always encouraged her, and the way he loved life and flirting with every girl young or old. He should be with his boys. She didn't want to think the worst, but his absence pierced her heart with a sharp pain.

Calm and so cool, Ford reached up with his right hand and touched his dark brown Stetson in salute to her. The simple gesture warmed her heart.

What did it mean?

She tried not to read anything into it. But she thought his intense stare and the slight tilt to his lips meant he'd missed her, too. Wishful thinking? Probably. Still, that dark spot in her soul lit with something that felt very much like hope.

She wondered if Ford told his brothers what happened. Maybe he'd told them why he changed his mind about leaving with her. Why he didn't ask her to stay, but made it clear he wanted her to go. Probably not. Ford tended to keep things to himself. But once upon a time, he'd shared his thoughts, his dreams, his plans for their future with her. Then suddenly something changed. She still didn't understand despite the lonely hours she spent at night thinking about it, him, everything.

She'd wanted that quiet, lovely life, living on a ranch with the man she loved, raising their children. The kind of life and family she hadn't had as a child. That dream still lived inside of her, even though she'd never found anyone she loved as much as Ford to share it with. She hadn't been strong enough to fight for it then, hadn't believed she deserved it, or him. So she'd run off to see something of the world outside of Montana and her mother's house, hoping to make something of the girl who always fell short of the mark like her mother always told her she did because Jamie Keller was nothing.

Well, maybe her mother was right all along, because Ford stopped seeing the girl he thought her to be, saw her for who she really was, and broke up with her—the girl who lived up to her mother's expectations and ended up nothing.

CHAPTER 2

Jamie followed her family into the restaurant behind Zac still thinking of Ford and what that tip of the hat meant. She wanted to take her nephew, Corey, into her arms, hug him close to her battered heart, and smell his powdery baby scent. She didn't trust herself to hold the sweet boy, despite the longing in her heart to connect with him.

She wondered if she'd ever be well enough to have a family of her own. This past year as her tour of duty came to an end, she'd dreamed of another life with a husband and children.

That thought took her back to Ford. He looked better than any man should in his cowboy hat, tight jeans, and boots. She'd wondered what it would be like to see him again and had known that coming home meant a high probability that it would happen. You ran into everyone eventually in a small town.

Still, she'd hoped she'd be better, stronger, able to deal with the riot of emotions swirling in her head and heart. Instead, she barely registered the people around her, because she was so focused on every little nuance of the moment she saw him again. The emptiness inside of her had briefly filled with the happiness of memories of the months she'd spent with him playing out in her mind in a matter of seconds.

"Stop acting like a zombie and pay attention," her mother ordered from across the table.

Jamie jumped and looked around, realizing the waitress stood next to her smiling and waiting patiently for her to say something.

"What do you want to drink?" Zac asked, helping her out.

"Uh . . ." She had no idea what she wanted. Sometimes the simplest decisions seemed so hard to make.

"Just bring her a Coke," her mother snapped when Jamie took too long to answer.

Pissed off, she glared at her mother and said to the waitress, "Iced tea. No lemon." The soda would have been fine, but she didn't want or need her mother to make decisions for her. She didn't need her mother's impatience and indifference to the many struggles, big and small, Jamie faced each day.

The waitress rushed off to get their drinks.

Jamie flinched when the bell over the door dinged behind her. Bad position. She hated not having her back to the wall. Exposed, vulnerable, she tensed, waiting for an attack that would never come.

Zac gave her a forlorn look. "Ford's here."

Ford and his family, judging by the number of footsteps behind her, walked in for lunch after the parade, too. She felt his gaze on her, but didn't turn around to acknowledge him.

Zac nodded his hello, but didn't say anything.

Sweat broke out on her brow, knowing Ford would see her again at her worst. She didn't want him to see the scars she couldn't hide and the ones he couldn't see but were obvious nonetheless.

She sucked in a calming breath, trying to regulate her heartbeat, which seemed to speed up every time she thought about Ford. She tracked him to a table several down from them with her peripheral vision. Jeans were made for his long legs and damn fine ass. He sat and took the menu with a smile from the same blonde waitress who'd taken their drink order. A zing of jealousy shot through her. He'd probably had a string of girlfriends since she left. The thought clenched her heart. She wanted to be the one he smiled at, the one he loved like back in the days when they ate here all the time. She'd order fries. He'd get onion rings. They'd pretend they didn't know one stole half from the other's plate. They'd end up in a spoon duel when he tried to steal bites from her hot fudge sundae.

They'd had so much fun together, which made it so hard to understand why he'd ended it. The rejection she'd felt the day he sent her away rose up again. The ache of missing him throbbed in her heart.

For sanity's sake, she shut off thoughts of Ford, the past, how good he looked, and focused on the menu as the waitress took her family's order. Didn't really matter what she ordered, she probably wouldn't eat it anyway. Not with her stomach tied in knots thanks to Ford's presence and her innate need to guard against anything and everything around her that could be a potential threat, despite the fact none existed. Not here.

Her mental reassurance that all was well didn't turn off her survival instincts.

She should have known the only person she needed to guard against sat at the table with her. It took less than half an hour for her mother to destroy the tenuous hold Jamie had on her emotions.

"I can't believe you let that man go. Not that you

have what it takes to hold on to him." Her mother wound up as the waitress finished handing out their meals. "Those Kendrick brothers are some of the most handsome men in the state."

No doubt. Jamie wanted to smack the leering grin right off her mother's face as she surveyed Rory, Ford, and Colt at the other table.

"Two of them found beautiful, sweet girls. Won't be long before Ford—"

"Mom. Don't," Zac warned.

"What? She's the idiot who left him."

He left me. She hadn't told her mother that to avoid giving her more ammunition to taunt Jamie.

"The man is good-looking and owns one of the largest ranches in the county. She could have been set for life. Instead she gives it all up to play soldier. Look how that turned out for you." She aimed her disappointment filled gaze at Jamie. "He's moved on. He won't even look at you. Why would he? You're a mess. You look like a boy with that short hair and that uniform. You're too pale and thin. Men like a woman with curves. You could use some makeup, not that it will hide that hideous scar on your jaw. You used to try to be pretty, but nothing will help now with that ugly thing slashed across your face."

"Mom." The edge to Zac's voice didn't deter their mother.

"It will be a wonder if you ever get a man to look at you again. Ford never will. You ruined that for good."

The rage exploded and Jamie slammed her hands on the table. "Shut up!" Jamie held her finger pointed at her mother and shook her head, knowing she wasn't worth it. Nothing Jamie said or did would change the spiteful woman who couldn't spare a kind word for her daughter who needed one more than her next breath.

Her mother sat back, not at all surprised by Jamie's outburst. She'd instigated it for a reason. To prove that she was right and better than Jamie. Her wide eyes narrowed and filled with triumph that she'd gotten under Jamie's skin. Again.

Zac reached over and placed his hand over hers. She yanked her hand free.

"Jamie, let it go."

If only she could.

Ford sat with his family across the diner from Jamie and her family, still in disbelief he could look up and see her sitting right there. He never thought she'd come back. It still felt like she was a world away. Seeing her today set off a wave of memories he'd tried to keep locked down all these years. One glimpse of her unleashed them in his mind. He tried to see all of them, but they flipped through his memory like a movie in fast-forward. He wanted to slow them down, savor them like he never had in the moment. He wanted to go over to her, say hi as though he had a right to talk to her despite the way he'd ended things. He wanted to touch her soft skin, smell her sweet spring scent, and hold her close—like he used to at their spot under their favorite tree—until the haunted look in her eyes disappeared.

The girl he used to know as well as he knew himself sat across the room, but she didn't look the same. Sure, she'd cut her long reddish blonde hair into a short pixie cut that suited her fairylike cuteness. She'd lost weight, or just transformed into all lean muscles that spoke to a strength that had become a part of her carriage. He liked the physical changes. They added to her beauty. But when he looked at her, he didn't see the bright, sweet, smiling girl he used to know. She looked uncomfortable and ready to jump out of her skin.

He'd read the article about her in the local paper. He'd scoured the internet for the few mentions of her in reports about the war and her return home with fellow injured soldiers, and what he'd discovered tormented him.

Every night she was gone, he would watch the evening news, looking for her in the meager war coverage. He'd never caught even a glimpse of her in one of those supply trucks, never saw her among the soldiers they showed. He'd prayed for her safe return. He should have begged for her to survive without a mark on her body, heart, or mind. He got his first wish, but not his last because she'd endured more than anyone should ask of one person and he saw it all in her eyes, even if her clothes covered the marks war left on her body.

"So, all three of you are destined to stare at the woman you want across this diner." Sadie's words snapped him out of his dark thoughts.

"Uh, what are you guys having?" Ford glanced around the table at his family.

Colt slid his hand over Luna's shoulders and pulled her close. He kissed her forehead, then turned and pinned Ford with a steady look. "Take it from someone who has been where you are now. No matter what happened in the past between you two, it will only get worse if you don't talk to her about it."

"We ended a long time ago."

Rory shook his head. "Nothing ended, you just went

in different directions. The way you look at her, there's still something there."

❧ Ford didn't acknowledge that statement. Didn't have to. His brothers knew him well enough to know how he felt about Jamie. What Rory didn't know was that he'd meant to leave them to be with her, and instead he'd let her go, and she'd almost died. He'd confessed to Colt long ago after a long night of trying to drink her out of his mind. Hadn't worked, it just loosened his tongue, and he'd dumped the whole sordid story on Colt. He wished he'd kept his mouth shut.

"Doesn't matter. She looks at everything and everyone in this place, but not me." Okay, that revealed more than he wanted. Luna opened her mouth to say something, but he held up his hand to stop her. "Leave it alone. She's back, but she's probably not staying."

She probably had a boyfriend back in Georgia where she was stationed. Maybe she'd even married, though the news reports said nothing about a husband and family. Still, he didn't know the details of the last ten plus years of her life. Some of that time, maybe most of it, probably included a man who made her happy. That man wasn't him, so he didn't really want to know, because then he'd want to kill the bastard who got to be her everything when once he'd been the lucky one.

He wanted to kill the fucks who'd hurt her. He hoped the guys still serving overseas took care of it for him.

"It's been a couple of months. How do you like your new place?" Sadie asked, changing the subject for his benefit.

He appreciated it, and the fact she'd fixed up her old house and asked him to move in and work her family's ranch. The last couple years, and especially since his brothers got married, he'd thought more and more about a wife and family. A home of his own. A ranch. A legacy to leave to his kids, the way his parents had left one to them. With Kendrick Ranch mostly in Rory's hands now, Ford wanted something of his own. He loved the fact that he finally had a chance to build a business from the ground up. He'd spent the last two months doing maintenance work on all the fence lines and outbuildings, getting ready to run cattle and horses on the property. The fields were in good shape. Sadie kept the grasses and hay fields in good order to help pay for her brother's many misdeeds and the debts and lawyers that came with them. In jail now, Connor had nearly gotten Sadie killed before Rory saved her—and Connor.

"I love it out there." He did, but he found it lonely after living with his brothers and granddad all these years. Rory and Sadie were married and expecting a baby in a few short months. Colt moved out and married Luna. She inherited Rambling Range from the old guy who used to come into the diner twice a week to have dinner with her. Crazy stuff happened when the old guy's family didn't take too kindly to Luna inheriting Rambling Range, but Colt helped her sort it all out.

So his brothers were settled with their wives, living their lives together, happy and in love, and he lived alone on the ranch he'd always wanted.

He got most of his dream. He should be happy, right?

But the dream in his head still included Jamie and wasn't the reality he lived. He'd let her go then. He didn't deserve her now.

He had work to do. If he didn't bust his ass every minute of the day, he'd never be ready for winter. He didn't have time to waste on a dream that would never be a reality.

He picked up the beer the waitress sat in front of him and took a long pull from the bottle.

"Hey, Ford," the waitress said in a sweet voice.

"Hi," he said back without really looking at her. He vaguely remembered dancing with her at Rory and Sadie's wedding. Nice girl. But not Jamie. None of the women he'd been with over the years had ever been as special as Jamie.

She'd never known how he truly felt because he'd been stupid enough to encourage her to leave. He never thought it would lead to this. Guilt settled like a stone in his gut. Her wounds, all she'd been through, might have been avoided if he'd begged her to stay. He'd never told her he loved her for all the many times she'd told him. He'd held himself back, too afraid to lay his heart and life on the line for her. She'd done so with him and it cost her dearly.

Lost in his thoughts, he jumped along with everyone else in the diner when Jamie slammed her fists down on the table, rattling dishes, silverware, and glasses, then leaned forward, glaring at her mother, and shouted, "Shut up!"

Tense silence ensued. Jamie clamped her hands on the edge of the table. He felt her vibrate with rage from across the room. He'd seen her angry at her mother a thousand times. A kitten with her claws out, not something you took too seriously. But this primal fury he'd never seen. Where had it come from?

All of a sudden, she stood, pushing her chair back with the backs of her legs. Zac reached over and placed his hand over hers on the table. She batted it away, then rushed off to the hall leading to the bathrooms.

Zac said something to his mother, pointing an accusing finger at her, then tossed his napkin on the table and stood to go after Jamie, leaving his baby in the high chair next to Rick, Jamie's mother's newest husband.

"What's it going to be?" Colt asked. "You going to find out what's up with your girl, or leave her to fend for herself against her twisted mother?"

Colt knew about some of the shit Terri pulled on Jamie, but not all of it. What Ford knew was enough to make him send Jamie away for her own good. Jamie didn't share everything. Ford didn't want to know the rest because then he might end up in a cell right next to Sadie's brother.

"She's not my girl."

"Then try harder," Rory coaxed in his direct way.

Not bad advice. Did he take it and risk Jamie's rejection?

Ford turned and stared down the hallway in time to see Jamie come out of the restroom, listen to whatever Zac was saying to her, then punch him in the face and push him up against the wall.

Ford moved without even thinking about it.

"You need help, Jamie," Zac gasped out, unable to speak clearly with his sister's arm braced across his throat.

"Let him go," Ford ordered, hoping to stop this scene before someone else in the restaurant saw them fighting and called the cops.

Jamie didn't respond, or even seem to know he was there.

"What she said was mean and hurtful. I get it, sis, but you've got to let it go. She's never going to change. But you have to. You've got to get a handle on your temper, this rage you can't control." Zac looked down at the arm she held against his throat. "Please, Jamie. One of these days, it's not going to be me you're punch-

ing, but someone who will make sure you're locked up.
I don't want to see that happen."

"What do you care? You were with her when she
ordered me out of the house."

"I wanted you away from her. Someplace you could
rest and recover and find your head again. I thought you
needed some space, but look at you. I'll say it again. I'll
keep saying it until you hear me. You need help."

All at once Jamie let loose her muscles and fell
against her brother, burying her face in his chest. Zac
wrapped his arms around her head and held her close,
his cheek on the top of her head. "How much pain do
you have to endure before you ask for help?"

Jamie pushed out of Zac's arms and glared at him.
"You don't know what you're talking about. You have
no idea what it's like for me now."

"Tell me. I want to know. I want to help you."

Jamie lifted her hand to her head, her fingers gripped
tight in her short hair. "You can't help me. No one can."
She turned to flee her brother, but came up short when
she nearly ran right into Ford.

He didn't move, just stared down into stormy green
eyes so filled with pain and sorrow her gaze felt like a
punch in the chest. "Jamie." Just her name, that's all he
could manage.

"What are you doing here?"

"I want to help you, too," he confessed.

She flinched and took a step back like he'd slapped
her. "You want to help me? You of all people?" The
anger he expected, but not the fathomless sorrow in her
eyes. "You saw it then, you can't help but see it now.
I'm not worth saving." Jamie pushed past him and ran
for the door.

Ford took two steps to go after her, hating the tears

that rolled down her cheeks as those horrible words came out of her mouth. Even now, he could barely breathe past the sadness those words evoked in him.

Zac grabbed his arm and held him back. "Let her go. She's in no frame of mind to listen to you, or anyone. You go after her now, she's liable to shoot you."

Ford scrunched up one side of his mouth. "She's upset."

"Yeah." Zac worked his bruised jaw. "She works out her upset by hitting things. Though I don't think it makes her feel better. Nothing seems to make her feel better."

"What the hell is going on?" Ford didn't get it. The woman who just left didn't resemble the girl he used to know at all. Jamie never used to be down on herself like that. He'd seen hints of it, mostly in reaction to her mother's abusive taunts, but not this kind of deep, desperate, dark, and hurtful belief that she was worthless.

"Mom said something nasty to her about no man wanting her now that she's all messed up and has that scar on her face."

Ford had seen it. A slash across the curve of her chin. "How did she get it?"

"Don't know. We don't know much about what happened to her over the years. I talked to her the most, but all I got was everything is good, limited details about her working in the military, which seemed more like a trucking job than anything else. Over the last six years of her serving overseas, I heard from her less and less. Whatever happened after that bomb exploded, she doesn't remember, but the military sure as hell wants to know whatever she knows. That blank spot in her mind torments her to the point she can't function. You saw her. She overreacts to the smallest things."

"Your mother has a way of tormenting her in a whole other way," Ford pointed out.

Zac planted his hands on his hips and hung his head. "Which is why I got her out of their house and moved her into my grandparents' old place. I thought she'd do better there. She looks worse than when she got home all bandaged up and quieter than I've ever seen anyone."

So, not married with kids. Good to know. Still didn't rule out a boyfriend back at base or still serving overseas.

As if Ford had a chance in hell of getting her back.

"How long was she in the hospital?"

"Five weeks."

Ford swore. "That long?"

Zac nodded. "Yeah. Several surgeries. Physical therapy."

Ford raked his fingers through his hair. "Jesus."

Zac looked off past Ford's shoulder to where Jamie had left through the front door. "I can't imagine what she's been through."

"And your mom throws insults in her face on top of it." Ford clenched his hands into fists. He wanted to defend her, but raging at her mother wouldn't change anything. Terri had no love in her heart for her own daughter. Jamie deserved better, but she wouldn't get it from Terri.

"I don't anticipate any more upcoming family dinners."

"Better keep your mom away from Jamie from now on."

Zac dragged his hand over the back of his neck. "Sorry to pull you into this."

"No problem." Ford cocked his chin toward Zac's jaw. "You should put some ice on your face."

Zac reached up and placed his hand over the dark red mark. "Yeah. She's got a killer right cross. I kind of wish they'd shot her on the other side of her chest."

"Why do you say that?"

"She can't raise her left hand past her shoulder."

"You're kidding me?"

"I wish I were. She's in so much constant pain, she chews on pills like they're candy. She drinks to fog the nightmare in her head. I'm really worried about her."

Ford stuffed his hands in his pockets, frustrated. He wanted to do something, but what? "Sounds like you have every reason to be."

"All I think about is the doctor's warning that veteran suicides are fifty percent higher than the civilian population in the first three years they leave the military. She's lost her purpose, her friends, the life she built for herself. I'm afraid she'll never find her way and be happy again."

The thought of a world without Jamie in it squeezed his heart and made it ache.

Zac shook off his thoughts and stared at him. "Sorry, man, how are you? It's been a long time."

"Long enough for you to have a kid."

"My son, Corey. He's nine months old and growing like a weed."

"Where's his mom?"

Ford couldn't quite read the emotions that zipped across Zac's eyes. He thought he saw pain, regret, sadness, rage, and resentment before resignation finally settled in them and stuck. "She's a long story." Zac sighed. "Look, I don't know what happened between you and my sister. I'm sure you had your reasons for breaking things off with her. If you cared about her then, maybe you'll do me a favor and if you see her around, make sure she doesn't get into any more trouble. That's all I ask."

"Done."

"Just like that." Zac eyed him suspiciously. "You still care about her."

"Never stopped. She wanted to leave, but I couldn't go with her."

"You never told her why."

Then, the ranch had been near foreclosure. Now, he was trying to get a ranch off the ground. He still had the same problems. Lots of work, limited funds, winter only months away. Then, his family had been counting on him. Now, Sadie counted on him to make a go of the business and help support her so she could stay home with the baby when it came and she could take a shot at a writing career. The list of things he needed to do ran through his mind, overwhelming in its magnitude, made even more difficult because most of it he had to do on his own. His brothers helped out, but they had their lives and their ranches to run, too. Plus, he liked a challenge. He wanted to do it on his own.

"Like you said, I had my reasons." None of which had ever stopped him from loving Jamie.

Her words rang in his head. *I'm not worth saving.* He'd tried to show her once that she was worth more than anything in this world. He'd have to show her again, because he couldn't live in a world where his Firefly wasn't happy, couldn't fly, and didn't shine.

CHAPTER 3

Tobin walked into the lieutenant's office, closed the door, stood at attention, and saluted.

Lieutenant Gedetti saluted back. "At ease, Sergeant. Take a seat."

"Thank you for seeing me, sir."

"How are you?" The lieutenant eyed him up and down.

Tobin hoped the lack of sleep and endless nights drinking didn't show on his face. He'd gone so far as to plunge his mug in a sink full of ice water to take down the swelling under his eyes and wake him up from the fog he'd been living in since the Army changed his orders, cut his deployment short, ordered him home and on leave.

"I'm well, sir. Ready to get back to work."

"You're on leave until Sergeant Keller is debriefed again."

"I've given my report of what happened. I don't understand why my life is on hold because her mind's a blank slate."

"We have your statement from the debriefing and her account of what she remembers. I understand she's been diligent about her sessions with Dr. Porter. It's only a matter of time before she's well enough to allow her mind to remember the events in full."

He hoped Jamie never remembered the hell they'd been through. "Who cares at this point the exact details of what happened? Let me come back to work. I need to work."

"The Army cares about what happened to those soldiers. The families of the deceased care what happened to their loved ones. You should care what happened to your friends."

Tobin raked a trembling hand through his hair, wishing for a drink to calm his nerves. "I do care, sir. I just want to get on with my life."

"Hard to do when you haven't dealt with what happened. You saved Sergeant Keller's life, not once, but twice. You witnessed that terrible attack, killed people, watched people you care about fall beside you. You've been ordered to take your leave and see the shrink."

"I finished my sessions, sir. I don't need to go back."

The lieutenant's eyes narrowed on Tobin's fisted hands on his thighs. "You might want to rethink that."

"If Jamie can't complete her debriefing, will the commander close the case?"

The lieutenant tilted his head, contemplating his next words. "There are conflicting reports coming in about the ambush and attack. We're waiting on some further information. The commander is concerned."

No one else survived, except the few insurgents captured when help arrived and the poor people who lived in that shit town. They had their own agenda. Who could believe anything they said?

"It's doubtful Sergeant Keller's memory will come back. She's in a bad place."

"You've spoken to her?" the lieutenant asked.

One side of his mouth drew back in a half frown as his heart throbbed with the regret he'd carried since she went home. He missed her. "No. She won't take my calls."

That raised an eyebrow on the lieutenant's suspicious face. "I thought you were *close* friends."

It appeared to a lot of people that he and Jamie had a *close* relationship, but he'd never been allowed to cross the friend line into something more. Not even for a few benefits, despite his best efforts.

"She's not talking to anyone right now. I'm surprised she talks to her shrink. She's home, trying to put her head back on straight." Though he wished she'd stayed here with him where he could watch over her.

"After what she's been through, I can't blame her." Lieutenant Gedetti pressed his lips together, his eyes filled with concern for Jamie. "Enjoy the rest of your leave. You're dismissed."

Tobin rose from the chair and exited the office. He hoped the lieutenant and the Army left Jamie alone and closed the matter soon so he could get back to the only thing he had left in his life if he didn't have her.

CHAPTER 4

Jamie drove into her yard and cut the engine with a flick of her wrist. She gripped the steering wheel tight and shook herself in a mini tantrum that didn't make her feel any better, then let her head fall against the top of the steering wheel. She'd made a complete fool of herself today. Again. And in front of everyone in the restaurant, the entire Kendrick family, and especially Ford. He must think her completely nuts.

"God help me."

Yeah, like God ever did anything for her. He'd dumped her in this life with a *you figure it out* dismissal.

Tears stung her eyes. The look of sadness and pity in Ford's eyes made her gut sour. She didn't want his pity. She didn't want him to think her so pathetic she couldn't get through one lunch with her family.

Well, her mother provoked her. She'd needled Jamie into losing her temper and making a complete fool of herself to show Ford he'd been right to leave her all those years ago. She wanted Jamie to know no man would ever want her now. In her mother's twisted mind, Jamie had always been "scheming" to "seduce" the men in her mother's life. Her mother wanted to see her brought low. Jamie had been brought down and dumped in a dark pit that collapsed on her every time she tried to claw her way out. No matter how hard she tried, the hole kept getting deeper, falling in on top of her at the same time. One day, she feared it would swallow her whole.

When will it end?

She slipped out of her truck and walked up to the dilapidated house. She should spend her time fixing it up. Instead, she let it sit with all its imperfections.

Exactly what she did inside those walls.

She went right through the front door and kicked it shut behind her, letting the darkness swallow her. She kept the drapes drawn, the light and outside world blocked out, so she could try to feel safe and protected in her cave, but nothing really made her feel either of those things. Not anymore.

She tore off her uniform, tossing the garments and her boots aside because she couldn't stand to be in them one second longer. In her panties, bra, and tank top, she went to her room, grabbed her gun off the sheets, because she needed it close at all times, and went back down the hall past her trail of discarded clothes to the family room. She sat on her sagging sofa, grabbed one of the bottles of pain meds she'd left on the scarred coffee table, and twisted off the safety cap.

Seriously, who are they kidding?

Nothing would keep her from getting to the only thing that dulled the pain and thoughts in her head.

That's all she wanted, to stop thinking and feeling. Anything. Everything.

Make it all go away.

If only for a little while.

She popped three pills into her mouth, unscrewed

the cap on the bottle of whiskey, and drank them down with one searing gulp and then another.

Her phone trilled in her fatigues pants pocket with yet another text message. Tobin. Just thinking about him took her mind back to the one place she couldn't get far enough away from to save her life.

She ignored the message and sat back, waiting for the numbness to overtake her, hoping this time the blackness cast out everything and allowed her blissful oblivion.

Please.

A noise startled her as she drifted off. An engine.

Someone was here. Coming for her. The enemy found them.

A surge of adrenaline washed through her, making time slow, the anticipation build. She raised the gun in her hand, pointed it at the dark shadow moving in to take them down. They wouldn't get past her. She'd kill them before they hurt her or someone from her team. She fired. The dark figure fell back and yelped in pain. She shifted her arm and fired again, hoping she finished him off before he got too close.

I have to save them!

"Fuck, Jamie. Stop shooting!"

The voice penetrated the fog in her mind and transformed the all too familiar interior of her supply truck into the house she remembered from visiting her grandparents as a kid. It hit her all at once. She wasn't driving down some Afghan road and falling under attack, she was home.

Oh God. Oh God, she shot Ford. His anguished voice blocked out the screams of her team echoing in her mind.

Where did Ford come from? Why is he here?
Did I kill him?

The thought sent an icy bolt of terror through her system, chilling her to the bone.

She leaped from the couch and ran for the door, stumbling on one of her discarded boots on her unsteady legs. The bullet hole through her flimsy front door made a cannon ball of dread drop in her stomach. Fear made her heart thrash against her ribs, rivaling the tempo of a hummingbird's. The sound echoed in her ears too fast to really distinguish the beats separately. It roared like the rush of a river through her mind.

Her trembling hand reached for the door handle, but her mind screamed, *Don't open it!* She didn't want to see what she'd done to the one man she loved so much it was the only thing that kept her heart beating. The one person she would die before hurting.

Ford lay on the porch, his hand over his upper arm, blood oozing out his fingers. He released his arm, revealing the long gash along the outside of his beefy muscle freely oozing blood, which dripped over his skin and onto the wood deck. He pinched the inch-long splinter of wood sticking out of his cheek and pulled it free. A trickle of blood ran down his face. He stared up at her, fear and pain and that same pity in his eyes. His gaze dropped to her thigh and the scars from the bullet that ripped through her leg. His eyes met hers again and filled with such sadness.

"No." She shook her head, feeling the booze in her gut threaten to blaze a trail back up her throat. She swallowed back the bile filling her mouth, but it didn't help, because the sight of Ford on the floor bleeding because she'd shot him made her ill. Not a mortal wound. But no relief came from that realization.

"No." The guilt she carried since that ominous day in Afghanistan intensified, tightening her gut and squeezing her heart. Right now, she hated herself for all she'd done, and most especially for hurting him.

She wanted this torment to end.

She didn't want to be responsible for hurting one more person.

The medication and alcohol still coursing through her system made her head swim. She tried to hold on to his image and not get lost in the wave of nightmares that swamped her mind. She wanted to make this right, but didn't know how. She wanted to take it back, take all of it back like it never happened, but she couldn't and the pain and guilt grabbed hold with sharp claws that tore her to shreds.

Ford rose up so fast, she didn't know what he meant to do. He wrapped his hand around the gun and held it away from both of them. She slammed her free hand into his chest to push him away, but ended up gripping his shirt in her tight fist and holding on to him for dear life.

"Damnit, Jamie, let it go," he ordered. "Please, baby, let it go. Don't do this, Firefly." His eyes implored her, but the sorrow and plea in his voice tore what pieces of her heart she had left to bits.

"Please, Jamie, I know the girl I used to laugh with and talk to for hours under the stars is still in there. Please, baby, come back to me."

If only it were that easy.

With his free hand settled on the back of her neck, his fingers gripped in her short hair, holding her so she'd look at him, their bodies pressed together in sweet agony.

"Do you see me?"

The overlay of past and present in her mind cleared and she stared at his face and the blood running down his cheek. She unclenched her fingers from his shirt and reached up and touched his face, then pulled her bloody fingers away and stared at them. All of a sudden it hit her like a wrecking ball.

I never should have come home. The people I love always end up hurt or dead.

She felt herself falling again. Her back hit the ground and everything went black.

Ford tried to hold on to her as her eyes rolled back in her head and she fainted and fell to the floor. The gun thumped on the wood beside them. He swatted it away and out of her reach just in case she woke up and made another grab for it.

He kneeled beside her and looked his fill at the troubled woman he'd longed for every day since he sent her away. Her chest gently rose and fell. Tears tracked out of her eyes and down the sides of her face and into her short hair.

"Fu-uck." He strung the word out and raked his trembling hand through his hair. He hung his head and took a moment to compose himself and breathe. The adrenaline still racing through his veins didn't help to slow his thrashing heart but did mask the pain in his shoulder.

Zac's words about the doctor warning him about veteran suicides, the devastation and pain he'd seen in Jamie's eyes when she saw him lying there bleeding, and seeing the gun in Jamie's hand and not knowing what she'd do next echoed through him.

He hoped she wasn't that desperate to escape, but

couldn't take the chance, so he'd tried to get the gun from her and make her see him and not an enemy.

She shot him. Why? Did she hate him that much?

He'd never seen anyone look so translucently pale. He leaned down and pressed his forehead to hers, his hands on both sides of her head. He held her close, hoping she felt his presence, knowing he didn't deserve to be this close to her again, but needing the contact, the touch of her skin against his.

"God, I missed you."

Her soft breath, tinged with whiskey, brushed against his cheek.

"What happened to you? Why would you do this?"

He kissed her forehead and leaned back, sitting on his heels. He stared down at her. She wore next to nothing. The scar on her thigh, the ones peeking out the black tank top straps at her shoulders, disturbed him. But the roundish scar on her chest tore him to pieces. The thought of what she'd endured, survived, ate at him like acid eroding his insides. To think of how she'd been hurt like this, how it still hurt her . . .

"I'm not worth saving."

Her words. She meant them, and it made him so sad his chest ached with a hollowness that filled him up, erasing all the good he had in his life because she had none.

She'd tried to kill him, but he didn't think she'd known it was him. She'd seen an enemy she'd fought once, one who still tormented her without actually being here.

He needed to believe that, because the girl he knew would never hurt him. She had to be in there still. Somewhere. He needed to find her and remind Jamie that she still existed.

He needed to do something. But what? He had no idea how to make her feel safe and happy again. He had no idea what to say that would make her forget, or at least help her cope with what she'd been through.

He stared into her place, at the bottles of pills and whiskey on the table. He had no idea how many pills she'd taken. How much did she drink on top of it? She needed help, but not the pharmaceutical kind. She needed to be shown that she was worth saving. She was worth loving.

Somewhere buried deep inside this angry, scared, broken soul lived the woman he loved. He'd bring her back. He had to.

Even if she didn't want to be with him again, he couldn't live with himself if he didn't try to save her from herself.

Maybe if he'd gone with her all those years ago, she wouldn't have ended up like this.

Guilt sat heavy in his gut. Things could have been different. For both of them. But second-guessing his choices didn't do him, or her, any good.

She'd never mentioned joining the military. He guessed when she got to her cousin's house in Georgia and discovered her options were limited the military had looked like a good and steady job. She'd be a part of something bigger than herself. She'd have wanted something like that, since she'd never felt like a real part of her family.

The pain in his shoulder penetrated his brain. He looked down at the deep gash and thanked God he'd caught her movement and the gun through the slit in the drapes and dove for cover as the shots rang out. If he'd stood in front of the door, she'd have shot him through the chest, too. Lucky for him, the bullet whizzed past over his head.

It scared the shit out of him.

The scratch on his face was the least of his worries. His throbbing shoulder hurt like hell and was getting worse by the minute as the adrenaline rush wore off.

He bit back the pain and tried to think what to do first.

Right now, he needed to take care of Jamie. He contemplated calling an ambulance, but discarded the idea. She passed out, but didn't seem in any physical distress. Plus, if he called 911 she'd be in a hell of a lot of trouble. He couldn't explain away his injury or the bullet holes through the window and door.

She wasn't likely to wake up for some time with the meds and booze in her system, so he stood and went into her house, past the clothes strewn on the floor, and into the kitchen. He grabbed the dish towel off the oven handle and tied it into a loose knot. He stuffed his hand in the hole and pulled it up his arm. Every tiny move-ment of his shoulder stung like a thousand bees. He held the towel in place against his ribs. He took one end of the towel between his teeth and held the other end in his free hand and pulled it tight around his wound to staunch the bleeding, groaning with the pain and gnashing his teeth around the fabric.

"Fuck." Man that hurt.

With more important matters to deal with, he left the kitchen and headed for Jamie's bedroom. The bullet holes in her door disturbed him and made him breathe out a frustrated sigh. Apparently, she couldn't sleep without waking up shooting at imaginary targets.

The whole place was a mess. He ignored the pain and stripped the tangled, sweat-stained sheets from the bed, mostly using his good arm. He dumped them on the floor with her dirty clothes and rummaged through the hall closet for a clean set of sheets and a blanket. He remade the bed. He went back through the house to Jamie lying on the floor just outside the front door. He slipped his arms beneath her shoulders and knees and scooped her up and held her close to his chest. Pain seared through his arm, making him hiss out a ragged breath, but God it felt good to hold her close again.

He rose and carried her to the bed and gently laid her on the cool, clean sheets. She rolled to her side, turned away from him. He stared at the burn scars on the back of her neck and shoulders. He didn't want to look, but had to see for himself how badly she'd been injured. His hand trembled when he reached for the bottom of her tank top. He pinched the material between his fingers and pulled it out and away from her back. He stared at the rippled and puckered scars, the still blotchy red skin mixed with patches of white that had healed, but would never look the same. He tried not to think too deeply about how she'd gotten them and wondered if it still hurt.

About to put her shirt back in place, he stopped and stared at the scar on her side. Different than the burns, he recognized the round pattern that matched the one on her chest. Another bullet hole. This one bigger. He leaned over and saw a smaller scar on her stomach. The bullet went right through her.

Ford leaned over and held his weight on one hand. He pressed a kiss to her shoulder, another to the soft spot behind her ear. The sadness inside of him expanded until it pushed against every inch of his skin. He just might burst with the overwhelming ache that made tears clog his throat and sting his eyes.

He kissed her temple, lingering with his lips pressed to her soft skin. She sighed in her sleep. He whispered into her ear, "Dream of me, Firefly. Dream of us. You're safe. You're home. I'll be here when you wake up."

He wanted to crawl in bed beside her and hold her, but didn't think she'd want him that close—or here at all. But he refused to leave her, not in this condition. Not until she was well again. If he was lucky, maybe never.

CHAPTER 5

The ancient bed creaked down the hall. Ford turned the stove on to heat the pot of stew he made after cleaning Jamie's house, tending to the front door and window, and driving into town for a grocery run. Jamie had only had a bottle of vodka in the freezer, a near empty bottle of orange juice in the fridge, plus two apples, a loaf of moldy bread, turkey bologna, and a wilted head of lettuce. Even the cereal boxes in the cupboard were either empty or stale, plus she didn't have any milk. The meager supplies and healing injuries explained her too thin frame. She needed to take better care of herself.

He'd taken one of her pain pills and used the first aid kit from her bathroom to patch up the gash on his shoulder. Half an inch the other way and he'd have a fucking huge hole in his arm.

Ford put the loaf of bread he'd purchased in the oven to warm. He grabbed the butter out of her now fully stocked fridge and set it on the table. Since he'd washed the mound of stinky, dirty dishes, he took two clean bowls from the cupboard and spoons from the drawer. He set them all next to the stove and waited for Jamie to come out and face him.

* * *

Jamie woke like she always did, with her heart pounding and an ominous nightmare scaring her out of sleep. The haunting images of war and losing her friends transformed into Ford lying dead and bloody by her hand at her feet.

She sat up in bed and made a grab for the gun she always kept close, but came up with nothing. Where the hell had she left her gun? Probably on the coffee table in the living room. That she'd gone to bed without it disturbed her. She always kept it close. She needed to keep it close.

Trying to orient herself, she rubbed at her gritty eyes and scanned the room. She didn't remember changing the sheets, but they smelled like spring, which only made her feel worse for some reason. Apparently, she'd picked up all her dirty clothes and dusted.

What the hell?

Why didn't she remember any of this? She must really be losing her mind if she'd been driven to sleep-cleaning.

She shook off random thoughts of her subconscious cleaning up the mess she couldn't deal with while awake.

The nightmare lingered, but something deeper made her hurt. It pushed against her hazy mind.

Her tongue felt thick and dry in her mouth. She needed something to drink, probably something to eat, since she couldn't remember the last time she'd attempted that without giving up after a few bites. She'd fled the restaurant after the fight with her brother and seeing Ford. Which probably induced the nightmare about him. That and the whiskey and meds that still fogged her broken mind.

A light glowed down the hall. She'd left her bedroom door open. She never left it open. She must have been really wasted to throw caution to the wind and pass out without making sure she was safe, secure, and unreasonably barricaded in her room when no threat existed except in her head.

Jamie swung her legs over the edge of the bed, ignored the rush of panic seeing the scar on her thigh evoked, and stood, stretching out her sore back and tight skin where the burns healed, but always seemed to pull. She went to her dresser and opened the drawer to pull out her sweats. Clean clothes sat in stacks, filling the drawer.

Great. Not only did I clean up, I even did the laundry without remembering.

Blackouts were a new phenomenon for her since leaving the hospital, but this, this was something else entirely.

Maybe she well and truly had lost her mind. She raked her fingers through the sides of her hair.

The savory smell of pot roast penetrated her foggy mind. No way she cooked in her blacked-out state. Besides, she didn't have any food in the house. Maybe Zac came by to check on her and brought food with him, knowing her fridge and cupboards were usually bare. What was the point of eating when you could barely summon the energy to get out of bed each day?

She quickly pulled on her sweats and headed down the hall. She spotted the cardboard taped to the window, the spotlessly clean living room beside her, and the wood patch on the front door. Her mind tried to put it all together, but it didn't make sense until she heard his voice.

"Hey, Firefly. How are you? Hungry?"

Jamie spun on her toes and stared into her kitchen

at the last man she expected to see in her house. The nightmare came back, of him dead at her feet. Blood covered his shirtsleeve and side. A bandage circled his upper arm above his bicep. She looked back at the window and door, then back at Ford. All at once, nightmare became reality.

She covered her mouth with both hands to stifle the agonizing wail. Tears flooded her eyes and fell down her cheeks. Her legs let loose and she fell hard to the floor, buried her face in her knees, wrapped her arms around her legs, and rocked herself back and forth wishing herself gone. If only she'd disappear and this never happened.

"No, no, no. I'm sorry. I'm sorry. I'm sorry," she chanted, hoping, wishing, begging God she hadn't done this. She hadn't shot the man she loved. Not Ford. She couldn't have hurt Ford.

Ford's hand settled on her head and brushed down the back of her neck, touching some of her scars. She scrambled back out of his reach and slammed back up against the front door, her hands up to ward him off. Her mother's voice rang in her head. *No man will want you now. Not with your kind of crazy and all those ugly scars.*

Ford remained crouched in front of her. Five feet separated them, but really a gulf of pain and regret kept them apart. Mostly her fault.

"You have to go," she pleaded. "I don't want to hurt you." Her gaze shifted from the deep gash on his cheek to his bandaged arm and back and forth again. The thought that she might have killed him made the pit of despair she lived in swallow her whole and drag her down to an exceptionally agonizing level of pain and misery. "I'm sorry. I'm bad. I'm no good. Call the cops.

They'll lock me up where I belong." She should turn herself in before she hurt someone else.

Ford shook his head, his eyes filled with sadness and the same regret she carried with her every day. "No, Jamie. You don't belong behind bars. You need help."

This time, Jamie shook her head. "What if I'm beyond help?" She leaned her head back against the door and stared blindly into that black hole in her mind. It held the secrets to what happened to her but refused to give them up, except for nightmarish images that made no sense. It drove her to do crazy, stupid things like trying to kill the man she loved.

"The girl you knew is gone. I can't find her." She stared around the room. This house. This place. "I should have never come back." From the war, or to Montana.

Ford shook his head. "You don't mean that." He didn't even want to think about the terrible things that happened to her and turned the girl who used to love to play Red Rover with the kids at day care and sing lullabies to the babies into a woman who was afraid of her own shadow.

"Yes, sometimes I do." She whispered her darkest truth.

Ford didn't know what to say or do to change her mind. He hated to see the defeat in her eyes, and worse, the deep belief that she'd be better off dead than living like she was right now. Her fear and sadness and grief and anger and desperation all showed in her eyes. The tumultuous emotions played out on her face like she couldn't settle on one. Not a single sign of happiness or even contentment—hell, he'd settle for boredom—

showed in her eyes. All of it was dark and bad and sad, and that was not his Firefly. She was bright and happy and yes, sometimes a little sad, but not in this tragic way.

Words wouldn't work, so he went with basic survival, because it seemed that was all she was capable of right now.

"Food's hot. I'll plate it up. Get up. Sit at the table. Let's eat."

Ford ignored Jamie's wide-eyed stare, stood, and walked into the kitchen. He went to the stove and filled the bowls he got out earlier. He pulled the bread from the warm oven, broke it into chunks for each of them, and set them on a plate he pulled from the cupboard beside him. He set the food on the table and took his seat.

Jamie hadn't moved from her position sitting in front of the door, sniffling back her tears, though she never wiped away the ones that trailed down her cheeks. She kept a wary watch on him while he got dinner ready. He wanted to go to her, wrap her in his arms, and reassure her everything would be all right. But those were platitudes she'd never believe.

She needed a push in the right direction.

"It's best to eat it while it's hot. You've got to be hungry. You didn't eat at the diner and crashed for the last several hours. Get over here."

She didn't move. Didn't say anything.

"You need to eat, Firefly."

Ford picked up his fork and a big bite of pot roast and stuffed it into his mouth. He chewed and ignored Jamie, hoping she'd come to her senses and eat a meal with him. After he forced himself to eat five more bites despite his growing impatience over her refusing to join him at the table, she finally picked herself up off the floor and came to the table and took the chair across from him. He'd set her plate next to him, but she pulled it across the table.

So, not going to even get that close to me.

Because of the way he'd ended things, or something more? She'd shot him. He'd seen how deeply that affected her. How sorry she was about what happened. Hell, she hadn't even really remembered it until she'd seen his arm, the holes in the door and window, and put all the pieces together. He imagined she'd thought she'd dreamed it. Just like she seemed to think this a dream based on the odd way she looked at him and around the kitchen, like this was some warped reality and not the way she'd been living the last month.

Ford took another bite of his food. Thirsty, he stood, making Jamie scoot her chair back two feet from the table, her body tensed and ready to fight or flee. He ignored her odd behavior and went to the fridge. He pulled out the jug of milk and poured two glasses. He put the milk away and set one glass in front of her plate and drank deeply from the other as he took his seat. He set his glass down and went back to eating.

It took two more bites before Jamie scooted her chair back to the table. Three more before she picked up her fork and took her first bite. He let out a sigh of relief when she tackled the meal and ate with some enthusiasm, sopping up the gravy with her bread and drinking all her milk.

She stopped midway to sliding the next bite on her fork into her mouth and stared across the table at him. He'd been very careful not to watch her directly, but he did meet her gaze this time with a questioning look.

"Are you okay?"

He wanted to ask her that very question. He wanted her assurance that she was all right despite what he knew and saw right before his eyes.

"What are you doing here? Did you clean my place? Why did you come?"

Ford stared at her, waiting to see if she rattled off any more questions. She ran out of steam, dropped her fork, and sat back, eyeing him.

"Eat, and I'll answer your questions."

Jamie bit her bottom lip, contemplating him and her options. He kept his patience intact, though he wanted to demand some answers of his own. Like what happened to her back? How did she get shot? What had she been doing the last ten plus years?

Did she miss him as much as he missed her?

So many things he wanted to know, but didn't ask because she didn't trust him enough to sit next to him, let alone open up and talk to him.

Jamie gave in and picked up her fork again, taking a small bite of the stew. He'd take what he could get. For now.

"I'm okay. Nothing but a scratch."

"I've been shot. It burns like a motherfucker. Hurts like hell."

He didn't want to think about her wounds, the scars he'd seen that had been imprinted on his mind. "Yes, it does, but in my case, it's nothing serious." He shrugged, though moving his arm made the searing pain inflame all over again. He didn't let it show. He didn't want to upset her more than she already seemed to be, even if she tried to hide it.

"I came over to check on you after that scene in the restaurant."

"I let her get to me. Every little thing gets to me

these days." Jamie shook her head and pinched her lips together, frustrated her emotions got away from her.

"I wanted a chance to say, hi, I missed you. Welcome home. And why the hell would you come back here?" Judging by the way her mother behaved toward her in the restaurant and Zac's statement that he'd had to move her out of her mother's place for her own good again, this was the last place Jamie needed to be if she hoped to recover after all she'd been through.

"The Army discharged me for obvious medical reasons. I served my time. Thanks for showing up. Now get lost." Sarcasm filled her voice. Her real family had dismissed her. Now the family she'd volunteered to join had let her go, too. "I'd been serving overseas for the last fourteen months, which means I didn't have a place to come back to, so I came here, hoping . . . Well, let's face it, hope is for people who believe that things can be different. I know better. At least I should have, but I needed . . ."

"What?"

Jamie shook her head. "Nothing. The only thing I need is to be left alone."

He ignored that, because that was the last thing she needed. "I cleaned up while you were sleeping. This place was a disaster."

"So am I."

He ignored that, too, because she spoke the truth.

"As for why I came, well, I'd think that's obvious." He waited to see if she'd say something, see in him what had always been true. The blank stare disappointed him, but didn't really surprise him. She didn't see what was right in front of her face. Maybe one day she would and they'd find a way back to each other. Maybe she'd forgive him for the way he'd ended things.

The guilt engulfed him. If he'd gone with her, made her stay, something other than sending her off on her own, maybe she wouldn't be sitting in front of him completely lost and broken and heartbreakingly sad.

"I'm your friend, Jamie. That's why I'm here. I care about you."

Jamie's lips pressed together in a derisive frown. "Right. Friends." She nodded. "Well, you'll find," she looked at his arm, "I guess you already know, I'm not someone you want as a friend. Friends don't try to kill you."

"You didn't know what you were doing. You didn't know it was me. When you realized what you'd done . . . I know you didn't mean it."

Jamie stared into space, silent tears streaming down her face. "I'd rather step on a land mine than hurt you," she whispered.

"Don't ever say anything like that again. When you opened the door and saw me, I thought you were going to . . ." He scrubbed his hands over his face, trying to wipe the image of her with the gun and what he thought she intended out of his mind.

"What? Shoot myself?" She shook her head. "I might be crazy, but I swore to Zac I'd never do that. I promised him." Conviction and anger filled her voice. That promise meant something to her. "I would *never* do that to him."

He desperately wanted to believe her. "Good. Because the last thing I want is for you to be hurt in any way. You dead and gone just might kill me."

Anger narrowed her eyes. "What do you care?" she snapped.

"Do you really need to ask?" After the way he'd treated her, she did. That was on him. "I guess you do.

I care more than you know or I ever showed you." Another mistake he'd like a chance to make right. He'd made so many mistakes. It would take him a lifetime to make them all up to her.

He reached across the table and laid his hand over hers, hoping the contact eased her in some small way. She snatched her hand back like he'd burned her, gasped, and sat back in her seat.

He held up his hand to let her know he meant no harm.

"You should go," she whispered.

"I'm not leaving you here like this."

"Believe me, *this* is better than I've been on many nights."

"Exactly why you shouldn't be alone."

"I'm alone because I hurt people. Look what I did to you." She flung her hand out toward his shoulder and let it fall back on the table with a thump. A fresh wave of tears filled her eyes and spilled over. "Go now, before it's too late and I do something else that will make you hate me even more."

Ford leaned forward and looked her right in the eye. "I don't hate you. I never did. Far from it, Firefly."

She slammed her hands on the table, making the dishes rattle, rose, and glared down at him. "I don't want your pity." She took three steps away, wrapped her arms around her middle, and hugged herself. Her head fell forward in defeat.

Ford didn't move. He wanted to go to her and wrap her in his arms, but she'd bolt or fight or break.

He didn't want her to do any of those things. He just wanted her to listen. "I don't pity you, Jamie. I admire your strength and perseverance, the will you muster up every second of the day to endure."

Her head came up and fell back. She stared at the ceiling, her shoulders sagging under the weight of the world she carried.

"You're still standing, Jamie. You're still here, fighting to get through each and every day."

"Yeah, I'm doing a bang-up job. I nearly killed the one person I . . . You." She gave him her back and shook her head. They still had so much distance between them. A distance he didn't know if they could bridge and mend.

Part of the pain she carried he'd caused her. He wanted to fix it, her, make it right and make her smile again. He really missed her smile. He wondered if she even knew how to smile anymore.

"What are you doing tomorrow?"

She turned and stared at him like he'd asked for the secret of the universe. "Why?"

"It's a simple question, Jamie."

"The same thing I've been doing every day since I got here. Dying a little more each day." She glanced over at the counter for the fifth time, to where he'd set her bottles of pills. Sweat broke out on her forehead and top lip. She must need another pain pill to take the edge off or just numb her brain because he made her think, and that's the last thing she probably wanted to do.

"Sit down. You look so damn uncomfortable, I feel like I need to tuck you back in bed or take you to the hospital."

"I'm fine," she bit out.

"Let's agree on one thing between us."

Her eyes narrowed to suspicious slits. "What?"

"We won't lie to each other anymore."

One eyebrow shot up in question.

He answered what she didn't ask. "I lied to you before you left. I regret it. I'm sorry as hell I did it, but I won't ever lie to you again. I hope you'll agree to do the same for me."

"What was the lie?"

He looked her dead in the eye. "That I didn't want to go with you."

She wrapped her arms around her middle and stepped back like he'd hit her. Her eyes widened on him and filled with shock and questions he wished he didn't have to answer, because what if nothing he said made her forgive him?

"What? What are you saying?"

"It's complicated and better left to explain when you're open to hearing what I have to say. Just know that I wanted to be with you. I wanted us to have that dream. But when it came time to make it happen, I couldn't be what you wanted and needed. I couldn't give you what you needed and wanted. But I wanted to."

Her gaze remained steady on some spot behind him, but she really looked back to that day, replayed it in her mind with what he'd just told her, and the confusion in her eyes remained, because she couldn't put it all together and make it make sense. He felt for her, because it no longer made any sense to him either.

Hindsight was a bitch who came back and kicked you in the ass.

"I'm sorry, Jamie. I'm sorry I pushed you away. I'm sorry I let you go. I'm sorry the life you found left you broken and unhappy. All I ever wanted for you is to be happy. I thought letting you go would give you that. I wish it had."

"I was happy here with you. Why did you tell me to go if you wanted me to stay?"

"You know the answer to that."

She tilted her head, staring at him, apparently no answer coming to her.

"You didn't want to stay here. You wanted to get away from your mother, this place, and find something better."

"I thought I did," she admitted. "For a while. But there always seemed to be something missing."

He wanted to believe she meant him. He didn't ask her. He didn't deserve to receive that kind of sentiment from her. "I couldn't go, but you needed to go. I wish it ended better."

"You and me both."

"You're here now. Do you plan to stay? Or are you going back? You must have friends, people missing you." He wanted to ask if there was another man waiting for her return. He didn't think so. If there was, the guy was a total asshole for leaving her alone in her condition.

Jamie scrunched one side of her mouth into a sardonic half frown, half grin. "It's not easy to admit that I'm kind of stuck here. I have no idea what to do now. I'm not capable of doing anything right now. My injuries prevent me from going back to the military. My mental state prevents me from doing anything but survive, and let's face it," she shrugged, "I'm barely getting by on that front."

"You need to take better care of yourself. You can't live on pills and booze. Which is why I stocked your fridge with actual food."

Her head fell forward again. "Thank you," she whispered. "It's been a while since someone . . ."

"Took care of you," he finished for her.

She shook her head. "Cared at all."

"I thought soldiers serving overseas were a close group. You must have friends . . ."

"They're dead. My whole crew. The guys assigned to protect us."

Ford sighed. "I'm sorry, Jamie. You must miss them a lot."

"I want to know what happened to them."

Ford eyed her. "What do you mean? You were with them when you got hurt, right?"

"Yes, but I can't remember anything past my truck exploding, except bits and pieces in nightmares that make no sense."

Ford frowned. "Maybe you don't want to remember because it's too awful to recall."

She didn't answer and her silence made the atmosphere charge with anticipation. He wanted her to talk about it because she needed to, because keeping it inside was killing her.

"Something happened," she whispered.

"You were burned and shot. You barely got out of there alive. That's what happened." He let his anger and frustration out in his voice. The fear seemed unreasonable since she was right in front of him, but it still lingered in his system. He wanted to let it go now that he knew she was safe, but he'd carried it so long he had a hard time releasing it. Looking at her now, sad and damaged and far from okay, he had reason to fear for her still.

Her gaze came up and met his. "Something else happened. Something very bad. I need to remember." Her eyes squinted as she looked into the past. "Every second of the day I feel like I did something, or didn't do something, or I'm supposed to do something, but I don't know what, and they're all dead, so what am I supposed to do?"

Ford stood to close the distance between them, take her in his arms, and hold her. She put up both hands to hold him off and shook her head. She didn't want to be touched. He wondered if it was just by him or everyone.

"Jamie." Just her name, because he wanted to say so much more, but didn't have the words to make her feel better.

"I'm sorry. It's not you. Well, it is you, but it's more me." She raked her fingers through her already disheveled hair. "So many things have happened since I saw you. Things I want to forget, but that show up and mess up my life all over again."

Ford didn't quite understand, but the "No Trespassing" sign she had up came through loud and clear. Still, he thought he saw a glimpse of her need for him to close the distance between them and hold her. Like she craved his comfort, but couldn't allow herself to give in to it—or worse, felt like she didn't deserve it.

One foot moved forward like she meant to take a step toward him, but then she pulled it back. She held herself back from him and it hurt like hell.

He went to the counter and grabbed the four bottles of pills. He set them on the table next to her unfinished plate of food. "Take what you need, Jamie." He hoped she understood he meant *anything* she needed, including the love and comfort he fought so hard not to force on her, despite knowing she needed both.

To allow her the space and time she needed, he picked up the dishes and carried them to the sink. He found a plastic tub to put the rest of the stew in and save in the fridge. He hoped she ate it over the next few days instead of starving herself rail thin.

She took a seat at the table behind him. He opened the freezer and pulled out the carton of Ben & Jerry's

Coffee Heath Bar Crunch and set it in front of her. He snagged a spoon from the drawer, set it on the table next to her hand, and went to the sink and washed the dishes, hoping she'd stop staring at him dumbfounded and take her pills and eat.

He took his time, knowing she needed it to settle down again. He made her nervous, but hoped that in some small measure his presence gave her comfort. At least she wasn't alone.

Kitchen cleaned, he picked out his own spoon from the drawer, sat across from Jamie, and went to take a bite of her ice cream. She smacked her spoon into his like a sword strike. Her gaze met his with a gleam of mischief to match the rusty grin barely tilting her lips.

"What do you think you're doing?" The lilt of humor in her voice did his heart good.

He eyed her, but didn't hide his grin. "That looks really good." He tried to take a bite, knowing how this would go and loving that she wanted to play.

Jamie's spoon tapped his away again. He parried her and nearly toppled the container when he tried for a spoonful. She blocked him and knocked his spoon back again with a soft giggle. "Watch it, tough guy."

"I want some." He meant a hell of a lot more than the sweet treat and she knew it by the steamy look he sent her.

She picked up the carton and tilted it toward him, all fun and games coming to an abrupt end because in the past they ended with a melted carton of ice cream, her in his lap, his lips devouring hers, and a long loving that left them both satisfied.

He let it go, not wanting to push. After what happened tonight, he just wanted to see one smile and he'd gotten it.

"Thank you."

He swallowed another bite. "My pleasure."

"I mean it. Thanks for not calling the cops. You could have put me behind bars for a long time. Instead, you cooked me an amazing meal I didn't do justice to by any measure. You bought me groceries, including my favorite ice cream, all with a gunshot wound that must scream with pain. I've known some tough, badass military guys and they have nothing on you."

That made him smile.

She turned serious again. "Thank you. For all of it. You didn't grill me for answers about what happened, or get on my case about how badly I'm living my life."

"I'm not here to give you a hard time. I came to help you out, because I wanted to see you. Because I care, Firefly. Maybe you feel like no one does, but I hope you see I do."

She gave him a nod, but her gaze never met his.

"You should take a shower and try to get some more sleep. It's late."

For the first time, she glanced at the clock. Her eyes went wide. "It's two in the morning."

He held back a soft chuckle at her surprise. "Not the first time we stayed up late together. I stayed to be sure you're okay."

"I'm not okay, but I'm not done either," she admitted.

Though Zac's warning rang in his head, he started to believe her. Maybe he had misread the situation earlier and she hadn't meant to harm herself after she shot him and lost it.

This time her gaze came up to his. "You wanted honest."

"Always. Do you feel better?"

She stood, scrunched her mouth into a frown, then

raised her gaze to meet his once more. "For the first time since I arrived here, I feel like I'm home."

Stunned, he stared at her, unable to string even a few words together to tell her what that meant to him.

Home isn't the place you are, it's the people you're with.

CHAPTER 6

Ford pulled into Dane's driveway just after dawn. The sun lit the pastures and trees in brilliant greens and golds, but didn't brighten his mood one damn bit. He'd caught a couple of hours' sleep on Jamie's couch after she snagged the gun he'd emptied off the top of the refrigerator and quietly retreated to her bedroom, closing the door on him and the world once again. Her groans, mumbled tormented words, and screams interrupted those few hours of fitful sleep. He wanted to help her, but didn't know how.

He'd thought he'd reached her, that she'd heard him and felt better for a short time, but then her eyes had fogged with her past once again.

For the first time since I arrived here, I feel like I'm home.

He wanted to be the beacon in her life that brought her back from the dark world her memories sucked her into every second of the day. He wanted to give her everything they'd talked about and planned back when things were simple and easy between them. Now, just getting her to eat seemed a complicated maneuver that involved convincing her he meant no harm and only had her best interests at heart.

She thought he pitied her. Not so. He admired her tenacity, but hated that her complicated past broke her down to the point her life became nothing but endurance.

She'd survived hell and come home, but hell followed her.

She couldn't escape, didn't know how, but she kept fighting. He'd help her. He wouldn't give up on her. He wouldn't let her suffer alone.

Dane walked out the front door, a cup of coffee in hand. Ford slid out of his truck, closed the door, and dragged his tired ass up to the porch.

"Morning, Ford. You okay?" Dane pointed to Ford's shoulder and shirt with his mug, his eyes narrowed in concern. "That's a lot of blood."

"Sorry for the early morning call, but I came to see your wife before she left for work."

"Looks like you need a doctor."

"Yeah. I hoped she'd check out my arm without writing anything down or asking any questions."

Dane opened the front screen door and waved him to go ahead in. "Let's see what she says. What happened? Some jealous boyfriend shoot you for sniffing around his girl?" Dane teased, but he wasn't far off.

"A girl I used to know shot me because she thought I wanted to kill her."

Dane's eyes went wide. "Seriously?"

One side of his mouth tilted up with the halfhearted smile he couldn't contain. Of course Dane knew he'd never hurt anyone, especially a woman. "It's a long story."

"I'm all ears," Bell said, coming out of the kitchen, Kaley beside her eating a muffin.

Kaley ran to him. Ford scooped her up with his good

arm, held her at his chest, and kissed her soft cheek. "Hey, pretty girl. What you got there?"

"Blueberry."

"My favorite." As soon as he got the words out, Kaley stuffed half the muffin in his mouth. Lucky for him, he opened it when he caught her intention or he'd have muffin all over his face. "Thanks," he mumbled as he chewed.

"Baby kicked." Kaley pointed to Bell's protruding belly.

"They do that," Ford said, nuzzling his nose in Kaley's neck and making her giggle. Just being with her made him feel better. He couldn't stay locked in his anger over Jamie's situation when he held the bright, happy little girl in his arms.

"Down, Uncle Ford."

Ford turned Kaley loose, though she didn't go far and wrapped her arms around her dad's leg.

Dane leaned down and patted her back. "Come on, sweetheart, let's go get Uncle Ford a cup of coffee and a muffin of his own while he talks to Mommy."

"O-tay." Kaley walked off with Dane, leaving him with Bell, who turned and walked toward her office just off the front entry. She picked up a large leather satchel from behind her desk and tilted her chin toward the plush chair by the sofa for him to sit. This room doubled as the library. Bookcases dominated the wall space, making this seem less like a doctor visit and more like a comfortable meeting with his friend.

"Listen, Bell, I know I'm putting you on the spot here. You're required to report . . ."

Bell held up a hand stopping him. She frowned and nodded toward his shoulder. "Nothing to report, since you haven't told me how you got hurt." She acted like she hadn't overheard him talking to Dane.

He appreciated that she gave him the benefit of the doubt. For now. He had no doubt she'd revoke that courtesy at any moment depending on what he said next.

"Let's have a look."

Ford shrugged off his shirt. Before he let Bell do anything, he planted his elbows on his knees and laid his head in his hands, rubbing at his gritty eyes. "I don't know what to do," he admitted.

Bell's hand touched his hair and rubbed down to his hand. She squeezed and comforted him because they were friends and this wasn't like him at all.

"What happened, Ford? Who did this to you?" Her gentle coaxing helped him to open up.

"Her name is Jamie. She came home from the military after some kind of assault. She's got burn scars all down her back. Three gunshot wounds that I could see. But none of that is as bad as her mind, Bell. She's . . . lost. Broken. Living in another world most of the time. She's scared and fierce and angry and looking for a fight and a way out all at the same time."

"PTSD?"

He finally looked up at her. "Absolutely. I showed up at her place. She shot first and didn't ask questions because she actually thought I was some enemy there to kill her. She was out of her mind and she didn't know what she was doing. She passed out when she figured out what she'd done. I put her to bed to sleep it off. But she doesn't actually sleep. She tosses and turns and fights off whatever is torturing her mind."

"Don't you think the cops need to know what happened?"

"I can't explain it, but she doesn't want to hurt anyone. She's protecting herself." He shook his head. "I know that doesn't make sense based on her actions, but it also makes perfect sense." He gave her a lopsided grin. "Even if I don't."

Bell unwound the gauze he'd used to secure the pad over his injury. "This doesn't look so bad."

"I cleaned it up the best I could, but I thought you should have a look to be sure it doesn't get infected."

Bell used the supplies she pulled out of her bag to clean the wound again, setting off another blazing ache in his arm. "I'll stitch it up and give you a prescription for antibiotics to be on the safe side."

Ford sat still, letting Bell do her thing. The second the last stitch went into the three-inch line across his arm, he breathed easier and unclenched his jaw.

"Are you going to call the cops?"

"This is serious, Ford."

"Please, Bell, give me a chance to get her help. We talked last tonight after she woke up. She was devastated by what she'd done. I think this might have been the wake-up call she needed."

"But you don't know that for sure. What she's been through, Ford, requires at the very least counseling. A medical professional should be looking after her."

"I checked out the doctors' names on her meds online. One of them is a psychiatrist. He specializes in PTSD."

"Good. I hope she's opening up to him."

"I'll find out. I didn't want to push too hard this morning before I left. I swear, Bell, I won't let up until I'm sure she's okay and not out to hurt herself or others."

Bell eyed him, concern and fear in her eyes now that he'd revealed his worst fear. "Ford . . ."

"Please, Bell. I need to do this for her."

Bell tilted her head, interested in why he'd go to these lengths to protect Jamie. "Who is she to you?"

"The one I let get away. I didn't fight for her before, but I will fight for her now, even if she doesn't want me back. I'll fight to make her better."

"What if you can't? What if what she needs is far more than you are capable or equipped to give her?"

"Whatever it takes, Bell, I will get her the help she needs, whatever that is, and see her happy again." He wanted Jamie well and back in his life and in his arms.

Bell sat quietly in front of him on the coffee table, no doubt contemplating what she'd do. Ford held his breath waiting for her decision.

"There's no magic pill that will make it all better. It will take time. A great deal of time for her to recover," Bell emphasized. "But she has to want to get better. It's work, Ford. Whatever happened to her left scars far deeper and more severe than the ones you saw on her body. If she's in a deep depression, she may need to be medicated to even begin to see that there is hope for something better in her life."

"She's on an antidepressant, two types of pain meds, and an anti-anxiety med."

"That's some cocktail. Do you get what you're dealing with?"

"I'm dealing with Jamie. She's not a lost cause, Bell. She just needs a safe place to find herself again."

Bell sighed, obviously still on the fence about what to do. "If you even suspect she's spiraling out of control again and will hurt you, herself, or anyone else, you will call the cops, or a medical professional, and get her the help she needs. Talk to her about getting help through the VA. See if you can get her to open up about what happened to her. Talking about it will help her cope."

"Right. I'll do those things. I'm starting with the basics, getting her to eat, sleep, and hopefully out of the house and her head. She's just out there with nothing to do. She's all alone. That can't be good for her."

"No, it's not."

"I'll take care of her, Doc. I swear."

"I hope you know what you're doing. If things get worse, let me know. Maybe I can help, or at least recommend a specialist who can work with her. You might want to contact her psychiatrist and let him know what happened."

"I can't do that, Bell. I can't chance that he'll hospitalize her for some evaluation that will do more harm than good."

"Not getting her evaluated and the proper care she needs could do more harm. Letting her spiral endangers herself and others."

"I swear, Bell, I'll keep an eye on her. She can't get into much trouble at her place. She's been out there for several weeks. I think the parade yesterday, a fight with her mom, and seeing me again was just too much all at one time. Some peace and quiet today should calm her down. Besides, I left her the gun, but hid the bullets."

Bell smirked and shook her head. "Smart man. Still, the fact you had to do that is what bothers me."

"The desolation in her eyes is what scares me, Bell. No one should look or feel that way."

Bell's eyes filled with sadness. "No one should ever feel that alone."

Bell would know. She'd been raised by her grandmother, a religious zealot who thought Bell was the spawn of the devil. She'd lived in isolation, made to feel like her very existence was evil. Dane changed all that for Bell. He fell hard and fast for her. It took some convincing for Bell to come around and believe the bull riding champion had given up the buckle bunnies and wanted something permanent with Bell. Now Dane gave Bell the things she'd never had—a family and infinite love.

Ford wanted those things for Jamie. He wanted to give them to her and spend the rest of his life making her happy. It seemed a long shot at the moment, but he'd do everything in his power to bring Jamie out of the dark and back into the light.

CHAPTER 7

Jamie wanted to slam her laptop shut and cut off Dr. Porter's incessant questions. She wanted to be left alone. She wanted everyone to stop worrying about her deplorable mental state. She wanted what happened to disappear from her mind entirely. She wanted some peace and quiet and the too-short periods of blissful oblivion she'd found in booze and pills.

Unfortunately, she had some need for self-torture, because she kept her video appointment with Dr. Porter and stopped self-medicating five nights ago when Ford showed up out of the blue, cleaned her place, made her dinner, and made her see the light.

She'd nearly killed him.

Her heart pounded in her chest every time she thought about it. No matter how bad she felt, how much the pain throbbed through her body, she'd never get that wasted again and lose control.

"What are you thinking about right now?" Dr. Porter eyed her from the computer screen.

Jamie shook off her dark thoughts and blinked back the tears she couldn't help. The thought of hurting Ford hurt her worse than the injuries she couldn't hide or escape. "What? Sorry. I got lost in thought."

"You do that a lot."

Jamie nodded. "I have a hard time concentrating on anything for long."

"How are the nightmares?"

"Vivid, scary, and incomprehensible."

"So no better."

"Nothing is better," she snapped. Well, that wasn't exactly true. For two hours every night she could breathe. Ford showed up at her place around six. He cooked, made her eat, but never made her talk. At first, she resented his intrusion. Checking up on her like she couldn't be trusted to live on her own. She didn't need or want a babysitter. So she gave him the silent treatment. He didn't care. Just took over her kitchen and sat at her table and ate like they did it every night. The third night, she finally asked, "What are you doing here?"

He answered with a simple "I'm hungry. You need to eat. Might as well eat together." He left that night with a "See you tomorrow."

Sure enough he showed up the next night, and the next. She expected him soon. She didn't know if she was stupid for feeling the butterflies of anticipation that she'd get to see him again, or for believing he came over for any other reason than he felt sorry for her.

"Jamie!" Dr. Porter shouted to get her attention.

"What?" She didn't hide the irritation in her voice.

"What is going on with you?"

Defensive, she gave him a sour look. "Nothing."

"You know, this doesn't work unless you talk to me. Something is different about you. What is it?"

"I'm not drunk off my ass." She threw out the words and meant for them to throw him off the scent of what she really had on her mind. Ford. Somehow he'd taken over her every waking thought. She didn't get him, or what he was doing coming around all the time.

"Why?"

"Why?" She scrunched her face into a questioning, narrow-eyed expression. "You prefer me drunk and so doped up I can't form coherent thoughts or sentences?"

"Of course not. I'm interested in what prompted you to lay off the sauce."

That's what she liked about Dr. Porter. He wasn't some stuffy, pompous doc. He said what he meant and not always in the most diplomatic way. Ex-military, he got her in a way some high-priced, fancily educated psychiatrist wouldn't. Of course, Dr. Porter had one of those fancy educations. He just didn't see the need to demonstrate it in some superior way that made her feel inferior. She'd rather he give it to her straight, even if she didn't like what he had to say most of the time. Mostly because he was right. But he never shoved it in her face.

"I did something," she admitted. "Something that almost cost me . . . everything." That's as close as she'd come to spilling her guts about shooting Ford.

A shiver raced up her spine and goose bumps broke out on her skin. She wrapped her arms around her middle. Her defensive, and at the same time comforting, posture told Dr. Porter more than her words.

"What happened, Jamie? Did you hurt yourself? Someone else?"

No hiding things from someone trained to sniff out your deepest, darkest secrets. If she admitted what she did, he'd have no choice but to have her arrested, or committed. Maybe she'd be better off locked up where she couldn't hurt anyone else ever again.

Still, she'd been living in survival mode for so long

she kept her mouth shut, because over the last five days the fog she'd been living in had begun to lift and a glimmer of hope that she might actually find something worth living for had sprouted in her heart—a part of her she thought lost a long time ago. But hope did spring forth from one of the broken, battered pieces of her heart. While she felt it, she tried to ignore it, because she couldn't afford to believe in it. Not when she'd lost so much.

One more disappointment just might break her irrevocably.

That little glimmer of hope glowing in her chest showed her like no words of encouragement from friends, her brother, or her doctors had that she could heal, she could one day be whole again, if a bit scarred and cracked.

She didn't delude herself into thinking she was okay now. She wouldn't be for a long time, but at least she didn't feel like the path ahead of her only led to her complete and utter destruction.

She owed Ford all the thanks for that. His unexpected return in her life shined a light in her dark world and woke her up. For a moment that night while sharing that pint of ice cream, she remembered what it felt like to be happy and wanted. *I want some.* Ford's words. But did he mean them? She wanted to believe he did.

"Jamie, I wish you'd share the conversation you're having in your head with me. I can help. I want to help. If nothing else, I'm here to listen."

"I don't want to die."

Dr. Porter sat quiet for a good ten seconds. "I'm proud of you. That's quite a breakthrough." Code for he'd been worried that she might off herself at any moment.

Just like Ford. The thing was, she didn't have thoughts of ending it all. Well, maybe once or twice in her darkest moments, but those thoughts disappeared behind the guilt she felt for surviving when her friends died. She should have died with them. At least, that's what she'd thought day in and day out until Ford showed up and said all those things to her nearly a week ago. Now the thought of dying actually scared her. Ford made her hope. People with hope didn't want to die. They wanted to believe that good things happen. She needed to believe that right now more than ever.

"It's kind of been messing with my head the last few days. I'm here. Alone. With nothing to do but think that I want to live again, but I don't seem to know how to do that anymore. I still feel overwhelmed by the simplest tasks. I'm still in constant pain. I still have nightmares. I want to move forward, but I'm mired in the past. I want to know what happened and I want to forget it all at the same time. I live with an unreasonable fear of being attacked, but I want to go out and see people, and I don't because I'm afraid. I want my mother to support me, not tear me down. I want to know why my brother didn't tell me I have a nephew. And where is that baby's mother? She should be with her child. I want to be able to call up old friends and have a drink in the local bar. I want to know why the guy who pushed me away all of a sudden can't stop coming around and says things that make no sense, but make me want to wish for things I thought would never happen. I want to have sex again. And damnit, I want to just be normal and not so screwed up that everything seems so fucking hard." Out of breath, she sucked in a gasp and let it out, her shoulders sagging as she stared at the wall across the room, completely forgetting Dr. Porter was still there listening to her spill her guts. She didn't think she'd strung that many words together in the last two months.

"Who's the guy?"

"Huh?"

"The guy you want to have sex with?"

She laughed, despite the need to squeeze her thighs together to ease the throb of need for Ford. "That's all you got out of that rant."

Dr. Porter's head tilted to the side. "That's the first time I've ever seen you smile, let alone laugh. So yeah, who is the guy? Because he seems important to you. You're different and he's the reason why. Tell me about him."

She stared out the window—able to do so because over the last few days she'd kept the drapes open and not closed herself off from the light and the world—and thought of Ford. The warmth that swept through her every time she thought of him eased her even more. He'd be here soon. Her heart fluttered in her chest and the tightness in her shoulders eased.

"So it's like that. Even the thought of him makes you feel better." He saw in her exactly what she felt. Ford did make her feel better.

"He's an ex. Someone I knew a long time ago. Before the military. Before everything happened."

"Does he know about *everything* that happened to you?"

"Only what he read on the internet. He doesn't know the details about the attack."

"Have more of the details surfaced in your dreams?"

Of course he wanted to know. The Army wanted to know. Well, she'd like to know what they knew, because maybe then she could put the pieces together.

The Army kept their answers classified. She kept her bits and pieces locked in a loop in her head.

"It's all still disjointed fragments that make no sense."

"How did you two reconnect?"

"I punched my brother in the face in a diner and Ford stepped in to stop me from decking him again."

Dr. Porter shook his head. "You need to control your anger."

"If I could, I would." She shook her head. "I'll work on it."

"Are you and this Ford rekindling the old flame?"

Ford definitely lit a spark in her every time she saw him. Even now, her fingers itched to touch all those hard muscles endless days working a ranch had sculpted. "Honestly, I don't know what we're doing. What I thought happened in the past doesn't seem to be reality."

"Did you ask him to explain?"

No, because she kept waiting for the day he wouldn't show up because she was too fucked up to bother with. So far, he'd kept showing up. She wondered if he knew how much that meant to her. More than she was able to admit. "We haven't talked about it."

"What do you talk about?"

"Nothing." *Because I'm too scared to say anything that might make him stop coming.* "He comes over. We eat. He goes home."

"Why don't you want to talk to him?"

"He doesn't seem to want to say anything."

"Could it be that he sees you aren't ready to talk, so he's waiting you out?"

Maybe there was nothing to say because they ended a long time ago. Though sometimes he looked at her with a longing she wanted to believe meant he still cared for and wanted her.

"Why doesn't he just say what's on his mind? He had no trouble the first night. Now he's, I don't know . . . quiet."

"Does it bother you that you eat together every night and neither of you says anything?"

"Yes." She let the word out without really thinking about it, but gave it a second thought. "No." She enjoyed their quiet dinners, the space he allowed her without leaving her alone.

Dr. Porter held out his hands, palms up. "Which is it?"

"I spend every day here in the quiet and it eats away at me. It makes me anxious and worried and I feel like I'm going crazy because my thoughts are all over the place. I want to run. I want to escape, but there's nothing to get away from because it's all in my head."

"Very insightful. You need to deal with those thoughts and your past and what happened to you."

"I know. But when he's here, the quiet is . . ."

"Comfortable. Bearable."

"Yes," she whispered.

"Sounds like you have a connection to this man that goes deep. Does he feel the same way?"

Jamie stared off into the distance and sighed. "I used to think so. And then I didn't. Now he comes over without me asking him to and I want to think there's something there, but I don't trust it. I don't believe in it, because I wonder if . . ."

"What?"

One side of her mouth scrunched into a sad half frown. "He just feels sorry for me."

Dr. Porter gentled his voice. "Is he the kind of man

who'd go out of his way to have dinner with you every night just because he feels sorry for you?"

Her instinct was to simply say no, but she second-guessed herself. "I don't know."

"Yes, you do. You're just having a hard time trusting your instincts. When he comes over tonight, put your gut to the test."

"How am I supposed to do that?"

"You trust him enough to let him into your house each night. Be brave, Jamie. Talk to him. Ask him why he keeps coming back."

"What if he tells me it's only because he's afraid I can't be trusted alone?"

"If he thinks that, doesn't that tell you he cares enough to check on you?"

"I guess."

"And if he cares that much, maybe he cares more. I think you don't talk to him because you're afraid if he does care, he wants something from you that you think you can't give him."

"I'm not the girl he used to know. I have nothing to give."

"Yes, you do. You just have to be willing to deal with the past so you can see that it is a small piece of who you are, not the whole. You can be happy. It's okay to be happy. That scares you. Him wanting that for you terrifies you, because you can't face the past."

"I have the scars to prove the past is a scary place I don't ever want to go back to."

"It's not going back when you are living in it each and every second of the day. You have to face it, Jamie. You have to look at it, deal with it, and find a way to let it go."

"You make it sound so easy."

"You know it's not. It takes time. And a willingness and a desire to do the work to make it happen."

Dr. Porter gently tapped the alarm, turning it off, signaling the end of their session. Ford's truck pulled into the drive out front. The engine rumbled then died.

"My dinner date is here."

"We'll talk again in a few days. You are brave, Jamie. Talk to him."

Ford honked the horn twice.

Dr. Porter touched his index finger to his ear and winced. The sound must have amplified through the speakers. "Why does he do that?"

An instant before she clicked off their session, she answered, "So I don't shoot him."

CHAPTER 8

Ford walked up the rickety steps to the porch and put his hand up to knock on the door, but it opened before he ever hit the wood. He took Jamie in with one long and swift glance, noting she didn't have a gun and she was smiling—kinda. Both things surprised him. He let loose the breath he unconsciously held every time he approached her door, unsure how it would go or how she'd be when he saw her.

But God, seeing her, cutoff shorts, white T-shirt, no makeup, the dark circles under her eyes fading, her soft pink lips slightly pulled back into a grin she tried to hide, and all those soft curves, punched him in the gut every time. He wanted to wrap her in a hug, pick her up off her feet, and hold her close.

"Hey."

"You're back."

He hated that every day his return surprised her, like she expected him to give up and just stop coming around. Not going to happen. Still, today, more so than any other day, she seemed happy to see him.

She eyed him up and down. One eyebrow went up with suspicion about the hand he kept hidden behind his back, but he ignored it, too taken with her bright eyes, the healthy pink color in her face, and that almost smile. Sexy as hell, standing there with her hip cocked and the V in her T-shirt dipped low to reveal the tantalizing swell of her breasts.

"You're up. Showered and dressed and . . . alert." He loved her bare legs and tiny bare feet. Reminded him of a summer day long ago when they'd had a picnic by the river, swam, and made love under a tree. Images like that kept him up at night in more ways than one.

"My shrink prefers me that way."

"I do, too. Your shrink?" He didn't want to let on that he'd looked up the doctors on her pills to see if they were just prescribing her meds or actually taking care of her.

"Dude who insists on talking to me three times a week."

Shocked, he tilted his head and studied her. "You went out?"

Jamie shook her head. "Video conference. A picture says a thousand words."

"Seeing you is more helpful than the few words you speak these days."

Jamie bobbed her head to the side. "You're probably right. What's the verdict today?"

"This version of you is a sight for sore eyes."

"This version isn't high and homicidal. Right now, anyway." Jamie ducked her head and stepped back, swinging her arm wide to welcome him into her house.

Another first. She'd been reluctant to let him in these last few nights. Always telling him to just go home, asking him why bother with her at all. He hoped all she'd needed was time to let the drugs and booze clear her system so she could think and see things for what they were and not as dark and devious as her thoughts.

Ford pulled the bouquet of flowers out from behind his back and held them up to Jamie. She instinctively jolted with shock, threw up her hands in defense, and stepped back until she focused on the flowers and saw that he hadn't pulled a gun on her.

The not-quite-a-smile bloomed into a happy grin. Her gaze shot to him, then back to the pink peonies he'd bought her at the flower shop in town.

"You brought me flowers?"

"I hoped they'd make you happy."

"They do."

"Mission accomplished. And I got to see your elusive smile."

Ford took her hand and placed it on the bundle of flowers. She sucked in a surprised gasp at his touch. He felt the electricity and heat between them, too. He wanted to slide his hand up her arm, over her shoulder to her neck, and pull her in for a kiss. Tempted, hot with the anticipation of doing it, he did the exact opposite and let her go because she'd been so surprised by the flowers and still didn't see the real reason he came by every day.

She kept the house clean now, the drapes in the living room open, and the shade in the kitchen up. The space felt open, inviting, homey, even though it needed a new coat of paint and an upgrade to make it more modern and less retro fifties. And that was being nice. Still, the place had great bones. Hardwood floors that would gleam and show off their knots and wavy lines if refinished. The arches setting off the rooms and hallway were a nice architectural detail. The stone fireplace in the living room when lit in winter would add a cozy feel to the small space. She could put some money into renovations and make this place really nice if she wanted to stay.

Big if.

Too much of an *if* for his comfort. He wanted her to stay, but wondered if her leaving was the right choice for her again.

The thought clenched his heart and soured his gut.

Something like hot peppers and garlic scented the air. "You cooked?"

"Well, I can't expect you to do it every night, now, can I?"

"I don't mind. I gotta eat, too."

"It's nothing fancy. Chicken tacos." Jamie walked past him and into the kitchen. Nervous, she couldn't quite meet his gaze. She didn't fully turn her back on him, even when she reached up to fetch a vase from the high shelf in the cupboard beside the sink and he got a really great view of her heart-shaped ass. He kept his distance and gave her the space she still needed but he wanted to eliminate.

What he wouldn't give to hold her in his arms again.

She filled the vase at the sink, unwrapped the flowers, and arranged them to her liking. She set the flowers on the table and went to the stove to stir the chicken concoction she'd mixed in the pot, always keeping him in her peripheral vision.

"I never asked. What do I owe you for the groceries?"

Shocked she actually wanted to have a conversation, he stood on the other side of the table to make her more comfortable. "Nothing. I got it. Besides, I'm the one who eats most of the food."

"I ate a couple of the brownie chunk cookies you bought me. They were really good."

"I thought you'd like them."

She kept eyeing him as she turned on the burner to

heat the refried beans. He tried not to crowd her. Hell, if he stood any further away, he'd be in the living room.

She opened the fridge and pulled out a bottle of beer and held it out as far as she could reach to keep him from getting too close. He moved forward slowly and took the beer at the end of his own reach. Ridiculous, but he did it hoping one day soon she'd settle down, relax, and be at ease with him again, the way she used to be.

"Um, would you sit at the table?"

"Will that notch your anxiety down a few levels?"

Her mouth tilted in a lopsided, self-deprecating grin. "I hope so."

He shook his head, but sat in the seat on the opposite side of the table from her spot in the kitchen. She tried to shake it off, but her hand trembled when she reached for the jar of salsa and set it on the table in front of him.

"Jamie."

"Yeah." She stared at her toes, embarrassed by her uncontrollable behavior.

"Relax. It's just me. It's just dinner. The same as we've had the last few nights. That's all. You don't want to talk, or even look at me, and keep a six foot no trespassing zone spread out in front of you, that's fine with me."

Her gaze darted to his, then back to her cute, bare toes. "Why are you here?" She whispered the words, but they still held a desperation to them.

"Stir the beans." He gave her a second to turn and do just that, because she'd asked the question, but it rattled her so much he saw the fear in her eyes despite the fact she didn't quite look at him still.

"I'm here because I want to be here. I don't like

eating alone every night. My guess is you don't either. Whatever else happened between us, I hope that at the very least we are still friends. You look like you could use one."

"Why are you eating alone? Did your brothers move off the ranch with their wives?"

Surprised she'd ask about him, he sat back and took a sip of his beer and relaxed himself, realizing he'd fed off her mood and stayed on guard these last few nights, too. If he settled the need to wrap her in his arms and comfort her warring with his desire to lay her out on the table and make love to her, maybe she'd settle down, too.

"Rory married Sadie a few months back. You might remember her from school. They're expecting a baby. A little boy if the ultrasound is correct. They live in the house now with Granddad. Colt got married about a month before them to Luna."

"I remember Sadie. She was two grades behind me. She has a younger brother, right?"

"That's right. Sadie's father passed several months ago. Her brother is in jail."

Jamie's eyebrow shot up in question.

"Long story. Rory saved her life and helped bring down a drug ring and stopped her brother from rustling all our cattle."

"Wow. And I thought Montana living was boring."

He grinned. "More steady than boring."

Jamie bobbed her head to the side. "True. Still, I think there's quite a story there about Rory and Sadie."

"Let's eat. I'll tell you all about it."

Jamie set the pot of shredded chicken with tomatoes, peppers, and chilies on the table next to the bowls of chopped lettuce, shredded cheese, sour cream, and flour tortillas. She took the seat across from him, grabbed a tortilla, and started stuffing it full of ingredients, more at ease with him than she'd been since they reconnected over ice cream that first night.

He followed suit and took the first bite. "Oh God, that's good. Spicy, but not too hot."

"You don't like hot."

"You do." And he didn't mean the food. She used to be wild for him to touch her. The more aggressive his need for her, the hotter her response. She used to love to sit across from him, her foot up on the chair, tucked between his legs, tormenting him as she playfully rubbed his throbbing cock. He'd drive her nuts, sliding his hand up her leg but never high enough to really satisfy her. Which made her torment him more. Most of the time, they didn't finish the meal, too hungry for each other.

He resisted the urge to reach for her now, which only notched up his hunger for her.

Judging by the heat in her eyes as she stared at him across the table, her thoughts ran the same path his did down memory lane.

Neither of them made a move, the tension growing between them. To distract them both from something neither of them were ready for yet, he told her about Rory and Sadie, then about how Colt and Luna shared a kiss after Luna's ex, who had been Colt's best friend, punched Colt, then they spent months apart thinking they'd crossed some line.

"Turns out, they both wanted each other." *Like we do.* "Now they're inseparable." *Like I hope we will be again.*

"So Colt is working for his wife on her ranch running Rambling Range, and Rory and Sadie live on the Kendrick spread. So where are you in all this?"

Did he detect a hint of jealousy in her eyes that he might have someone special, too?

He put any thoughts she had about that to rest. "Sadly, alone. Don't get me wrong, I love seeing my brothers happy and in love with their wives, but that kind of leaves me the odd man out at the moment."

"Do you still want to get married?"

After their long-ago plans never materialized, he guessed her question made sense, especially since he'd never found anyone else he wanted to spend the rest of his life with.

He nodded and gave her the simple truth. "I do. To the right woman."

"I guess you haven't found her yet." He hated that she didn't believe he'd wanted to marry her.

I'm looking right at her. I will make you believe in me again. "I'm working on it," he said instead of his first thought.

Jamie eyed him. To keep her from backing off again, he went back to her original question. "Rory and Colt have what they want and Sadie gave me what I always wanted."

"Really? What's that?"

He eyed her across the table. "You already know."

"Your own ranch?"

"Sadie kept her family's place, fixed it up, and moved me in to take over. I've spent the last few months working on the place, getting it ready to run cattle again. I've still got a few projects to complete, but I'll have the business up and running soon." He hoped.

He'd fallen behind this week taking care of Jamie. He had to have everything in order before winter set in. "Colt just delivered three horses. I've got two hundred head of cattle coming next week." And more in another two months if he could get the rest of the fencing done. The schedule he'd set cut things close. He might have to rethink his plans if Jamie needed more of his time. It meant that he'd either have to put out more money he didn't really have up front to hire help and meet his deadline, or wait to add to the herd, which might complicate the breeding program he wanted to implement in the spring.

He still needed to cut and bale enough grass and hay to get through the winter.

Didn't matter. He'd made the mistake once of putting ranch business before Jamie. He wouldn't make that mistake twice. Still, the stress settled between his shoulders. He'd make it work. No matter what, Jamie's health and well-being had to come first.

"Wow. You must be so happy to finally have what you wanted."

"I am. For the most part. I mean, I've got the ranch, but the dream's not complete."

She wasn't there. She was the missing piece that would make it all worth it. He wanted to tell her that, but she'd shut down again and shut him out, because she wasn't ready to hear that from him. She wasn't ready to give him anything more than the tenuous friendship they held on to now. Though they'd spent the last several days together, they'd barely done more than exist in each other's company. Until tonight.

He ate up more than the delicious food. He devoured every bit of her attention and interest in his life, the way she relaxed as the seconds ticked by, and the building interest in her eyes that she couldn't hide behind her instinctive urge to pull away, because she wanted to be close. To him, he hoped, and not just anyone who made her feel less alone.

"I have no doubt you'll get exactly what you want out of that place."

With every fiber of his being, he hoped so. But even having a thriving business didn't compare to what he'd feel if he got her back.

What did any of it matter if he didn't have her beside him to share it?

Why the hell did I let her go?

If he felt this connected to her even when she kept her distance, how could he have ever thought he could live his whole life without her? He couldn't. He didn't want to. He wanted her back. He wanted to make her happy. He wanted the life they'd once dreamed about to be their future.

He wanted everything his brothers had found with their wives.

"You're a hard worker, Ford. You don't give up. You don't quit. I always liked that about you. I wanted to be like you in that way."

"You are like that. Look at you, Jamie, and all you've endured. You're still here. You survived."

"The Army taught me that. Looking back, I realized I needed to toughen up and fight for what I wanted. I let my mother insult me and accuse me of things I didn't do. I let her chip away at my self-respect and self-esteem until I ran." Her soft, imploring gaze met his. "I ran away from what I really wanted instead of standing up to her and for what I wanted." She looked down at the table. Her fingers traced the lines in the wood. "I believed the terrible things she said about me. I still hear her in my head. Every mistake I've made, every time I fell short of being and doing what I thought I should, I let her win because I believed what she said about me was true."

"It's not, Firefly. Deep down, you always knew that. That's why you endure and survive. It's *your* voice that speaks to you and pushes you to move on."

"Too often these days, my voice is a whisper I barely hear and hers is a shout that rings in my head."

"But you do hear that whisper. All you have to do is believe in it, Firefly, and it will drown her out."

"It seemed so much easier to hear when I was away and living the military life. I loved my work, the people I served with, the sense of being a part of something bigger than myself. I needed that after I left. I thrived on it."

"What you did was courageous. Driving in the supply line with a target on your back every time you went out . . ." Ford shook his head. The same sense of dread he'd carried with him since he found out what she did for a living washed over him again. He'd lived in fear of something happening to her. It had, but she'd survived and come home. To say that he was grateful to have her alive and sitting in front of him didn't begin to describe the depth of feelings he had for her.

"I worked my way up to what you'd know as a management role. I hadn't driven in the convoy for a long time. But that day, a few of us covered for other soldiers who came up sick with food poisoning. You know, adapt and improvise when things don't go your way."

"That change in personnel cost you in the end."

"It cost several soldiers. Friends."

"I'm sorry for that. I'm sorry you got hurt and you're still hurting."

Jamie's gaze fell away again. She fidgeted with the collar of her shirt, trying to pull it up over the scars on her neck. Noticing his gaze, she stopped and sat back. "I'm trying."

He took a chance and reached across the table, putting his hand over hers. "I see that, Jamie."

She flinched at his touch, but overcame her initial reaction, leaned forward, and set her hand on top of his on the table. She hesitated a moment, taking her time to get used to touching him, someone, like she hadn't done it recently enough to remember the comfort it offered. Her fingers softly traced the veins on the back of his hand like she'd done the lines on the table.

He tried to coax her out of retreating on him again. "You can tell me anything. I think you need to talk to me about it. I know you've got your shrink, and I'm happy you're working with someone who can help you, but you used to tell me everything. I hope I made you feel better then. I'm trying to do that for you now, but you push me away even though you want to pull me close." He pointedly looked at their joined hands, then back at her.

Jamie didn't respond. She didn't even look at him.

"Tell me I'm wrong." He pushed, hoping she'd open up. Wishing she'd take one small step toward him instead of always retreating.

"You're right. But I don't know how to start. Where to start. I don't like to talk about it because it makes it real all over again. What do you want me to do? Dump all my crap on you and prove I'm more trouble than I'm worth, that you have every reason to walk away again?"

Ford squeezed Jamie's hand and didn't let up. "I won't walk away this time. I won't send you away. I won't let you go. I promise."

Her lips scrunched into a sardonic smile. "It's not that simple, Ford. I'm different. You're different. Everything is different."

He leaned in, wishing the table didn't separate them,

wishing nothing else did, kissed her palm, and pressed it to his cheek. "Then let's be different together."

The pained look on her face made Ford's chest tighten with dread. He anticipated her next move, but hated that she felt the need to retreat from him again. She pulled her hand free, stood up, and took three steps away from the table, her hands up to ward him off despite the fact he didn't move to go after her. He'd made progress with her these last few days. He anticipated they'd go through some ups and downs. He just wished the tenuous trust they'd built didn't feel this close to breaking. Still, he needed to know how hard he could push her without sending her into a downward spiral. Right now, she needed space, but she hadn't blown up on him for talking about them being together—something he thought she wanted as much as he did.

"I'm not the same woman you used to know. You didn't want her. There's no way you'd want me now."

He remembered Zac telling him what their mother said to her at the diner. "You're dead wrong, Firefly. That's your mother speaking, and you know it."

She shook her head. "You should go."

"Jamie, honey, it's okay to . . ."

"Go. You need to go." The pulse at her neck beat faster than her breath sawing in and out. He'd sent her into a panic attack.

He rose from the table, making her eyes go even wider. She braced for a fight or to run. He didn't know which and didn't want to think about it too much. It would only make him mad to think she wanted to do either of those things because of him.

"Leave. I want to be left alone."

"No you don't." Ford stared at her from across the

room for a full ten seconds. She barely held on to her composure as she slowly unraveled in front of him.

"Don't come back." The soft words barely made it past her lips.

She didn't mean them. But they ripped through his heart and made it bleed.

"I'll see you tomorrow." He hoped those words, the reassurance he put into them, finally penetrated and sank into her mind and heart. If he had to start all over with her tomorrow, so be it. He'd settled in for the long haul. One setback wouldn't deter him from his goal—Jamie, healthy and happy again. And just maybe, his again.

CHAPTER 9

The ringing phone sent a jolt of adrenaline through her system. Jamie rolled over and stared at the pretty peonies Ford had given her. A much nicer view than the dead fern Ford had tossed out. She waited out the four rings, for it to go to voice mail before she picked it up. Missed call. From Tobin. Again. Because she couldn't bring herself to talk to him. He reminded her too much of what happened. Even his call sent her mind back to that one moment in time when she was lying on the ground shot and bloody and staring up at the attacker who killed all her friends.

A man she couldn't bring into focus.

A man she should have killed before he killed all her friends and tried to kill her.

He'd tried damn hard.

She rubbed her finger over the scar on her chest.

The phone chirped with the inevitable text message from Tobin because she hadn't answered his call. Guilt swamped her for ignoring the only friend she had left. Well, except for Ford. Maybe. She hoped they were still friends, especially after she'd ordered him out of her house last night when things got too personal and too scary.

Tobin wouldn't be her friend much longer if she kept ignoring him, but her need to distance herself from the past kept her from answering his calls.

TOBIN: Pick up the phone call me back or I'll come to Montana

Direct. To the point. Just like Tobin. A man of few words. Jamie rolled to her side and grabbed her sour stomach. She did not want to see Tobin. He wouldn't come here, she tried to convince herself, but the more she thought it possible, the harder it was to breathe and fight the need to run from him and a past she didn't want to think about anymore.

She tossed her phone back on the nightstand and tried to think of something less . . . overwhelming. She didn't want Tobin to invade her solitude and haul all the things she tried to keep shoved in the back of her mind to the forefront. She wanted time to deal with them in her own way, in her own time.

The only good thing to take up residence with the ghosts in her mind, the only person she wanted to think about, was Ford.

Jamie went to bed last night, tossing and turning, with one thought rattling around her brain—she and Ford had both changed. Nothing in her life seemed the same. His life wasn't exactly the same as when she'd last seen him. Could they really be different together?

She didn't know if she had it in her to love someone again. She'd only ever loved him. She'd seen other men after him, but they never seemed to measure up to the one man who'd stolen her heart. The man who still held it, despite how battered and broken it had become these past years. She didn't know if she had it in her to put the pieces back together and give him what he seemed to want.

Did he really want a second chance with her? Did he want to be together again? He sure made it seem that way, but why would he want her back after all this time when she was so much worse than the girl he sent away all those years ago? It didn't make sense. He didn't make sense.

What the hell am I doing here?

She needed to leave, find someplace new, someplace where no one knew her and she didn't know anyone. No one to pressure her. A place she could breathe—if that even existed.

Her phone chirped again. She leaned over and read the message.

TOBIN: Call me!!!

She needed to move to someplace without cell service.

She'd find a job. Something easy. Thanks to her medical disability and the money she'd saved, she could afford to take a low paying job and still get by if she kept her expenses down. She didn't need much. A roof over her head, food, and her meds. She'd get by. She didn't need anything extravagant. Look where she lived now. More shack than modern home, the place needed a lot of work, but she couldn't even muster up the energy to paint the walls, let alone renovate the place.

It had good bones. It would be a great place to live. If she fixed up the barn out back, she could even get a horse. She used to love to ride. Especially with Ford. She missed those long rides, challenging him to a race, and ending up kissing under a tree, or splashing and laughing in the river.

Her grandmother had a thriving vegetable garden on the side of the house back in the day. She could put one in, but she'd have to start with plants from the nursery. It was summer now, and soon winter would be upon them and nothing would grow until after the snow thawed.

If she bought a rocking chair, she could sit on the porch and watch the sunrise while she drank her coffee. She and Ford could sit out there and watch the sunset.

Wait. What? She didn't want to stay. She wanted to go. Right?

Two honks blasted out front. Ford. Her heart fluttered and another bolt of adrenaline shot through her system with the anticipation of seeing him again. After she sent him away last night, she didn't expect to see him this early in the morning. Or at all.

But he came back. He kept coming back.

What did it mean?

Unable to figure that out without accepting what Ford kept trying to tell her, she turned and stared at the clock. Just after eight-thirty. What was he doing here now? He should be working his ranch. The one he'd always wanted. The one she'd thought she'd live on with him.

Not going to happen. Right? She didn't know the answer to that question, or the millions of others rattling around her brain in some random whirlwind.

The front door opened and closed. Ford turned the water on in the kitchen sink.

What the hell is he doing? How did he get in?

That last question scared her, because she was sure she'd locked up before going to bed after spending far too long staring at a bottle of whiskey and her bottle of pills, listening to the silence in her empty house and her even emptier soul, scolding herself for sending Ford away when she'd have liked to stay locked in that moment when he kissed her palm and pressed her hand to his rough cheek. The warmth that simple touch had sent through her system should tell her more than anything how much she wanted to be with him again.

Logically, she knew the dark moments that dragged her deep into the black pit in her mind would pass. She fought her way through her dark thoughts to find a glimmer of light to hold on to. Most of the time something, anything worth living for was hard to find, but lately, one thing always emerged and lit up that blackness. Ford. She clung to him and memories of what they used to share. She didn't spend every second of her day lost in the past anymore. She'd even caught herself thinking about the future, and the possibility of one with him.

She didn't know which was more dangerous, wallowing in her past, or risking her heart to be with Ford again.

Worth it? Yeah, probably. But it meant working even harder to be the kind of woman he'd want and deserve. Her heart really wanted to try.

"Firefly, get up," Ford called down the hall. Probably too afraid to come to her door for fear she'd shoot him again.

On a positive note, this morning she didn't wake up with the gun in her hand. She woke up sighing out his name, wishing she could sink back into the dream of her with him in this bed, tangling up the sheets. His warm hands on her skin. His hard body pressed on top of her, rocking into her.

She'd much rather dream about that. Though reality would be a hell of a lot better.

He was here, in her house, and she didn't know why, but she wanted to believe it was because what she thought they shared so long ago actually existed in some small way between them even now.

Jamie rolled out of bed, stretching her back side to side to loosen up the tight muscles and scarred skin. What she wouldn't give for a massage. A bubble bath in a luxurious tub. The one in the master bath here had seen better days and staring at the outdated gold flecked Formica counter and god-awful lime avocado green paint depressed her more.

She raised her right arm and stretched her shoulder. She tried to raise her left, but only managed to get her hand level with her face. She needed to get back to her physical therapy before she lost even more of the mobility in that arm.

She dragged on a pair of old worn sweats and adjusted the T-shirt she'd slept in up on her shoulders to cover as much of the burn scars as possible. She stood and walked to her closed bedroom door, catching a glimpse of her rumpled self in the mirror over the dresser. She stopped and raked her fingers through her disheveled hair. Too thin, lines on her face, dark circles under her eyes, ugly scars, and a bad attitude.

Every guy's dream.

If she had a hope of keeping Ford's attention, she needed to work on her physical and mental state.

She ran the brush through her hair, dabbed some concealer under her eyes, and slicked some tinted lip balm over her lips. Far from a beauty queen, but a hell of a lot better than the zombie she usually looked like, she opened her bedroom door and walked down the hall to the kitchen. She turned the corner and found Ford standing with his back to the sink, drinking a cup of coffee. On the table in front of him, he'd set a plate with scrambled eggs, sliced strawberries, and her favorite glazed donut holes.

She stood staring at him, her heart melting in her chest at his kindness. God, just the sight of him made her feel better. She wanted to walk right up to him and lay her head on his wide chest, feel his strong arms around her, hear his steady heartbeat against her ear, and let it all go.

A single tear slipped past her lashes and ran down her cheek. Still, she didn't move. Couldn't really. She just wanted to look at him and feel this way. Happy. Grateful. Relieved he was here.

He came back.

"Morning." His deep voice resonated through her body.

That bit of happiness in her heart grew three sizes in her chest. She just might get used to it again.

"Hungry?"

Unable to speak or dismiss his kind gesture, she swiped the tear from her face, sat at the table, and picked up the fork. She slipped the first bite of warm eggs into her mouth. They practically melted on her tongue.

Ford sighed next to her. He set his coffee mug on the counter beside him and reached for something out of her sight. She tried to remain calm, relaxed, but her focus remained on his every movement.

She placed another bite into her mouth and froze with the fork on her tongue when Ford's hand settled on her shoulder and that familiar electricity shot through her system. On guard all the time, she slipped the fork out of her mouth and breathed in his clean, rain in a forest scent.

He leaned over and set her bottles of pills on the table next to her mug of coffee. Her focus settled on the warmth and weight of his hand on her. That warmth spread through her like smoke from a fire filling an enclosed space. Nothing was as empty as her before that happiness settled inside her, but now something even better washed through her. Heat. Need. Longing.

His fingers brushed across her back as he stood and went back to the counter, grabbed his mug, and came back to the table and sat across from her.

Only then did she try to swallow the sweet strawberries.

"Relax, Firefly, I've touched you a million times, a thousand different ways. You know me. I know you."

Several of the ways he used to touch her came to mind and heated her cheeks. "I'm not the same. You're not the same. This isn't the same." But God, how she wanted it to be.

He leaned forward and kept his steady gaze locked with hers. "The way I touch you is the same. I will never hurt you." He sat back in his chair and sipped his coffee, completely at ease, except for the intense gaze he kept on her. A stare that dared her to believe and asked her to trust.

"I'm trying."

"I know you are. I'm asking you to keep trying."

She hadn't realized she spoke her thought out loud. What he asked was exactly what she told herself each and every day—multiple times a day. Don't give up. Never give up.

Easier said than done.

She went back to eating the lovely meal he'd made her. He sat across from her watching without making it seem like he studied her every move and every nuance of her expression. Which she tried to keep blank, but feared every random thought in her head showed on her face.

"I ran into your brother in town while I was picking up some supplies and getting you donuts."

Jamie popped one into her mouth, savoring the sweetness and light doughy texture. "Thank you." She didn't know what else to say right now. He'd completely thrown her off balance with that one simple touch.

"You're welcome. Zac asked about you. He said you haven't called him back in days."

"I didn't have anything good to say."

"Really? Nothing new or good happening in your life this past week?"

"What do you want me to say to him? 'Ford's back in my life. I sit around the house alone all day getting my crazy on and waiting for him to show up and make it all seem normal and better, hoping he doesn't see that I'm a mess despite how obvious that is. And how was your day, Zac?'"

Ford's smile spread across his face and lit up his hazel eyes. She replayed what she'd said in her head and sighed. Damn the man for making her say things she didn't want him to know.

"Well, under that mess is someone who wants to get better. Without the booze mixed with meds, the crazy has turned down, despite the thoughts you still listen to in your head and the fact you sent me away last night when you really wanted me to stay."

Despite how much she loved that cocky grin, it pissed her off sometimes, especially when he was right.

"You're awful sure of yourself, tough guy."

He nodded his agreement. "For all the one step forward, two steps back, I see you working to move in the right direction, but I worry about you sitting here all day fighting the thoughts in your head and the memories of your past."

"I miss having something to do, but I'm still in so much pain."

"Zac mentioned you're supposed to do physical therapy for your injuries. You always seem physically uncomfortable. You need to move, not waste away on the couch staring at the TV. Half the time, you're not even paying attention to what you watch anyway."

She couldn't argue with anything he'd said, so she didn't say anything.

"So, get dressed. You're coming with me."

"Outside?"

The unexpected chuckle bubbled up from his gut. "Yes. In the fresh air."

"Ford, I don't want to go anywhere. Being around people . . ." She shook her head, the panic rising in her chest. Her heart thrashed against her ribs. She could barely breathe, thinking about the parade, the level of anxiety that had caused until she exploded and punched her brother in the face. She didn't want to have another total meltdown in front of Ford, let alone the whole damn town.

Ford placed his hand over hers. "Jamie, breathe. Please, baby. Take a short breath and let it out."

She tried. She really did, but the thought of going out, being around a bunch of people, feeling like the enemy was out there waiting for a chance to hurt her when she knew it was all in her mind . . . *Oh God, please, I can't.*

Ford rose and came around the table and crouched beside her. He laid his hand on her shoulder. She flinched, but didn't make a break for it. Her breath stopped and her heart skipped several beats. Something inside of her throbbed. It pulsed out to him and back. It made the missing him worse, the wanting him stronger, the need to reach out to him overwhelming because she feared him pushing her away again.

She tried to focus on the connection to him and concentrated on the feel of his warm hand on her shoulder.

"You feel me, Firefly. I'm right here beside you. I will never let anything happen to you. I'm not taking you to town. We will be alone. You and me. At my place." Ford squeezed her tight shoulder. "Come with me today. Let me show you the ranch I'm building." So much pride and anticipation filled his voice.

She stared straight ahead, her heart thrashing in her chest. One simple thought took hold in her mind that had the power to destroy her if things didn't go well. She'd get to spend the day with him.

"What if I can't do it? What if I freak out and get lost in the past and . . ." She didn't know what else, but something equally terrible, like her trying to hurt him again.

"So you do. We get through it. We keep moving forward. We stick together."

We. That sounded so good to her.

But could she do it?

"Stop talking yourself out of it. You can do it. You want to do it. You're scared. I get it, Jamie, but you need to fight that fear and learn to live again. Baby steps, like you coming over to my place where it will be only me and you."

They used to be an "us." They used to stick together. Until he didn't want her anymore. The old wound opened and bled. How long before that happened again?

"That scares me, too."

"I know it does. You'll get used to it. Just like you're getting used to me touching you."

Lost in her head, she hadn't paid attention to him brushing his fingers up and down her back. It felt nice. Familiar. Her muscles loosened. The tension she fought every second of the day eased.

Afraid to give in to her urge to believe it meant more than simple comfort and touch him back, she rose and headed for her room, calling over her shoulder, "I'll be dressed in a minute."

She didn't even make it to her room before another seed of hope sprouted out of her battered heart. That bomb had blown up her truck and someone had shot her. Those things froze her in that moment and drew a black curtain over her future, but Ford had managed to pull it back and give her a glimpse of a future she thought she'd lost.

She wouldn't allow herself to hope for more than a chance to spend the day looking at him and remembering what they used to have, the way they used to be. Maybe that was all she'd get. She'd take it, because he was the only good and bright thing keeping her from falling back down into that deep dark pit she'd dragged herself out of a few short days ago.

She'd go. She'd try. And maybe, even though it felt like it, it wouldn't kill her.

CHAPTER 10

Ford pulled into the driveway and stopped the truck in front of his house. Jamie remained smashed against the passenger door—as far away from him as possible. He tried not to take it personally. Especially after the way she'd hesitated at the threshold of her door, afraid to go outside and leave her hideaway where she felt safe. Afraid she'd lose her shit and embarrass herself or hurt him again. But she stepped out and climbed in his truck anyway. The girl still had guts. She had more strength than he'd ever given her credit for, and he should have because she'd been brave enough to leave everything behind and find a purpose and direction in her life that she loved. Part of the reason she felt lost and disconnected was because she'd been so wrapped up in her job and the family she'd become a part of with her military friends. He doubted she'd spent many days alone in the military. Here, she isolated herself. The nights they had dinner together, she ignored the calls coming into her phone. He doubted she called her friends back. She hadn't even called her brother back.

He wanted her to start living again. That meant getting her out of the house and out of her head.

Every night he drove over to her place a ball of

nerves and deep concern, afraid that she'd be in a bad place, lost in some nightmare, or simply gone again, too distraught to stay here anymore. He worried he'd never get a chance to make things right and see if what they had in the past could be the foundation for an even better future.

These last few days he'd seen glimpses of the Jamie he used to know. This morning, she'd actually seemed happy. He wanted more of that for her.

He wanted to share this place with her.

She understood his need for something of his own to pass on to the family he wanted to have, a family she'd wanted with him a long time ago. He hoped she still wanted that, because he needed her sweetness and tender care back in his life. All that love that used to pour out of her had filled the void his parents, and especially his mother, left in his life. His brothers and grandfather cared for him and about him, but until Jamie came into his life and showed him that a kinder, gentler kind of love could mean so much and sink so deep, he hadn't realized how much he'd missed and craved it.

He wondered if she thought about the dream they'd once dreamed together that evaporated the day she left and he was trying to rebuild right now.

"Jamie, this is Sadie's old place. I moved in a few months ago. What do you think?" Until this moment, he hadn't realized how much he wanted her to like it. How much he wanted her to be here with him.

Sadness filled her eyes and tilted her lips into a soft frown. "I always wanted a house with a long, wide porch."

"I know. And a swing." He pointed to the one he'd put up two days ago between the living room windows. "The vegetable garden still needs to go in."

Her gaze shifted to the tilled earth surrounded by a wood and wire fence to keep the critters out. A soft smile touched her lips. The dreamy look in her eyes told him she was picturing the lush plants and abundant vegetables, too.

They'd talked a lot about the house they'd share, the land he wanted, the business they'd run together. When Sadie offered him the house and property, he'd instantly thought of Jamie and how perfectly this place matched the dreams she'd shared with him about the kind of home and life she wanted with her husband, kids, and horses. The kind of life she wanted with him.

Here it sat, ready for her to accept it, if only she could look at him again the way she used to. If only she could believe in and trust him again. If only she loved him the way she did before he turned his back on her when he should have held on to her. To love.

"Sadie and Luna fixed up the inside for me. It's really nice."

"Big."

"Yeah, sometimes the place feels like way more than one person needs."

"A place like this needs a family."

He wanted that more than anything. Ford stared at the house and land. "Yes, it does. I'd love to see my kids playing tag in the yard and riding horses in the fields."

Her gaze swept over the house, stables, and pastures in the distance. "This is a great place, Ford. Everything you ever wanted."

"Almost." He didn't elaborate, but her nod told him without words that she understood he meant that she was still missing from this perfect picture.

"You know what I miss most about the military? My

friends, but also the routine and having a purpose. You said Colt delivered some horses. Want some help with them? I can do some of the easy chores. I need something to do." Hope lit her eyes.

The shock of her words made him question if he'd heard her right. He'd thought to ease her into coming here. Start with today, get her to come again tomorrow. He'd tempt her with the horses she adored, keep her close, until she enjoyed being here with him.

"You're hired."

"I didn't mean that. You probably have several people working here."

"Not yet. I need to hire some help soon, so I'll start with you."

"Ford, I have some money saved up. I have a place to stay. You don't need to pay me. I just thought this would be a good start for me to get back to work."

"It's a hell of a lot of hard work. It's a chance for you to be productive and a part of something again. A part of this." He nodded toward the ranch spread before them. "With me."

She pressed her lips together so tight, they disappeared into her mouth until she made up her mind to say what was on her mind and clouding her eyes with second thoughts.

"I don't know how much help I'll be. I can't raise my left arm very high." She adjusted her shirt, trying to pull it up and over the scars on her shoulders and neck. "The burns . . ."

"You can tell me anything, Jamie. What about the burns?"

"The skin is tight, gnarled in some places with scar tissue. It makes it hard to move sometimes. My muscles lock up. It hurts."

"Zac mentioned you need physical therapy. You need to work on your range of motion in your arm, shoulder, and back. Rebuild the muscles and your strength. You can do that here. We'll start off slow. You'll do what you can. No pressure."

She shook her head. "Ford, I'm happy to give you a hand here and there, but taking on the big jobs, you need someone who can actually do the work. Not me."

"I want you." He let that hang between them in the silence filling the truck cab. When he got nothing but her confused stare, he opened his door, got out, shut the door, and rounded the hood, going to her side. He opened her door and held his hand out to her.

She sat back, staring at him. "You're asking too much."

"I'm asking you to try. I'm asking you to believe in me again." If she believed he could do this, put this ranch back together and make a real go of it, he knew he could do it. And maybe in rebuilding this place, he'd find a way to rebuild their relationship, because he couldn't fail again. Not with her.

He reached for her hand. And just like the old Jamie, when something scared her, or she thought it too hard to do, she dug deep and marched onward. She put her trembling hand in his, sucked in a steadying breath, scooted off the seat, and stood in front of him. Close. He gave her hand a little tug to draw her with him. She pushed the door closed and walked with him to the stables, her hand in his.

Ford pushed the barn doors open and stepped in with Jamie right beside him. Three horses nickered their hellos and hung their heads over the stall gates.

"Meet the guys." He pointed to the horses in turn. "Dusty, Mo, and Ash. They need to be brushed. Check their hooves for stones. Dusty likes to kick over his water bucket. It probably needs to be refilled. Ash has a sore on his right hind leg. The medicine is on the counter outside his stall. Clean the wound before you put the ointment on it.

"You need a purpose, a daily routine, and a place where you belong. Everything you lost. Here it is, Firefly. This is where you belong." He hoped someday soon she thought so, too.

"I don't want to disappoint you."

"Never, Firefly. You do what you can, work on getting better, that's all I ask."

"Um, what are you going to do?" Her hand trembled in his. Her gaze took in every inch and dark corner of the interior. He hoped it was being in a new place that was making her so nervous and not him.

"Muck out the stalls and get to work on some of the other items on my huge to-do list." He squeezed her hand, then reluctantly released her to go to Ash's stall door and give the big gray gelding a pat down the nose. "Let's get to work," he ordered, hoping that would get Jamie moving before she bolted out the door. He slid the stall door open and hooked the lead rope to Ash's halter and led him out into the alley. "Come here, Jamie."

Drawn to the horse like he hoped she would be, she slowly walked over and brushed her shaking hand down Ash's side. She used to love to go riding with him. She loved to pet the horses and talk to them at Kendrick Ranch.

He loved seeing the soft smile on her face. He should have thought of this sooner, but it mattered so much more that Jamie wanted to work here despite the way she second-guessed herself. One more step forward.

Ford tied off the lead rope and backed away from Jamie, giving her space to settle down and relax. She dropped her purse on the table outside the stall and grabbed the brush he'd left out for her. She held it in her right hand and stroked it down Ash's long neck.

"Use your left hand to do the front of him. As you move around to the other side, use it to do his back end."

"Ford, I told you . . ."

"You need to work the muscles to build them back. Take your time. When your arm gets tired, switch to the right. He's not that tall. You might be able to do his back. If not, you'll work your way up to doing it over time."

Jamie stared at him over the horse for a good ten seconds. "You won't quit, will you?"

"Not on you."

Her eyes filled with a soft warmth. She took the brush in her left hand and raised it up the horse's side. She slid the brush along Ash's coat in slow, awkward, and deliberate motions. He tried not to stare, and grabbed what he needed and went into Ash's stall to clean it out. It gave him the perfect excuse and line of sight to spy on her without being obvious.

The way her eyes winced with pain as she worked tore at his insides. He wanted to tell her to stop. He'd do it. She should just rest and let it be. But that was exactly the opposite of what she needed. So he sucked it up, endured the nagging instinct to protect her from any more pain, and let her do the job. She did the best she could, working the brush over Ash's coat, but it was far from what Ash needed. He'd have to go over him again later tonight. That wasn't really the point. This was about Jamie and what she needed.

By the time he finished cleaning out the stall, Jamie had finished brushing down Ash. A fine sheen of sweat glistened on her face. The seemingly simple task had sapped her energy and left her weak. He went to the tack room down the aisle and pulled a bottle of water out of the small fridge. Most of his supplies and tack needed to be sorted, organized, and hung or stored. He hoped Jamie would help him out and take care of the task. He hoped that despite how hard this seemed for her, she came back tomorrow and kept at it. He wanted to see her healthy and well and this was a means of making her strong again in body and mind. If she felt a sense of accomplishment and pride in a job well done, no matter how long it took her to finish the task, then she'd get better.

God, he just wanted her to feel better.

Ash rubbed his big head against Jamie's shoulder, pushing her back a step with his affection. Jamie pressed her fingers to her chest, rubbing at the pain that also filled her eyes.

"You okay?"

"Sore. Tired. But in a good way."

Ford handed her the bottle of water. She tried to squeeze it in her left hand and twist the top off with her right, but muscle fatigue made her left hand shake and the bottle slipped free. He caught it before it hit the floor, twisted off the top, and handed the bottle back without comment. She took it and drank deeply, glancing over at her purse on the table.

"If you need your meds, Jamie, take them."

She took another deep swallow of water, eyed him, then went to her purse and pulled out the bottles of pills. Figuring if she couldn't open her water bottle, no way she'd get through the childproof safety caps, he walked up behind her and reached for the first bottle of pills. Jamie sidestepped, jumping away, and putting him square in front of her rather than at her back.

Shit. His mistake.

"Easy, sweetheart. I just wanted to help you."

"Ford . . ." She held up her hand and let it fall, staring at him with a look that begged him to understand everything she didn't know how to say. "I'm sorry."

"Nothing to be sorry about." He handed her one of the pain pills. "I shouldn't have come up behind you like that."

"It seems so stupid and unnecessary and crazy."

"It's a survival mechanism. One you've been taught due to extreme circumstances. I get it, Jamie. For now, take that pill. Take a break. I'll put Ash back and bring out Dusty if you're up for more."

"Sure. Just give me a few minutes." She opened and closed her left hand several times to work out the soreness he read on her face.

He took her hand in his. "Jamie, if you need to rest, I'm fine with that. You can hang out while I get some things done. I'll take you home if you want me to."

Jamie pressed her lips together and stared at the ground. "Would you do something for me?"

"Anything."

She tilted her head to the side just enough to glance at him with one eye and squeezed his hand. "Get out."

His head whipped back with surprise. "I'm sorry."

"Go away. Leave me with them. I can't relax and focus on the movements I need to make to work my shoulder when all I can focus on is your eyes on me. I'm self-conscious enough as it is, but feeling you makes it harder."

He squeezed her hand back. "You haven't really felt me yet, Firefly."

A soft blush tinged her cheeks pink.

He used his free hand to brush a thumb over her soft skin. "Okay." Ford turned to go.

Jamie tugged on his hand. "Okay?"

With his back to her, he smiled, but let it fall when he turned back to her. "Did you want me to stay?"

Her hesitation in letting go of his hand only made him grin.

Jamie dropped his hand, but she didn't back away. "Sometimes I want to smack that cocky smile right off your face."

Kiss me and I won't be able to smile. At least not on the outside. They weren't quite there yet, but they'd made progress. One step forward.

For all her nerves and wanting to be alone, she actually wanted to be alone with him. She wanted him there, but not watching her. Nearby, but not underfoot.

"I've got a gate to repair out in the corral." He pointed just out the wide doors, turned, and went out to do the job, so he could let the horses out later.

Three steps away from her, he stopped in his tracks and shook his head.

"What is it?" she asked.

"Nothing." Except he must really care about her if he was willing to go through all this to spend time with her. As much as she wanted him near, he wanted to be with her even more.

Jamie breathed a sigh of relief when Ford walked out and gave her some space, but it only took a minute for her to feel the walls close in on her as the quiet and unfamiliar shadows unsettled her.

She stared out the big door to where Ford used a

hammer to bang out the pins on the gate hinge. Once he had both pins out, he braced his hands on the gate's crossbar and lifted the gate free, carrying it back several paces to lay it out on the ground to repair the broken, weathered boards and attach the new latch lying at his feet. The muscles in his arms turned rock hard from the hefty weight and strength it took to lay the gate down without just dropping it. Her eyes ate up the expanse of rippling muscles in his arms and back. He didn't seem winded or even remotely strained by the exertion.

Heat pooled low in her belly. The connection she'd felt to Ford so long ago pulsed in her chest. A strange pull made her want to go to him and touch all that strength and somehow take it into herself. Acutely aware of his scrutiny while he'd been in the stables with her, she'd asked him to go, hoping she could stop thinking about him and what they used to have, but distance didn't lessen the thoughts in her head—it amplified them.

She wanted so much to go back in time and change the course of her life. She wanted Ford to ask her to stay, not tell her to go. She wanted to have the life they'd dreamed about, but now it seemed like some other woman's wish because she wasn't that person anymore. She wanted to be that hopeful girl again, but couldn't fight reality. She'd never be the same again. This version of herself wanted to run. From the nightmares. That terrifying black hole in her mind. From Ford. Herself.

Damnit, she was so tired of fighting herself, the dark thoughts in her mind, and the feeling of defeat that swamped her sometimes, and especially fighting what she felt for Ford. She didn't want to do it anymore.

Time to declare a cease-fire with herself.

I'll take care of myself.

I'll be kinder to myself.

I'll allow myself to believe good things still happen.

She needed this job. Time outside with the horses, doing something productive. Her shoulders and back ached, but it felt like a workout that would get her the results she wanted if she just stuck with it.

Get with it, Keller. Push, push, push.

Drill sergeants could be so unrelenting. She'd made it through basic training—she could do this.

Instead of overthinking it, she got to work and lost herself in the rhythmic motion of brushing down the horse, the feel of his big strong body under her hands, and the steady billowing of his breath as she steadied herself against his side. She brushed down his head. Dusty blew in her ear and nuzzled her cheek.

"Hey there, sweet guy. Are you flirting with me?"

Dusty nudged his nose against her chest. She instinctively swept her fingers over the spot and felt the puckered scar where the first bullet hit her. She fell into the past, seeing her best friend Catalina lying dead. Blood covering the side of her face, her dark eyes empty and blank. Pedro ducked behind a vehicle, rose up, and shot toward the incoming fire. One shot hit him in the chest. He gasped as all the breath pushed out of his lungs. The next bullet sliced across his neck. He dropped to the ground face-first, blood pooling all around him. He was the last of her group to fall. Everywhere she looked lay her dead friends. Ahead, she saw herself falling from the top of an armored vehicle and hitting the ground on her back.

A hand clamped onto her and dragged her back. She

fought the enemy, striking out with her fists, wishing she had her gun.

"Jamie! Jamie! Come back!"

She couldn't breathe. Someone held her tight even as she fought to get free.

"Jamie! Stop! You're safe. Please, Firefly, come back."

Firefly. No, that's not right. Everyone called her Keller. Catalina called her Jamie when they were in the mess tent or alone in their bunks.

But Catalina wasn't here. None of them were here anymore. She was all alone and the loneliness throbbed in time with the guilt swamping her.

"They're dead," she wailed, giving in to the tide of grief that washed over her. Ford's strong arms surrounded her and held her close. For the first time she realized her feet weren't touching the floor but dangling at his calves.

"Ssh, baby, it's okay," Ford crooned.

Unable to allow the grief to suck her under, she went with the rage that rose up in its place. "It's not okay." She pushed against his shoulders and leaned back.

He released her, but held on to her shoulders to keep her within reach. She swung her arms up and out, breaking his hold on her. Ford's eyes went wide with surprise by her defensive move.

She fisted her hands and stamped her foot, her body rigid with the rage roiling inside of her. "They're dead. All of them." And somehow it felt like it was all her fault.

"I'm sorry, Jamie."

"Sorry! Sorry. What the hell did sorry ever do? What the hell did I do? Nothing." She should have done something. "I see him up there spraying bullets everywhere. People are yelling, then they're silent. Nothing but the crack of gunfire. Over and over again." She placed her hands over her ears to block out the sound, but it didn't stop the echo in her head. "It hurts like hell, but I go after him. I need to stop him. Stop! Stop!"

"Do you reach him?"

"I don't know. It all goes black. Like I can't bear to see what happens next."

"Did anyone else survive with you?"

Her hands fell limp at her sides as the glimpse at her lost memories faded along with her energy. So much for a cease-fire with her dark thoughts.

"Tobin survived."

"What did he say happened?"

"The shooter got away."

"Is that what you remember?"

"I can't remember anything," she shouted, her frustration overriding the roiling fear and urgency building inside of her, pressing against her skin, until she felt like she'd explode. "I failed. They're dead."

The grief swamped her again. Her knees buckled from the weight of guilt on her shoulders. Ford caught her before she hit the ground and pulled her into his chest and wrapped his arms around her. His lips pressed to the side of her head again and again. Those sweet kisses eased her in a way she'd never thought possible. His strength and comfort wrapped around her. She buried her face in his neck and breathed in his spicy scent mixed with the hay and horses surrounding them. She held his shoulders in a tight hug that had her fingers digging into his tight muscles.

"It's okay that you lived, Firefly. Your friends would have wanted you to survive. They'd want you to go on living and be happy. They'd want you to live the life they lost. For them, Firefly. For your friends, if not for your-self and for me, you've got to keep trying to live again."

"It all comes back. I can't shake it. I feel like I should have done something. I should remember something."

"There is no making sense out of war. You fought. You survived. War is a battle that goes on but solves very little and makes even less sense the further you get away from what started it and why it seemed so necessary in the first place. Being over there and seeing the things you saw changed you, but that one event hurt you in a way that goes deeper than the wounds on the surface. It goes deep into the kind of person you are, who can't fathom the reason for those deaths. They were good people. Friends who had families and lives beyond that place.

"You're home. You got away. You feel guilty for having what they don't. You have to find a way past that and believe that you deserve a long life as much as they did because you are a good person. Your happiness isn't a betrayal of them. It honors them. You fought for them to get home. They fought just as hard for you. Don't let their efforts and their sacrifice go unappreci-ated. Live, Firefly."

"I feel so numb. Nothing feels real."

Ford squeezed her tight against his chest. "I'm real. This is real." His lips pressed into her hair in a soft kiss.

She held on tighter, not ready to let him go and stand on her own. She needed him to remind her that there were good things in this world. Amazing things like the flush of warmth sweeping through her body. The tingle of awareness and need that grew as her breasts crushed against his hard chest and his corded thighs pressed against hers.

He brushed his hands over her head. She managed to suck in a ragged breath and look up and into his sad and reverent hazel eyes.

"Ford. Hold on to me."

He granted her wish and wrapped his arms tight around her again, his hands clamped onto her sides, crushing her to his chest. It felt so good. So right. So familiar. Like home.

"You are worth saving." He leaned down and pressed his lips to hers. Warm. Soft. Filled with a depth of emotion she hadn't felt in years, not since they were together.

It seemed a lifetime ago.

He drew away, just a breath between them, his gaze locked with hers. Passion and something she didn't want to acknowledge filled the hazel depths. Drawn to him, the hot rippling sensations spreading through her, the sweet agony of needing and wanting more, she closed the distance, her eyes, and sank into him. His tongue swept along hers in a tempting invitation to take more. The kiss transformed from the novice ones they'd shared as teens into hot, demanding, sensual caresses that promised heaven.

Ford's hands brushed down over her hips, then pulled her up and closer to him, their bodies pressed together. His hard length pushed against her belly. She rocked against him, falling into the past and the way they used to be—just like this. Hot for each other. Lost in each other. Completely consumed with the feel of the other, so close she breathed in time with him.

She slid her fingers up his neck and into his sun-kissed blonde hair. The silky strands slipped through her roving fingers. His hands gripped her ass tight and pulled her close, then rose up her hips and dipped under her T-shirt. The second he touched her scarred and gnarled skin she planted her hands on his chest and shoved him away. She tugged at her shirt to pull it down and cover herself and backed away several feet, breathing heavy and staring at the floor, hoping he hadn't seen the scars and realized that he'd touched them.

"Jamie, what's wrong?" He panted out the words, his breathing as labored as hers.

The question took her off guard. She didn't know what to say, or how to answer. "I'm sorry."

"Trust me, I'm sorrier."

Right. He'd gotten carried away, but it didn't mean anything.

She bit her lip and tasted him. "Just take me home."

"I don't want to take you home. I want you back in my arms."

Stunned, she blurted out, "What?"

"You tell me what."

"I don't understand."

He held his hands out to his sides, then let them fall back to his thighs with a slap. "Me neither. Why did you push me away?"

She tilted her head to the side and narrowed her eyes. "You know why."

"Uh, if I knew that, I wouldn't be asking."

"My back. Everything."

He took a step closer, his hand held out. "Did I hurt you?"

She instinctively took his hand and stared up at him, his questions and demeanor not computing at all. "Maybe I took too many pain meds again. You make no sense."

"Maybe you did, because you're not making sense,

so here's my side. One second I have you in my arms and I'm kissing you, the next you shove me away. Did I misread the situation and the way you kissed me back?"

She didn't know how to put her emotions into words. How it meant everything to her to feel how much he wanted her. How when he touched her scars everything got confused in her muddled mind. But looking at him now, all confused lines on his face and questions with answers that seemed obvious to her, but not to him, it didn't make sense. She narrowed her eyes and stared right at him, trying to read what was really going on here.

"You touched my back."

That cocky grin came back. "I wanted to touch a hell of a lot more of you."

"You touched my back," she repeated, not believing he didn't get it. "Trust me, you don't want to touch it, let alone see it."

"Jamie, I saw your back the first night I came to your house."

"How?"

"You passed out on the floor. I put you to bed. In a tank top, it's not hard to see the marks on your shoulders. Even in your T-shirt I see them spreading up the back of your neck. I understand they make you uncomfortable. They may even still hurt you. I imagine it will be a while longer before they're fully healed and start to fade. Especially from your mind."

It took everything she had not to let her jaw drop to the floor. "You saw them and you still touched me?"

His hand tensed around hers, firm and unrelenting. "Do you think me that shallow and loathsome that something as insignificant as the scars on your back would turn me away from you?"

"No."

Ford raked his fingers through the side of his hair. Frustration pulled his lips tight and narrowed his eyes. "Every time I see you, I catch my breath, my heart beats faster, and all I want to do is touch you, taste your lips on mine, and feel your hands move over me." He reached up and traced the scars snaking up the side of her neck and slid his fingers through her hair. "I love the way your hair changes to a million different shades of gold and red in the sunlight. The freckles on your cheeks drive me to distraction when I look in your beautiful green eyes. You have got one scxy set of legs, but I do so love to admire the swing of your hips when you walk away. Don't even get me started on your tiny, little feet. I used to love to see what color you painted your toes. Looking at you builds a hunger inside me I have had a damn hard time fighting these last days. Thinking about you distracts me from everything. Dreaming about your body pressed to mine keeps me up every night.

"The scars are nothing compared to the way you look at me. Sometimes just one look is enough to bring me to my knees when you show me how much you want me. The scars are there, but I don't see them as anything more than a mark of what you survived. They remind me of all you've been through. They tell me how strong you are. When are you going to finally get it?" His thumb brushed against her jaw. "You lived, Jamie. You're here. With me. And I am so damn happy to have you back. Scars and all."

Jamie leaned into his palm and stared up at him. "I must be out of my mind to think this is real."

Ford looked her in the eye. "We have something, Firefly. I've lived without it far too long. I don't want to live without it anymore. Tell me you didn't feel exactly what I felt in that kiss. Tell me you didn't feel something and I'll back off, but I won't leave you alone. I promise you that."

She sighed. "I haven't felt anything in a long time."

The disappointment in his eyes and tilted lips touched her.

"But when we kissed, I felt like the person I used to be with you. For a moment, I felt light enough to fly."

Warmth and understanding filled his golden-hazel eyes. "I made you feel better?"

"Ford, you made me feel like the sexy woman you just described, and I want more of that. Of us. But the last thing you need is me mucking up your life, especially now when you're trying to make a go of this place and I'm slowing you down."

"I have a good life, but it tends to get boring as hell. Since you've been home, I've been shot, pummeled, yelled at, and kissed. I think we're heading in the right direction." He leaned down and kissed her forehead. "You're certainly not boring."

That made her chuckle, but the reminder of what she'd done to him sobered her quickly. She let go of his wrist and traced her fingers up his bicep to his shoulder, pushing his T-shirt sleeve out of the way and revealing the long scar on the outside of his arm. She gently brushed her thumb over the barely healed wound.

"I'm sorry."

"I know you are. It's better. Doesn't even hurt anymore. One day, you'll say the same about the marks on your body. They tell a story about who you are, but they aren't all you are, sweetheart. You are so much more than them."

"I want to forget how I got them. But at the same

time, I'm trying to remember. My head is a really huge fucked-up mess."

"You're not that bad."

A silly grin crept across her face. "If you think so, there's something messed up about you."

"Maybe I'm just crazy for you." He smiled back, clearly trying to ease her mind.

She released his arm and touched his face, her palm against his rough jaw. She swept her thumb over his bottom lip. "That's the first real smile I've seen from you. It looks good on you."

"Got any more affection in there somewhere? That's sure to make me smile."

"I didn't think I had anything worth a damn inside of me until you came back into my life."

"You should kiss me again. I'm happy to help you find all kinds of good things inside of you."

"Is that right?"

Ford's mouth drew back in a lopsided grin. "It's worth a shot."

She swept her thumb over his bottom lip again, her gaze locked on his. His jaw tensed beneath her hand. Hope filled the depths of his eyes. He wanted her to kiss him.

Anticipation crawled from her belly and spread through her system until all she wanted to do was press her lips to his and rub her hands over every strong muscle in his body. She wanted to taste him on her tongue, feel him move against her, inside her.

She used to be brave. She pulled from some deep place within her the last stores she had of that particular trait and leaned up and pressed her lips to his. Warm. Soft. Tempting. She kissed him again and again until her mind went blank of anything and everything that wasn't him. Lost in his taste and touch, she gave herself over to him and the warm wave of passion and happiness that washed through her.

Yes, this was what she wanted, what she craved.

Ford ended the kiss by placing his big hands on each side of her face and pressing his forehead to hers. He kept his eyes closed for several breaths, then opened them and stared into her eyes.

"Come with me." He took a step back toward the huge doors that led out to the yard and his house.

Jamie tugged back on his hands to stop him from pulling her along after him, afraid to move too fast.

All of a sudden, it became all too real. Making all those erotic images in her mind a reality . . . Well, she didn't know if she had it in her to be that bold and brave.

Yes, this was Ford, but she wanted to do this right this time. She wanted to be better, more herself, less . . . fractured. "Ford, I can't just . . ."

"What? Come up to the house for lunch," he suggested.

She stared at him blankly.

He tugged her to get her to follow him and gave her one of those irritating grins. "What kind of guy do you think I am that after a few kisses I'd just sleep with you? Seriously, Firefly, you're gonna have to get to know me much better before we hop into bed together. I mean, we've got history, but you don't leap into my bed without a little more friend time."

She laughed because everything he said was what she would have said if she was any kind of normal. Instead, she used the things that happened to her in the past to keep from living in the here and now. Time hadn't changed who he was, even if it had changed her.

"You're right. I mean, you're a good and decent man

who lives his cowboy creed: manners, principles, honor, all kinds of good stuff. You'd never take a relationship to the next level unless it was on solid ground."

"Damn right. Especially when you're anything but solid right now. But I'm hoping now that you've felt something good again, you'll want to keep feeling it, and we'll work our way back . . . Actually, to something better than we had before, because I've got all kinds of good stuff to show you."

That made her smile. "I've seen your good stuff, tough guy." And she wanted to see it again, but she couldn't help reaching out and touching his wounded arm. "Ford, no matter what happens, the last thing I ever want to do is hurt you."

He took her hand and brought it up to his lips and kissed her palm. "I know, Firefly. You smiled like three times today. That's progress. You'll get there."

Where? She sometimes wondered what she was trying to get back to, because it seemed so hard to remember a time when she was happy. It always seemed to be Ford's image in her mind that settled her and gave her a sense of belonging and contentment.

He was her happy place. Being with him was everything she wanted.

If she wanted to keep him and not break this tenuous hold she had on him, she needed to work harder to be the kind of friend he deserved—and maybe she'd find the strength and courage to love him again with all the passion and need filling her up that she wanted to lavish on him.

Fear held her back. She needed to find the strength to trust him again. To trust herself. Maybe then they'd have a shot at forever.

CHAPTER 11

Tobin walked into Dr. Porter's office unannounced, slammed the door behind him, and took the seat in front of the wide-eyed man. Tobin crossed his arms over his chest, letting the doctor know he'd come for a reason and wouldn't leave without getting what he wanted.

"What are you doing here?" Dr. Porter leaned back in his chair and studied him across the desk. Anger filled his eyes that Tobin would dare intrude like this.

Desperate times. Desperate measures.

"I'm here about Keller. She won't answer any of my calls or texts and I want to know why."

"I can't discuss her with you. She's my patient."

"Don't give me that doctor-patient confidentiality crap. I don't need details, but I do want answers." He raked his fingers through his close-cropped hair. "I'm worried about her."

"All I can say is that she's been in a very bad place since the attack. She needs time and space and distance to process what happened to her."

And that told him exactly what he already knew, but not what he wanted to hear. "Is she coming back?"

Dr. Porter shook his head. "I can't tell you what we discuss in our sessions."

"It's a simple yes or no." Tobin missed her more than he thought possible.

The damn woman had kept him at arm's length the last five years, but the weeks leading up to the end of their tour, they'd grown closer than ever. Catalina had talked nonstop about getting married to her fiancé and having a baby right away. He'd seen the jealousy and want in Jamie's eyes to have the same for herself. A time or two he'd caught her looking at him and had hoped she'd reach out and take what he'd made so plain he wanted to give her.

Then that damn attack happened and she'd completely cut him off.

"Tobin, are you okay?"

He didn't need Dr. Porter's concern or him getting into his head. He'd done his required sessions and bullshit his way right out of more. Stupid shrinks thought they knew everything. Well, Porter might know a little more since he'd served in the first Gulf War. Porter might see more than Tobin wanted him to know.

"It's not like Keller to disappear and not return my calls," he covered. "All I want to know is if she's okay."

"She's getting by. A little better these days, now that she's got someone to look after her."

Tobin nodded. "Her brother. She talked about Zac a lot. She missed him."

"She's seen her brother, but he's busy with his baby. Home turned out to be another battlefield for Jamie with her mother, so Zac moved her to her grandparents' old house."

"Alone."

"She was until an old friend came back into her life."

Tobin wracked his brain for girls Jamie used to be friends with before she left home for the military.

The only people she talked about were her family, the cousin she stayed with in Georgia before leaving for her tours of duty, and the old boyfriend she couldn't seem to forget. Tobin didn't come up with anyone who stood out back home. "Who's taking care of her?"

"A guy she used to know."

"Not Ford." He bit out the name of the bastard who'd broken her heart and made her reluctant to give any other guy a shot. Including him.

Dr. Porter neither confirmed nor denied.

It had to be him. Tobin's hands ached, so he released his fists and gripped his thighs instead of wrapping his fingers around the doctor's throat and shaking the answers he wanted out of him.

"He'll use and hurt her again. Call her. Let me talk to her. I'll straighten her out. He's no good for her."

Dr. Porter shook his head before Tobin finished his sentence. "I'm not calling her on your behalf. She isn't ready to talk to you. Give her the space she needs to heal. When she's ready, she'll pick up the phone."

"Bullshit. If she's back with that asshole, she's making shit decisions. I won't let him make things worse for her."

"It's her life. If he makes her happy, you should be happy for her."

"She thinks she's still in love with the guy." Why couldn't she get over him? He'd made it clear he didn't want her and sent her away. Tobin did everything he could to be her friend, someone she could trust and rely on, but still, she went back to Ford.

"Love is a powerful motivator. It's what brought you here today, isn't it?"

Tobin wished Jamie saw how he felt about her as easily as Dr. Porter did.

"We have a history. Everyone wants her to remember what happened. I'm with her, nothing good will come of her remembering what happened. It's best locked away and forgotten. It's time for her and me to move on."

Dr. Porter's gaze remained steady. "She needs to remember to move past it."

Jamie needed to forget the past forever. Including Ford. That asshole had to go.

CHAPTER 12

Jamie rolled her shoulders and stretched her back. After two days working at Ford's place, her muscles were sore, but in a good way. She felt looser, even if the persistent ache made her uncomfortable. At least she'd earned it.

"Why do you keep fidgeting?" Dr. Porter leaned forward in his chair and eyed her, his face large and a bit distorted on her laptop screen.

"I'm sore."

"The meds aren't working?"

She twisted this way and that until the pain eased. "They do, but I've cut back."

"Too much if you're in too much pain to sit still."

"The job doesn't help, and helps, all at the same time."

Dr. Porter fell back in his chair. "We've been on this call for fifteen minutes and you're just now bringing up the fact you got a job?"

"You didn't ask."

Dr. Porter blew out a breath. "Why would I ask that?" He narrowed his eyes. "The last time we spoke, you hadn't left the house in more than a week."

"Well, I've spent the last few days at Ford's place.

But he still cooks me dinner here every night. We have lunch together, too."

The surprise and confusion on Dr. Porter's face made her smile, which only made him frown harder. "You're smiling again."

Her smile notched up a few more degrees. "It seems to happen more and more these last few days."

"Why?"

This time she eyed the doc. "Why?"

Dr. Porter's dark brows drew together again. "I ask the questions. You answer them."

She rolled her eyes at his teasing and impatience. "Ford's fixing up his place. He took me to see it and his horses. I needed something to do, so I offered to help him out."

"You offered."

"His idea and mine about what I could actually do were vastly different, but then he got me working, stretching my arm and shoulder, doing a little more each day. He might have been right about pushing myself and how it would help me both physically and mentally. I feel stronger, but don't tell him I said so."

"You work for Ford?"

She nodded. "On his ranch in the stables. I take care of the horses. It's working, too. Since I came home, I haven't had any physical therapy or done the exercises they suggested. Brushing down the horses, lifting their feed and water buckets, putting on their halters and lead ropes means a range of motion in both arms that I can do with the specific moves the therapist taught me, but it's so much more effective when it's for a purpose. My legs are sore, my back, my shoulders, and arms, but it feels like progress rather than a punishment for what happened."

"This is the most positive I've heard you. You said since you came 'home.' When you left base, you said you didn't think you'd stay there."

"I knew staying with my mother probably wouldn't pan out. It lasted just short of a month and me going ballistic." She rolled her eyes. "Believe me, longest month of my life. I hoped things would be different, but I guess I knew they wouldn't be. She's not capable of nurturing and compassion."

"Two things you desperately needed when you left here."

Jamie tilted her head and pulled one side of her mouth back in a half frown. "Probably. I guess I still do. But I came to the wrong place for that."

"Until Ford showed up. In just a few short days, you're different. He gives you the nurturing you need."

"I think you'd classify it as tough love. I take a step forward and he pushes me to take more."

"You're trained to follow orders. He knows you well enough to know that's the only way to get you to do anything."

"You give me orders all the time and I don't follow them."

"True, but I'm asking you to relive something painful. He's asking you to play with his horses. Much easier to deal with than your past."

"Actually, it helps with that, too."

"How so?"

"When I'm working with the horses, brushing them down, in the monotony of it, I relax. My mind wanders. My time in the military comes back to me in daydreams. When I'm doing the menial tasks, it's not so overwhelming."

"What comes back to you the most?"

"Ordinary things. Inventory with Catalina before a convoy run. Scheduling, routing, and change request with Tobin. Letting off steam with the gang while we listen to a visiting band. Toby Keith put on one hell of a concert for the troops. Catalina and I danced with some of the guys. I remember thinking it felt so . . . normal and odd at the same time considering where we were and what we were doing."

"Was Tobin there, too?"

"Sure. Catalina, Amy, Jo, Pedro, and I danced the whole time and drank beer. We let everything go and had some fun."

"How long was that before you were hurt and they were lost?"

"Lost." That word didn't feel right. She wanted to use "gone," but it felt so final, and she still felt like she needed to do something for them. "They were killed a month after that concert. It seems strange to have a concert in the middle of a war, but I kind of get it now. We needed the distraction. A moment to breathe and not think about what might happen. I needed that then."

"You've found it now working with Ford and the horses. A space to breathe and let your guard down. You think about your friends and the way things used to be."

"I guess."

"But you still can't bring yourself to think about what happened."

"I don't want to dwell on the bad anymore. Isn't that a better way to recover?"

"No. It's putting off the inevitable. You have to reconcile your past to have any chance of moving forward unburdened."

She didn't say anything. You can't fight right. But she

finally felt lighter. Better. She woke up the last two days with a sense of anticipation rather than dread. When Ford touched her shoulder or took her hand, she leaned into him instead of pulling away. When he kissed her, she felt like a woman again. She felt desirable and loved though she hadn't convinced herself he actually loved her. He cared. She needed that. She needed him.

Her cease-fire with herself helped. She didn't dwell on bad thoughts or stare at herself in the mirror cataloguing all the flaws. She'd painted her toes pink with white polka dots last night to add a little whimsy into her life. Just looking at them now made her feel happy and pretty.

"Why don't you want to talk about Tobin?"

Just the mention of his name took her back to that day. She tried to fight the memory of them in the supply truck driving down the road. His incessant drone about how bad things were getting and how someone needed to fuck those bastards up. She rolled her eyes then and now. So much fierce indignation and frustration about the war dragging out, gaining and losing ground, always fighting to get the upper hand and hold on to it.

"Mind clueing me in to the thoughts rolling around your head with your eyes?"

"Huh? Oh. Nothing. Just remembering the last time Tobin and I were in the truck together."

"You look like you ate roadkill."

She let loose her narrowed eyebrows and tight lips. "Just thinking about my last conversation with Tobin."

Dr. Porter leaned forward. "What did he say?"

She found his intense interest odd. "A lot of stuff he'd said before that I ignored." She thought about his words.

Someone should take the bull by the horns and bomb the fuck out of this whole fucking place.

If I had the chance, I'd cut them all down.

Why the hell are we here?

She tilted her head thinking of the days and weeks leading up to that moment. "We were all on edge, counting down the days to the end of our tour, dreaming about being back home. I wanted a pizza so bad I could taste it."

"Is that what he talked about, wanting to come home?"

"We all wanted to come home."

But that wasn't entirely true for Tobin. While she loved the routine of what they did, Tobin wanted some action. He'd joined the wrong division for that. Supply wasn't glamorous or exciting most of the time. Danger dogged the convoy, but she and Tobin and others of their rank were in charge of planning and organizing. The tedious stuff. If he wanted to really get in the action, he should have moved over to the infantry.

It didn't matter. Not anymore. What relevance did it have now?

"He needed to blow off steam. Everyone at one time or another boasted in some way about how they'd take down the enemy, end the war, go home to the people they love, and have a normal life again."

Lost in thoughts of working with Tobin, his increasing need to go out with the convoys, she shook off the one thought that always hung in her mind. They weren't supposed to be there. Circumstances, fate, had put them in those vehicles that day. Nothing could change that now. She couldn't fix what happened.

"Why won't you take his calls?"

That got her attention. "How do you know that?"

"He came to see me and asked me to talk to you on his behalf. He's worried about you. You were friends, yet you won't speak to him."

"Just thinking about him brings the nightmares too close to the surface. It feels like a tidal wave that will suck me under."

"Maybe if you face it head-on, you'll finally be able to let it go."

"Or I'll suffocate from the fear and terror that claws at me even when I just remember small glimpses of that day. It's all I can do to deal with those small pieces."

"You think talking to Tobin will bring it all back and you're not ready."

"No. I'm not ready." Some of the strength she'd gained these last two days seeped away with the knowledge that she wasn't mentally ready to look at the past rationally and dispassionately. Until she could, this sense of failure would stick with her.

"Why are we talking about him? I thought you were supposed to be asking about me."

"Okay, talk me through what you remember about the blast."

She shook her head. "We've talked about it a dozen times. You know what happened from the reports."

"I want to hear your version of what happened and how Tobin helped you. You're not loopy on pain meds or drunk or filled with anger. You're calmer and clearer today than I've ever seen you."

She smoothed her hands up and down her thighs, wiping the sweat from her palms.

Right, calm. Not.

She sucked in a deep breath and let it out. Either she talked now, or Dr. Porter would continue to badger and probe until she did open up. Frustrated with him, and herself for putting off what she needed to face, she tried. She wanted to be well.

"We drove into the town on our way to drop supplies for one of the Ranger teams. We followed the lead security vehicle. It turned a corner. I turned to follow, but a man stepped out of a doorway a block up with a rocket propelled grenade launcher on his shoulder. I remember staring at him in disbelief like it couldn't be real. You know it could happen. You even expect it. But when it happens, and you're staring at death, it's kind of surreal.

"I remember thinking if not for the food poisoning that hit the group, I wouldn't be there. I'd be safe back at base."

"There is no rhyme or reason for the way things happen, Jamie. It's just life happening."

She didn't have an answer for that, except that if it hadn't been her driving that truck, someone else would have been and they might have died or been hurt in her place. Nothing would have stopped the events. It was just dumb luck she was the one behind the wheel that day. Otherwise, it would have been someone she put in that seat.

"The enemy fired," Dr. Porter prompted when she got lost in thought.

"I couldn't go forward. The security vehicle was blocked ahead of us, too. I yelled for Tobin to get out. I made a run for it. The rocket hit the truck moments after I opened the truck door and jumped out. I didn't clear the blast fast enough. A wave of heat and fire took me down. My clothes caught on fire. Tobin tackled me and smothered the flames with his body. He suffered some minor burns. Nothing significant. He saved my life."

The words didn't relieve her in any way. They amped up the adrenaline and fear and desperation coursing through her veins. Tobin's heroic actions should make her feel grateful, but something ominous swept through her like a premonition of death that left her cold. Those pieces of the puzzle that left black holes in her mind.

"Then what happened?"

"Everything at once. Slow. And fast. Out of sorts and strange and incomprehensible."

"Think it through. You're on the ground. Tobin is with you, lying on your back. Does he administer first aid? Call for backup? Say anything to you? What does he do?"

"It burns and I'm screaming in pain." She shook her head, trying to erase the images from her mind and the echo of pain that seared her back. "He pours a canteen of water all over my back. My head is swimming, ears are ringing. I'm dizzy and disoriented from the explosion. People are shouting and screaming. There's the rapid fire of guns everywhere. The security team is fighting the insurgents pouring into the area to get to the supply trucks and take everything.

"Smoke clouds us in cover, but all I want is for it to clear so I can breathe. It hurts to breathe. The blackness crowds in, but I try to stay awake. I'm scared to pass out. What will happen to me if I pass out?"

A comforting hand settled on her shoulder.

"A bellow of pure agony rips from Tobin's throat. I've never heard anything like it. I want to tell him I'm okay, but the pain and the burning and the smoke choking my throat make it impossible to speak." She stared at nothing, seeing everything in that moment so clearly it scared her all over again. "He thinks I'm dead. I want to be to stop the pain."

A warm hand brushed up her shoulder and neck to her cheek. Callused roughened fingertips swept away the tears streaking down her face. Soft lips pressed to her temple bringing her back to reality and her living room. Not the war zone that changed her life forever.

She closed her eyes and whispered, "Ford." The feel of his head pressed to the side of hers, his hand on her face, the strong presence of him behind her, leaning over the couch, warmed her from the outside in, all the way to her frozen bones. "When did you get here?"

"A few minutes ago. You didn't hear me when I pulled up and honked. Are you okay?"

She sighed. "I am now."

"Jamie, you did really well." Dr. Porter sat back in his chair. "Nice to meet you, Ford. I'm glad you showed up when you did. I'd hate to leave Jamie alone after such a breakthrough."

"I hate to leave her alone anytime."

Dr. Porter smiled. "She told me you've been really good for her. Work is helping her heal."

"It's selfish really. I get her to do the chores and I get to spend time with her."

"Noble, I see," Dr. Porter teased along with Ford.

Their easy manner helped to settle Jamie even more. With Ford beside her, touching her, she breathed easier. The past slipped away, and she settled in reality with him. Just where she wanted to be.

Something jumped up and pawed at her legs. Jamie looked down and into the big brown eyes of a chocolate Lab puppy. She gasped and reached for the dog, pulling it up on her lap. It immediately climbed her chest and licked her face.

"Where did you come from?"

"Now you'll never be alone, Firefly."

"You got me a puppy?"

"If you don't want her, I'll take her home with me. I've got a huge ranch for her to run around on, you know."

"No way." She held the puppy up in front of her, staring at the tiny creature's cute little face. "You're staying with me, aren't you?"

Dr. Porter smiled on the laptop screen and nodded his approval. "What's her name?"

Ford patted the puppy's head. "She doesn't have one yet. It's up to you, Jamie."

Jamie nuzzled her nose into the dog's soft fur. "Zoey."

"Zoey, meet Jamie. You're in charge of making her smile." Ford rubbed behind Zoey's ears.

Jamie realized she was indeed smiling.

"Looks like she's good at her job." Dr. Porter tapped off the alarm signaling the end of their session. "We'll talk again soon. You did really well today, Jamie. I'm glad to see you're opening up. One last thing. If Tobin calls, are you going to talk to him?"

She held the puppy at her chest, her soft head beneath Jamie's chin. "I need more time and distance so it doesn't suck me back into that dark place I can't escape."

"You did escape it, Jamie. Look at you right now. Look how far you've come in just a few short days. Keep doing what you're doing." Dr. Porter turned his gaze to Ford, who still leaned over the back of the couch and kept his hand on her shoulder, his thumb absently brushing against her face. "You're good for her. Keep doing what you're doing. Slow and easy so she has time to adjust."

Ford nodded. "Whatever she needs."

"Expect setbacks and resistance."

"She's very good at that." The humor in Ford's voice didn't undermine the truth in his words.

Dr. Porter nodded his agreement and ended the video chat.

Ford kissed the side of her head again. "Let's take Zoey for a walk and get you some fresh air."

Jamie turned and kissed Ford. Zoey got in on the action, licking his chin. Ford pulled back, smiling and chuckling.

Jamie stared up at him. "I'm glad you're here."

Ford leaned down and kissed her again. "There's no place I'd rather be. Come outside with me."

Jamie stood with the puppy in her arms. She came around the couch and took Ford's outstretched hand. He pulled her out the door and down the porch steps. Jamie leaned down and set Zoey on the grass. She high stepped, unsure of the texture beneath her paws. So cute the way she tried not to touch it, but was unable to escape it. Then she made a run for it, stumbling over her own huge paws and tumbling. Jamie laughed along with Ford at her unsteady antics and happy yapping.

"I think she likes it here."

Ford wrapped his arm around her shoulders and pulled her against his chest. "I hope you're starting to like it here."

A week ago she wanted to leave this place for good. Now, more and more she wanted to stay and make a life with Ford. If only she could face her past so she could move on with her future, unburdened like Dr. Porter said. She wanted to shove her past into the closet and never look at it again. Today she realized that dealing with it, examining it objectively, could be the path to leading a healthy, happy life again.

The puppy helped. She couldn't be mired in the

dark with such a sweet and happy little puppy bouncing around her feet, begging to be loved.

Ford helped, too. With him beside her, she breathed easier and let the weight of her dark thoughts go because she could rely on his strength and comfort to get her through anything. She didn't want to lose him.

If she wanted to keep him and build a life with him, she needed to face her past. She hoped she had the strength to do so without messing up what she had with Ford.

She wouldn't squander this chance at a real and happy future with him. Not like she'd done before. This time, she wouldn't run away. This time, she'd hold on.

CHAPTER 13

Ford walked out of Dusty's stall and closed the gate, trying to figure out how the horse managed to bust the latch on the outer gate and escape this morning. He spent an hour chasing down the horse, which led him to the second downed fence line in two days. Once he'd caught Dusty, he spent another hour rounding up the cows that got out of their pasture. It took two more hours to get the fence fixed on his own. By the time he made it back to the stables, Jamie had driven over and stood waiting for him, concerned because he hadn't picked her up. He didn't like to make her worry. He'd done enough of that for both of them these past weeks, trying to be there for Jamie while getting things done here before winter. All these little mishaps set him back more and took him away from being with her. If he didn't know better, he'd think himself jinxed. That or the animals had turned on him, hell-bent on escape.

He shook off the silliness of it and focused on the many jobs still left to do around here. Jamie worked in the tack room sorting out the bridles, halters, blankets, saddles, and other horse supplies Sadie left behind and he'd brought from Kendrick Ranch. He'd asked her to organize everything and put it up on the pegs and shelves, and in the bins he'd bought. Zoey snoozed in a wood crate on the blanket Jamie bought her along with her favorite stuffed squirrel with the squeaker in the tail. Zoey loved to carry it around with her, though she tripped over it most of the time. In another month, she'd find her coordination. In a year, she'd be bounding all over the ranch after him and Jamie.

The thought made Ford smile. Though he took Jamie home to her place each night, she'd settled in here with him and the horses. She loved working in the stables. He'd seen a real change in her the last week. Especially after he walked in on her talking to her shrink about what happened. She still didn't remember everything. In fact, she'd asked her doctor to back off on going deeper into the shooting. She needed time to settle what she did remember in her mind.

Part of her resistance had to be from the calls she received but never answered. Ford asked about it, the way she tucked the phone away, out of sight, like she just couldn't go there yet.

Tobin. He'd caught the part of her conversation with her doctor about the man who'd saved her life.

If he'd saved her, why didn't she want to talk to him?

She denied any problem with the guy. She made it absolutely clear that she wanted to be here with Ford, in the moment, and let the past rest until she was ready to wake that beast again. Like her doctor, Ford didn't push. She'd finally settled into her routine. Every day she smiled a bit more and spent less time locked inside her head and more time interacting with him, the horses, and Zoey. Best thing he'd ever done was give her the dog. The puppy demanded so much of her attention, Jamie didn't have time to sit and wallow. Ford no longer worried about leaving Jamie home alone at night with the time and solitude to fall back into her anger and grief and guilt.

"Hey, pretty girl, I'm headed out to unload the supplies from the truck."

"Okay," Jamie said over her shoulder.

"I was talking to the dog," he teased.

A laugh bubbled up from Jamie's gut and brightened her flushed face. The temps had gotten hotter as July pushed toward August. Working on the ranch and in the sun gave her a healthy glow, though he constantly had to remind her to put on sunscreen to keep his redhead's fair skin from burning. No matter how hot it got, she always wore a shirt that covered her back, shoulders, and upper arms. He hoped he'd convince her one day soon that the scars didn't bother him.

Jamie planted her hands on her hips. "You're so infatuated with her now, I pale in comparison, is that it?"

The intense attraction between them sizzled. Tired of fighting it, Ford closed the distance between them and stood a breath away from her but didn't touch her. "I spend every second of the day fighting the urge to pull you into my arms and kiss you."

"Why?"

"Why do I want to kiss you?"

She smiled. "No. Why do you fight it?"

Surprised she'd want him to give in to his impulses and touch her the way he wanted to, he studied her inquisitive stare. "Mostly because you need a friend and time to heal. Sometimes when I reach for you, I feel the way you hesitate or hold back."

Her gaze fell to his boots. "I don't mean to."

"Listen, I think we need to clear the air about the way we parted. The things I said to you."

"Ford, it's all right. We were different back then. You had your reasons."

"I did, but none of them had to do with not wanting you."

Her gaze swept up him and settled on his. "Do you mean that?"

"Yes. Missing you is a sea of memories that flood my mind. You used to love to sing Aerosmith songs at the top of your lungs with the windows down on the back roads. The way your eyes used to light up when you saw me."

"I couldn't wait to get my hands on you the second I saw you."

Ford held his hands out wide. "Have at it, honey."

Jamie's soft laugh died far too quickly.

He turned serious too and tried once again to reassure her that what they shared was real and true. "I felt the same way about you, wild to get my hands on you and feel your soft skin against me. Which is why most of the trips we took into town took twice as long, because we'd hit that back road with the secret turnoff to our favorite spot under that huge tree."

"You made me late for work more often than not. I think about those stolen moments all the time. They saved me."

His chest ached. If he could have been with her all those moments she'd needed him, he'd have moved heaven and earth to get to her.

"I'm glad you were able to still think of all the good times we shared even though things didn't turn out the way we wanted."

"You say 'we,' but you're the one who changed his mind about leaving."

"I couldn't leave."

Finally ready to hear him, she asked, "Why?"

"Two reasons. The ranch was in trouble. The money I saved, I sank back into the business so we didn't lose the ranch. And I helped pay my grandfather's medical bills."

"Oh my God," Jamie gasped, clapping her hand over her mouth, then sliding it down her neck. "Is he okay? He wasn't at the parade or diner. You haven't mentioned him before now."

"I avoided it, hoping to have a chance to talk to you about this when you were ready to hear it." He reached out and touched her beautiful face, her eyes filled with concern for his grandfather. "Granddad is fine. Now. When you came to the ranch that day, I had just come from seeing him in the hospital. He'd gotten dizzy, fell in the house, and hit his head. He suffered a concussion. High blood pressure combined with what we prayed wasn't heart failure."

"Ford!" She smacked him on the shoulder. "Why didn't you tell me? I would have stayed and helped you through that difficult time." Tears flooded her eyes. "Why would you keep that from me? You knew how I felt about you and your family."

"Exactly. Your mother had become unrelenting. You kept pushing to leave, but I had to stay to help my family hold on to my parents' legacy and get my grandfather through his medical emergency. It took him months to get his blood pressure and other issues under control and begin getting back on his feet. It took nearly two years for the ranch to recover from the drop in cattle prices and start making enough money to give us some breathing room. I couldn't abandon my family in their time of need. I hated to let you go, but I felt it was the right thing to do *for you*."

Jamie opened her mouth to protest again. But then regret and understanding filled her eyes and she stopped herself from speaking.

She turned and gripped one of the shelves, her head bent, and took a moment before she turned back to him. "I never stood up to my mother the way I should have. It's hard. She's my mom. I want her to act like it, but with every scornful word out of her mouth my hope that we'll ever have a decent relationship dies a bit more. She will never be there for me the way I need. I'm better off on my own than with her in my life, but I'm not alone. I have Zac."

"You have me."

She took his hand and held it in both of hers. "I'm so happy I have you, but you want more than friendship and my working here." She cocked her head just enough to glance back up at him.

"You know I do. It will happen in your own time."

"Such confidence."

"You've made amazing progress."

"I'm just trying to impress you," she teased with a soft smile.

"Your strength and determination and fight impress the hell out of me, Firefly."

"You think I have all those things locked up, but I falter more often than not. Without the meds and counseling, I'd fall apart completely."

He caressed her soft, pale, lightly freckled cheek. "Needing help isn't the same as being helpless, Firefly. It takes a lot of strength to admit you can't do everything yourself."

"Maybe you're right."

"I am right."

Jamie sighed and squeezed his hand, holding something back, or just not able to say what she wanted to say.

He really didn't want to know, but asked anyway. "Does this have something to do with Tobin? Are you two—"

"No." Jamie shook her head.

"Tobin saved you during the attack on your convoy. That's got to mean something to you."

"It does." Affection mixed with something he couldn't read mixed in her bright eyes. "We've worked together for a long time."

Her gaze fell away.

"He's more than that to you." The thought made him uneasy. She might have left her old life behind to come back here, but that didn't mean she'd left everyone behind. She didn't take his calls. Maybe they'd had a fight and Tobin wanted her back? Ford's gut tightened with dread.

"Ford, we're standing here beating around the bush about taking this relationship forward in a real and meaningful way. Do you really think I've got a thing for Tobin and want to be with you at the same time?"

No, but he wanted her to say exactly what she did want from him. "You tell me."

"It's always been you."

He'd hoped that was what she'd say, but hearing it made so plain and blunt hit him straight in the heart like a sledgehammer. He wanted to reach for her, drag her into his arms, and hold on to her forever, but she took a step back, distancing herself from him. He had an idea why. He'd find a way to make her trust him again.

"I dated after I left here. Nothing too serious, just trying to forget you. Didn't work." She gave him a pouty frown that made him smile. "Tobin and I spent a lot of time together, working in the same unit. We got to know each other really well. He has a thing for me, but for whatever reason, I never encouraged or pursued a deeper relationship. In fact, for the most part, I ignored it and acted like it didn't exist."

"Why?" He didn't know why it mattered. She didn't want a relationship with the guy. Good enough for him, but something about why she'd told him this extra information seemed relevant to why she refused Tobin's calls now despite the fact the guy saved her life. His actions should prove to her that he cared deeply for her, yet she avoided him. She didn't want to talk about him. Why?

"I can't explain it. He's a nice guy. Kind of intense. Possessive where I'm concerned. It seemed sweet at first, but because we work so much together, it became uncomfortable. I wanted some space and distance from work. You know, to decompress after a long day. Spending all my time with him seemed confining."

"Friends is one thing. A relationship is another. You like him, but you weren't attracted to him to the point where you'd fall for him. How did he take it?"

"We never really discussed it. We shared a silent conversation where he'd slowly push for more and I'd allow it to a point, then back off when it became too much. It's one thing to listen to my gripes and comfort me when I'm upset, but another to push for something I'm not willing to give."

"You've said it a dozen times to me since you came back. You wanted to be left alone. What you really wanted was for everyone to stop asking you for something you didn't want to or couldn't give."

She nodded. "I guess. When I left here, I wanted to stand on my own. I did."

"You still do, Firefly."

"Given half a chance, Tobin would rule my life. He's just that type of guy. That's not the kind of relationship I want."

"What do you want, Firefly?"

"I like the easy way things have been between us lately, but . . ."

He didn't want to hear the but.

"I want more."

He liked that but.

She tilted her head, adding, "You're holding back. I guess I am, too, because I'm afraid of doing or saying something to push you away. Although I'm better, I'm always aware that something could set me off. I'm constantly on guard for a threat even when there isn't one and that puts distance between us even though that's not what I want. Hell, I still search for snipers in the rafters." She stared up at the tall ceiling overhead, shaking her head with self-deprecation.

Ford held out his arms wide. "Come here."

Jamie didn't hesitate to walk into his arms. He wrapped them around her and held on tight. She placed her hands on his back and pulled him close, nestled against his chest.

"Here, you are safe, Firefly." He kissed her on the top of the head. "I promise, I'll never let you go again."

She sighed so heavily he felt her relief in his own body. He didn't push to take things further. He just stood with her, the horses nickering and swishing their tails in their stalls, and let her work it out in her mind and heart that this was the way things could be from now on. Her. Him. Them together and building a life they both wanted. Happy on their ranch.

She buried her face in his neck and inhaled his scent.

Her soft murmur of contentment made him smile. Such a simple thing meant so much to her.

In the last few weeks he'd noticed she responded best when he took things slow and let her have the distance and time she needed to step out of the space she'd been in and adjust to something new—or something familiar but long put on hold. He hoped he had the will to restrain his desire to drag her to his bed and the patience she needed to adjust to being back in his life permanently.

"I missed this," she whispered, hugging him close.

"I missed you every day you were away. I don't want to miss you anymore."

She leaned back in his arms and smiled up at him. "You know what else I missed?"

"What?"

"The long rides we used to take. Let's take a break."

"I'll saddle the horses." He moved to release her and get the horses ready, but she held on to him.

"I'm sorry you had to go through all that, taking care of your grandfather, holding on to the ranch, alone. I know what they both mean to you."

God, she had such a good heart.

"You mean that much to me, Firefly."

He leaned down and kissed her softly. He meant it to be a thank-you for understanding, for forgiving him for what he'd done to her, but like every other time he had her close the hunger built until he was desperate for more. He slipped his tongue past her sweet lips and took the kiss deeper. His hands slid down her back and over her round bottom. Her fingers dove into his hair and held his head to hers as they got lost in each other.

He needed to be closer to her. With his hands gripping her ass, he pulled her up to her toes. She nestled into him, her hips rubbing against his. He backed her into the wall and pressed her against it with his body.

"Ow!" Jamie tried to pull her arm down between them, but had little room to maneuver with him crowding her.

Ford leaned back and stared down as she squeezed her arm to her side and rolled her left shoulder.

"Sorry. I can't move like that yet."

He touched her cheek and tried to get a hold on the lust coursing through his veins. As much as he wanted her, he didn't want their first time back together to be a wild romp in the tack room. He wanted her laid out in his bed where he could take his time.

"I'm sorry, baby. I should be more careful with you."

"I'm fine." To prove it, she tugged on his shirt so he'd come in for another soft kiss.

This time, he kept it soft, slow, and way too short for his liking. He'd find the perfect time, the perfect way for them to make love again.

CHAPTER 14

Jamie rode Dusty next to Ford and his mount, Mo. The wind blew her hair back. The sun felt warm on her skin. The land spread out before her in fields of green and gold with trees dotting the landscape. She'd missed this. Being with Ford out for a ride in the wide-open space.

She kept her impulse to find cover in check. She stopped looking for snipers and focused on the beautiful day and the man beside her, who'd made it clear he wanted her by his side. She felt lighter. She'd hold on to the good memories and set aside her hurt about him sending her away. He'd been needed here, and she'd had to go. Simple and complicated, they'd needed to do for themselves so they could come back together now knowing how much they'd given up and appreciate this second chance even more.

She'd almost died thinking he didn't want her anymore. Now she knew better. This time, she wouldn't let anything or anyone tear them apart. She'd been fighting her way back to being well. She'd fight just as hard to keep Ford.

"You're awful quiet, Firefly."

They rode at a slow and steady pace. While the ride hurt her back, she wanted a little more action.

"Just scouting out my route."

Ford's worried gaze landed on her. "Jamie, honey, I don't think—"

She pointed into the distance. "Last one to that tree does the dishes tonight." Jamie kicked her mount and leaned over Dusty's neck as the horse took off. The speed sent a bolt of adrenaline through her veins. Her heart pounded along with the horse's hooves over the ground. The wind in her face made her eyes tear up, but that didn't stop the laugh bubbling up from her gut as Ford gave chase, gaining ground beside her. Jamie gave Dusty another nudge. They pulled out to the lead just as they approached the cluster of trees.

Okay, maybe Jamie had the faster horse and weighed less than Ford, giving her the advantage, but he'd given her a real run for her money.

Exhilarated, she reined in close to the trees, jumped off Dusty's back, and turned to face Ford. She pointed at him, smiling and still laughing. "I beat you!"

Ford dismounted next to her, smiling, too. "Yes, you did."

"Ha!" The rush of adrenaline and just pure fun made her smile so big her cheeks ached.

Ford's steady gaze filled with awe. "Look at you, Firefly. You shine." He wrapped his arms around her middle, picked her up, and spun her around. "God, how you shine." He let her body slip down his until she came face-to-face with him and he took her mouth in a searing kiss.

She wrapped her arms around his head and held him close, losing herself in the sheer joy. She hadn't felt this free in a long time.

Ford set her back on her feet and stared down at her, the worry she always saw in his eyes gone. Seeing her happy eased him. If their talk earlier hadn't convinced her, his peace did. He cared deeply for her. Not just her recovering, but also her truly being happy again mattered to him.

"I need to get you out of the sun before you burn. Your cheeks are already pink." He unstrapped the saddlebag from his mount and led her to the copse of trees.

She pulled the hat he insisted she wear off her head and tossed it on the grass. She undid the scarf around her neck, protecting her healing skin from the sun, sat, and tugged Ford's hand so he'd join her in the shade.

He pulled out the sandwiches and bottles of water they'd packed before they left the ranch. He handed her one. She dipped her hand into the bag and pulled out her bottle of pills. She took one, so she'd be able to ride back.

"You must be sore. Was that too much for you?"

"Stop worrying," she scolded. "I'm fine. Better than fine." She bumped her shoulder into his arm. "Thank you for dropping everything and coming out here with me."

Ford swallowed his bite of sandwich and smiled down at her. "My favorite thing to do is spend time with you."

"I love being with you, too. But I know you've got a lot of work. So much so, you got delayed coming to get me this morning. Maybe Dusty's ride will tire him out and keep him from escaping again."

Ford's eyes narrowed as he stared off into the distance. "I still don't get how he busted the gate the way he did."

"Didn't he kick it open?"

"The lock was busted, but he didn't do any damage to the gate itself. It's odd."

She gave him a lopsided frown. "He didn't leave any marks on the wood?"

"No."

"That's strange."

"Even stranger is the two fence lines that were pulled down. One by the road. I'm surprised one or more of the cows didn't get hit by traffic on the blind curve. With them in the road, someone could have had a bad accident. I had a devil of a time getting the cows back into the pasture."

"Do you think someone messed with the fencing?"

Ford stared off into the distance shaking his head. "I don't know who would have done it. The drug dealers who rustled cattle at Rory's place know this used to be Sadie's brother's place, but with him in jail, what could they want here? Unlike the Kendrick land, this place is too open to hide a meth lab. None of the cattle were missing, so it doesn't appear someone was after making a quick buck off them. It's more likely something spooked the cattle and they rushed the fence line and took it down."

Jamie glanced up at the sprawling tree branches overhead. "Mountain lion, maybe."

Ford followed her gaze to the empty branches and chuckled. "Doubt it. I didn't see any tracks." Ford ate more of his sandwich, lost in thought, staring at the pretty landscape before them. "I've had a string of bad luck the last week or so."

"Including my kicking your ass in that race," she teased.

"I just like staring at your ass, sweetheart."

They laughed together, but Ford sobered. "The electrical on one of the water pumps went out."

"Another thing that needs maintenance and an upgrade, huh?"

"I checked it when I first moved onto Sadie's spread. It worked perfectly."

"Sometimes things wear out."

Ford shook his head. "Sadie replaced the pump last year. It's practically brand-new." Concern clouded Ford's eyes and the heavy burden of getting the ranch up and running filled his deep sigh.

He put in some long hours, but always found time for her. Like today, sneaking away for a ride and a picnic lunch under the trees. She helped out, but more often than not she felt like she held him back.

She stood and held her hand out to him. "Come on, let's go. Days a wasting and we've got work to do."

Ford took her hand, but instead of her pulling him up, he pulled her down into his lap. "Work can wait. I may have to do the dishes, but I was hoping you'd ease the sting of defeat."

"And how am I supposed to do that?"

He rolled to his side, laying her out on the grass next to him, with his body down the length of her side. "Kiss me."

"Now, that's *my* favorite thing to do." She reached behind his head and pulled him close, her lips brushing his in a soft sweep before she settled her mouth against his. This was how it used to be, them sneaking away to a secluded place under a tree. Lost in sweet memories, she melted into him, taking the kiss deeper.

His hand swept up her arm, over her shoulder, and down her chest to cover her breast. She leaned into his hand, sighing out her pleasure when he squeezed her aching nipple between his two fingers. He kissed his way down her neck. His hand swept down her belly and back up under her shirt. He pulled the bra cup out of his way and squeezed her bare breast in his rough palm.

She lost herself in the waves of heat every lick of his tongue, every caress of his fingers over her sensitive skin created. His head dipped and took her exposed nipple into his mouth. He licked and sucked until she writhed beneath him wanting more.

"Ford."

In answer to her call, his hand slipped down her belly to the button on her jeans. He had it undone and the zipper down with her next breath. By the next one her jeans and panties were at her knees and pulled over her boots.

"Sorry. I can't wait to taste you again."

Before she understood his intention, he slid down her, pulled her legs up and over his head, and buried his face between her legs. The first lick made her forget that her boots were digging into his back. He didn't seem to care. The second his tongue plunged into her throbbing core she didn't care about anything. His tongue came up and circled her clit. She moaned his name.

"I'm going to light you up, Firefly."

He slipped his hands beneath her bare bottom, lifted her to his mouth, and lit her up so bright she exploded like a supernova.

CHAPTER 15

Jamie found herself listening for Ford's truck, thinking about their afternoon under the tree as she made dinner. Everything had changed this afternoon, or so she'd thought until she'd found her breath and the energy to reach for Ford after he did in fact light her up. In that moment, she'd felt as close to him as she had before they parted years ago. But he hadn't made love to her today. Instead, he'd kissed her, helped her get dressed, and said they needed to get back to the ranch.

He wanted her. The evidence of how much had been pressed to her thigh. The torment of holding back had shown in his eyes. Still, he'd pulled away from her, cleaned up their picnic, and lifted her into her saddle, leaving her feeling completely satisfied in one respect, but also incomplete.

"We have all the time in the world."

His words to her before they rode back to the ranch. Apparently work couldn't wait, but they could. No. That's not what he'd meant. Ford wasn't like that at all. He wanted to give her time to settle into their relationship again. He didn't want to move too fast. She appreciated his consideration, but she also wondered if maybe he'd seen her apprehension about him seeing the scars on her body. He'd stopped because she hadn't been bold enough to show him how much she wanted him. She'd hesitated, and they'd lost the moment.

What the hell am I doing?

She had a chance for a real future with Ford. About time she immersed herself in all the love and comfort he offered her. If she wanted to keep Ford, she needed to put her heart on the line and believe in him, them, again.

Ford wasn't the kind of guy to reject her based on some physical flaw. He told her the scars didn't bother him. Why didn't she believe him? Not because he lied, but because she had trouble looking at the scars. That was her issue. Her problem to solve by seeing them for what they were—a badge of survival. A reminder that she was stronger than the events that hurt her.

She was strong enough to let Ford back into her life and her bed. Silly though her insecurities may be, they were real to her, but she wouldn't let them define her, or keep her from having the life she wanted—with Ford.

Time to fight to keep Ford.

She wrapped up the lettuce, grabbed it and the tomatoes, and put them back in the fridge. She turned the oven down on the Southwest casserole and ran for her bedroom. She needed to hurry if she wanted to be ready before Ford arrived for what he thought was just another dinner together. She had other plans. Bold plans for her, but she'd go through with them because being with Ford meant finding another piece of herself.

She wanted to be the woman who'd reveled in Ford's arms this afternoon all the time.

If she could cross this threshold, be brave and bold, maybe she could see herself for who she was and not what she looked like. If she let go of the guilt, healed the pain, maybe she'd find herself again. She could be the woman she wanted to be, not the victim she felt like all the time.

She could be the woman Ford deserved.

In the bathroom, she brushed pink blush over her cheeks. She didn't need much, thanks to her days spent outside at Ford's ranch. Next, she darkened her lashes with mascara, making her green eyes stand out. Ford used to love her long hair. Now that it was cut short, she didn't have many choices for style. She grabbed the gel to slick the sides back, but tossed it back in the drawer, deciding to go with something softer, more feminine. She brushed the soft waves back and away from her face, thinking the next time she got it cut she'd keep the top a bit longer than the sides and back. Give it a little more edge, but still keep it feminine.

Maybe she'd grow it out again. Ford used to love to run his fingers through the long, thick mass. She loved the feel of his fingers stroking her hair. It always comforted her.

The last thing she did was dig out the bottle of her favorite perfume. She spritzed her neck, wrists, and cleavage for good measure. Feeling and smelling pretty and ignoring the flutter in her belly, she went back into her room and opened her closet. Most of her clothes were still in boxes in the spare room. She slid one hanger after another aside, looking at each top and discarding it, trying to find the perfect item. She stopped on a sky blue sleeveless top that was a double layer of sheer material over the cotton shell. Lovely in its simplicity, she almost discarded it, too, because the scars on her shoulders and upper arms would show.

Be kind to yourself, Jamie. The scars don't matter.

The butterflies in her belly turned into hummingbirds, but she pulled off her plain T-shirt. She frowned at the simple cotton bra and went to her dresser and found the pretty pink lace bra and satin panties Catalina had bought her for her birthday last year. She could almost hear her friend say, *Go get him, girl!* It brought a sad smile to her lips and a soft glow to her heart.

Bolstered by thoughts of her friend and how she used to prod Jamie to find a man, or at least get laid once in a while, she put on the bra, took off her jeans, and swapped her simple bikini panties for the cheeky satin pair that showed off her ass. Ford liked her ass.

Really starting to feel sexy, she slipped the blue blouse over her head and down her torso. She smoothed the soft material and studied herself in the mirror over the dresser. The color made her eyes stand out even more. Her hair shined bright, with the golden and red colors warring with each other in the soft sunlight streaming through the window.

She rummaged through her closet once more and found the skirt she'd bought but never worn. The navy blue silky material fell in tiers of waves to her knees. She loved the effect of the wavy material and the dark against the light blue of her top. She left her feet bare, showing off her polka dot painted toes.

Why not? One less thing for Ford to take off.

Maybe she should put them on.

No.

Nervous and impatient all at the same time, she couldn't wait to hear Ford honk his arrival. She smiled just thinking about it and took one last look at herself in the mirror, admiring how pretty she looked.

Something moved in the background and caught her attention. She spun around, hands up ready to defend herself, but didn't see anything out the window. She could have sworn she'd seen a man spying on her.

She rested her hand over her fluttering stomach. "Just your ghosts," she assured herself. Out here, who would be sneaking around like a Peeping Tom?

She'd left her gun tucked in the drawer beside the bed for more than a week. She didn't need it to feel safe anymore. She had her sanity back. Most of the time. She wouldn't give in to destructive thoughts and imagined visions. She had a new mission tonight: seduce Ford.

Zoey woke up in her bed in the living room and yapped out once and bounded for the front door. She scratched against the wood, hearing Ford's truck before Jamie did.

"Good girl," she called to Zoey, who bounced around in front of the door waiting for her other favorite person.

Jamie gave one last look to her perfectly clean room, forced herself not to focus on what she thought she'd seen out the window, and settled her gaze on the bed. She'd endured too many nights alone. Ford probably didn't like it any more than she did. Tonight, they'd both get what they wanted. Each other.

Ford honked twice, then slipped out of the front seat of his truck with the two pots of daisies he bought her in town after picking up a new automatic timer for the irrigation system. Another thing that had worked fine for months then decided to go on the fritz with the water pumps. Another coincidence, a stroke of bad luck, a quirk with the electrical, or someone fucking with him? Sadie's brother's drug dealing buddies hoping to drive him off the land so they could set up another meth lab?

He didn't know and couldn't prove anything because it all looked like a bunch of freak accidents or prematurely worn-out parts.

Zoey yapped at the front door. Jamie opened it and unleashed the energetic puppy on him. Zoey bounded down the steps and awkwardly ran toward him. Ford smiled at the spunky pup, but his mouth fell when he spotted Jamie standing on the porch waiting for him looking better than he'd ever seen her. He loved the pretty blouse and skirt. Her beautiful face made him forget all his problems. She'd made herself up for their dinner tonight. He appreciated her efforts, but he didn't need or expect her to go out of her way for him. No matter what she wore or how she looked, she was always the most beautiful woman he'd ever seen.

And maybe he should tell her that more often.

He leaned down and gave Zoey a pat on the belly, but didn't take his eyes off Jamie. "Hey, beautiful. Look at you, so pretty. If I'd known you were going to get dressed up, I'd have taken you out to dinner."

She shook her head. "I don't want to go out. I want to be alone with you." The bold words matched the intensity in her eyes.

He stopped on the step right below where she stood on the porch and stared down at her. She wasn't that much shorter than him now. "Are you sure? You look really great. We could go into town and eat at one of the restaurants."

"I like staying in with you."

"Did someone stop by before I arrived?"

Her brilliant green eyes narrowed. "No. Why?" She

tensed. Her gaze swept the yard and driveway, every tree and bush along the way.

"I thought I saw a car pull out of your drive. Must have just been someone turning around on the road."

Her lips pressed into a grim line, but she shook off whatever unnerved her, then smiled at him, though it wasn't quite as bright. "Are those for me?"

He held up the pots. "So you have something pretty to look at when you sit out on the porch, drinking your coffee in the morning."

She brushed her fingers across the delicate white petals. "Daisies are the happiest flower of them all."

"They certainly make you smile."

He watched her, fascinated by the change in her. He didn't know what was different, but something was and it reminded him so much of how she used to be.

Instead of taking the flowers, her hands came up and cupped his face. She leaned in and pressed her soft lips to his, kissing him for a long moment. She leaned back just enough to look him in the eye and smile again. "Thank you."

Before he could say, "You're welcome," she kissed him again, sliding her hands around his head and wrapping her arms around his neck.

Ford dropped the pots on the porch on either side of her feet so he could pull her close. He needed her close. The kisses they shared before made him want more. This one made him think his knees might buckle and he'd sink down and beg her to finish what they started earlier today.

Slowly losing his mind, hoping he didn't push too hard, too fast, he swept his hands down her back and over her hips. She pressed closer, rocking her hips into his. His fingers dug into her soft flesh. He tried to be gentle, but she moaned at his touch and he gripped her tighter, crushed her body against his, and kissed her like his life depended on it.

His tongue swept along hers and he explored her mouth, savoring her sweet taste. She matched him, and they lost themselves in the kiss, the feel of their bodies pressed together, the excitement and anticipation of being together again. Still, he held back, letting her take the lead.

Jamie broke the searing kiss and planted kisses along his cheek to his ear. "Do you want me?"

In answer, he pressed his aching cock into her belly. "Desperately."

Her tongue swept across his earlobe, sending a shiver of need down his back. She whispered, "Take me to bed."

Before the last word escaped her lips, he picked her up right off her feet, walked through the front door, waited longer than he wanted to for Zoey to follow them in before he kicked the door shut, and carried her to her room all the while kissing her neck. She locked her arms around his head and sighed out her appreciation. A soft tremble went through her body when he set her on her feet at the end of her bed and stared down at her.

He swept his hands up her sides, set them on her shoulders, and softly rubbed his thumbs along her jaw. "Are you sure?"

"I loved what we shared today, but it just wasn't enough. I want to be close to you again, Ford. I miss you. I miss us."

"So do I," he whispered a breath away from her lips before he kissed her again.

Her hands settled on his wrists and squeezed.

He drew back and stared into her hesitant green eyes. "What is it, sweetheart?"

"I can keep my shirt on if it helps you to not have to look—"

He kissed her to stop the ridiculous words coming out of her mouth. "I don't care about the scars. I care about you. I want to be with you. Not halfway. Not most of the way. All the way."

To prove it, he leaned down and kissed the scar on her chin, slipping his hands beneath the hem of her blouse and sliding his palms up her sides and over her silky skin, just the tips of his fingers brushing the scars on her back. She tensed, but settled when his lips pressed to the top of her breast.

Her fingers slid through his hair and held him. "Ford, I'm a little scared."

The softly spoken admission made his chest tight and his heart ache. He stood tall, stared down at her up-turned face, slid his hands around her back, and planted his palms and fingers wide over her scars. "You are brave and beautiful. I'm nervous, too, but this is you and me. We know each other." He leaned down and kissed her softly. "I've missed the way you taste." He kissed her again, brushing his fingers down her back and over her bottom, pulling her close. "I've missed the way you feel against me." He slid his hands back up her sides, bringing her shirt up and over her head. He leaned down and pressed a kiss to her chest above her breast and inhaled her sweet meadow scent. "I've missed the way you smell. Sweet flowers and spring days."

He'd gotten a taste of her today, but he hadn't gotten her naked, free of all the barriers, physical and emotional, separating them. Tonight, they'd bare it all and take another step toward their future.

He unhooked the pink lace bra at her back and slipped it free of her arms. He bent and took one peaked nipple into his mouth and sucked softly. Her fingers combed through his hair, held him to her, and gripped the strands, letting him know how much she liked it and didn't want him to stop. He couldn't if he tried. His need for her grew with each sweep of his hand over her soft skin. Each taste of her made him want another until he had to lay her out on the bed, peel away the skirt and silky panties that distracted him but didn't halt his progress to his real goal—making her his again.

Her hands rubbed down his back as he leaned over her and kissed her belly. She gripped his shirt in her fingers and dragged it up his back and over his head, tossing it away so she could slide her hands over his skin.

"Ford."

Just his name on her lips and he was gone all over again, mapping her stomach with kisses down to her hip. He hooked his arm around her leg and kissed a trail down the inside of her thigh. The bullet hole scar didn't stop him or make him hesitate. He kissed it, too, hoping that in some small way it made her feel better. She stilled at his touch, but he distracted her by palming her breast and squeezing as he kissed his way back up her leg to the very place he wanted to sink his aching flesh into right now. He held back, hoping to keep hold of his patience and make this better than any other time they'd been together. She needed to see, to feel, to believe that nothing had changed in this way between them. They could have what they shared in the past, and it could be better, because the future they'd once given up was within their reach now.

He squeezed her nipple between his fingers. She sighed with pleasure, arched her back, pressing her breast into his palm, then lay back down, raising her hips, seeking his touch. He gave it to her, licking her wet center with his tongue, delving between her soft folds. She cried out at the sheer pleasure, driving him on to do it again and again until she writhed on the bed.

Her fingers dug into his shoulders. Her nails bit into his skin. He sank his tongue deep in her center, stroking, taking her up and over the edge with a wild howl of satisfaction that made him smile against her thigh before he kissed her hip and belly softly again and again to bring her back down. She relaxed into the bed as he drew away.

"I love to make you shine, Firefly."

He sat on the edge of the bed, her hand softly brushing up and down his back as he removed the rest of his clothes. He pulled the condoms he'd carried around with him these past weeks out of his pocket. Yes, he was an optimistic man, desperate for any chance to be with Jamie, but holding off until she was ready.

"Ford, you okay?"

He glanced over his shoulder at the woman lying behind him with the soft glow of happiness radiating from her pretty green eyes. He'd never seen her more relaxed.

"I have a beautiful, brave, strong woman like you in my life. What could possibly be wrong?"

Her eyes shined with unshed tears. He didn't let her speak. He didn't need her to say anything, just wanted her to take his words in and believe in the truth of them.

His body covered hers, and he kissed her as the wave of pleasure and heat raced through him. Skin to skin, her hands rubbing over his back and sides, every contour and tensed muscle, making him near mad to have her. He nudged her thighs wide with his knees and rocked his hard length against her soft center. She rolled her hips against him, driving him insane. He left the sweet temptation of her breast to tear open the condom and sheath himself. Settled against her again, he took her nipple into his mouth, sucked, and slid his hard length into her wet center in one long glide that had him buried to the hilt. He gritted his teeth, giving her time to adjust to him, but she sighed and moved against him, setting off a wave of pleasure that provoked him to move. He lost himself in making love to her, drawing out every sweet moan and soft whimper.

Lost in her sweet temptation, the feel of her body moving against his, the feel of her hands moving over him, her soft mouth pressing kisses to his neck, he drove them both up to the brink. Her hands gripped his ass and pulled him close, rocketing them over the edge as he thrust into her hard and deep and lost himself in her.

His breath sawed in and out at her neck. He held his weight off her on his arms, his fingers toying with her soft hair. "I think you're trying to kill me again."

Her chest vibrated against his with her sweet laugh. "If I do that, I don't get to do *this* again with you." She rocked her hips against his, setting off a new round of spasms in her body. She sighed and smiled at the same time.

He stared at her in wonder that this beautiful woman had come back to him. "Stay with me." Those were the words he should have said to her all those years ago. He'd held them back then. For good reason. But he wouldn't do it now.

She wrapped her arms around his back and hugged him close. "I'm right where I always want to be."

He kissed her again, soft and sweet. He drew out the kiss for a long moment, telling her without words how much he'd missed her. How grateful he was to have her back.

She squirmed beneath him, squished by his weight. He moved to her side and pulled her close, draping her over his chest with her head on his shoulder. Unable to help himself, he brushed his fingers up her back and neck and through her soft hair, taking the same trail back down. He rubbed between her tense shoulder blades with his palm, massaging her sore muscles.

"Working in the stables with the horses must leave you hurting every day."

"It does, but look at the way I'm lying."

He stared down at her. She had both arms up by her head, her hands rested beside her face. The left arm was slightly lower than the right on his chest, but when she'd first returned, she couldn't put that hand over her shoulder at all.

"You're getting better."

"I am better, thanks in part to you." She sighed, her back rising and falling under his hand. He kneaded and rubbed. She relaxed more and more.

He leaned up and kissed her on top of the head. "Better?"

"You do so many good things to me with those hands."

He chuckled, happy she'd finally let go of her worries about him seeing and touching her. "It's really selfish. I like touching you too much to stop."

She lifted her head and stared at him, her green eyes filled with heat. "Don't stop."

He didn't. He loved her long into the night, stopping for an intimate dinner naked in bed, until they reached for each other again and eventually collapsed in exhaustion. Best night of his life, and he wanted more of them. A lifetime of them.

CHAPTER 16

Jamie pulled into Zac's driveway happy to see her brother and nephew for the first time since she stormed out of the restaurant. She gut-checked the urge to turn the truck around and head straight back to Ford's place when her mother turned from Zac and narrowed her disapproving gaze. The anger came along with the resentment. She hadn't done anything to deserve that look or her mother's scorn. As quickly as those feelings surfaced, they dissipated with the heavy sigh Jamie breathed out. Jamie didn't want to fight with her mother. She didn't want to carry the burden of past hurts. She just wanted to let it go. If her mother couldn't do the same, so be it. She wasn't going to miss out on seeing her brother and nephew anymore. She'd stayed away for years, settling for phone conversations and emails rather than coming home to see Zac too many times to count.

Their relationship suffered.

She still didn't know how Zac ended up a single father to his son.

Jamie slipped out of the truck and walked the short distance to join her family. While being with Ford again had made her feel at home, the disconnection she felt from her mother persisted. She wished for a real and loving relationship, but knew deep down she'd never get it. But that didn't mean she had to continue to feed the animosity between them.

"Jamie, you're here." The surprise in Zac's voice matched the shock in his eyes.

"I hate that you find it so odd I'd come to see my brother." She softly poked Corey's belly and made him smile. "And this little one." She smiled at the baby and brushed her fingers over his golden hair. A longing in her heart for her own child glowed warm and bright.

"What is that thing on your face?" Zac pestered her about the smile she gave him that used to be rare, but came much easier now.

"Shut up," she teased back. "Hi, Mom. How are you?"

Taken by surprise by her easy manner, her mother eyed her suspiciously. "Just fine. What are you doing here?"

Jamie squashed a smart comeback. Defensive had become her default. She hit reset and tried nice for a change. "I just wanted to say hi and pick up something from the things Zac is storing for me."

"Always depending on your brother." Her mother shook her head, her mouth scrunched into a disapproving line.

She wanted to remind her mother that Zac had relied on Jamie growing up to provide him with the mothering and love every kid needed, but they'd lacked as their mother pursued one man after the next. Her mother desperately wanted to be loved, but had never been capable of giving it to her own kids. Sad really, but Jamie had needed time and space and a clearer head to see she'd never change her mother, but she could change herself.

Tired to the bone of always fighting—with her mother, against an enemy only in her mind, for her life—she wanted to live her life the way she had the last several days—filled with peace.

She may have only been able to depend on her mother's consistently bad attitude, but Zac had never failed to give her his constant love and support. "I'm lucky to have Zac." She smiled at her brother, who seemed taken aback by her changed attitude.

"You look different. Working with Ford looks good on you, sis."

Jamie lifted her arms and flexed her biceps like a weight lifter. "I'm getting stronger every day."

Zac chuckled. "And happier."

"It won't last. Ford's just feeling sorry for you. Eventually, he'll find a true beauty like his brothers did."

"Mom," Zac warned.

Jamie cut him off. "You know what, Mom? It takes a hell of a lot more than a pretty face to keep a man interested."

"Your face sure isn't pretty," her mom shot back.

"Maybe not to you, but Ford doesn't look at my scars and see something ugly. He sees them as a badge of strength and survival. He cares about me because of who I am, not what I look like. You of all people, with three failed marriages under your belt, should know that love withers and dies under unrelenting jealousy and anger and just plain unhappiness."

Her mother gasped and wound up to fight back, but Jamie didn't let her. "I don't care what you think of me, Mom. I don't want to fight with you anymore. I won't fight with you anymore. I hope you can see that I'm happy with Ford. I love him. I've always loved him. I'm trying really hard to make a life with him. I have no interest, nor have I ever had any interest, in the men in *your* life. I want *you* to be happy. I wish you could say the same to me."

"You think what you have is better than what I have. You think you're better than me. You always have."

"Mom, you're the only one comparing our lives. Believe me, I wouldn't wish my nightmares on anyone." Though having Ford back in her life made all she'd been through worth it. "I love you, but I won't let you continue to tear me down. I don't deserve it. You do your thing, and I'll do mine. Though we'll share Zac and Corey, we'll stay out of each other's way. Let's just leave it at that for now."

Jamie turned to Zac. "I'll be in the shed, looking for what I came for." She walked away from her stunned mother. Maybe next time they could actually have a cordial conversation.

She slid the shed door open and walked into the cooler, darker interior and checked the stacked boxes, looking for the one she wanted.

Corey's sweet babbling announced Zac's arrival a few minutes later as she ripped the tape off a tall box.

"Mom gone?"

"I don't think I've ever seen her speechless," Zac teased.

Jamie turned and faced Zac. "I can't do it anymore. I'm going to follow your advice and just let it go."

Zac titled his head and his lips in a lopsided grin. "Who are you? And what have you done with my sister?"

She chuckled. "It's me. In fact, this is the most me I've felt in a long time."

"When you came home, I didn't think I'd ever see you happy again. In fact, I wasn't sure how long you'd . . . Never mind." Zac nuzzled his nose into Corey's hand, playing with the little boy who reminded Jamie so much of Zac as a wild runt running after her years ago. It seemed like a lifetime ago now.

She gently touched his arm. "I gave you every reason to be scared and worried about me."

"I didn't know how to help you. You were always there for me, and I just didn't know what to do for you. Nothing worked. I guess all you needed was Ford." Zac's sad voice touched her.

"You helped me more than you know, Zac. Seeing Ford again made me feel something I hadn't felt in a long time. I found the strength to want to be the woman I became after I left here again. I'm not completely there yet, but it's getting better."

"I can see that. So, you two are back together?"

"Yes. But it's still new." She pinched her lips, then sighed. "I'm trying not to screw it up."

"You won't. You love him."

"I found out the first go-around that sometimes love isn't enough. A relationship is work. Ford deserves an equal, someone he can count on. I want to be that woman more than I can say."

Zac bounced Corey to calm his fussing. "You'll get there, Jamie. You've come so far. Give yourself time to heal. If he loves you, he'll be patient. He'll pick you up when you fall. Let him help you, sis, so he doesn't feel like you're pushing him away."

Zac spoke of more than her relationship with Ford.

"Where is Corey's mother, Zac? What happened?"

The tumultuous emotions whirling in Zac's eyes made her stomach clench. "It's a long story. We'll get to it soon. Right now, I need to feed him." Corey whined and squirmed in Zac's arms.

"When you're ready." She knew all too well that pushing him when the emotions were so close to the surface would only make him defensive. He needed to talk about it. He just wasn't ready to put words to the confusion a simple question like, *What happened?* evoked in him.

She'd give him time. Time she still needed herself to get through her own trials and troubles.

"Did you find what you needed?"

Jamie pulled out the manila envelope containing her belongings from her stay in the hospital. She opened it and pulled out the horseshoe she'd taken with her every-where she went after leaving home. Tobin brought it to her in the hospital and hung it on her bed when those first few hours had been touch and go. "Got it."

"Is Ford running low on supplies?" Zac joked.

Jamie shook off thoughts of those agonizing days in the hospital. "He gave it to me a long time ago after I had a particularly bad fight with Mom and went run-ning to him. He said it would bring me luck. I hung it everywhere I ever lived, even on the door to my bar-racks overseas."

Zac cocked his chin toward the scar on her face. "Looks like you could have used a bit more luck than that thing gave you."

"I'm still alive," she pointed out. Others hadn't been that lucky. She'd suffered, but they'd lost their lives and left behind the people they'd loved. She had a second chance to be with the ones she loved.

"I'm sorry, Jamie, I didn't think . . ."

"It's okay. You wish nothing bad ever happened to me. I feel the same way, but I can't change what hap-pened, no matter how hard I wish it away." She needed to face it, accept it, and find a way to move on. She only wished this dreaded sense of guilt didn't hang on like eagle talons ripping through her heart.

"So you're going to hang that up at your place?"

"No. I'll hang it at Ford's. He's thought about his own ranch for so long. I want him to have it, but it's not easy. He needs all the luck he can get to make it a success." Especially with all the oddball things happening at his place. Ranching was a tough business, and most didn't last. Not the way the Kendrick Ranch had lasted all these years, partly because of the sacrifice Ford had made to stay and fight for his family, the business, and the legacy that meant so much to him and his brothers.

Jamie closed the box lid and walked with Zac back out to her truck.

"You ever going to take all that stuff and fix up Grandma's place?"

"Maybe. Right now, I'm working on me." And her relationship with Ford. Maybe one day soon, she'd do more than just work at his place. One day, maybe that place would be theirs.

CHAPTER 17

Ford wiped the sweat from his brow with the back of his forearm. He picked up the jug of iced tea Jamie had made before she left to visit her brother and drank deep right out of the container. He'd worked like a demon the last two hours to get all the hay and grass he'd bailed yesterday stored in the barn he, Rory, and Colt had spent the better part of the last couple of days repairing, or practically rebuilding. He'd thought it would need a few new beams and columns for bracing, but the place had required much more work and it had taken three times as long to get it done. Without his brothers' before dawn help, it would have taken him more than a week to do it, if he could have done it at all on his own.

Rory smacked him on the shoulder. "You need to hire some help, or let me send a few of the guys over from our place for a few weeks. At least until you're set up here."

Ford wanted to say yes, but wasn't sure Jamie was ready to have a bunch of guys roaming the property. She'd gotten so much better the last couple of weeks. He didn't want to set her back, but if he didn't do something soon, he'd be so far behind he'd never catch up before he lost everything.

He wondered if Rory's offer and the concern behind it were because he didn't think Ford could pull this off. Sadie was counting on him to provide her with an income from this place, which meant big brother was looking out for his wife's interests as much as he was trying to help out Ford.

"Look, man, I'm doing the best I can here. I'll get it done, and Sadie will get her cut. I won't let you down. I just need more time."

"What you need is help." Rory pointed out the glaringly obvious. "And this has nothing to do with you paying Sadie. As long as she can pay the taxes on this place, she's good. She doesn't want to lose it, and she won't."

Meaning Rory would step up and pay to make sure his wife kept her family's land if Ford couldn't pull this off. He would pull it off, because he wanted it. The ranch, Jamie, the legacy he wanted for their family, come hell or high water. However many hours of sleep he gave up, he'd get it done and provide for Jamie and the family he wanted to have with her.

"I told you when you took over here, you don't have to do this alone," Rory reminded him.

Colt sat on the grass nearby, Zoey gnawing on his fingers as Colt played with the pup. "We've got your back, Ford. We can keep tackling these big jobs in small chunks, but time is running out before winter sets in and a lot of what needs doing will have to wait for spring."

He knew all that, but still hesitated because he needed to put Jamie's needs first.

Or maybe he had to give her a little more credit and recognize that the strides she'd taken these last weeks, each and every day, meant that she could handle having a crew working here full-time.

Jamie pulled into the driveway. Zoey jumped up, her tail wagging.

"Mama's home. Go get her," Ford coaxed.

Zoey ran full out to Jamie, who scooped her up, laughing and trying to dodge Zoey's face licking. The sound of Jamie's laughter tightened his gut and lightened his heart all at the same time.

"So, this is home now?" Rory asked, one eyebrow cocked up.

"Did she move in?" Colt eyed him.

"I thought you were taking things slow," Rory added.

He understood their concerns and dismissed them. He wanted this to be her home. He needed more time to get this place together, but he didn't need more time to know this was exactly where he wanted Jamie to call home.

"I'm working on it."

"You keep working the way you have been, you'll work yourself into an early grave. I'm worried about you." Concern narrowed Rory's eyes as he studied Ford's face.

"You can't do this alone," Colt said under his breath as Jamie drew closer, her approach cautious.

"I got this." Ford appreciated their concern. He'd never been more tired in his life. He tried his damnedest to get the work done and be everything Jamie needed. He wouldn't fail. Not this time. Yes, it was hard, but he'd put the work in now for the payoff later. He'd have what he wanted and would take care of Jamie for the rest of her life—if she'd let him.

Jamie eyed the stacks of bales behind him. "I don't

know how you do it, Ford. You guys got all this done in just a couple of hours."

"Yeah, Ford's a slave driver," Colt complained, rising to his feet with a groan for all the heavy lifting Ford made him do.

Jamie surprised him and walked right past his brothers and straight to him for her kiss hello. She set Zoey at her feet, stood tall again, and planted her hands on her hips and eyed his brothers. "So, are you both avoiding me for some reason, or is all the late night and early morning work you guys do while I'm not here Ford's doing?"

Rory and Colt both turned to Ford to answer that loaded question.

"Uh . . ."

Jamie cut him off, an edge to her voice. "Do you really believe me so far off my rocker that I'd go off the deep end if your brothers came over to help you while I'm here?"

"No. I didn't think you'd be comfortable with a bunch of men around."

She tilted her head and eyed him. "I worked with mostly men in the military, you know."

"I know, but . . ."

She tilted her head. "I might embarrass you if I lost it in front of your brothers?"

"No, Jamie. I'm trying to make things easy for you."

Her hands went up, then fell and slapped her thighs. "Nothing is easy for me, Ford. You know that, but treating me like I'll break or fall apart at any second doesn't help."

"I don't think that at all. I don't want to do anything that triggers another flashback or sets you back."

"I work with the horses to build back my strength.

How do you expect me to learn to be around people again if you never let anyone come here when I'm here?" One eyebrow shot up along with one side of her mouth in a tilted grin, like she'd got him with those true words.

"I'm sorry. I thought I was doing what's best for you."

"I know. I appreciate it. And until now, maybe you were more right than I'd like to admit, but you need to do what you need to do and stop making decisions for this place based on your fear that you'll harm me in some way."

"I swore I'd never hurt you again."

Her eyes narrowed. "You've made it your mission to help me get better."

"I'll do anything to make sure you're well and happy again."

She held her hands out. "Don't you think I want you to be happy, too?"

"I'm happy being with you, seeing you get stronger every day."

"I'm not happy you feel like you can't have your family over when you want. I'm not happy you still haven't gotten the help you need here. I'm not happy to see the worry and exhaustion in your eyes because you're working so hard and not getting everything done you need to, to make this place into what you want. I won't be happy if you lose it because of me. You think I don't see what's going on, but I do, and I can't let it go on any longer."

One side of his mouth pulled back in a lopsided frown. "You do realize you're saying all that while keeping my brothers in front of you and standing ten feet away from them."

"I might need my space, but I don't need an entire

ranch." She turned her back on Rory and Colt and reached up and touched her fingertips to the dark circles and puffy bags he'd seen under his eyes himself in the mirror this morning. "If you're not happy and well, how can I be? I want you to have everything you ever wanted."

"She's standing right in front of me." He reached up and cupped her face in his hand, her soft skin against his rough fingertips.

She placed her hand over his and leaned into his palm. "Don't hold on to me by letting everything else go. You'll resent me if you do, and this will all fall apart."

"I won't let that happen."

She gave him a quick kiss. "Good." She stepped back and held his hand between them and glanced over her shoulder at his brothers. "Then I'll see you guys more often and a few new faces around here soon." She looked back up at him, a question in her eyes. "Right?"

He looked down at their joined hands. Hers trembled in his, but she gave him a squeeze to reassure him that despite this being difficult for her with his brothers at her back, she meant it. He sighed, giving in, hoping he made the right decision. "Yes. I'll hire some help."

Jamie let out her pent-up breath and pulled a horseshoe out from her back pocket and held it up to him. "Remember this?"

Surprise spread a smile across his face. "You kept that."

"Took it with me everywhere I went. You never know when you'll need a little luck."

He frowned. "You needed more than that gave you."

"It was enough to bring me back to you." She squeezed his hand, another soft smile on her tempting lips.

He drew her in close, leaned down, and kissed her softly. "I think that makes me the lucky one."

The love that filled her eyes matched the outpouring in his heart, then turned to a flirty twinkle. A promise of things to come later tonight.

Jamie turned back to his brothers. "What do you guys think about rounding up your wives and Grandpa Sammy and having dinner with us tonight? I've got groceries in the truck."

Rory and Colt glanced at him. He stared down in shock at Jamie. Not only did she push him to hire help, she wanted to cook dinner for his entire family.

"Granddad has poker night with his buddies, he'll be sorry to miss it, but I'm sure Sadie would love to come."

"Luna's been working on paperwork for the ranch all day. She'd probably love to get out of the house."

Jamie beamed them both a smile. "Great. See you back here in a little while." She walked over to the toolbox he'd left near the barn door, picked out a small hammer, then a nail out of the coffee can beside it.

She looked over at the chicken coop he and his brothers had put up yesterday morning before Jamie came over. She'd spent ten minutes cooing over the chicks and holding them. "What happened?" she asked, pointing to the damaged wood frame and hastily repaired wire.

"Something tried to get the chickens."

"Did any of them get hurt?"

Ford shook his head. "No. They're fine." For all the damage done, not one chicken or chick appeared harmed. Not a single one had gone missing, taken by a predator. Nor had whatever had done the damage left a single track. He added the odd event to the other strange things happening on the ranch.

Rory waited for Jamie to head up to the house and

out of earshot before he said, "So, we're supposed to ignore the fact that she broke out in a sweat being that close to us?"

"Yes, because she overcame her fear and did it, because she trusted me to protect her."

"From us?" Colt asked, appearing surprised and annoyed she'd think that about them.

"She knows she's imagining the threat, but it doesn't make it any less real for her. I'll make the calls to the guys I talked to about working here already and see if they're still available." A few more people to keep an eye on things.

"You're sure?" Rory asked, concerned as he was that Jamie may not have been as serious as she'd sounded about him hiring help.

"Yes. She's right. I don't want this place to come between us. I won't let it. No matter what, she'll always be my priority. But if I don't get things moving here, I'll lose it, and she'll think it's her fault."

"She's not like I remember," Colt said. "I don't think I've ever seen that kind of . . . caution and . . . despair in her eyes. She just can't hide it, can she?"

"No. And she can't control the thoughts in her head, or the fear that sweeps through her, or the nightmares that make her scream in the night. So if you guys are here and you see her do something strange, just know it's not you. Give her the space she needs. She's better, but she's not over it."

"Whatever you and she need, you got it." Rory clamped his hand on his shoulder in a show of support.

"Let's keep dinner simple and short. Ease her back into the family nice and slow. Don't walk up behind her. Don't startle her. Don't stare at her. Don't ask her about the Army, or what happened to her. If she freaks out for some reason, duck and cover." He smiled on the last sentence to let them know he was kidding. Mostly.

Colt smacked him on the shoulder. "We got this."

"Great. Now I'm going to go show that girl how much I appreciate her."

"Go get her, bro," Colt coaxed.

He didn't need the nudge when everything in him was drawn to the house and the woman hanging a lucky horseshoe over his front door. The woman he wanted to keep forever.

CHAPTER 18

Jamie set the last set of utensils on the table, stood back, and admired her work. Simple white dishes, gleaming silverware, navy napkins, and pretty wildflowers in three crystal vases down the center of the plank table. The roast chickens in the oven scented the air with garlic and butter. Potatoes boiled on the stove. She'd mash them once done. Fresh green beans sat on the cutting board waiting for her to steam them.

Ford wrapped his arms around her waist and pulled her into his chest. Fresh from his shower, he smelled of soap with a hint of citrus and mint. "Are you sure about this?"

"Ask me again, and I'll shoot you." He'd asked her a dozen times since his brothers left to pick up their wives if she was ready for a house full of guests. But they weren't guests, they were family. She needed to get used to being around them again.

"I believe you will," he joked, kissing her neck. "The table looks great. The food smells even better."

"I'm nervous."

The doorbell rang. "No time or reason to be nervous. They're here. You know my brothers. You'll love their wives."

"Yeah, but will they like me?"

"What happened to your cease-fire?"

Be kind to yourself. She swapped her uncertainty for courage. "I can't wait to meet them."

Ford turned her in his arms, kissed her softly, then went to open the door.

Everyone came in one by one.

Rory first, with his beautiful, pregnant wife's hand in his. When Rory stopped in the living room, Sadie passed him and approached her. Rory held her back, but Sadie tugged her hand free and closed the distance with her hand held out. "Thank you for inviting us, Jamie."

Jamie took her warm hand, smiling back at Sadie. "I'm glad you came by while I'm here." She looked around Sadie at Ford. "Instead of when Ford sneaks you over when I'm not."

Sadie chuckled. "We wondered how long Ford would keep you all to himself."

Luna scooped up Zoey and held her close. "Oh my God, I want her." Zoey wiggled in pure bliss as Luna tried to hold on to the growing pup and scratch her belly. Pretty soon, no one would be able to handle the chocolate Lab.

Sadie put her hand to her swollen belly. "Oh my. Someone is hungry for whatever smells so good."

Jamie reached out but pulled her hand back. She used to love working at the day care, seeing the expectant mothers come in and pick up their toddlers. She had longed for a child of her own. It seemed so long ago now, but being back with Ford uncovered the hope that it could be a reality someday.

Sadie smiled and pushed out her belly. "Go ahead. He's kicking up a storm."

Jamie pressed her palm to the mound and felt the baby kick and move under her hand. The wonder of it brought a smile to her face. "He'll be as big and strong as his dad." She winked at Rory, who stood protectively close to his wife.

Ford caught her eye. His gaze softened and he relaxed, seeing her with his family.

"I want in on this." Luna stepped forward and put her hand next to Jamie's on Sadie's belly. "Oh my. Look at that, he kicked me."

"Are you and Colt going to give Grandpa Sammy his second wish?" Sadie asked.

Colt hugged Luna from behind. "Grandpa Sammy and his pushing and prodding and meddling."

Jamie eyed them, seeing the inside joke in their eyes. "What's this about?"

Ford joined the group. "Nothing."

"Nothing?" Luna scoffed. "The man won't rest until he's got his three grandsons married off with his three great-grandbabies on the way."

Jamie nudged Colt's shoulder. "No pressure though, right?"

Ford frowned. "Jamie, you know Granddad. He's ornery as hell."

"And bound and determined to see you join your brothers in wedded bliss." Rory covered Sadie's mouth to keep her from saying anything more.

Jamie got why. Ford must be feeling the pressure to fulfill Grandpa Sammy's wishes now that she'd come back into his life. "So you guys didn't come for the chicken. You came to make sure I have honorable intentions toward Ford."

He actually groaned.

"Mostly to be sure you won't murder him in his bed," Luna teased.

Ford groaned again.

"Oh, I kill in bed," Jamie teased back. "Which is why Ford is missing out on so much sleep."

Ford sighed out his relief that she played off the jokes with humor rather than taking offense or getting upset that they knew she'd lost it and tried to kill him. That seemed a long time ago and a far different woman than she felt like now.

Rory and Colt high-fived Ford. Luna and Sadie rolled their eyes.

"Who wants a drink?" Now that they'd broken the ice, everyone seemed to relax and stop anticipating her total meltdown.

"We'll help," Sadie said, going to the fridge with Luna to grab beers for their husbands, soda for Luna, and a glass of lemonade for Sadie.

The guys settled on the sofa and chair in the living room. She went to the stove and stirred the potatoes, checking to see if they were done. No use telling Sadie and Luna she had dinner under control. They helped out anyway. Sadie put the green beans on. Luna dumped the boiling water from the potatoes, mashed them with salt, pepper, and lots of butter. Jamie took the chickens out of the oven and cut them into pieces on a platter.

Chatting with them about simple things eased Jamie into the evening even more.

"Sadie, where did you get those cute sandals?"

"Online. I'll write down the name of the site before I go. They have great shoes. Not too expensive either. These are so comfortable, even for my swollen feet and ankles."

Jamie laughed along with Luna. Sadie was the picture of a glowing expectant mother.

"I love your pink polka dot toes," Luna commented, showing off her own dark purple pedicure.

"Ford mentioned you're putting together an equine therapy program." Jamie hoped they could connect on their mutual love of horses.

"Colt found me this gorgeous palomino. She's a sweetheart. I've been training her the last few days. The kids are going to love her."

They fell into easy conversation about horses. The ache she carried in her heart throbbed, thinking about working with Catalina and Jo. She missed her friends so much, but found she enjoyed making new ones with Ford's sisters-in-law. The future she wanted with Ford included his brothers and these ladies. Having them over tonight showed her what life with him would really be like. She wanted it even more.

The three of them brought dinner to the table, which brought the men as well.

Everyone sat and filled their plates. Ford put his hand on her thigh under the table and gave her a soft squeeze, silently thanking her for dinner and inviting his family. She held his intense gaze. She smiled, letting him know she got it. This night was important to him. Having her beside him, his family at the table, it was what he'd always wanted. She'd wanted to take him away all those years ago, but she should have known leaving his brothers would have made him miserable. This was where he belonged.

She felt like she belonged, too.

"Happy?" she asked him.

"More than I can say."

She leaned in and kissed him. Sadie and Luna both

went, "Awww." She and Ford smiled with their lips pressed together. She pulled back, then moved her chair to get up.

He stilled her with his hand on hers. "Where are you going?"

"To get my meds so I don't murder you in your sleep." Sarcasm dripped from her words, but everyone stilled around the table and stared at her. "Joking." She put all her humor into the single word. "I forgot the gravy for the potatoes on the counter."

The collective sigh made her shake her head and laugh. The rest of the evening went by with easy conversation, good food, and even better company. She really enjoyed it. Judging by the many thanks and requests they do this again soon as everyone left, so did Ford's family. The warmth and expectation in their words told her they really meant them.

She stood on the porch by Ford's side, his arm wrapped around her. He leaned down and kissed the top of her head and right there in the quiet said the words she'd longed to hear for too long. "I love you."

Surprised, her heart all aglow with a warmth that spread through every cell of her being and lit up her soul, she put all she felt into her reply. "I love you, too. So much. This is how it should be." She hugged him close. "Us, just like this."

Ford took her hand and turned for the house. Something in the shadows by the barn caught her attention. That feeling of being watched crept up her spine, raising the hairs on the back of her neck.

"Jamie?"

She scanned the darkness one more time, wishing she wasn't spotlighted in the porch light. The urge to shove Ford inside and take cover overwhelmed her.

"Jamie!"

Ford's sharp voice jolted her out of the rising need to protect herself and Ford from whoever spied on them. Even though she knew no one was really there she had a hard time fighting that primitive part of her mind.

"Sorry. I'm coming." She wished she could trust her instincts. "Do you mind if we stay at my place again tonight?"

Ford stood behind her in the open doorway. "Sure, Firefly. Whatever you want." Disappointment filled his words, even though he tried to hide it.

He wanted her here with him. She wanted that, too, but when she stayed, she wanted it to be forever. She hoped he understood. She hoped he didn't realize she wanted him away from here tonight because her radar had gone haywire again.

CHAPTER 19

Ford didn't know what spooked Jamie last night, but he had a feeling whatever it was had to do with the strange things happening at the ranch. Like the fact that he suspected his patch job on the chicken coop had been torn apart by a two-legged culprit rather than the four-legged predators that normally did those kinds of things. Not a single damn track on the ground. He didn't want to go there, but he had to consider someone had done this deliberately to provoke him. Unsettled as Jamie looked last night, he searched the yard again for any evidence to support his growing concern that Jamie's paranoia that someone was out there wasn't all in her head.

The chickens and chicks had escaped their pen and roamed the yard, but were safe and all there by his count. Not one foot print from a predator out for an easy meal.

Another task to attack, he went to the tool shed to grab a hammer and staples to repair the broken boards and wire. The second he stepped through the door, it swung closed as something scraped against the wood followed by a thwack as the shovel he'd left propped against the outside wall fell and blocked the door. Ford pushed against it, but only managed to lodge the shovel firmly against the handle.

Another fucking fluke? This made one too many co-incidences. Frustrated, he tried the door again, shaking the weathered wood, then punching it when it didn't budge.

Ford listened intently as something rustled in the grass outside.

What was that?

Probably one of his now free-range chickens.

He rubbed his stinging knuckles and tried to think of the best way out of there. He needed a tool, something he could use to pry one of the weathered boards off the wall by the door and free himself.

Tired of bumping into things in the dim light coming through the narrow window at the peak of the low roof, he reached for the light switch, hoping the bare bulb wasn't burned out and the damn thing worked. Seemed everything he touched went haywire lately. He flipped the switch. A spark and hiss alerted him to danger a split second before the gasoline soaked rag lying over the outlet box caught fire and it spread up the desert dry wood walls.

Who the hell put that there?

He thought the gas smell had come from one of the old lawn mowers.

Smoke filled the small space quickly. Ford tried to kick the door open, but the shovel handle held firm. Coughing, trying to think through the panic, he searched for something he could use to bust out one of the boards in the back wall.

He grabbed hold of the worktable and tried to move it from the wall, but with its drawers filled with tools, spare parts, and junk from years gone by, he barely moved it an inch at a time. The effort it took sapped his energy and made him cough harder through the thickening smoke. The heat from the fire licking across the walls and up to the ceiling made him sweat.

"Jamie!" The bellow only made him cough harder.

She was too far away in the stables to hear him, so it wouldn't do him any good to scream his head off, but reason quickly escaped his mind as overwhelming fear pounded through his veins. With three walls engulfed and the fire closing in on him, he kept working at moving the table, trying not to think of the blistering heat baking him alive.

"Ford! Ford! Are you in there?"

"Yes," he gasped, though his voice came out rough from all the smoke. He dropped to his knees, trying to get some air by a crack between the boards. "Jamie," he called weakly.

"I'm here." She slammed something into the board a foot away from him. "Watch out."

The sharp edge of an axe cut through the wood, splitting it. She yanked it out and swung it back through the cut she'd already made.

The flames raced toward the opening Jamie was making with quick, efficient hacks at the wood. She hooked the axe around a board and yanked once, then twice, and pried the board off. Smoke billowed out the opening, cutting off the bright light. Jamie wacked another board, then pulled it free. He could barely contain the urge to leap toward her, but he couldn't act on that impulse as his vision blurred and the smoke filled his lungs until he could barely take a breath. The darkness surrounding him crowded into his vision.

Just when he thought he'd pass out and die, Jamie grabbed his arm and pulled. He used the last bit of energy he had to lean toward her and get his feet under him enough to push his lagging body toward her.

A sickening crack sounded behind him a split second before he dove through the hole Jamie had made in the wall and the other side of the building collapsed in a blast of heat and flames. Jamie pulled his arm harder. He stumbled forward and fell onto the dirt and grass, gasping for breath. Jamie fell beside him and rolled him over and over until he ended up on his back once again.

"What the hell?" His head spun.

"Are you okay?"

"Why are you rolling me around like that?"

"To make sure all the sparks went out." She patted his jeans in a few smoking places.

It hit him all at once. She'd saved him. He'd nearly burned to death. If that wall of fire had fallen on him, he'd be dead. He stared with incomprehension at the ten-foot-tall flames. It seemed so unreal.

Jamie cupped his face and leaned in close. "Ford. Are you okay?"

He coughed a few more times, his lungs aching from the exertion. Instead of trying to talk when his throat still felt like it was on fire, he grabbed her to him and hugged her close as the fire consumed the rest of the building.

"Ford, you're scaring me." Panic filled those words.

"I'm fine. You saved me."

"I couldn't get to the door. The flames were too hot. The fire . . . I almost lost it . . . The fire . . . You were in there." She stumbled over her words and thoughts. Her body trembled against his, or maybe that was him, because that near death experience had taken ten years off his life.

"What the hell happened?"

He wished he knew. "A shovel fell against the door and locked me in. I hit the lights and the whole place went up."

"What shovel?"

"Didn't you see it against the door?"

"No. I grabbed the axe you left out and ran for the other side of the building. I guess I missed it."

If she grabbed the axe from where the shovel had been beside the door, how did she miss seeing it? He'd think about it later. Right now, he was happy to be alive and to have Jamie in his arms. "Are you okay?"

"I'm never going to sleep again. But I got you out." Jamie spread her hands over his chest and moved them over him, assuring herself that he was really okay.

Ford wrapped Jamie in his arms and held her close. He couldn't imagine what nightmares that fire brought back to her. Feeling the scars on her back through her shirt, he could only imagine the pain and fear she'd suffered. He got a small taste of it being trapped in that room. He got off lucky with a few minor stinging burns on his bare arms and where the sparks had burned through his jeans before Jamie patted them out. In her case, she'd barely escaped with her life.

He held her tighter until he could breathe without imagining her on fire or him dying in that shed.

Sirens sounded in the distance.

"You called the fire department?"

"I'm just glad the dispatcher understood me. I called during my run up here from the stables."

"Did you hear me call for you?" He didn't think so.

She shook her head. "I felt like something was wrong. I'd already begun to investigate when I smelled the smoke, then saw the flames." The distress came back into her eyes.

Ford sat up with her and held her close. "I'm sorry I scared you."

"Enough, Ford. Hire someone. Ten people. Fix this place and make it safe. What if you'd been here alone, or I hadn't come out of the stables and given in to my . . ." Tears choked off her words.

"I'm so glad you listened to your instincts, Firefly. They saved my life."

"I am, too, even though most of the time I'm chasing ghosts."

"I'm not so sure about that considering everything that's been going on around here. You thought you heard or felt something last night on the porch."

"I think things like that all the time, but it doesn't mean they're real. Ask my shrink."

Maybe he was grasping at straws.

By the time the fire department drove onto the property moments later, the shed had burned to the ground, leaving behind a charred and smoking mess. Some of the grass caught fire, but he and Jamie were able to stomp out the hot spots. The fire department sprayed down the rest.

He gave his account to the guy in charge. The fire department and cops took down everything he said. He didn't add his suspicions, only telling exactly what had happened as the events unfolded. His story raised a few eyebrows, even from Jamie, and opened an arson investigation. The cops promised to investigate the other odd happenings on the ranch.

Ford couldn't prove anything. He didn't know who'd mess with him, but he'd find out, and whoever it was would be sorry they'd put that haunted look back in Jamie's eyes and added one more nightmare in her mind.

CHAPTER 20

You overcame your fear and saved Ford, Jamie," Dr. Porter praised.

Jamie tried not to dwell on the fire from a week ago, but like her other nightmares, it hit hard sometimes.

"I almost lost him." She didn't want to think of a life without him. Ford's near death experience had brought them closer together. He had a renewed sense of living life to the fullest, fixing the ranch, and making every moment count. He'd certainly made the quiet nights they shared into memorable moments this past week. He made love to her with a passion and need that told her how deeply he felt and how almost losing her made him want to hold on all the more.

She felt the same way.

"You're smiling."

Jamie jumped at the sound of Dr. Porter's voice and the trace of accusation in it.

She shook herself out of thoughts of her in bed with Ford, his hands on her skin, his lips pressed to hers, his body moving over her, under her, against her until passion burst from them and they clung together in the magic they made each night.

"You're blushing and smiling even bigger now. I'm concerned."

Jamie didn't hide her joy. She couldn't. She reveled in it, because the darkness didn't crowd in and turn her mind black with negativity and doubt. She had hope. She had dreams. She had love in her life again.

"Why are you concerned about me smiling?"

"Don't take this the wrong way, but your recovery seems rather fast. From deep depression to all smiles in just a few weeks."

"Is that so bad?"

"I'm concerned that such a swift change won't last, that it's not sustainable when you haven't dealt with your past."

"Can't you be happy that I've found something that brings me more joy than I've felt . . . ever? Now that I'm consistent with my meds, eating regularly, getting exercise, I'm actually leveling out. You said the meds take time to work. They're working."

"How is your pain level?"

"Hovers around a three to a five most days because of the physical labor I'm doing. I don't mind the pain so much because I'm making progress." To prove it, she raised her arm up to a forty-five degree angle from her body. Major progress. Soon, she'd be able to raise it all the way up to the side of her head.

"Nice. How are the headaches?"

"Gone. I haven't had one in five or six days. Before that, they'd tapered off considerably."

"How are you doing with the extra men working at Ford's place?"

Ford finally hired help. Four guys to start. "The first couple days were hard, but it's getting better." She didn't look over her shoulder a hundred times an hour now. Mostly because Ford kept the guys working away from her. Still, she hadn't completely freaked out, so that was something. "I had one scary moment," she admitted, using her time with Dr. Porter wisely now that she'd given herself over to the process and grudgingly admitted to herself that talking things out with him helped.

"What happened?"

"Nothing really. The guys were walking back toward the stables from fixing a fence line. They were carrying a bunch of tools and posts in their hands and the past and reality collided. I thought they were carrying rifles. I thought they were gunning for me. I shoved Ford into a stall and he spent the better part of five minutes convincing me we weren't under attack. Totally embarrassing. I lost my shit."

"How did Ford handle it?"

"Like he handles everything: with infinite patience and more love than I probably deserve."

"Why do you say that?"

She touched her fingertips together and pressed the point of her hand into her chest. "I still feel this weight, this something pressing on me." She sat back, trying not to let her emotions get away from her, but thinking things through. "I think it has to do with the recurring nightmare I can't shake either."

"Tell me about it."

"It's after the explosion. I'm out of the truck. I'm crouched behind another vehicle. I'm looking around, seeing everything as it happens. It's too much to take in all at once. I look up at the shooter, but I can't see him. He's just a black figure."

"The attack happened in the middle of the afternoon. Broad daylight."

"Yes. But in my dream it's all grey, and the shooter is black as night, bullets spraying everywhere like bursts of fire."

"Vivid, yet obscured."

"Yes, exactly."

"You're still too afraid to see it and face it."

"Why do I need to now? I feel better. I've found a new life. I want to focus on my future, not keep looking back." Stuck in denial, she didn't want to switch gears and feel the pain anymore.

"And what is that future, Jamie? Working in the stables at your boyfriend's place? Is that the life you want?"

"I want a life with him. What I do doesn't matter."

"It does matter. You're working there now to be close to him. You're using him and the job to block out the things you don't want to deal with because he does make you happy. But that's not going to change the fact that you have to deal with your past so you can move forward without the past haunting you. Without it eventually infecting your life. It will, Jamie. You know it will."

"Right now, I need the routine. I need Ford's strong and steady presence. I need the way he makes me feel."

"What happens when that's not enough to keep the past only in your nightmares and you start acting out again because you can't deal with the nightmares, flashbacks, paranoia, and other effects of PTSD? The Army thinks you have intel they need."

She held up her hands. "What could I possibly know?"

"They seem sure you know something. All they'll tell me is that they expect some lab results soon."

"Great. I don't know what they're testing, but maybe they can give *me* some answers."

"Tobin called me again. He really wants to talk to you."

Jamie held up her hands and let them fall in frustration. "Everybody wants something from me."

Dr. Porter cocked his head to the side. "Do you include Ford in that?"

"No. He pushes, nudges, he's even provoked me a time or two, but it's always to get me to take a step toward being healthy again. He wants my happiness more than anything else."

"Then you need to continue to work on you, so you are the best you can be for yourself and for him. If you aren't, how can you be what he needs without harming yourself?"

"Dr. Porter, what we have is really good. I mean it. He reads me so well, it's easy for me to communicate with him exactly what I need, even when I'm unable to put it into words. He's patient, because he knows we have a lifetime to get this right."

"Do you believe that?"

"I want to." Hope filled her voice.

"Come on, Jamie, look at what you have accomplished and what you have in your life. Give yourself permission to believe in it. Acknowledge the love you feel for him, the love you feel from him, and validate what you share. You deny the past. You deny the present. You deny the possibility of a future. Stop living in denial and find acceptance and understanding. Own it. Say it out loud. Make it real."

"Yes, I love Ford. It fills me up, but there is still this blackness inside of me that I try to hide and ignore. Yes, okay, I need to deal with it, but I don't want to. I want it to go away so I can be with him and be happy and have everything I lost and found again. I want us to live on his ranch and have babies without this thing living inside of me.

"I want it to stop nagging at me. I want it to go away!" She sank into the couch, her chest rising and falling with every pant as she tried to catch her breath and slow her throbbing heart.

"Breathe, Jamie."

"I can't breathe when I'm suffocating. You say 're-member' and all I do is see myself on the ground staring up at the dark figure. I can't catch my breath and all I want to do is scream at him." She sucked in a ragged breath and let it out, yelling at the top of her lungs, "Stop!"

"Keller!"

The rat-a-tat-tat of gunfire sucked her into the past. The wretched smell of smoke and burned flesh. The incessant ping of bullets off metal. The screams of men being hit and falling, injured and dying, gasping for their last breaths. The eerie silence from those lying dead around her.

The smoke billowed overhead, obscuring the bright blue sky. The feel of the gun in her hand, a familiar weight and sense of security. She stumbled up and raised the gun and pointed it at the dark man and squeezed the trigger.

"Jamie!" Dr. Porter's voice echoed through the too-bright room.

Someone held her close in a tight hold she couldn't break.

"Firefly, come back to me. Come on, sweetheart. You're okay. You're safe. You're here. I love you. Come back to me, Firefly." Ford's soft voice whispered against her ear.

She shook free of the past and felt Ford's hard body

pressed against hers. Her arm ached. Ford held it pinned between his arm and side so tight she couldn't move or slip it free. She relaxed her arm and hand. The gun slipped through her tingling fingers and clunked on the hardwood floor. Ford kicked it away and let loose on her arm. She leaned away from him, checking him over, running her hands over his chest and arms to be sure she hadn't shot him again.

"Jamie, Ford, is everyone okay?" Dr. Porter yelled from her laptop on the table.

"We're fine. Jamie, honey, say something."

"Where did you come from? When did you get here?"

"Just now. What's going on?"

Zoey danced around their feet barking and yapping.

"Uh, I don't know. I was . . ." She shook her head to clear the cobwebs from her muddled mind. "I don't know."

"Sit her back on the couch," Dr. Porter ordered.

Ford held her to his side and guided her to the sofa. She sat and raked her fingers through her hair, trying to breathe and find her sanity again. Her head swam with images that overlapped and made little sense.

Ford set the gun on the table next to her laptop.

She looked all around, the window, the door, and walls, but found no new bullet holes.

"I emptied the gun, remember, sweetheart?"

She buried her face in her hands. "Oh God, I could have shot you again."

"Again?" Dr. Porter asked, leaning forward toward his laptop, his arms braced on his desk.

"What the hell is going on here?" Ford demanded, sidelining any talk about her shooting him. "I walk in and she's in some sort of state. She doesn't hear you yelling her name or me talking to her. What did you do?" Ford yelled at Dr. Porter.

"We were talking about the attack and her night-mares."

"Let me guess, you pushed her to remember until she lost it."

"I . . ."

"Fuck. She was doing so well, and you've got to take all that progress and flush it down the toilet."

"She needs to face the past."

"Yes. In her way. You have to let her do it in her time. You push and push and she fights it. Give her a nudge and time to let it come to her, time for her to slow things down to her pace, and she'll remember more and incorporate it in her mind without it hurting so much. Without it sending her into a tailspin and looking for her goddamn gun!"

"Ford, you're upset." Dr. Porter's voice held a calm that didn't show in his eyes.

"I'm fucking pissed off that you'd do this to her."

"You might want to turn and look at her."

Ford turned to her. She couldn't help the smile on her face, despite the anger in his eyes and the grim line of his lips.

"You're really sweet to be so worried about me."

"Of course I'm concerned. I love you. God, Jamie, come here." Ford dragged her into his arms and held her close, his face buried in her hair and neck. "Don't ever scare me like that again."

"I'm sorry. I kind of blacked out or something."

"We were talking about . . ."

"Enough," Ford cut off Dr. Porter. "No more. Not now. Give her time to let it settle. Let her process what happened. She'll talk about it again when she's ready."

Jamie brushed her hands up and down Ford's wide shoulders. "Ford, it's okay. I'm okay now."

"We need to discuss—"

"I said later." Ford tapped her keyboard, ending the session. Dr. Porter's image turned into a blank blue screen.

"Ford, that wasn't very nice."

"I don't care. You can talk to him at your next session. You heard the bell, his time was up. Now it's my time."

Jamie held Ford's wrists and leaned into his hands on her head. "What do you want to do?"

"This." He leaned in and kissed her softly, his thumbs sweeping over her tearstained cheeks as she settled into him and the kiss that demanded nothing but said so much. His lips met hers again and again in soft, sweet sweeps until he settled in for a deeper kiss, his tongue gliding against hers. Lost in his touch and taste, she sighed and let the last of the fear and panic dissipate as Ford's love and the passion he invoked in her filled her up.

"I love you," she said against his lips.

"I know," he answered back. He held himself a breath away and stared into her eyes. "No matter what happened to you, you came back to me. As long as you want me, I will never let you go. I will do everything in my power to make you happy, because I love you too much to live without you ever again."

"Show me," she pleaded because she needed to feel him and his love wrapped around her.

"Always." He stood and pulled her up with him, leading her down the hall to her bedroom. He gave her those few seconds to shake off the last of her waking nightmare and let the anticipation build between them with each stroke of his thumb against her palm. Warm tingles resonated up her arm and spread through the rest of her body.

He stopped at the end of her bed and turned to her. The love and tenderness in his eyes made her heart melt. His hand came up to cup the side of her face. "You sure you're okay?"

She leaned into his warm, rough hand. "I'm okay."

"Jamie." His coaxing tone made her reach for him to reassure him.

She laid her palm on his chest over his heart. "When I'm with you, I'm better than okay." To prove it, she slid her hand down his chest and rock hard abs to his belt buckle. She pulled his shirt from his jeans and used both her hands to slide it up his body and over his head, though he had to help her at the last because she was short and couldn't raise her arm that high.

She smoothed her hands over his bare chest, down his tight, tanned muscles. He stood before her, his hands loose on her hips, and let her have her way with him.

Emboldened by his stillness and patience, she took hold of his belt buckle and undid it, the leather letting loose with a rasp and slide. She glanced at Ford. His gaze held hers and burned with anticipation and need. His whole body tensed at her touch, just the back of her hand against his stomach while her fingers worked the button and zipper on his jeans. She slipped her hand inside and palmed his ever-growing rigid flesh. His deep groan prompted her to lean in and kiss his chest. Her lips pressed to his warm skin over his heart. As she stroked his hard cock, she used her free hand to drag his jeans over his lean hips and down his thighs.

Without warning, Ford grabbed her under the arms, lifted her right off her feet, spun around, and dropped her on her back on the bed. She bounced with a laugh bubbling up from her gut.

"Enough. My turn."

"But I was just getting started. You didn't give me a chance to really drive you crazy."

"Mission accomplished, Firefly. I'm crazy for you."

Her clothes and the rest of his hit the floor with amazing speed, but Ford took his time kissing his way up her leg, over her stomach to her breasts. He spent a great deal of time lavishing one and then the other with soft kisses, long stokes of his tongue, and sweet suckling that had her hips bucking on the bed, and her fingers pulling Ford's hair to keep him close.

"Ford, now you're driving me crazy. Come here." She pulled his head up and took his mouth in a searing kiss.

Ford broke the kiss, rolled to his side to find the condoms in the drawer beside the bed, and she rolled up behind him, bit his shoulder, then smoothed her tongue over the small hurt.

"You're playing with fire."

"Mmm."

Her fingers fit around his rigid length in a wide grasp. She worked her hand over his cock, her body pressed to his warm back. She trailed kisses over his shoulders and up his neck. He brushed her hand aside to sheath himself before he rolled toward her and right on top of her. She giggled, then sighed as he settled between her thighs, kissed her hard and deep, and thrust into her in one smooth motion then stopped. Each of them moaned into the other's mouth and lost themselves in making love. His body moved over hers in soft but demanding sweeps, his broad chest brushing against her hard tipped breasts. She held his hips pressed to hers, her fingers digging into his ass. She spread her legs wide, took him deep, and reveled in the uninhibited passion they couldn't contain when they lost themselves in each other.

Spent, wrapped up in his warmth and strength with his arms around her and her head on his chest, her ear pressed to his thumping heart, she smiled softly at the sheer joy and satisfaction being with him brought her.

"I love you," she whispered because the feeling overwhelmed her and the words burst from her lips.

"I love you, too." His lips pressed to the top of her head in a long kiss before his head fell back to the pillow.

"I didn't mean to shoot at you."

"Don't ever do it again."

She smiled against his chest. Yes, her tough-talking cowboy would dismiss her reckless behavior with a simple order to do better. Be better.

She was better. On her own. For him. With him.

CHAPTER 21

Tobin wore the tread off his tires, tearing down the Montana back roads in his rental car. He didn't mind the long drives it took to get from one place to another out here, but he would much prefer to take them with Jamie at the wheel like when they were overseas. He would sit and stare at her, daydreaming about the life he wanted with her when they got home.

He'd hoped to carry their relationship to the next level once they were free of that dreadful place. But it all got fucked up on that damn supply run. It wasn't supposed to go down that way.

He slammed his hand against the steering wheel. Jamie had barely survived. If she'd died in that firefight he'd have never forgiven himself. They shared a deep connection because of all they'd been through. She understood him in a way no other woman could or would now. They were partners, and he wanted her back.

He took the turnoff down Juniper Road and counted down the miles, anticipation building in his gut, making it hard for him to sit still.

The second she saw him, she'd give him one of those big smiles, the ones where her eyes lit up and her cheeks flushed pink, making the tiny freckles atop her cheeks stand out. She'd run to him, wrap her arms around him, and hug him tight, her body pressed to his. Maybe her excitement would overcome her and she'd kiss him.

He couldn't wait to see her. He needed to see her.

He'd protect her always.

Especially from that no-good fuck who'd broken her heart and thought he could take advantage of her now that she'd come home. Jamie was in no condition to think clearly when it came to her ex. She needed someone who understood all she'd been through. Someone who knew her inside and out. Someone who'd been there with her through it all.

Once she saw Tobin again, she'd know.

They were meant to be together.

He loved her.

He'd do anything for her.

He'd die for her.

CHAPTER 22

Zoey bounded off Jamie's chest and woke her from her nap with a jolt. The pup leaped to the floor and barked incessantly at the door. Three minutes after five. Either Ford was early for dinner, or Zac had come calling. The unfamiliar rumble of a big V8 engine sent a shot of adrenaline through her system and had her scrambling off the couch and on the run for her bedroom. Zoey barked at her heels. She snapped up the gun from the bedside table and fell to her knees beside her dresser, pulling out the bottom drawer, and finding the stash of bullets she kept hidden there.

With her adrenaline pumping, her nerves frayed, and her mind splintering into thoughts of the past, the present, reality, nightmare, and the overwhelming rush of fear coursing through her veins, she couldn't think straight, so she acted on instinct to protect herself even if it didn't seem wholly rational at the moment.

She loaded the gun in seconds, tossed the box of bullets back in her hiding spot, pushed the drawer back into the dresser slot, and ran for the front door. A pounding fist echoed against the door. That's all it took to break her tenuous hold on reality.

The thump on the door became the explosion of

a bomb. She reeled back, raising the gun, but Zoey jumped on her legs, barking and begging for her attention. One part of her brain dragged her into a living nightmare. Another held on to reality and the bouncing puppy at her feet. She sucked in a breath, tried to calm her racing breathing and heart, and picked up the puppy. Zoey licked her face and pawed at her shoulders. She focused on the oversize pup and not the irrational thought that she was under attack.

"Open up, Keller."

Jamie jumped. Tobin? Here?

"You can't ignore me anymore."

No. Not when her past came calling out of the blue like this and upset her life once again.

Uneasy and still feeling that sense of unreality— past, present, and nightmare mixed in her mind—she pulled her cell from her back pocket and texted Ford.

JAMIE: Tobin's here. Come over. Now!

Tobin was her friend, but his presence tore open the wound she'd tried so hard these last weeks to heal so she could find a way to live without feeling so . . . raw . . . responsible. Guilty. And some other feeling she couldn't name but hurt deeply. She tried to hold on to this moment and not black out like she had the other day with Dr. Porter—tried not to do something stupid because Tobin triggered her nightmares. She barely hung on to reality now as images flashed in her mind, a crazy slideshow of death and destruction. Her lungs burned, and she finally inhaled a ragged breath.

Tobin banged his fist on the door again. "Come on, Keller. Open up."

Jamie kept Zoey tucked against her side and reached

for the doorknob, but stopped when she saw the gun in her shaking hand. Yep, crazy. She sucked in another breath and tried to muster up the calm she'd found with Ford.

While she was aware of herself loading the gun in a desperate need to protect herself, it felt very much like a dream.

She hated when reality no longer felt real.

She didn't need to protect herself from Tobin.

Still, her heart jackhammered in her chest as she tucked the gun in her waistband at her back, covered it with her shirt, and reached for the door once again.

She forced herself to turn the knob, scolding herself for being afraid of letting a friend into her house. For not being able to cope with such a simple, mundane thing as welcoming a guest—even an uninvited one. She thought she'd made progress, but this felt very much like a setback and an eye-opener, showing her that while she'd found peace and happiness with Ford it was tenuous at best. The second her past intruded on her present, everything fell apart.

It took all her strength to open the door and face Tobin for the first time in months. The second she saw his face, she knew all her hard work was for not. Dr. Porter's declaration that if she didn't deal with her past now it would come back again and again and muck everything up in her life was coming true.

"Hello, Tobin."

He reached for her, coming in for a hug, but she put her hand on his chest and held him off.

"What are you doing here?"

"I came to see you." He reached out and patted Zoey on the head.

The pup wagged her tail and licked his hand. Zoey

had no fear of the big man. Jamie had to fight for every breath and scrap of calm she could muster, though most of it had washed away due to the shot of adrenaline racing through her system. Her hand trembled against Tobin's chest. He didn't move back. She didn't budge from her spot in front of the door.

"Why are you here?"

"Keller, seriously, I know you're having a hard time. I am, too. I came because I needed to be around someone who gets it. Someone who lost the same friends and thinks about them all the time." His hand settled over hers on his chest. "You've been avoiding me because I remind you of them."

She hadn't considered her maniacal aversion to everything having to do with her past a way of avoiding grieving. A great weight shifted in her chest and set off a wave of sadness unlike anything she'd felt since waking in the hospital and finding that she'd survived while others hadn't been so fortunate. She'd wallowed in her anger in a futile attempt to not feel the loss and sadness. She felt it keenly now with an ache that tore her heart open.

Tobin's thumb swept across her cheek as she stared into the past. Catalina belting out a Taylor Swift song at the top of her lungs and completely out of key. Jo swiping on her favorite cherry lip balm and smacking her lips and pressing them into a sexy pout, then giggling. The sweet sound echoed in Jamie's broken heart even now.

Long conversations under the stars about the lives they wanted when they returned home. Catalina couldn't wait to go home to her fiancé, get married, and start a family. Jamie had felt that same pang in her heart for those things and envied Catalina for finding the love of her life when Jamie had lost hers. Jamie would never be her maid of honor now. Who would be hers if she ever got married? Jo had wanted to start a family with her husband. After two years of marriage and months apart, Jo couldn't wait to hold a baby in her arms and settle into life as a soccer mom, driving a minivan instead of a Humvee.

Pedro had written love letters to his girlfriend on their long drives, trying out sexy lines on Jamie, making her laugh, but secretly melting her heart. What she wouldn't have given to get a letter from Ford letting her know she was missed, wanted, loved so deeply that his every thought included her.

And Tobin. Her constant companion, always there to lend a hand with the heavy supply boxes. The guy who always remembered how much she loved chocolate and always seemed to have a candy bar stuffed in his pocket. She'd had no idea where he'd gotten them half the time, but anytime she'd needed one, he'd handed it over with a smile. The guy who'd read her moods and knew when she needed to hear a joke, needed a push to get back on track, or simply needed a hug and the easy silence they'd shared in the truck.

She'd told Ford they were just friends, that she didn't think of Tobin that way, but that hadn't been entirely true. Sometimes she had let her mind wonder if moving on with Tobin and making a life with him was possible. Those daydreams always ended the same as they did when she thought of any other man. Their faces all turned into Ford's.

It wasn't anything about Tobin that kept him in the friend zone. Dark hair, whiskey colored eyes with flecks of gold. Tall, though several inches below Ford's six-two height, and broad with just enough muscle to make a girl take notice, but not too much to make him seem stocky. She liked her guys tall, lean, and ripped. Like Ford. It always came back to Ford. So Tobin had become her dearest friend and the guy she could count on to watch her back.

"Here you are," she whispered, warmed from within because he'd come to check on her and be the friend she remembered but had ignored for far too long.

His hand cupped her cheek. Those whiskey eyes stared down at her filled with compassion and an understanding that didn't require her to explain all he saw in her.

"Here I am."

She stepped back and let him in the door.

He dropped his Army duffel on the floor by the sofa and glanced around the room. "Nice place. Definitely better than some of the places we've slept."

She stared at the peeling paint on the wall and the faded wallpaper in the dining area. "It needs some work, but it's home. For now." She hadn't started working on the house because she didn't want to stay here. She hoped to move into Ford's big house, the one she'd described to him so long ago that he'd made his, but could be theirs soon.

Tobin took a step closer. "I came, hoping to talk you into coming back to Georgia. Everybody misses you. I bet your cousin would love to see you again. I sure would love to have you back." The words were matter-of-fact with hints of coaxing and hope mixed in, but underneath the simple statement she read a whole lot more.

He'd never hidden the fact he wanted them to be something more. He joked about it mostly, but the truth lay in those tossed-out jests. She used to laugh them off to keep things easy between them. She didn't ignore it or let it go this time.

"Um, Tobin, you should know—"

"You're back together with Ford." Tobin rolled his eyes. "Yeah, I got the memo on that one. I'm surprised I caught you alone." The sarcasm didn't mask the underlying disappointment and anger in his voice.

"Why do you keep asking Dr. Porter about me?"

A crease formed between his brows as his eyes narrowed on her. "I'm concerned about my best friend, who won't speak to me."

"I'm sorry. I've been . . ." She slid her fingers over her forehead, unable to put into words how lost she'd been until Ford. Yes, until Ford. Everything changed when he came back into her life and made it easy to breathe again.

"Me, too," Tobin answered, knowing what she wanted to say without her having to say all the words to describe what she'd been through. His gaze softened on her face and his mouth dipped into a forlorn frown. "That's why I came. I don't want you to go through this alone. You couldn't help it. You froze. It happens."

That odd sense of dread and the feeling that she was missing a piece of the muddled puzzle in her mind flared to life, knotting her gut. "What are you saying?"

"Don't worry, Keller, I didn't say anything in my debriefing. It's war. Things happen that are out of our control. Maybe a few more of us would have survived if you'd acted, but you were out of your head with pain, barely able to think through the agony, let alone move and do what needed to be done. It's okay. No one needs to know."

"I can't remember . . ."

"It's better you never remember what happened."

The intensity in his words and body struck her. "You keep telling the Army that and you won't get in trouble. Just keep it to yourself. Don't tell anyone. It's our secret. People like Ford, who have never been to war, seen the things we've seen, done what we've done in the name of freedom for them, won't understand. They'll condemn you, Jamie." His voice softened. "But I'm here now. I'll protect you. I'll make sure no one ever finds out."

Jamie tried to put what Tobin said and the pieces of the nightmare together in her mind, but her brain shut down. She didn't want to believe what Tobin said was true. She'd been responsible for some of her friends' deaths. She'd frozen and they'd died.

She hadn't done what needed to be done to save them.

Like the months home she'd spent not doing what she needed to do to be well. Because deep down she didn't believe she deserved to live and be well again. And now she finally understood that nagging feeling inside of her. It wasn't just survivor's guilt. She really was responsible.

Tobin stared at her. His eyes didn't hold a bit of censure or hate. He genuinely believed it wasn't her fault because she'd been in bad shape when it all went down. He forgave her because of that, but she couldn't forgive herself.

A man of action, one willing to sacrifice for his family the way he had when he sent her away, would Ford understand her weakness and inability to help her friends when they needed her most?

Oh God. "I . . ."

Tobin took her face into his hands again. "I'm here to help, Jamie. I'm here for you. I was there. Right beside you. You had my back, and I've got yours." His gaze fell to his feet, then swept back up to meet hers. "I will keep your secret, but you've got to be careful what you say to Dr. Porter and Ford. I won't let anyone hurt you again."

Red-rimmed and shadowed eyes held hers. Too much booze, not enough sleep. He'd lost some weight since she'd seen him. His ready smile didn't come so easily, or at all as time passed and they reacquainted themselves with each other. His body remained tense and on edge. His gaze swept around the room and darted out the door more times than she could count.

Yeah, she got that on guard behavior innate to someone who'd been to war, that feeling that a threat lay around every corner.

She didn't want to face her past with this new knowledge and the roiling anger, guilt, and agonizing pain in her gut for what she'd done—or hadn't done that she should have to save her friends no matter what. But she needed to know the truth. Once she knew everything, maybe then she could find a way to live with it and herself.

Tobin knew what happened. He'd give it to her straight. With a sick heart, she finally welcomed the one person who knew the worst about her, who hadn't turned his back, but had come to protect her from herself.

"Are you hungry?" She'd feed him and get the answers to those black spots in her mind.

"Are you cooking?" His words held little enthusiasm.

She gave him a mocking frown. She might not be a gourmet chef, but she could put together a decent meal. Or at least an edible one. "I won't poison you." She glanced at the clock, remembering they wouldn't be alone long. She needed to get her answers fast. "Uh, Ford will be here soon. He's a great cook."

"What's he going to say about me staying here with you?"

Presumptuous, but she couldn't toss him out after he'd come all this way.

Ford might object. Ford would definitely object. Shit. She had some explaining to do when he showed up.

She needed more time.

Would he see it in her face now that she knew why she'd fought so hard to forget her past? Would he leave her because of what she'd done?

You can't go back and fix what you did wrong. He forgave you for leaving, but will he forgive you for the lives you took, the ones you didn't save?

Bile rose to the back of her throat. She choked it back and tried to pull it together.

"Ford left a couple of steaks in the fridge. I'll make the salad and put the potatoes in the oven to bake." Her stomach turned at the thought of food, but she needed to do something mundane, normal, or she'd go completely crazy with the thoughts and feelings swirling in her mind.

"What can I do to help?"

"Take a seat at the table. Fill in the blanks for me. What happened out there?"

Tobin dropped into the chair. "It's best to let it be, Jamie."

"I can't."

She set Zoey on the floor. The puppy bounded over to Tobin's big booted foot and pounced on it, growling at the black laces and biting them as she danced back, then went in for another attack.

Tobin batted Zoey away with a swat of his big hand. "Beat it, Killer."

Jamie froze in place. Her heart dropped into her stomach and her throat seized on the scream rising up inside of her. A great black wave stole reality from her and dumped her on her back in the middle of that street, staring up at the dark man looking down on her.

CHAPTER 23

Keller!" a man shouted from inside Jamie's house.

Ford ran up the steps and straight through Jamie's front door, making it slam against the wall and bounce off it nearly hitting Ford's arm, but he didn't stop until he got between Jamie and the guy who must be Tobin. It took some effort to pull the guy's hand off Jamie's shoulder and step in front of her, backing the guy up with a cold glare. Ford's insides turned to ice-cold rage at seeing Tobin with his hands on Jamie and the blank stare on her face that meant she'd blacked out and gone to another place. A place he hoped he could reach her once again.

"Back off," Ford bit out, hands fisted at his sides, holding his ground in front of Jamie.

Tobin took two menacing steps toward him, his eyes narrowed with fury and lips drawn back in a threatening snarl. "Something's wrong with her."

Jamie's arms wrapped around Ford from behind. Her hands pressed to his chest and pulled him back against her. She buried her face in his spine between his shoulder blades. He quit glaring at the man in front of him and turned to take care of the woman he loved. His gut ached seeing her like this. Clinging to him, she pressed her forehead to his chest.

He slid his hands up her arms to her neck and used his thumbs pressed to her chin to get her to look up at him. "What happened?"

"Nothing. I—I'm fine."

"It's not nothing. You're not fine."

She turned to the half open door and his truck out in the driveway. "You're early. When did you get here?"

"While you were blacked out again. What triggered you this time?"

"Jamie, are you okay?" Tobin asked, stepping up beside them.

She pulled Ford close, turned her head away from her friend, and held Ford tight. "I'm sorry."

Ford kissed her on the head. "No sorries. Talk to me."

Her grip on his sides tightened. He didn't mind the small pain.

"I didn't know. Now I do. It hurts so much. I don't know what happened. I fell back in time. I have to live with it."

Ford didn't understand that convoluted line of thinking. He'd get her to explain when she was calm again. He brushed his fingers through her hair to soothe her, then ran his hands down her neck and back, rubbing her tense muscles until he got to the gun in her waistband. He leaned back and stared down at her, though she didn't meet his gaze.

"Well, at least we've made some progress." She hadn't pulled the gun on Tobin, or shot anyone. "You didn't—" She pressed her fingertips to his lips, cutting off his words.

"I'm okay now." She pulled his hands away from her back, the gun, and sidestepped so Tobin didn't see what she'd tried to hide from both of them. He read the narrow-eyed look on her face. She didn't want Tobin to know about the gun.

Great. What the hell did he step into between these two?

"Someone want to explain what just happened?" Tobin persisted.

"I suffer flashbacks. I don't remember everything that happened. You know that. But sometimes it comes back like a living nightmare."

Tobin eyed her. "Some things are better left buried."

Ford didn't get the look Jamie and Tobin shared, or the deep grief that filled her eyes. He sure as hell didn't like the way Jamie couldn't even look at him.

"Jamie loses time, her ability to see reality, and does things she shouldn't without thinking." Ford felt that strange undercurrent between Jamie and Tobin intensify.

"What kinds of things?"

"Those aren't woodpecker holes in the doors and window." The sarcasm in his voice belied the deep concern eating away at his insides that Jamie needed her gun close when she'd left it in her room this last week. Well, except for that incident after she lost time talking to Dr. Porter. And now this. He'd really thought she'd improved these last weeks. It just proved how tenuous her progress was and that every hard-won victory could be laid to waste with these setbacks.

Tobin surveyed the front door, the bedroom door down the short hallway, then settled his worried gaze on Jamie behind him, her back against the wall, her eyes cast down to her feet.

"Why didn't you tell me you were having this much trouble?"

"I didn't want anyone to know. I didn't want anyone to see me like this."

Ford leaned down and picked up Zoey to stop her from jumping on his legs. He turned and handed her to Jamie. "There you go, Firefly. Hang on to her."

Like always, Zoey's puppy kisses and undying devotion and love eased Jamie. She took in a slow breath and let it out, hugging Zoey close. Ford rubbed Jamie's arms up and down a few times to calm her even more. "Sit down. Breathe. I'll make you something to eat."

She took the seat at the table closest to the kitchen and shared another of those knowing looks with Tobin across from her. Whatever he'd missed between those two before he arrived seemed to have driven a wedge between Ford and Jamie. He didn't understand it or like it one bit.

He definitely didn't like this change in Jamie's attitude. She'd been so positive and strong, yet today she'd slipped back into thinking she should have died over there. Not good. He wished he knew what to say or do to make her feel better.

Tobin's unannounced visit sure as hell hadn't done her any good. He needed to go. Soon. Now would be better, but not Ford's call.

Tobin scrubbed a hand over his face. "Mind if I grab a beer?"

"Help yourself," Jamie offered.

Tobin pulled two from the fridge, unscrewed the caps on both, and handed one to Jamie. Tobin downed half of his in one long gulp.

Jamie took a sip of hers and didn't look up from Zoey, probably because she didn't want to see the surprise he couldn't hide on his face. She hadn't had a drink since she shot him. Nothing but a sip or two from his beer.

This is going downhill fast.

He didn't want to put her on the spot in front of her

company, so he snagged the beer from her hand and drank a long swig like she did from his all the time before setting it in front of her again.

"I take it you're staying for dinner," Ford said to Tobin, trying to keep his anger in check and out of his voice.

"I'm staying for a while," Tobin shot back.

Ford wanted to punch the smug smile right off his face.

"You know, to make sure Jamie is okay and doing better."

She was until you showed up.

Ford held his tongue for Jamie's sake. He didn't want her to think this incident meant anything more than the other ones. She'd gotten through those. She'd get through this one.

He'd get that damn gun away from her again.

"I guess the spare room has your name on it." *As in, don't even think about moving in on my girl.*

Yep, Ford wanted to punch the smug smile right off Tobin's face. This was not going down the way Tobin wanted it. He'd come for a reason, and Ford didn't think it all had to do with Tobin checking in on his good friend.

He wanted Jamie.

Never going to happen.

"You know, I owe you a debt of gratitude."

Suspicion filled Tobin's eyes. "You do?"

"Absolutely. Thanks to you saving Jamie, I got a second chance to build a life with her."

Tobin cocked his chin at Jamie and the scars peeking out from under her shirt, crawling up her neck. "They look a hell of a lot better."

"They're not as bad as Jamie thinks they are,"

Ford added, reassuring her once again that they didn't bother him.

"Pretty damn bad when it happened. After she got shot, I thought she was a goner, but Jamie's tough. She made it." Tobin's eyes unfocused and stared into the past just as Jamie's eyes too often did.

"Where were you when Jamie got shot?"

Tobin didn't miss a beat. "Pinned down by gunfire like everyone else. I barely got out of there alive."

"From what Jamie remembered, it doesn't sound like anyone but you and her made it."

Tobin and Jamie shared another of those strange looks. "We were lucky."

Ford brushed his hand over her soft hair. "You need to eat. It's time for your meds." He took another swig from her beer, nearly draining it for her. The more he drank, the less she did.

He went to the fridge and pulled out the steaks. Too late to bake the potatoes, so he set them on the cutting board, then chopped them into cubes, dumping the whole lot into a cast iron fry pan on the stove.

Jamie got up and served herself and Tobin a second round of beers, anything to break the silence between them. Ford let it go. For now. He'd keep an eye on her, and especially Tobin. The guy tried to pull off being relaxed and just here to see a friend, but Ford caught the edge to his words, the way he couldn't stop staring at Jamie, and the not-so-subtle glares he darted at Ford while Jamie stared at her lap or fussed with Zoey.

Maybe Ford had it all wrong and the guy was just looking out for his friend's best interests. Ford could relate, because he too wanted only the best for Jamie. Then why didn't Tobin see the worry and hesitation in Jamie's eyes, understand that drinking and taking her meds wasn't a good idea, talk to her about something that didn't bring all the nightmares back?

He cooked and gave them some space, hoping Jamie would settle down. Tobin drew her out of her head, talking about old friends. The stories and shared memories seemed to ease Jamie and make her sad all at the same time.

Ford left the potatoes frying on the stove and went to her, sliding his hand over her shoulder and neck and settling it over the scar on her chest.

Tobin glared at the intimacy between them. "So, you really don't remember anything about being shot." Tobin leaned back in his chair, his head bowed, but his gaze sharp on Jamie's face.

"No." Jamie picked at the label on her beer bottle. "It pushes at my mind, but I can't see it. I thought I wanted to remember, but now . . ." Jamie shook her head.

Ford leaned down close to her ear and whispered, "You did everything you could under the circumstances. Living your life, being happy, honors your friends, Firefly. Live for them."

Jamie clasped her hand around his forearm and kissed the healing burns on the back of his hand. "I should have done more."

Tobin pointed his beer at Jamie. "He's right. Dwelling on the past won't change what happened. They'd want us to move on."

Jamie flinched under his hand. A tremble rippled through her. He squeezed her shoulder to let her know he was there, to anchor her in the here and now, but he didn't understand her reaction.

Weary, Jamie stared into space. "Every time I think I have a hold on my mental state, something takes me back there. You should know that I tend to hurt people when I'm lost in the past. I lash out when I get angry."

"You didn't exactly roll out the welcome mat." Tobin seemed so sure of himself, but his eyes narrowed with concern.

"What she's trying to tell you is that she can't help herself. She's not really there sometimes. In those moments, she doesn't see the person in front of her. She isn't in the moment, she's in her head battling what you can't see but she remembers so clearly and wants to stop."

"I can't stop it," she snapped. "It's done. I didn't do what needed to be done, and they're gone."

He didn't like the sound of that at all. Ford crouched beside her and slipped his hand behind her neck. He massaged the tight muscles and pulled her forehead to his. He stared into her eyes, telling her with just a look how much he loved her, hoping his presence helped her get through this.

For a second the connection they shared pulsed strong and true, then Jamie retreated into her head with a look so filled with regret and sadness he felt the weight of it in his chest, too.

Zoey woke from her nap on Jamie's lap and licked his chin and Jamie's face. She smiled and laughed at the pup, though it didn't ring quite true.

"There's your smile."

She touched her hand to his cheek, the soft smile on her face brightening when she looked at him this time. "Stir the potatoes before they burn."

He kissed her softly and went back to tend to dinner.

"I'm sorry, Jamie. If I'd known you were having this much trouble, I'd have come sooner. Come home with me to Georgia. Surround yourself with the people you know, the ones who understand what you've been through and can help you through this."

Jamie is home, asshole.

"Believe me, I've had my own dark moments and had to lean on friends, or had someone shake some sense into me when I've gone off the rails."

"My brother, Zac, has a little boy. Corey. I want to get to know him, spend time with my brother, and hold on to what little family I have left. I've been gone so long, I hardly know Zac anymore."

Why didn't she mention wanting to stay with him?

"Spending time with him must help. Unless big, bad boyfriend keeps you all to himself."

"I saw Zac not that long ago. I even spoke briefly with my mother without losing it. Things have been going really well." She briefly glanced at Ford, but still didn't hold his gaze. "Ford keeps me sane. When I can't keep the thoughts in my head from taking me to that dark place, he distracts me."

"I bet he does." The suggestive tone implied all kinds of dirty ways Ford distracted Jamie.

Sometimes, it was like that. Especially at night when she couldn't fight off the nightmares. He pulled her out of them and gave her a real life fantasy. In those moments, he felt the closest to her because her guard went down and she made love to him with an openness and honesty that rocked him to the core.

Before Ford leaned across the table and punched Tobin in his smart mouth, Jamie spoke up. "Grow up, Tobin, I'm serious," Jamie snapped. "You got a glimpse of me falling away. Believe me, you got off lucky today coming here without letting me know and walking up to the door. It could have gone a whole lot worse than me being unfriendly."

"What are you going to do to me, little bit?"

"Shoot you dead," she shot back, deadpan, a little of that hair-trigger anger coming back into her voice.

"Right." Tobin shook his head with disbelief and took a long pull on his beer.

Ford shut off the burner under the potatoes and walked over to the table determined to prove to Tobin that Jamie spoke the truth. He pulled up the sleeve of his black T-shirt and showed Tobin the long scar across the outside of his shoulder. "She nearly took my head off, too."

"Maybe you deserved it." Tobin pointed to the burns dotting his forearms from the sparks from the fire. "And whatever left those marks."

The not so nice smile Tobin shot him made Ford wonder if Tobin knew exactly how he'd gotten the burn marks on his arms. Ford shook off his unwarranted suspicions. Someone had to be truly desperate to do something as deadly serious as setting a building on fire to kill someone. If Tobin wanted a piece of him, he could come and get it right now.

To prove the severity of Jamie's condition and give Tobin a warning he'd better heed, Ford reached behind Jamie and pulled the gun from her waistband. She gasped and tried to turn and take it back, but he held it out of her reach and set it on the table with his hand over it. "Maybe you deserve it."

"Holy fuck." Tobin leaned forward, staring at Jamie. "Were you really going to shoot me?"

Jamie turned her guilty gaze away and didn't say anything.

"It's not you she wants to kill, but the guy who attacked your group."

Tobin fell back in his seat. Ford thought he saw fear

in his eyes, but Tobin masked it quickly with yet another dark glare.

"She sees the guy who killed your friends and shot her. She wants him dead. So when she gets scared, when she falls into a waking nightmare, she tries to kill him and doesn't know what she's doing, or who she's shooting at. Lucky for you, the gun isn't loaded."

Jamie wrapped her arms around her middle and hung her head with a heavy sigh.

Ford glanced from her to the gun under his hand. He picked it up and pulled the clip free. The fucking fully loaded clip. "Jamie." He bit out just her name, too pissed to say more without going off on her with a string of curse words.

She'd lied about not having any more bullets hidden in the house. He'd let her keep the gun as a security blanket kind of thing.

"I'm sorry," she said to her lap. She raised her head and gave him a halfhearted, lopsided grin. "I didn't shoot him. I didn't even pull the gun on him. That's something."

"You could have killed him," he barked out, trying to drill into her the possible consequences. "Do you want to spend the rest of your life in jail?"

"No." She shook her head, her gaze falling away again. "I want to be with you."

"Do you?"

"Yes." Desperation punctuated the emphatic reply.

He stuffed the clip in his pocket and racked the slide, popping the bullet in the chamber out, catching it midair. Furious she'd had a round chambered and ready to fire, he glared down at her, too pissed off to say anything at all.

Tobin downed the last of his beer. Finally getting the severity of the situation, he said, "Damn, Keller, you don't fuck around, do you?"

"No, she doesn't, so you'd do well to keep her rooted in the here and now and not push her on the attack and what happened."

"Let's both forget the whole damn thing." Tobin held up his beer in a salute to get her agreement, saw that it was empty, and turned to Ford. "I think I need another." Tobin raked his fingers through his short hair, wiped the sweat from his brow, and let out another heavy sigh.

Jamie jumped up to get one out of the fridge. Ford turned his back on both of them and flipped the steaks on the grill pan on the stove. Jamie came up behind him, placed her hands on his back, and ran them up to his shoulders, pressing her forehead into his spine. He dropped the fork he used to turn the steaks on the stove and turned to her, taking her in his arms and holding her close.

Tobin watched from the table, his eyes narrowed.

Ford tried to read the myriad of emotions in them, a jumbled mix of jealousy, anger, and resentment.

Go fuck yourself, asshole. She's mine.

Ford wondered how long before Tobin undermined his relationship with Jamie. It had already started the minute Ford showed up. Before, really. Maybe all the way back to the days the two had spent working together, when Tobin wanted her but she'd still been Ford's in her heart.

No fucking way would Ford let Tobin come between him and Jamie. He'd given her up once. He wouldn't make the same mistake twice. If Tobin tried to take her from him, he'd be in for one hell of a fight.

Ford held her closer and kissed her on top of the head. "I love you, Firefly."

She hugged him tight, making his sides ache, but he didn't care. He held her in his arms, letting her know he understood she was sorry for what she'd done. She didn't want to fight with him. She didn't want to put space between them.

But something had her rattled tonight. Something more added a desperation to her embrace. He wished he knew why and understood the undercurrent running between her and Tobin.

"Sit down, sweetheart. Let's eat."

She looked up at him. He brushed his fingers through her soft, golden-red hair, gave her a smile to let her know they were okay, and leaned down and kissed her softly.

She fed Zoey before returning to the table. The pup ate greedily at her bowl while Ford plated up dinner and set it on the table.

"This looks great, man. Thanks." Tobin dug into the potatoes.

"You're welcome." Ford set Jamie's pill bottles in front of her.

She dumped the ones she needed into her hand, popped them in her mouth, and washed them down with her beer.

Tobin held up his bottle to her. "To old friends."

Jamie hesitated, her eyes filled with regret and sadness. She tipped her bottle and clinked the neck to Tobin's beer. "Old friends." She drank deeply, polishing off half the bottle.

Disappointment settled in Ford's chest when she didn't turn to him to toast old friends. She was his first love. He was hers. They'd found their way back to each other, but right now, she made him feel like the odd man out.

The food he ate soured in his stomach as the night wore on and Jamie and Tobin lost themselves in stories about the places they'd been, people they knew, their adventures, and games they'd played. Grateful for the change in sentiment to happier times and inside jokes, Ford grew quiet, laughing and smiling when appropriate, but ever aware of how Jamie slowly eased into the conversation, then participated with open enthusiasm. She warmed to Tobin's presence with little resistance once the topic changed to things much easier for her to deal with, things she could remember without any trauma.

The stories gave Ford great insight into the past few years of Jamie's life.

Tobin kept up a stream of topics and jokes, engaging Jamie nonstop and holding her attention.

Never one to be jealous about any of the women he'd dated, he found that his protective streak for Jamie ran deep and true. Her paying absolute attention to Tobin, every laugh and smile she graced him with, all the inside jokes and anecdotes they shared, made that green-eyed monster stand up and roar inside of him until he didn't think he could take it anymore.

"I gotta take a leak." Tobin stood and walked around the table, reaching out to Jamie. His hand clamped onto her shoulder. She didn't even flinch. "I'm so glad I came. I missed you."

Jamie stared up at the man, a soft smile on her face. "I missed you, too."

Tobin leaned down and kissed her on the top of the head.

Jamie shoved him toward the hallway. "Stop flirting with me."

"It's my favorite thing to do." Tobin took off down the hall, that smug smile back on his face.

Ford held on to his temper and tamped down the urge to tackle Tobin to the floor and punch his lights out for kissing his girl. He only had a minute to talk to Jamie alone.

She turned to him, the bright smile on her lips dying when her gaze collided with his and she read his simmering anger. "I'm sorry. We got caught up."

"I need to go home and check on the horses. They need to be fed."

"You always do that before you come here."

"Yeah, except when you text me in a panic to 'come now.'"

"No I didn't."

Ford pulled his phone from his back pocket, swiped the screen, and showed her the text. Her face paled and went blank.

"You don't even remember. Do you remember loading the gun?"

She shook her head, pressed her lips tight, her gaze darting away from him.

He leaned forward, planted his elbows on his knees, and took her hand. "Come home with me—"

Her head shook before he even finished the sentence. "I can't leave Tobin here by himself."

"But you expect me to leave you alone here with him?"

She placed her hand on his. "Yes. I do. I need to ask him about what happened. I need to know."

"Fine. Ask him, then I'll take you home with me."

"He won't open up with you here. He'll brag and play up the story, trying to look strong and indestructible in front of you. It's got to be just as hard for him to relive that time as it is for me. When it's just him and me, he'll drop his guard and talk. Please, Ford, do this for me."

"I don't trust him."

"I need to know, Ford. He won't tell me everything if you're here."

"Talking about it will leave you sad and raw. I want to stay and help you through it."

She gripped his hand tight. "I'll be okay. Besides, you already disarmed me. If things get bad, what can I do?"

"This is a bad idea."

"It has to be done. I can't go on like this anymore."

He stood to take his plate to the sink, taking a minute to think. Everything in him told him to take her home with him. Protect her. He couldn't protect her from her own mind. No matter how content and happy she'd been lately, this remained a storm cloud waiting to thunder and rain down on her, to wash away her progress and hard-won confidence a little at a time.

He closed the distance between them, braced his hand on the back of her chair, and leaned down close. "You'll call me if you need me."

She reached up and touched his face. "I always need you."

He growled his frustration and undeniable need for her, then planted a searing kiss on her lips letting her know all the things he'd like to say: *I love you. I don't like this. I wish I could spare you any more pain and sadness. I want you in my bed. I need you more than I can say. Stay with me.*

The door opened down the hall. Out of time, Ford broke the kiss and stared down into Jamie's eyes and saw the understanding in their depths. She knew this wasn't easy for him.

Though it bothered him to go against his instincts to protect her, he'd give her this chance to find out the truth so she could put it to rest once and for all.

"I hate to leave you like this."

Tobin grabbed two beers from the fridge and set one in front of Jamie. "She'll be fine. Won't you, honey?"

Ford gnashed his teeth and glared at Tobin. He glanced back at Jamie. "You took your meds," he said under his breath, warning her about drinking on top of them.

"Don't worry. I'll be fine."

He hoped so, but the growing ball of worry souring his gut said otherwise. "I'll see you first thing in the morning. We have plans."

She cocked her head. "We do?"

"Yeah." He kissed her again, then walked out the door without saying goodbye to Tobin. Something about the guy rubbed Ford the wrong way. Something that went deeper than the fact the guy wanted to steal his girl. Tobin had an agenda. What he wanted, besides Jamie, Ford didn't know, but he'd be damned before he let Tobin come between him and Jamie.

CHAPTER 24

Tobin hid the smile tugging at his lips. Finally, that asshole left him alone with Jamie. Without her watchdog, he hoped Jamie would finally relax and they could talk. Jamie wanted to believe she could move on with Ford. He wanted her to come back to Georgia with him. God, how he'd missed her these last few months. Being stateside, dealing with the aftermath of what happened overseas alone was driving him insane. He needed her. They needed each other to get through this.

Jamie's eyes filled with questions he had no intention of answering. She leaned toward him, took a fortifying drink of her beer, set it aside, then folded her arms on the table. "Tell me what happened after the explosion?"

He didn't want to go there and trigger her memory, or some fucked-up episode where she tried to kill him, so he distracted her. "Remember the time you and Catalina cut out a cardboard Christmas tree and made all those silly decorations with bottle caps and plastic utensils and shit?"

A soft smile touched Jamie's lips. "Yeah. I really enjoyed that Christmas. The ones here with my family weren't that fun."

They'd had a good life on base. A family rooted

in honor, duty, trust, and camaraderie. Better than where either of them had come from. They had that in common.

He wanted to go back to that life, get back in the action, but he'd give it all up for her.

"What are you doing here, Jamie? You belong in Georgia with the people who really care about you." *With me.*

She didn't say anything, just sat back in her chair, legs out, eyes on the black window behind him, staring at the past he saw in her eyes and the lines etched on her forehead.

He got up and grabbed the bottle of whiskey off the counter. If he couldn't distract her, he'd get her drunk until she passed out.

He found two glasses and set them on the table as he fell into the seat Ford had vacated next to her.

She turned her head and gave him a halfhearted smile. "I shouldn't drink anymore."

"One toast. To our friends, the life, being part of something bigger than ourselves."

Jamie took her glass and held it up to him. He clinked his to hers and they downed the shots. He poured another for both of them.

"I'm done." Jamie didn't just mean drinking. She was done with the military.

Tobin didn't want to believe her, but the ache in his heart told him he'd lost her in that part of his life. If he lost her completely, he didn't know what he'd do.

Jamie downed the other shot, found her courage, and asked again. "What happened?"

"You really lost all that time?"

She bobbed her head up and down like it weighed

too much on her shoulders. "Except for disjointed fragments, everything after the truck exploded."

"It's probably better that way."

"The longer I'm with Ford, the easier it is to remember. I don't get lost in that dark place, because I know I've got him to bring me out of it."

Ford wasn't helping her—he was making it damn impossible for Tobin to convince her to forget. That shit needed to stay buried.

She'd never looked at him the way she looked at that damn cowboy. It stung. What the hell was it about the guy that drew her to him and made her blind to what was right in front of her? He could make her happy. They'd shared the last several years together. Still, she only wanted to be with the asshole who'd broke her heart once and would do it again.

"I always see myself on the ground, shot, and staring up at the guy on the armored vehicle. Something about him nags at me."

Tobin poured her another shot. "Shut that shit down. Forget him. Remember our friends. Know that you wanted to help, but in your condition, you were in no shape to do anything." He hated to keep saying that to her and seeing the deep regret in her eyes.

Jamie absently picked up the drink and downed it, hissing out a breath as the whiskey burned down her throat.

He understood her need to drown out the memories and the guilt.

She rolled her head on the back of the chair and stared at him. "What happened after all the shooting stopped?"

He hated reliving that time as much as her. "I got to

the radio in one of the vehicles, called in our location and ordered a medivac for you. I put pressure on your wounds and prayed they'd get there in time."

"I can't imagine how difficult it must have been for you to be the only one left standing." The haunted look in her eyes told him she got it.

The memories tightened his chest, flooded his mind with dark, grisly images, and filled his heart with regret that she'd been hurt. He wished he could take that back.

Hoping he didn't trigger any more memories, he said, "Mostly standing. I took a few hits to my vest and a bad knock to the head." Tobin traced his finger over the side of his head where he'd been bashed with a gun butt and temporarily knocked out.

"That damn black spot haunts me. What you said about how I froze . . . it kills me." She scrunched her face into a frown, drawing the furrow between her eyebrows out.

"If I can look at it, see how it happened, maybe one day I'll forgive myself." Her eyes drooped, then squinted. "You got me to safety behind one of the trucks. Bullets pinged off the metal. Pedro got shot. The blood poured out of him."

Tobin slammed his palm on the table to rattle her out of those dark thoughts before she got swept away under a tidal wave of nightmares. Jamie jumped, her eyes wide with fear.

"Shit happens, Jamie. You did the best you could. Leave it alone," he ordered. More softly he added, "I don't want to go back there anymore." He scrubbed his hands over his eyes to erase the images flashing in his mind. "I don't want to see you bloody, burned, death trying to steal you away from me. No more," he pleaded.

She laid her hand softly on his arm and squeezed. "I'm sorry, Tobin. I'll stop."

He hoped so.

"Tell the commander you don't remember what happened, get them to believe you have nothing more to add to your statement, and move on with your life. Promise me you'll let it go."

She nodded her agreement.

He poured her another shot and held his aloft, hoping she fell back on old times and forgot to be smart and just got shitfaced to get through the night. He nudged her. "Let's hope we always get what we want and never what we deserve."

They clinked glasses and downed the shots. Feeling the effects more keenly than her thanks to the many beers he'd consumed during dinner and their trip down memory lane, he stood and held out his hand. "Come on, I'll put you to bed."

She put her hand in his. Warm. Soft. He wanted to touch all of her, but held back the urge, not wanting to push for too much. He helped her stand.

She swayed on her feet, drunk and nearly ready to pass out. "I hate sleep."

"Me too, but you need to sleep it off, Keller." He held her to his side and guided her down the hall, Zoey yapping at his heels. He nudged the mutt out of his way so he and Keller didn't tumble to the floor. The room spun, but he kept his feet under him, barely.

He was drunker than he'd thought.

Jamie face-planted on the bed, her legs dangling off the end. Zoey jumped and attacked her shoes. "She needs to go out." The mumbled words barely reached him.

"On it." He picked up the pup, carried her down

the hall to the front door with the patch over the bullet hole. A shiver danced up his spine, thinking he'd escaped another attempt on his life after his bulletproof vest saved him the last time. He dumped the dog on the porch, closing the door as she dashed off to the grass to do her business.

He walked back into her room, ready to crawl into bed and sleep off his latest night of drinking. But first he needed to ensure his future with Jamie. Ford had to go. He'd only hurt her anyway. Tobin was doing her a favor. She'd see that in the end.

He stripped Jamie's clothes down to her tank and panties and hauled her up to the top of the bed, gently laying her head on the pillow. He stood over her and touched the scar on her chest, then the one on her thigh.

"You've been through so much. I hate to put you through more, but it has to be this way." He leaned down and kissed her on the lips. She'd never let him do such a thing when she was awake and sober. He took advantage now, lingering over her soft lips, closing his eyes, fantasizing about all they could share if only she'd turn to him the way she'd turned to that damn cowboy.

Undressed, his cock hard and aching for her, but not a big enough asshole to cross the line and tired to the bone, he slipped into bed beside her. His weight sank into the mattress, drawing Jamie toward him.

She jolted from the sudden movement. "What are you doing?" she mumbled, her eyes squinted and barely open as she tried to bring him into focus in the dark room.

"I hate sleeping alone."

"Me too," she sighed. "Nightmares."

"I have them, too. We'll be here for each other and keep the nightmares away."

"You need to go," she mumbled and tried to push him away, but she didn't budge him one bit before she passed out.

He didn't want to go anywhere without her.

He stared at her in the dark, wishing for things that she'd denied him too long. It wouldn't be long before he got Ford out of the picture for good and he'd have Jamie all to himself again.

CHAPTER 25

Ford pulled into Jamie's driveway, his gut tied in knots, his eyes scratchy from lack of sleep. He'd tossed and turned, thinking about Jamie, talking himself out of coming back here in the middle of the night.

Tobin had fucked everything up by coming here. That asshole had to go. Ford wasn't going to let anything get in the way of Jamie's recovery, or his and Jamie's future together. Not this time.

He hoped she'd gotten the answers she needed last night and they unburdened her heart. She deserved that. She needed it.

If Tobin gave her that, he'd happily send the man on his way in one piece. If he added to Jamie's despair, Ford would kill him.

He slipped out of the truck and walked up to the porch. Zoey jumped up from the mat where she lay curled into a tight ball to keep warm in the early morning fifty-something degree temperature. The poor pup ran to him, yapping with excitement. He took the stairs in one leap and picked her up. She licked his face, happy to be rescued from being locked outside.

Anger roiled in his gut, but he held it together and

rubbed Zoey with his hand to warm her up. He tucked her close against his chest and walked right through the front door. He stopped in the entry, staring at the open bottle of whiskey and glasses on the table amidst the beer bottles and dirty dinner dishes no one had cleaned up. With a disgusted shake of his head, he walked down the hall to Jamie's room and stopped in his tracks in the open doorway, too shocked to move another step.

The wave of pain overtook his whole body and pulsed into intense rage then back into the hurt he didn't want to feel. He truly couldn't believe his eyes. Jamie, in bed with another man, Tobin. It didn't make sense. He didn't want to believe it.

They'd been building something real. She wouldn't throw that all away. He had to believe Tobin had manipulated her, this situation, taken advantage of her vulnerability. He barely contained the overwhelming urge to kill the man lying in bed with his girlfriend.

Jamie fidgeted in the bed, caught in a nightmare. As angry as he was, he still wanted to comfort and free her from her demons. She screamed his name and woke with a start. Breathing hard, she jolted with awareness and turned toward the snoring asshole beside her. Face-to-face with Tobin, she gasped, turned away quickly, and spotted Ford staring at her.

He couldn't seem to take his gaze away from the horrible scene. "You left Zoey locked outside all night. Now I see why."

Her surprise at finding Tobin beside her and not him left a glimmer of hope in his heart they'd work this out, that what he thought happened hadn't really happened, but right now he couldn't think through the red haze of rage roiling inside of him.

He needed to get out of here. Now. Before he did something he'd regret, or that landed him in jail for the rest of his life.

Panic seized Jamie's heart and squeezed it so tight she couldn't breathe or feel anything but the agonizing ache. Ford set Zoey on the floor, gave her a look so filled with disappointment and pain she felt the impact like a punch to the heart, turned, and walked away.

"No. Ford. Wait!"

She tried to scramble from the bed and go after him, but Tobin had one leg over hers, his knee jammed in her crotch. His hand had slipped up her tank top and rested on her bare stomach, his fingertips brushing the underside of her breast. The second she moved away, he held her still, wrapped his hand around her side, and pulled her closer. She fought to get free, grabbing his hand, pulling it out of her shirt, and tossing it over his back. He never stopped the incessant snoring, or blowing whiskey tinged morning breath on her face. She scrunched her nose and clamped her hand over her mouth to fight off the urge to puke burning up her windpipe.

Ford's truck rumbled to life outside. His tires kicked up gravel as he tore out of her driveway. She never even made it out of bed before he was gone.

"Fuck! No, no, no," she wailed, tears streaming down her cheeks, blurring her vision. The best thing in her life just walked out the door. This time, he hadn't sent her away for her own good. She hadn't left because she needed something different. She'd pushed him away.

He loved her. He'd shown her in too many ways to

count how much he cared and wanted to be a part of her life. He put up with her mood swings, the scary things she did without knowing it, the nightmares that plagued her sleep and made it impossible for him to sleep through the night with her. He'd seen what she needed and given her a job, a purpose that helped her heal and put her with the horses she loved. He'd given her sweet Zoey so she'd never be alone, even when he couldn't be with her.

All she wanted to do was hold on to Ford.

And now she might have lost him forever.

What had she done?

What the hell happened last night?

She scrubbed the heels of her hands over her gritty eyes to her forehead and the pounding headache that would not cease. The emptiness spreading through her chest like a river of doom sucking her under hurt like hell.

She'd woken up with the wrong man in her bed and the right one walking out the door. That was what needed to be fixed. But first, she needed to fix herself.

Bleary-eyed and fogged in by the unrelenting hangover, she took stock of her situation, starting with herself. She didn't remember coming to bed last night. In fact, the last thing she remembered was Tobin pouring her another drink from the bottle of whiskey she hadn't touched since she shot Ford.

She sat up and kicked the blankets and Tobin's leg off her. She wore nothing but her tank top and underwear. Tobin lay beside her in his ridiculous red and green plaid boxers and nothing else. She'd seen him in this state of undress many times out in the field when they had little time and even less privacy to take care of personal matters. Most of the time on a long haul, they changed clothes, brushed their teeth, took a camp bath in the truck. Still, it didn't explain why he was in her bed.

Her muddled mind couldn't make sense of it, which made her even angrier at herself.

The thought of them actually having sex made her stomach queasy. Not just because it would mean she'd been so far gone last night that she'd go against everything she was, everything she stood for and betray Ford and cheat on him. She couldn't fathom doing that to him.

She couldn't see Tobin taking advantage of her when she was drunk out of her mind and not capable of consenting, let alone participating. Still, creepy crawly tingles rippled over her skin and danced up her spine.

The last thing she wanted was Tobin in her bed. So how had he gotten there?

She closed her eyes tight and tried to trudge up even one memory from last night. All the snippets that flashed against her scratchy eyelids showed Ford sitting next to her at dinner, quiet and watchful as always as she and Tobin talked about all the people they'd lost and good times gone by but never forgotten. She'd liked that talk a hell of a lot better than thinking about the consequences of what Tobin told her she did, or rather didn't do, during the attack.

Why would he tell her that and make her feel worse? Why say anything about it when she'd forgotten? Why make her believe Ford wouldn't understand? Why was he really here?

Why hadn't she asked herself these things last night before she lost it?

Why wouldn't he tell her what really happened?

That something strange hit her in the pit of her stomach. A nudge in her brain told her that she should know something, but she couldn't quite catch the fragment in her mind that pushed in before getting swallowed by the darkness once again.

Maybe she really didn't want to remember failing her friends. Still, that wasn't the feeling she got when she started remembering the attack. Deep inside, she felt as if she'd done everything she could to stop it.

So what was the truth?

She didn't know.

What she knew for sure: Tobin should not be in her room, let alone her bed.

The ache in her chest grew too much to bear. The thought of losing Ford again tore her heart to shreds and left it bleeding and aching and barely able to beat in her chest. Like a wounded, dying animal, she let the adrenaline sweep her away into anger to fight to live— and get Ford back.

She hauled back her arm, fisted her hand, and socked Tobin in the shoulder as hard as she could. He grunted, rolled to his back, and stared up at her through bleary eyes. She swung again, this time at his face. He caught her hand in midair and held tight.

"What the fuck, Keller?"

"Yes. What the fuck are you doing in my bed?"

"I'm trying to sleep." He released her hand and let his arm fall over his eyes. "It's too damn early to be up. What the fuck time is it anyway?"

She checked the bedside clock. "It's just after six."

"Fuck, Keller, go back to sleep."

She whacked him on the chest. "Answer me. What are you doing in my bed?"

"I didn't want to sleep alone. The nightmares get me, especially when I've been drinking." He moved his arm from his eyes and stared up at her. "We drank a lot last night."

"That I remember. This," she spread her hands over the bed they shared, "not so much."

"You said you hated sleep because it scared you. I feel the same damn way. There is no peace in sleep. It's just an easy way for my mind to replay . . . everything." Tobin reached over and touched his fingertip to the scar on her chest.

She flinched away. A flash of the dark man standing over her sparked in her mind. She ruthlessly pushed it out again.

What he said rang true. She remembered bits and pieces of that conversation, feeling like he got it. Ford understood her pain and despair, but Tobin lived it, the same as her.

"That doesn't explain why I'm nearly naked in bed with you."

"You were so wasted last night, you literally fell face-first into bed. I undressed you to make you more comfortable and tucked you in. That's all, Keller, so get a grip."

Tobin rolled to his side and levered himself up on his elbow. His free hand settled on her thigh. She batted it away.

He held it up in surrender. "Hey, I'm not the enemy here. I was just trying to be a friend and put you to bed. I didn't want to sleep alone. Neither did you. We made it through the night without incident. No harm. No foul."

"Except Ford walked in on us a few minutes ago."

Tobin fell back on the bed. "Sorry." He didn't sound upset about it at all. "I don't know what you see in that guy. Nothing happened. Fuck him if he doesn't believe you. You didn't do anything wrong." Tobin scrubbed his hands over his face. "Better he walks out now than in a few months when you're so tied to him you've got nothing else to fall back on. Come back to Georgia with me."

She had everything. The happiness she'd found in her life and in her heart again. The love she'd discovered had grown over the years into something so deep it came from her soul and connected her to Ford in a way she couldn't explain and didn't want to lose.

"You're a real asshole."

"We agreed on that a long time ago," he teased. He rolled toward her, hooked his arm around her waist, and pulled her down and against his chest. He spoke into the back of her neck. "You don't belong here, Keller. You belong with me and your friends in Georgia. Come back with me. I need you. You need me."

I need Ford.

It took some muscle and a bruising elbow jab to his ribs to extract herself from Tobin's embrace, but she rolled out of bed and stood before him, staring down at a man she considered more than a friend. He was family. A brother. Always there for her. Sometimes annoying. A pal to mess around with, grab a few drinks, and share some laughs. A guy she shared a lot of memories and experiences with.

But deep down, he was looking out for him, not her.

"Your idea about getting me through this is getting me drunk and making me feel guilty about something I don't even remember. You see me with Ford, the bond we've forged these last weeks, the happiness he brings me, and you want to tear us apart because you don't want to lose our friendship."

"Hell no, I don't. He wants to keep you here, away from the people who care about you."

"No. He doesn't. He wants to give me a safe place to heal so that when I'm ready I can face my past. You included."

"Me?"

"Yes. You. A text, a call, looking at you reminds me of the last time we were together and my mind takes a dark turn and I do things I shouldn't."

"Like nearly shooting me last night when I showed up?"

"You got off lucky. I almost killed Ford twice."

"What does that say to you, that you want to shoot him dead?"

She raked her hand through her mussed hair. "It's not him I'm trying to kill. I love him, Tobin. With everything I am. I am so broken inside I can't hold on to the pieces of me that slip through my fingers. But every time I look inside for the best pieces of myself, there is Ford and the way he makes me feel, the joy he brings into my life, the constant support he gives me even when I'm at my worst."

"He doesn't love you. He let you go."

"Yes, he did. Because I needed him to let go even if I didn't know it at the time. I would have stayed with him. Loved him. And discovered that I couldn't hold on to him because I wasn't happy with myself, so how could I make him happy?"

"You're in the same place now, Jamie. You can't be that girl again."

"I don't want to be her. I want to be this me, only better." She squeezed the tight muscles in her neck. "I was getting better."

"Until I showed up."

"No. Until I let the past tear down all the progress I made these last weeks. Until I let the fear and anger drag me down. Until I gave in to the easy way out of avoiding that stuff instead of facing it, dealing with it, and trying to find a way to live with it."

"He's not going to forgive you for what he saw this morning."

"Yes, he will." Her voice reflected the lack of conviction she felt in that statement. She hoped Ford forgave her for her stupidity and total lack of consideration for him.

She hoped he knew that she loved him above all else and that even when she acted out, her compass home always pointed to him.

Tears stung her eyes. She couldn't breathe past the ones clogged in her throat.

"Even you don't believe that." Tobin reached out to take her hand.

She stepped back and turned for her dresser. "I'm not going to give up until he does forgive me. I won't stop until I'm well again either. Until I'm the best version of me I can be, so that I can love him the way I want to love him. The way he loves me."

"You're fooling yourself, Keller. You can't just snap your fingers and change who you are now, or what you did. Not after all that's happened."

She shimmied her jeans over her hips and zipped and buttoned them. "Maybe not. But that doesn't mean I have to stay stuck in one place. I can move forward. And the only place I want to go is wherever he is."

"You've lost your mind."

"Maybe. But I know who I am. The good, bad, and the ugly. So does he, and he loves me anyway. All of me." She pulled her shirt on over her head, grabbed two more from the drawer, along with some other essentials and a clean pair of jeans and shorts, and stuffed the pile of clothes in a duffel bag. "I know what I want, and I'm going after it."

She headed down the hall, picking up Zoey on her way to the front door.

"You're just going to leave me here."

"There's food in the fridge, satellite TV, and a bed for you in the *spare* room."

"When are you coming back?" he bellowed down the hall.

Not until she had Ford by her side again.

CHAPTER 26

Jamie tried to stay focused on the road, but her thoughts swirled with all the things she wanted to say to Ford. No magic words came to mind that would excuse her behavior or make him forget what he'd seen this morning. Her stomach ached with the acid eating away at her insides along with the guilt sitting heavy in her chest.

She had to find a way to convince him she'd never hurt him. She'd do anything he wanted just to get a chance to talk to him.

Just around the next curve she'd come to Ford's beautiful house with the wide porch, gleaming new paint, and the blooming flowers his sister-in-law had planted. He'd be in the barn or out in one of the fields with the cows. Now that he had help, she hoped he got caught up. She'd step it up, overcome her fears and apprehension, and help him and the crew, because she wanted Ford to have everything he wanted.

The ranch, a wife, a family to leave the legacy he was building to. How could he have all that if the woman he wanted couldn't be the partner he needed?

She would give everything to be that woman right now.

She'd work even harder to be her from now on.

The house came into view and her heart called out that this should be home.

Grandpa Sammy's truck sat pitched over a small hill, the front end crashed into a huge pine. The old truck hadn't suffered much damage, but the man in the front seat lay over the steering wheel. Her heart lurched, and she slammed on the brakes. Poor Zoey tumbled to the floorboard, found her footing, and barked her excitement that something was afoot.

Jamie jumped from the truck and ran the short distance to Grandpa Sammy and yanked open the door. He didn't move. Blood covered his forehead and the side of his face. Her hand trembled as she reached out to touch his neck. Relief swept through her at his warm skin beneath her fingertips, but disappeared when she didn't feel a pulse.

"Oh God, no."

Too heavy for her to pull him out of the truck, she pulled him back from the steering wheel and pushed him over onto the bench seat. It took considerable muscle and awkward twists to lay him out flat, but she managed, despite the pain it caused her. Training kicked in and she unbuttoned his shirt to his sternum and rested her head over his heart. No sound, not even a soft thump.

Still warm, he'd only been out for a short time. She prayed she could bring him back. For Ford's sake. For all the Kendrick boys.

"Come on, Sammy, you can't do this to me."

She clasped her hands together, one palm on top of the back of the other hand, linked her fingers, and began compressions on Sammy's barrel chest. She didn't have a lot of headroom in the truck cab, but she made every compression count. She kept up a quick and steady pace, then bent to Sammy's face, pinched his nose, tilted his chin back, and blew into his mouth, filling his lungs. His chest rose and fell, but he didn't wake up.

"Come on, Sammy. You come back to me now. I can't lose another person I care about."

She went through the motions and kept up the CPR, desperately praying that the man who'd treated her like a granddaughter and shown her more kindness than her mother ever had lived again.

"Please, Sammy." Her tears dripped onto his cheeks as she leaned down for another breath of air to fill his lungs. On the second one, he sputtered, his eyes blinking up at her.

She brushed her hand over his forehead, not caring that she got blood on her hand from the small wound he'd received when he hit his head on the steering wheel.

"Hey there. Remember me? It's Jamie."

"What happened?" Sammy asked, confused and twisting his head from side to side to orient himself.

"You hit a tree."

"I don't feel right." His too-pale skin didn't pink up the way she'd hoped. His breathing still seemed shallow and a bit labored.

She put her hands under his arms and tried to pull him up and into the corner of the seat and against the door. A shocking pain flashed through her back, making her yelp. Sammy tried to help with his minimal strength, but she hoisted the bulk of his weight. She got him situated and fell back into the seat next to him.

"What are you doing?" he grumbled.

"Taking you to the clinic."

Sammy touched his fingers to his head. "I still feel dizzy."

"Don't you worry. I'll take care of you."

Jamie slid from the truck just enough to pick up Zoey as she stood with her front paws on the running board ready to go for a ride. Even her small weight made Jamie clench her jaw against the throbbing in her shoulder and back. She set Zoey on the seat next to Sammy and hopped back into the idling truck. It seemed in working order, so she put it in reverse, backed up from the tree, stopped, threw it into drive, and sped back down the road, past her truck with its driver's door still wide-open.

"Where's Ford?" Sammy's voice came out weak and slurred.

"I don't know. His truck wasn't up at the house."

Sammy pressed his lips together, his eyes narrowed in thought. "He's at Colt's. He asked me to feed the horses. I thought you went with him. He said you'd love your surprise."

A surprise. News to her. Another thing she'd ruined. "Yeah, well, I surprised him this morning and haven't seen him since."

Sammy's heavy eyelids closed.

Fear squeezed her heart. She reached over and placed her hand on his chest, over his heart. Sammy's hand covered hers and held it in place.

"I'm still kicking, honey."

Jamie drove one-handed at speeds that defied the law, but she didn't care. Sammy needed medical attention now. If his heart stopped again, she wanted professionals there to do whatever it took to save him. He needed more than a hungover, practically insane woman who couldn't keep herself rooted in reality to save her life, or from doing the one thing sure to lose her the only man she'd ever loved.

She wanted to call Ford. He'd come. He'd take care of this. He'd make it all right. But she didn't dare take her hand from Sammy, who seemed to take comfort in holding on to it.

"We're almost there, Sammy. You stay with me, you hear?"

"I hope you stay with Ford this time. He needs you."

She spoke her worst fear. "I'm not so sure he needs the chaos I bring into his life. He needs someone who can love him the way he deserves to be loved. Someone who's not broken."

"You're not broken, honey. Maybe a bit damaged. But damaged can be fixed." Sammy held her hand in both of his and squeezed. "It's a terrible thing to take a life even in the name of war. It's a terrible thing to watch the ones you love die. You are not the terrible thing. You did your duty. You honor the dead by living, honey."

The words came from a man who'd served. A man who knew her heart and just what she needed to hear. She squeezed his hands back and pulled into the clinic, grateful she'd brought him back and he'd given her those words.

"Stay put. I'll get someone to come out and help you inside."

"I'm not going anywhere, honey. And neither should you."

She didn't want to go anywhere. She wanted to stay with Ford. Forever. If he'd still have her.

Jamie dashed out of the truck and ran inside the new clinic she'd passed several times on her way into town for one errand or another. A doctor stood writing in a chart by the reception desk. Several people waited in the room off to her right.

"I need help. Sammy Kendrick had an accident. He's in the truck. He needs help."

The dark-haired pregnant doctor dropped the chart on the counter and approached her. "I'm Dr. Bowden. I know Sammy. Is he conscious?"

"Barely. He . . . he died. I brought him back, but he's not breathing well. He's listless and pale. Something isn't right."

"Dorothy, bring a wheelchair and ask Rico to help me get him."

Dr. Bowden followed her out the door to the truck parked right in front of it. Jamie opened the door slowly, hoping Sammy didn't fall right out on the ground. He managed to shift his weight and sit up, though his head swayed from side to side.

"Sammy, it's Bell. Are you okay?"

"Hey, sweet thing, I'm not really myself right now." Again, the words came out soft and slurred.

"Okay, we'll get you inside and checked out."

Rico arrived with the wheelchair and muscled Sammy out of the truck and right into it. Sammy sat back heavily in the chair, his head hanging down. Dr. Bowden touched her fingers to his wrist as they pushed Sammy into the clinic.

"Jamie, come with me. I need to ask you some questions."

Jamie followed. "How do you know my name?"

"I guessed you're Ford's girlfriend. I, uh, patched him up after he hurt his shoulder."

Right. Dr. Bowden stitched up his arm after she shot him.

"I didn't hurt Sammy. I swear."

"Never said you did. Tell me how you found him."

Dr. Bowden stood back while Rico helped Sammy out of the chair and onto the hospital bed.

"I found him unconscious in his truck, not breathing, no heartbeat. He struck his head on the steering wheel when he hit a tree. The engine was still idling. He was still warm, so I did CPR right there in the truck cab. He came back on the second round of CPR. He spoke, seemed lucid, though slow."

"I'm right here," Sammy grumbled. "You can ask me."

Dr. Bowden softly touched his face and looked down at her patient like he was family. "What happened leading up to the accident?"

"I fed the horses. Took care of the chores Ford asked me to do. Started feeling funny. Slow. Dizzy. Thought I'd get on home and lie down for a while. I don't even remember getting in the truck."

"Okay. Did you take your medication this morning?"

"I forgot, so I took one while I was in the barn."

Dr. Bowden eyed him. "Sammy, did you take one this morning, and then take another?"

"I told you I forgot, so I took it when I remembered."

"I have a sneaking suspicion you forgot you took it in the morning and took it again. That explains the symptoms you experienced. You dropped your blood pressure way too low."

A nurse on the other side of him ripped the cuff off his arm. "Ninety over fifty-seven."

"That's much too low for you, Sammy." Dr. Bowden directed the nurse, "Let's draw some blood, start an EKG, and clean up that cut on his head."

Jamie pulled her phone out of her pocket. "I'll call Ford and let him know what happened. You said he's with Colt, right, Sammy?"

"Yeah. Rory's at the ranch."

"I'll call him," Dr. Bell volunteered, leaving the room.

Jamie dialed and prayed Ford picked up. The phone rang once, twice, three times before the voice mail picked up on the fourth ring. She hung up. She didn't want to leave this kind of message. He was probably ignoring her call because of what happened. She texted him.

JAMIE: Grandpa Sammy at Crystal Creek Clinic. Come now. He's okay.

Jamie took the chair next to Sammy's bed and held his hand as the nurse cleaned and dressed his head wound. Ford didn't call her back. He really didn't want to talk to her. She set aside thoughts of how badly she'd mucked this up and tried to be there for Sammy as they drew blood and checked his blood pressure again.

The nurse kicked her out when they set up the EKG, and asked her to take a seat in the waiting room. She walked in that direction, spotting the truck illegally parked out front. Zoey had her nose pressed to the window. Jamie hadn't even bothered to take the keys out of the ignition.

She went to the truck and opened the driver's door. Zoey rushed over to greet her and lick her face. Jamie actually smiled and felt better with the puppy's happy exuberance lavished all over her chin, though it did nothing for her pounding headache that she deserved for what she'd done to herself last night.

"Sit," she ordered and Zoey complied, plopping her butt on the seat. "Good girl. At least one of us follows Ford's instructions."

Ford had been working with Zoey to teach her some doggy basics. Zoey was a quick learner, anxious to win Ford's approval. Jamie should follow the dog's example. It might keep her out of trouble.

She moved the truck to a parking space, picked up her furry friend, gingerly lowered herself out of the tall seat to the ground, and walked back into the clinic.

"You can't bring the dog in here," the receptionist said.

Jamie stopped and looked down at Zoey's happy little face staring back up at her. "She's my emotional support dog."

Dr. Bowden walked out of Sammy's room and held back a laugh. "It's fine, Dorothy. Jamie is a vet."

Dorothy cocked her head. "Huh, a vet who can't go anywhere without a pet."

Jamie didn't feel the need to correct the receptionist's misinterpretation of what Dr. Bowden called her.

Dr. Bowden shook her head. "Not a veterinarian. A soldier. Jamie recently returned from overseas."

"Oh," Dorothy said. That "oh" said so much. "Thank you for your service."

Jamie gave a curt nod, uncomfortable accepting the gratitude, especially knowing what she knew about her culpability in the attack and her fellow soldiers' deaths.

"Does the puppy need some water?" Dorothy asked, warm and cordial now that she knew Jamie had a reason to keep Zoey with her.

Yes, she'd abused the service dog allowance because Zoey certainly wasn't certified in anything but eating, napping, and chewing shoelaces. But she did provide Jamie with a great deal of love and support that helped her when the flashbacks overtook her and when the grief and guilt became too much to bear.

Right now, sick at heart and worried about Sammy

and wondering if Ford would ever speak to her again, she needed all the support she could get.

Dr. Bell approached her. "Jamie, are you okay?"

"I'm fine."

"It must have been traumatic for you to find Sammy like that. What you did for him . . . you saved his life. I'm sure that's got to have a profound effect on you, especially under the circumstances." Dr. Bowden reached out to touch her, but Jamie flinched, and Dr. Bowden patted Zoey's head instead, sticking close so Jamie didn't have to raise her voice to speak.

"It hasn't really hit me. I just kicked into that mode and got the job done. You know?"

"Yes, I do. Procedure, protocols, these are the things we rely on in an emergency. It's why we train."

"Yes." So why did she freeze when her friends needed her? It didn't make sense.

Relieved the doctor understood, Jamie smiled to reassure her that she wasn't about to go postal in the middle of the clinic. She had her head screwed on straight for once. Mostly. "I'm okay."

"Good. I'll go check on Sammy, see how the EKG is going. I spoke with Rory. The guys are on the way."

"Maybe I should go." Jamie glanced at the door, then back at Dr. Bowden, then the door again.

"Sit down. I may need to ask you some more questions. And Rory wants to talk to you when he gets here."

Ford's big brother could intimidate a general. "Uh, why?"

"Probably to find out what happened from you directly."

"Uh, okay." Jamie took a seat in the corner of the waiting room away from everyone else. She needed some space. Zoey lay content on her chest for a few minutes, then opted for the cool tile floor, jumping off

Jamie's lap, tumbling on her unsteady legs, and plopping down flat.

Nervous about seeing Ford and his brothers and thinking about poor Sammy alone in the other room, she leaned forward, hung her head between her shoulders, her forearms braced on her legs, stared at her bloodstained hands, and lost herself in a war-torn world only in her mind.

CHAPTER 27

Ford opened the gate on the trailer he'd backed into Colt's yard at Rambling Range. On his way over, he'd picked up a horse as a favor to Colt's wife, Luna. He took the horse's halter and backed him out of the trailer. The horse was to be a new addition to her equine therapy program. He'd wanted to bring Jamie with him, so he could hopefully get her involved in the program. He thought helping others might help her.

It seemed a perfect fit, but now he didn't know if he'd ever bring her here.

Everything had seemed so sure in his life yesterday. Today, he felt adrift, uncertain, and pissed off to keep from feeling the unrelenting pain that had settled in his chest.

The fury he felt this morning seeing her in bed with that fucking asshole Tobin nearly made him snarl at Colt instead of nodding his head in greeting when Colt came out of the barn.

"Hey, where's your girl?" Colt looked around him and the horse to see if Jamie was still in the truck.

His girl. He didn't know if she was his anymore. He wanted her to be. He wanted to believe that what he'd seen this morning didn't mean what he thought it meant. He tried to give her the benefit of the doubt, but the image of Tobin with his hand up Jamie's shirt had burned in his brain.

"She's not here."

Colt's eyes filled with concern. "Oh. Bad day for her again, huh?"

Ford had kept Colt and Rory in the loop about his seeing Jamie and the issues facing her. She'd done so well at the ranch when she ran into his brothers again. And the family dinner remained one of his best recent memories. She'd adjusted to the guys he hired working at the ranch. He'd wanted to bring her to Colt's place today and ease her into the family a little at a time. Luna and Jamie had hit it off talking horses. Completely on board with his plan, Luna wanted to invite Jamie to join the equine therapy program.

Colt's head tilted as he eyed him. "What's with the pissed-off glare? I thought Jamie was getting better."

"She was until an Army buddy showed up last night and thought it a great idea to talk nonstop about the past."

"Shit."

"Not even close. Fucked up is more like it."

Colt leaned against the wood rail fence. "Care to share what happened?"

He needed to get it off his chest. Colt had always been a great sounding board. Maybe if he talked about it, he could get it to make sense. "The guy is crazy about her. You can see it in the way he never stops staring at her."

A curious frown tugged one side of Colt's mouth back. "How does Jamie look at him?"

Ford didn't want to believe there was something there, but as the evening wore on last night her initial trepidation wore off and they were like best friends.

Ford didn't say that. Instead he went with Jamie's initial reaction to Tobin, which still didn't make any sense when put together with the obvious bond they shared.

"She nearly killed him when he showed up."

Colt's eyes went wide. "Did she shoot him, too?"

"No. Apparently she saves that for me." He shook off some of his anger and tried to explain. "He set her off. I thought I'd taken all her bullets, but she must have had some stashed away. She loaded the gun and had it ready to fire when she let him in the door."

"Did she actually pull the gun on him?"

"No. She had it tucked away at her back."

Colt's head tipped to the side again. "Okay. Well, he made her nervous and scared. She armed herself, but she didn't shoot first without thinking."

That's how he'd felt last night. She'd had a major setback, but she hadn't totally gone off the rails and lost it completely.

"She drank a few beers and took her meds. She barely ate anything. She ignored me most of the night."

Colt eyed him. "She ignored you? Or she spent time catching up with a friend who understands what she's been through and related to her better than you can?" Colt's one shoulder shrug punctuated the rhetorical question.

Okay, Ford hadn't thought of it that way. "When did you turn into Dr. Phil?"

Colt mocked him with a lopsided grin. "Did I touch a nerve? They have history. That incited your little green monster."

"I was not jealous." The conviction in his voice didn't erase the lie in his words. Yeah, he'd seen her with Tobin and the easy way they spoke and finished each other's sentences when relating a familiar story about an event or one of their other friends. It pissed him off that he'd sat there with nothing to say because he didn't know that part of her life.

"Deny much?"

Ford held up his hands and let them drop. "Fine. I don't like the guy. He's pushy."

"You're pushy with her. You said it yourself, you make her face things to help her get through them."

"Not when it comes to the attack. That's dangerous territory. She will shoot if she loses herself in that time."

Colt's eyes filled with suspicion. "This is the guy who was there with her, right?"

"Yeah?"

"So why is he pushing her to talk about what happened? I'd think he already knows and doesn't want to talk about it either."

Ford cocked his head and thought about it. "I think he said something to her, or asked her about something that happened that made her . . . I don't know . . . feel guilty. I got the feeling he wanted to know just how much she remembered, or didn't."

"Why does it matter? He already knows what happened."

"Right. He saved her. From the fire and after she was shot."

Colt gave him another of those knowing looks. "See? She's nice to the guy because she owes him her life. She loves you."

That actually made a hell of a lot of sense and eased Ford's aching heart.

His phone rang. He ignored it.

"You're not going to answer that?"

"I'm not in the right frame of mind to talk to her right now. I don't want to say something I'll regret."

Colt's eyebrow shot up. "Like what?"

"I don't know." He also didn't want to hear her say goodbye. He really didn't want to hear that she planned to stay with Tobin. He really hoped that didn't happen.

"What else happened last night?" Colt eyed him, knowing he'd held something back.

Ford didn't want to tell his brother that he'd found Jamie in bed with another guy. If they managed to fix this mess between them, and that was a big *if*, if she'd slept with the guy, then he didn't want his brother always looking at her knowing what she'd done to Ford.

"She asked me to leave last night so she could talk to him alone and get some answers to those missing pieces in her mind."

"You didn't trust the asshole to keep his hands to himself without you there."

Exactly. And look what happened. Well, he actually didn't know what happened.

His phone chimed with a text message.

Colt pointed to the phone poking out of Ford's pocket. "Answer her."

Ford shook his head. He needed a little more time to let his anger, disappointment, and the deep hurt she'd caused him settle so he could think things through and talk to her with a clear head.

This time Colt's phone rang. He pulled it out of his pocket and smiled. "Big brother is calling." He swiped his finger across the screen and put the phone to his ear. "Hey, big bro, what's up?" Colt's smile died and his eyes filled with worry.

"What is it?" Ford asked, his stomach tying in knots just seeing the devastated expression on Colt's face.

"We're on our way. Ford is here. I'll fill him in, and we'll meet you there." Colt hung up and let out a catcall whistle toward the stables. Luna walked out. Colt waved her over, telling her with that signal to hurry.

"Colt, man, what is it?" Ford demanded.

He waited for Luna to run over to them. "Grandpa Sammy is at the clinic. He crashed his truck at Ford's place after he had a dizzy spell and his heart stopped."

Luna gasped and covered her mouth with her hand, her eyes filling with tears. "No."

"He's okay," Colt assured her, then turned to Ford. "Jamie saved him."

"What?" Ford felt the bottom drop out of his stomach. One second he thought his grandfather dead, the next he discovered Jamie saved him.

She'd gone to his place looking for him.

Oh God, if they'd come here to Colt's as he'd planned, his grandfather would be dead right now.

"Ford." Colt clamped a hand on his shoulder and shook him. "Whatever happened between you two last night, I don't know, it doesn't matter right now. We need to get to the clinic. He's stable, but Bell is running some tests."

Ford turned to leave, realizing he still held on to the horse he'd come to deliver. "Uh . . ."

Colt took the horse's lead rope and ran the horse down to the barn.

Luna touched his arm. "Unhook the trailer. Let's go."

Ford acted, doing what he had to do to get to his grandfather, but all his thoughts dwindled down to two things. He prayed his grandfather was really okay. And he needed to see Jamie and thank her for saving his grandfather's life. Everything else could wait. For now. But soon they'd have to talk, and he didn't know how that would end. He hoped it didn't end everything.

CHAPTER 28

Ford walked into the hospital behind Colt and Luna just as Rory and Sadie's truck pulled into the lot. Colt spotted Jamie in the waiting room and headed toward her. Zoey saw Ford, leaped up from her nap on the floor, and came running, attacking his boots. Ford scooped her up and stared at Jamie.

Colt nearly reached her, but stopped when Ford called, "Stop. Don't go near her."

Jamie sat very still with her hands in front of her. She rubbed her thumb over the red stains, but they didn't go away. Lost in her own world, she didn't look up as Colt approached her. Ford feared if startled she'd come up fighting.

She didn't do that though. Her head came up at his order for Colt to stay clear and her tear-filled eyes met his. "I'm not going to hurt him." Her head dropped again and she continued rubbing at her hands.

Rory walked right past Colt and went to Jamie, kneeling in front of her so she didn't have to look so far up to see his face. "Hey, Jamie. It's good to see you again."

Jamie nodded but didn't really respond.

"I heard what you did. You saved Granddad. You gave him CPR, brought him back."

"That's what I'm trained to do." Her sad eyes came up and met Rory's. "I'm supposed to help people, save them from bad things happening, but I didn't save my team. They're dead. I should be dead, too." A tear slipped down her face. She pursed her lips and the sadness disappeared. "You should go see him. He's just down the hall. Room two."

Her head fell between her shoulders and tears fell silently to the floor between her feet.

Rory looked back at him, one eyebrow raised in question about her odd behavior. Ford's chest ached so bad he thought it might crack, split clear open, and spill out all the sorrow he had for Jamie inside of him.

Ford walked over and tapped Rory's shoulder to get him to move out of the way. He took Rory's place in front of Jamie, kneeling with Zoey between his legs. He didn't know what to do or say. This wasn't the usual way Jamie broke down. She got angry. She got homicidal. She blacked out. She came back fighting. She did not get sad and quiet like this.

Her head came back up and her eyes went wide when she saw him sitting in front of her and not Rory. "Go see your grandfather. He's waiting to see you. He needs you."

"Jamie."

Tears flooded her eyes again. "I'm really sorry. It wasn't at all what it looked like, I swear. I would never do that. Ever." She shook her head from side to side. "Never. I love you." She swiped her finger over her tear-streaked face, leaving behind a wet, red mess.

It hit him all at once that the stain on her fingers was his grandfather's blood.

Her gaze dropped to her hand and her eyes went wide. She wiped her hands on her jeans, trying to get the stains off. Her breathing became erratic as a full-blown panic attack kicked into gear.

"Colt, get something to clean her up," he called over his shoulder. His family had moved away to talk to Bell and give him a minute with Jamie, but now they all stared as she broke down in front of him, desperately trying to get the blood off herself.

He grabbed her hands and hid them in his. He leaned close so all she saw was his face. "I love you, too."

Her breath stopped altogether, then whooshed out on a sigh. "You do? Still? After last night?"

"We will talk about that, but right now I need you to calm down."

She cocked her head and studied his face. "I'm okay."

"You sure?"

"I'm a little here and there, but I'm mostly here."

He actually understood that. The past was intruding on her thoughts, but she was still in control of her mind.

"He died." Her eyes implored him to understand all she didn't say and what that meant. "I didn't panic. I didn't freeze. I brought him back. For you. For them." She cocked her head toward his brothers. "He's okay. I saved him. This time I saved him."

As in she hadn't saved her friends. He saw that in the depths of despair in her eyes. How much she wanted that to be untrue. How seeing Tobin last night brought the fact their other friends were missing from that reunion into sharp focus. Jamie couldn't face the pain, so she'd tried to numb it, drinking with Tobin.

Colt handed him a wet towel. Ford picked up Zoey and set her in Jamie's lap to distract her while he cleaned her hands and blood-smeared cheek. To distract her more, he asked, "How'd you get them to let Zoey in here?"

"I told them she's my emotional support dog. Dr. Bowden backed me up. She's nice."

Ford rubbed Zoey behind the ear. "It's the truth. Zoey helps you."

"And you're angry she got left outside last night because I was too wasted to hear her, let alone remember to take care of her."

"I'm not talking about this now." He tucked the bloody towel at his side so she didn't see it. "You okay to wait here while I go see my grandfather?"

"I'm leaving. You need to be with your family, not taking care of me. I've taken up far too much of your time and made you put off important things you need to do too often. Be with your family, Ford. Don't worry about me."

"And just how are you getting out of here?"

"I have the keys to your grandfather's truck. I'll drop it off at your house and get my truck."

He sucked in a deep breath trying to remain calm and avoid having the fight brewing between them explode here in the middle of the clinic waiting room.

"And go home to Tobin?"

Her eyes went wide. "I forgot about him."

Well, that was a relief. She'd come to find him and she'd forgotten about her so-called friend.

"Maybe I'll go to Zac's."

"You're coming with me." He pulled her up by the hand he hadn't realized she'd kept in his this whole time. Zoey tried to wiggle toward him, but Jamie held the pup close, nuzzling her nose into Zoey's soft fur.

They found Rory, Sadie, Colt, and Luna in Grandpa Sammy's room. Ford set the bloodied towel he'd used to clean Jamie up on the counter by the sink and walked to the end of the bed, Jamie still beside him.

Granddad held out his hands. "What do we have here? Is that the pup you got for your girl?"

Ford took Zoey from Jamie's hands, though she looked reluctant to release her. "Go get him," he ordered Zoey, setting her on the bed beside his grandfather's leg.

Zoey rushed up the length of him and promptly pounced on his chest and licked his face. Grandpa Sammy laughed, tried to dodge the puppy's tongue, and rubbed her back, enjoying the attention.

Who didn't love a puppy?

"Jamie, we really can't thank you enough for what you did," Luna said, reaching out to touch Jamie's shoulder.

Jamie didn't flinch away, but her breath held for a split second before she breathed again. "I'm just glad it worked out and you're okay," she said to his grandfather. "You scared me."

"He scared all of us," Rory added. "Really, Jamie, thanks. I'm so glad you were there."

"We all are," Colt said, taking Luna's hand and holding it.

Rory had Sadie at his side, his arm around her back, and his hand on the side of her pregnant belly.

His brothers had the women they loved next to them for support and comfort. They looked so connected. Ford had Jamie here with him. Hell, she'd saved his grandfather. If she hadn't, this would have been a very different scene. Still, he wished he could pull her into his arms and hold her, knowing there was nothing standing between them. But after what he'd seen this morning, the hurt still tightening his chest, he held back and hated it.

"Jamie, honey, I'm really okay, but you look a little worse for wear. Are you okay? I hate that what happened reminded you so much of your past." Sammy absently pet Zoey as she slept at his side.

Jamie went past Colt and Luna and leaned over his grandfather. "I'm okay, because you're okay. He loves you so much." She looked around at all of them. "They all do. You're really lucky to have so many people to love and support you."

"Anything you need, honey, we're here for you." Granddad reached for her hand and held it tight.

Jamie surprised Ford and leaned down and kissed his grandfather on the head next to the bandage without an ounce of reluctance. "I'll leave you with your family. There's something I have to do. Thank you for what you said in the truck. It helped."

Ford had no idea what she meant. Judging by the faces of his family around him, neither did they, but his grandfather nodded in acknowledgment.

Jamie walked toward the door, leaving Zoey on the bed and not saying anything to him. He stopped her before she left. "Where are you going?"

"I need to ask Dr. Bowden something."

He finally put together her tense stance, inability to move fluidly, and the crease in her brow drawing her pain-filled eyes together.

"You're in pain."

"I forget to bring my meds with me." She leaned in close and whispered, "I hurt my back and shoulder lifting him. It's not that big a deal compared to what he's been through. Take care of him. I'll take care of me."

He grabbed her arm before she left. "Jamie," he pleaded, but he didn't know what for. He wanted her to let him back in, not hold him off because of what happened between them. Right now, he didn't care about any of it. He only cared about the misery etched on her face, stiffening her body, and pulling her away from him.

She pried his hand from her arm. "There's something I need to do. Stay with your family."

"Do not leave. I will drive you . . . wherever you want to go." He hated that he didn't know where she wanted to be right now.

She slipped out the door and closed it. He kept his back to his family trying to figure out his own head and heart.

"Is everything okay?" Sadie asked.

"No. Yes." He turned to them, gripped the end of his grandfather's bed, and squeezed his hands tight. "I don't know."

"She looks haunted," Luna said. "She's really having a rough time. I feel so bad for her."

"Yeah, well, it doesn't help that something happened and it's driven a wedge between us," he admitted. He looked at his grandfather. "What did you say to her in the truck? What helped her? Because sometimes I feel like nothing I say or do is right or helpful or even gets through to her."

"You don't believe that." His grandfather continued to pet Zoey's head as she slept. "Zoey helped. Your love helps. Even your anger and frustration helps. You have no idea what it's like to take a life. To watch someone you've fought beside and lived with die right before your eyes in such a brutal way."

They'd all heard stories of their grandfather's time in the military, but nothing too terrible. Mostly stories about buddies he'd served with and some wild antics. Probably because their grandfather didn't want to scare them with war stories.

"She never said she shot anyone. Did she tell you that?"

"She didn't have to. I see it in her. She's a soldier, Ford. She's trained to fight in combat."

"She drove a truck."

"A very dangerous job when the enemy not only wants you dead, but what you're carrying, and they'll stop at nothing to get both. Cut off the supply chain, you gain ground, supplies, and you can win. She was a target every day she did her job. You think she drove back and forth and nothing ever happened. That girl has more guts than you can possibly imagine. Every day she fights to stay alive. Every day she remembers who she is, what she did, what she lost. Those thoughts are so heavy in her mind, processing anything else is just too much sometimes. She's rooted in discipline and duty. You've given some of that back to her, but it takes time to settle into a new life, a new routine. She's done well. You've said so yourself, but you have to expect setbacks.

"Pick the worst thing that ever happened to you and amplify it by ten thousand. That still isn't enough to compare to what happened to her in the middle of that war. Your mind isn't meant to endure the things she's seen and done. That's why we call the flashbacks in her mind nightmares. Let me tell you, that doesn't begin to describe the terror she goes through."

"Granddad, I know she's hurting. I've seen her in the grips of one of those nightmares. They scare the shit out of me and I don't even see what she's seeing."

"No. But you see what she goes through and it scares you to not be able to protect her from that recurring trauma. That's a mild version of what she feels about not being able to protect the friends she lost."

"I hadn't thought of it that way."

"You are a good man, Ford. You have done everything you can for her. Keep doing it. In time, her mind will heal. I hope you can hold on long enough for that to happen because she's a remarkable woman."

"I know that. There is no way in hell I'm letting her go. Not this time."

"You never said, Grandpa Sammy, what you told her in the truck." Luna squeezed his hand.

Grandpa Sammy looked up at Ford. "Deep down, she believes she's broken. I told her she's damaged. Damaged can be fixed. I told her that what she saw, what she did, was a terrible thing, but she is not the terrible thing." Granddad's gaze bored into Ford's. "I don't know what happened between you two, but if it's not completely broken, it can be fixed if you want it."

He did want it. He wanted her and the life he dreamed of, with them living on the ranch and raising a family, just like his brothers had found with their wives, the women they'd fought to hold on to, too.

He left his grandfather's room without a word in search of where Jamie had run off to earlier. She'd said she needed to talk to Bell. He found the doc standing outside one of the draped cubicles on the other side of the reception area.

"Bell."

"Ford. Everything all right with your granddad?"

"Yes. He's fine. Did Jamie come and find you?"

"A little while ago." Deep concern filled Bell's eyes. "She needs to get some sleep."

"Did you give her the meds she asked for?"

Surprise filled Bell's eyes. "She didn't ask me for any meds. She asked to use a computer."

"What?"

"She said she needed to contact her psychiatrist."

Surprised, he scrunched up one side of his mouth.

It wasn't her usual day or time to talk to Dr. Porter. "She did?"

"It's a good sign, Ford. She had a difficult day. Instead of letting it overwhelm her to the point where she can't cope, she wants to speak to someone who can help her make sense of it."

Yeah, she needed the kind of help he couldn't give her. He wanted to make her better. He wanted to be the reason she got better. But he really needed to face the fact that Jamie needed to do it herself. He couldn't fix everything, though he tried damn hard.

Though she faltered last night, she found her inner strength again today to come after him to make things right, to save his grandfather. She knew she needed help and asked for it from her doctor. She needed him, but he needed to be with his grandfather, and she'd pushed him to do that for his sake.

She put him first, not herself. "Where is she?"

"In my office in the adjoining building. Second floor."

"Thanks, Doc. I appreciate you helping her."

"I just lent her my computer. She literally brought your grandfather back from the dead."

Ford took a second to absorb that statement. He raked his fingers through his hair. "I can't believe after all she's been through, she ends up saving him like that."

"She's trying to save herself, too, Ford."

"I know she is. She's so damn strong. Sometimes she doesn't give herself enough credit for everything she does to get through the day."

"She's got you to remind her. When are you going to marry her?"

"I still have to ask her." The answer surprised not only Bell, but himself.

He planned to do it when she was well again. But

what if what his grandfather was trying to tell him was true, that her healing was a long road with many setbacks and turns with no real end in sight? That Jamie would have to find a way to deal with what happened and work to make the good days outnumber the bad. He could live with that, so long as he had Jamie by his side. They'd make a life together. The best life they could have despite the obstacles they'd face. They'd do it together.

CHAPTER 29

Jamie clicked off the call to Dr. Porter and sat back in Dr. Bowden's chair. The office was filled with books and plants, a nice place to enjoy the quiet for a few minutes. She needed time to compose her thoughts about what she'd say to Ford.

"Jamie."

Her gaze shot up to him standing in the doorway, hesitant to come in and see her.

"Are you done, or do you need more time to talk to your doctor?"

She sighed. "I'm done. How did you know I was here?"

"Bell told me you needed someone to talk to." He hung his head. "I'm glad you turned to your doctor, but I'm sorry I made it hard for you to talk to me."

"*I* made it hard for me to talk to you, because I acted irresponsibly."

He looked up at her again, his lips tilted in a sardonic half frown. "I can't imagine the toll it takes on you physically and mentally to work so hard every single minute of the day and have all that hard work fall apart on you the second an old friend knocks on the door."

"I lost it."

He nodded. "Yes, you did. But that doesn't mean you've lost all the ground you've made up since you got home. It doesn't mean you start over. You start from where you left off and keep working at it." Ford walked into the room, took the chair in front of Dr. Bowden's desk, and brought it around to sit next to her.

She spun the swivel chair to face him, though it cost her to move. A rippling fire of pain burned in her shoulders and down her back.

Ford read the pain in her eyes. "You're really hurting."

"It's nothing compared to how I feel about losing you."

Ford leaned in and took her hand. "You haven't lost me, Jamie."

"I know you're grateful I saved your grandfather, but that doesn't excuse what happened last night."

"Did you have sex with Tobin?" He bit the vile words out.

The thought made her stomach quiver. "No. Absolutely not." She pressed her lips together. "I didn't remember very much this morning, thanks to the epic hangover, which I deserve, but over the last several hours more and more has come back to me."

He touched the worry crease between her brows. "What's bothering you?"

"He wanted you to think we slept together."

"Yeah, I got that."

"I made it very clear I plan to stay here. I told him that I love you. Not that it was any surprise to him. I've been in love with you forever."

Ford brought her hand to his lips and kissed her palm.

"You're very sweet, but please stop moving me." She clenched her jaw.

He gently set her hand back on her thigh. "You're really in a lot of pain."

"I don't pop those pills for show."

He looked around for her purse, which she'd left in her truck at his house. "Where are your meds?"

"I left them at home. I forgot to grab them on my mad dash out to find you."

"Come on, we'll go get them. Maybe Bell has something she can give you before we go."

"No, wait. I have to tell you what happened."

"What?" He didn't sound like he wanted to know if it had to do with Tobin.

"Before you arrived for dinner, Tobin told me that I froze in the middle of the battle. My friends needed me, and I didn't do anything."

Ford's eyes narrowed. "That can't be right."

It didn't feel right. "Why do you say that?" She really needed to hear his thoughts.

"A guy's pointing a rocket propelled grenade launcher at you. You don't sit there, you make a run for it and jump out of the truck."

True.

"You sense a threat at your door, you get a gun, ready to shoot whoever is on the other side."

True.

"The shed is burning and you know I'm in there, and the fire doesn't stop you from busting me out, despite how it reminds you of what happened to your back."

True again.

"You find my grandfather dead in the truck. You bring him back. Jamie, you don't freeze. You act. Every time, even when you aren't in your right mind. Even if you did freeze that one time, you were burned, in terrible pain, scared, and under attack, an imminent threat all around you. You can't blame yourself for your brain being unable to process all of that and more and still act in such dire circumstances. And why the hell would he tell you that, knowing you were in a bad place?"

"He made it sound like I was to blame, but I sensed an ulterior motive."

Ford's eyebrow cocked up. "Like what?"

"He's very adamant about you being bad for me."

"He's jealous."

"A little, but it's something else."

"I don't know where you're going with this, Jamie. He wants you." Anger flashed in his eyes. "He slept in your bed last night to let you and me know that's where he wants to be."

"I think he did it more to make sure you left me."

"If he doesn't want you for himself, why?"

"Because I told him that because of you I've been able to recover more of my memory of that time and not fight it because I know no matter how dark my world gets you'll pull me back into the light."

"Ah, Firefly, you're the one who lights up my world."

She smiled and sighed out her relief that she hadn't irrevocably damaged the bond they shared.

"I wish I could express how much your love lights me up inside."

Ford squeezed her hand. "When you smile, I can see it."

"You make me want to smile all the time, even when I can't see any reason to smile."

"I want to kiss you so damn bad, but I don't want to hurt you."

"You should really stop talking yourself out of kissing me." She'd said something similar to him in the stables in the early days, when their relationship had been even more tenuous than it was this morning.

Ford stood, planted his hands on the chair arms,

and leaned in and kissed her softly. His warm lips brushed hers in a soft caress, then settled over hers and held. Love poured into her in a soft warm wave that temporarily numbed the pain and made everything all right. He broke the kiss, leaned back, and stared down into her upturned gaze. "I love you. Everything else we can figure out, but that I know."

"I love you, too. That's why I think you should stay away from me."

"What? No."

"Tobin wants me away from you because he thinks that I'll remember my past if I have you to help me break through the block in my mind. He doesn't want me to remember something. What, I don't know, but if he's willing to come all this way to make sure it doesn't happen, what will he do if he thinks I will remember and you can help me with that?"

Ford fell back into the seat in front of her. "Jamie, that's a little far-fetched, don't you think? Isn't it more reasonable to think that he wants to break us up so he can have you for himself?"

"I'm telling you he doesn't want me to know something about what happened that day. He wants me to believe I'm better off never remembering."

"If you truly believe that, then I'm definitely not leaving you alone. If he thinks you will remember, what if he comes after you next?"

Jamie hadn't actually considered that. "What could I possibly know that would make him want to stop me from remembering?"

"I'm not convinced that's really what he's doing here. He has to know that seeing him might spark your memory."

"His arrival sparked my survival instinct. I went

full-on defensive and got a loaded gun. Even when I saw him, something inside of me resisted. I tried to talk myself out of it. Tell myself over and over again that he's a friend. I overreacted. But still, it took everything I had to let him in that door and not shoot him on sight."

"Jamie, baby, why didn't you say anything to me when I arrived?"

"I was being crazy. Unreasonable. Irrational. Pick your favorite. If you hadn't shown up, I don't know what I would have done."

"You called for backup."

"What?"

"You went on the defensive and you called for backup by texting me. You fell back on training. My grandfather said something about you being rooted in discipline. It makes sense."

"So you believe me."

"I believe that you've been living on instinct for a long time. Something about him tripped your enemy meter. Why?"

She let her head fall back against the chair. "I wish I knew."

"You're exhausted, baby. Come on, I'll take you home."

"I can't go home. There's a bad man in my house."

That made Ford smile. "I meant home with me."

"Really?" It seemed too much to hope that they'd gotten past this with one conversation, though she had tried to be as honest and forthcoming as she could to show him she had nothing to hide.

"You're sorry. I'm sorry. You won't do it again. I won't do it again. Let's move on. I missed you so damn much and it hasn't even been a day."

"I feel like it's been a month."

He tilted his head, reached out and swept his thumb across her cheek. "You look like you haven't slept in one."

"I think a hot shower will help."

"How about a hot bath? I'll wash your back and give you a back rub."

"I must be dreaming, because you're too good to be true."

Ford stood and took the chair back to the front of the desk. He came back and held his hand out to her. "Do you need help up?"

"I got it." She rose, but a tremble of pain quaked through her shoulder and back.

Ford ushered her out of the building and to his truck. He helped her inside and buckled her in. "Stay put. I'll go get Zoey, say goodbye to my family, and take you to get your meds."

"But Ford, don't you want to stay with your grandfather?"

"Rory and Colt will stay with him. They'll call me if his condition changes. Granddad will want me to go with you."

"I really don't want to take you away from your responsibilities and your family."

"I told you, you need me, I'm there."

Ford helped Jamie into his truck, closed the door, and ran back to the clinic.

Bell stopped him in the hall with her hand held out. "Dr. Porter called and said his session with Jamie went well and that she needed these." Bell dropped several pills in his hand.

"Thank you. You have no idea the kind of agony she's in."

"That should take the edge off and get her home. She needs to sleep."

"She'll get it, I promise. How is Granddad?"

"It's what I suspected, he took his blood pressure medication twice by accident. His blood pressure dropped too low, which made him dizzy and lethargic, so he tried to go home. I told Rory and Sadie to set up a system where he can keep track of the pills and they can monitor to be sure he doesn't make this mistake again."

"His heart is okay?"

"Still ticking. No signs of blockage or irregular arrhythmia. I'll keep him overnight to monitor his blood pressure and make sure it's stable. He'll probably go home tomorrow."

"Great. Thanks."

Bell went to see her next patient and he walked into his grandfather's room. Everyone looked at him expectantly and all their faces dropped when they didn't see Jamie with him.

"She's in my truck. She's in a lot of pain because she forgot her medicine." He held open his hand. He didn't want his grandfather to know she'd hurt herself helping him. "Bell helped me out with that, but I need to get her home."

"Go on, son, take care of your girl. I'll be fine." Grandpa Sammy still stroked the puppy, who tried to bite off the armband the clinic had put on him.

"Thanks for understanding, Granddad."

"You need anything?" Rory asked.

"Time. We worked out our problem. She knows what she needs to do and she's trying, but it'll take time."

"Bring her around our place soon," Colt coaxed. "When she's ready, we'll talk to her about the equine therapy program."

Ford clamped his hand on Colt's shoulder. "I'm going to talk to her about that soon. I think that's a stepping stone she needs to good health."

"I like her, Ford. We'll work something out," Luna promised.

"Bring her by the house for dinner once Grandpa Sammy is home," Sadie suggested. "She'll want to see that he's okay."

"You guys are amazing. Thanks for the support."

"We're your family," Rory said, explaining it all.

Ford picked up Zoey, making his granddad frown. "Maybe I need to get you an emotional support dog," Ford teased.

Grandpa Sammy gave a lopsided frown. "It's not a bad idea. I like that little one."

"She's Jamie's, but I'll see what I can do. My nephew might like a dog around the house."

Sadie smiled and rubbed her hand over her protruding belly.

Ford ran back out to the truck, climbed in, set Zoey on the seat between him and Jamie, and held his hand out to her. "Bell sent you some relief."

Jamie snatched the pills from his hand and popped them in her mouth, crushing them once with her teeth and swallowing them with a swig of water from the bottle he handed her from the console.

"Hold on, Jamie. Just a little while longer and I'll have you settled in for the night."

"It's barely past lunch."

"Does it matter? You probably haven't even eaten anything."

"Zoey needs to eat."

"I've got her food at my place, but I'm stopping by yours to get your pills."

"Tobin is there."

"You don't even have to get out of the truck, baby. I'll handle him."

Ford didn't mind the quiet drive to her place. She fought the pain, waiting for the meds to kick in and give her some relief. He'd not only make sure Rory took care of monitoring Grandpa Sammy's meds, he'd make sure to check in with Jamie to ensure she took hers on time. It had worked up until last night. She'd found a steady balance between the pain and the acceptable intervals for taking the meds. Yes, after a hard day in the stables working her muscles she sometimes needed an extra dose, but those days were becoming few and far between the more she strengthened her body.

He turned into her driveway, unhappy to see Tobin's black Camaro still parked in the same spot. Zoey lay on Jamie's lap. She lazily pet the dog and stared at her place dispassionately.

"You okay?"

"Tired. Meds are starting to work."

"Give it another ten minutes and maybe you'll stop clenching your teeth."

She gave him a halfhearted smile, all she could manage right now.

He leaned over and kissed her softly. "Be right back."

It cost her, but she reached over and grabbed his arm before he got out. "Ford. Just get the meds. Remember how I am when I'm in a flashback. He told me he suffers from them, too."

"Where's the gun?"

"Last I saw it, on the kitchen table, but you took the clip and bullets."

"But you have another hidden in the house, right?"

She ducked her head. "Maybe."

Ford growled out his frustration and walked toward the door, stopping next to the Camero when he spotted the rental papers on the dash. He read the date. It didn't make sense that Tobin rented the car weeks before he arrived at Jamie's last night.

Tobin probably watched him from the windows the second they pulled into the driveway, so Ford didn't linger by his car. He went in through the front door and stopped just inside, eyeing Tobin as he sat up from what looked like a nonchalant lounge on the sofa.

Ford didn't believe it for a minute.

"Where is she? Is she okay?"

"If you cared one bit about her well-being, you wouldn't have pushed her last night and plied her with drinks."

"She needs to let off steam. A couple of drinks isn't going to set her back."

"That's how little you know about her condition. Your little stunt hurt her because she thought she lost me, but I'm not going anywhere, asshole. So get used to it, or get out."

Tobin stood and faced off with him, the couch between them. "Fuck you."

Ford rolled his eyes. "I don't have time to do this with you right now. Jamie needs me, so stay out of my way, and we won't have a problem."

Tobin's eyes narrowed into a feral glare, but he was smart enough to read that anything he started, Ford would finish. Ford had several inches on the guy and a clear head, not fogged by a long drinking binge. Ford was stronger, faster, and smarter. He could take this guy, no problem, but he didn't want to cause one more worry for Jamie by going after her "friend."

Ford gave Tobin a dismissive shake of his head,

not giving Tobin the opportunity to test him, walked
down the hall to Jamie's room, and grabbed her bottles
of pills. He walked back to the kitchen, grabbed the
gun off the table, stuffed it down the back of his jeans,
and walked out the front door, slamming it behind
him, hoping that Tobin had the same hellish hangover Jamie nursed and the loud bang made his head
feel like it would split in two. He didn't worry about
Jamie. She'd taken her pain meds. Nothing close to
what Tobin might have taken, unless he'd stolen some
of Jamie's stash.

He jumped back into his truck, gave Zoey a pat to
get her to stop jumping on his shoulder, and started the
truck.

"Any trouble?" Jamie asked.

"None. He's watching TV and drinking beer on the
couch." A little hair of the dog. Tobin had a hard night
and morning.

"Did you know Tobin's been in Montana for a couple
of weeks?"

"What? No."

"According to the car rental agreement, he's been
here a hell of a lot longer than last night."

Jamie's eyebrow shot up. "An awful lot has happened
at your place the last few weeks. Including the fire."

Ford didn't argue or deny his thinking followed that
same train of thought.

"Let's get out of here." Jamie sighed and sank back
into her seat.

Tobin would never fess up to anything, and beating
it out of him would only get Ford arrested, so he drove
her to his place. Jamie was in no shape to confront
Tobin and toss him out. They'd take care of it when she
had her head straight and her strength back.

He stopped just behind her truck with the driver's door wide-open in the drive.

"I'll move my truck," she volunteered, trying to sit up without showing how stiff and sore she'd become over the last few hours.

"Leave it. I'll close the door and drive us up closer to the house." He didn't want her to have to walk any further than necessary.

He hopped out of the truck, spotted the damaged bark on the tree his grandfather hit in the accident. His grandfather's near death experience hit him all at once again with a punch to the chest. Jamie saved him. It amazed him and made him love her even more.

About to shove the door closed, he spotted her duffel and purse on the seat and grabbed both. He closed up the truck and went back to his. "You brought a bag?"

"I hoped to make things right with you and to stay here to show you that I want to be with you, not him."

He gripped the steering wheel, hung his head, and sighed out his frustration. "I know you want to be with me. Last night, things got muddled, but I never thought you'd . . ."

"But it looked that way this morning and I don't blame you for believing the worst."

"I'm sorry I didn't stay and talk to you. I wasn't in the right frame of mind. I didn't answer your call because I didn't want to say something I'd regret."

"We're okay now, right?"

He turned and stared at her. "Yes. We're okay. If you hadn't come looking for me, you wouldn't have found my granddad. We would have been over at Colt's place and we would have lost him."

Jamie reached over and squeezed his hand. "I'm glad that, for once, I helped."

"You help me all the time. You insisted I hire help even though I know how hard it is for you sometimes to be around them. I am catching up around here. That's because you work harder and harder every day, not only with the horses and the odd jobs you do around here, but by accepting the guys' presence and doing your best to work with them. Some days are harder than others, but you fight through it because you want to help me."

"I want you to be happy, Ford."

"Just being with you makes me happy, Jamie. Believe that. Believe in us, and we'll get through this."

Ford drove them up to the house, took her bags, and picked up Zoey, closing the truck door behind him. Jamie eased out of the truck and joined him at the front. They walked up the steps to the front door together, him feeling a growing sense of eagerness to get her inside where she belonged. Where he wanted her to stay. They hadn't really talked about their living arrangements. He got that she wanted to go home each night after a long day working here on the ranch. She needed familiar things. Her space. He didn't mind spending his evenings and most nights with her there. But he really wanted her here.

They stepped into the house. Ford set Zoey on the floor. She ran for her bowl of water in the kitchen. Since he and Jamie had lunch here every day, Ford had set Zoey up to do the same. Jamie followed her through the living room, into the kitchen, and filled her bowl with kibble from the bin beside the counter.

"I'll put your stuff in my room. Come on back. You can take a bath and crash for a few hours while I take care of the horses and get dinner ready." Ford went straight back to the master bedroom and set Jamie's bag on the bed. She'd never come down to his room. She'd never stayed the night here. He didn't know why.

He wanted her in his bed every night.

Jamie walked in behind him. "Ford. Are you sure about this?"

He turned to face her, the confusion he felt no doubt showing in the frown that drew back one side of his mouth without him even thinking about it. "Why would you ask that?"

"This is your home."

He tilted his head, trying to read her. "I stay at your place all the time."

"It's different."

He didn't get it. "Why is it different?"

"Because this is the place I always thought we'd be."

He felt the same way. "And here we are, Firefly."

"I know. It kind of feels unreal."

Drawn to her, he closed the distance between them, cupped her face in his hands, and kissed her softly. "It actually feels a bit more real now that you're here." He kissed the soft smile on her lips, falling into her and the moment, pouring all his love for this beautiful woman into the sweet caress.

She tried to raise her arms up over his shoulders, but she winced in pain, and fisted her hands in his shirt at his chest. He kissed her one last time, melding his mouth to hers as he dug his fingers into her tight muscles between her shoulder blades.

She sighed, but he didn't think it only had to do with the searing kiss they shared. He tore his mouth from hers, shut down every dirty thought he had about laying her out on the bed two feet behind him, and stepped toward the bathroom with his hands covering hers tangled in his shirt. "Come on, baby. You need a bath."

He pulled her shirt up and over her head, dragging it forward toward his chest instead of straight up to keep her arms from going over her head. He cupped her breast in his palm and swept his thumb over her tight nipple. "I am going to do something that is going to make you feel so good."

He went to the tub and turned on the water. He turned back to her, unzipped her jeans in one slow drag down, shifted his hand, and cupped her in his palm, rubbing softly against her. Teasing. Tempting. Distracting her from everything else but her and him and this moment.

He pulled her jeans down her legs slowly, kneeling as he went and brushing soft kisses on the silky skin he exposed down her thighs. Shoes, socks, jeans out of his way, he slid his hands up her legs, hips, and stomach as he rose and covered her breasts with his hands.

"Get in the tub." He turned her in his arms and held her hand to steady her as she stepped into the tub and sank into the steaming water.

Eyes closed, a soft smile on her face, she let the warmth sink into her sore body.

"God, you're beautiful."

"I've been dreaming of soaking in a tub for a long time."

He stripped with her heated gaze locked on him and tossed his clothes aside. He slipped into the tub behind her. Not much room for the both of them, but he'd make it work. He used the bar of soap all over her back, set it back on the shelf, then massaged her slippery shoulders. She melted under his hands working all the tight muscles and scar tissue she told him sometimes pulled and always ached. He'd seen the pain in her eyes in Bell's office earlier. Every tiny movement hurt, but she'd held it together. Such strength under all her beauty and in her small body. His heart both ached and swelled with love for her.

"Oh God, that feels fantastic." Not an ounce of self-conscious hesitation in her voice that he was not only staring at but touching her back.

"I make good on my promises."

Her hands rubbed over his thighs in soft circles and caresses. It felt so damn good to have her hands on his bare skin and his body swelled with wanting her, his aching cock pressed hard against her bare bottom.

"You have something else for me." The smile in her words made him smile behind her.

"That's for later. Right now, I'm going to work on this." He rubbed his thumb hard up the muscles bracketing her spine, all the way to her neck.

"Mmm." Not even coherent words anymore.

He took his time working his hands over her whole back, concentrating on her bad shoulder a little longer than the rest. She sat quietly, enjoying the attention. The more she did, the more he wanted to pamper her. He managed to snag the bottle of shampoo off the shelf with the tips of his fingers. He poured some in his hand, then washed her hair, working his fingers over her scalp, continuing the massage.

He raked his soapy fingers through his own hair and gave it a scrub. Jamie was so tired she didn't even move, just sank down, her knees coming out of the deep tub, and let the hot water wash the suds away. She came back up with her head back, the water sluicing down her back. She scooted forward just enough for him to copy her dunking. He settled back against the tub and Jamie lay against his chest, letting the heat relax her even more.

They sat like that, her fingers softly caressing his thigh, his brushing over her silky belly. They enjoyed the closeness they both needed until the water cooled.

He helped her out of the tub, tugged a towel off the nearby bar, and wrapped it around her. He made her stand there and let him softly dry her. He pulled the towel over her head and dried her hair until it stuck up in all directions. She laughed and smiled up him, her face soft and innocent.

He dragged the towel over his body in quick sweeps up his legs, over his torso, and down his arms. Jamie grabbed his brush off the counter and ran it over her head. He leaned over, letting her brush his hair for him. Done, he grabbed the bottle of lotion out from the cupboard.

Her sweet smile warming his heart, the meds and bath easing her pain, he picked her up into his arms, making her giggle.

"What are you doing?" Her tiny feet dangled over his arm.

"Taking you to bed."

"It's not even dinnertime."

"I didn't say we were going to sleep." He set her down beside the bed, but kept one arm wrapped around her. He set the bottle of lotion on the bedside table and pulled the covers back all the way to the end of the bed.

She slid her hands up his bare chest, pressed her naked body close to his, and rocked her belly against his hard length. He hissed in a ragged breath, leaned down, and kissed her softly, sliding his tongue past her welcoming lips and reacquainted himself with her taste, though it never seemed to leave his lips.

"Ford." His name on her lips pressed to his sent a wave of heat rushing through him.

He reined it in and gently laid her back on the white sheets. She raised her arms, inviting him to come to her, but he held himself over her. He traced his fingers up her arm and along her collarbone, detouring at her throat. He skimmed his hand down her chest and over her breast. She arched into his touch. He cupped her breast, pinching her tight pink nipple between his index and middle fingers, massaging the firm mound in his palm. Her eyes fell closed and she sighed.

He feasted on every line and curve of her body, softly touching every inch of her with his fingertips until she melted into the bed.

He slipped his hand around her hip and cupped her bottom, his fingers spread wide. He pulled her over to lie on her stomach. She kept her arms close to her sides, her hands near her face.

"Ford?" she questioned why he didn't lie over her and make love to her.

He leaned down and kissed her shoulder, not caring one bit about the scars beneath his lips. The contrast between her front and back was striking, but he'd long since stopped being surprised by the marks.

"Trust me."

Her eyes closed and she relaxed into the mattress with every stroke of his hand over her back and down over the soft slope of her bottom.

He grabbed the lotion off the bedside table and squirted a generous amount into his hand. He rubbed his hands together to spread it evenly and warm it a bit, sat beside her, laid his hands on her shoulders, and rubbed the lotion into her skin, massaging the tight, gnarled scar tissue to help keep it pliant and prevent it from pulling against her skin.

"You are amazing."

He smiled and kept working her back. "Will you say that when I leave my socks on the floor?"

"No," she answered honestly. "But I will always think overall that you're amazing."

"Everyone's got a flaw, right?"

"Well, if the worst thing you ever do is leave your socks on the floor and think you can fix everything on your own, I can live with that."

"Will you live with me?" He hadn't intended to ask her now. Someday. Soon. But the words left his mouth before he really thought about it. He waited for the need to take the words back to strike, but instead he held his breath waiting for her answer, hoping she'd say yes. Knowing that if she did, his life would change for the better.

She rolled to her side, leaned up on her arm, and stared at him, her head tilted in that way that spoke of disbelief. "Are you asking me to move in here?"

"I'll settle for that for now."

"You seriously want me here? All the time?"

"Yes." That came so easily. Why were the butterflies in his stomach still swirling? Why didn't she just say that one word and put him out of his misery?

Tears flooded her eyes. "I never expected this. Not after . . ."

"I love you, Firefly. Is it so hard to believe I'd want you with me all the time?"

"With the way that I am, yes."

"Just say the last word again."

She pulled her mouth back into a line, unsure of what he wanted her to say, until it dawned on her. She smiled softly and said, "Yes."

He let out a heavy breath. "Good. That's settled." He leaned down and took her mouth in a searing kiss, sealing the bargain. He slowed things down, sliding his body down the length of hers. Cupping her cheek in his hand, he stared down into her vivid green eyes. He didn't have the words to tell her how much she meant to him. So he showed her.

Her lips were soft below his, hungry for each of the kisses he pressed to them before he dove in for something much more tempting. Her body rolled toward his, her hips pressed against his. She arched into him, rubbing her belly against his aching cock. He slid his hand around her side and over her bottom, his fingertips diving deep to caress her soft folds.

She moaned into his mouth. He slid one finger deep into her wet center. She slid her foot up his calf, pressing her thigh up and over his, opening to his urgent caresses as his finger slid in and out of her tight core. He used his body to press her upper body back and kissed his way down her neck and chest to the tight bud begging for his kiss. He licked the tip, then sucked her softly into his mouth.

God, she tasted sweet.

"Ford," she called to him, her small hand rubbing down his chest, over his stomach, and down until she wrapped her fingers around his hard shaft and stroked him up and down.

Unable to endure the sweet torture for long despite his attention on her pink-tipped breast, he grabbed her hand and moved it back to his chest. He took her mouth in another hot, wet kiss, his tongue sliding along hers as he stroked her soft folds, sent one finger, then two deep into her, his thumb softly rubbing that tiny nub that made her body coil before it snapped with release.

He wanted to be inside her when she found the pinnacle of pleasure he desperately wanted to give her and grabbed a condom out of the drawer. He sheathed himself, distracted by Jamie's hands roaming over his back and arms. He loved that she never stopped touching him, never stopped participating, and always loved him.

Settled between her thighs, he joined their bodies in one smooth thrust. She sighed and he stopped, savoring the feel of her body locked around him. He slid out slow and back in with another long sweep of his body into hers. He lost himself making love to her slow and easy, the intensity unlike anything he'd ever felt. He didn't need to rush. Didn't want to, not with her hand softly stroking his skin, sliding down his back, and gripping his ass.

She pulled him close with each thrust and he buried himself deep in her welcoming warmth. He rubbed his hips against hers, creating a sweet friction against her clit, then pulled out and plunged back in, doing it all over again. Her body tightened around his and he thrust deep, faster, harder until they were both racing toward that blissful peace and, with her, a connection he'd never felt in his life.

He fell to her side, not wanting to crush her under his weight when she'd been so sore today. He held her close to his chest for long minutes while their breathing evened out and they enjoyed being locked in each other's arms.

"I've got to go out and take care of the horses, but you get some sleep."

She snuggled in close and held him to her. "Stay until I fall asleep."

He kissed her on the top of the head and her body softened next to his.

"Thank you for saving my granddad."

Her lips pressed to his chest in a soft kiss, then she

was out. He held her for a few minutes, just staring at her in wonder, memorizing every slope and plane on her pretty face.

He slipped out of bed, trying not to move or awaken her. He stood staring down at her in his house, in his bed, and smiled. She'd said yes to moving in. They were finally going to have the life they'd talked about so long ago. The life they both wanted. Nothing and no one would get in the way this time. He'd make sure of it. And if Tobin tried to mess things up again, Ford would take care of him, too.

CHAPTER 30

Tobin tossed his cell on the coffee table. Jamie didn't answer his call. Again. Tobin picked up his heavy work boot and chucked it against the front door. The loud thump didn't ease the frustration and hurt Jamie's absence inflamed.

He braced his hands on the back of the couch and hung his head between his tense shoulders. All the time they spent together, the stories they shared, the memories they created . . . and every time she chose that damn cowboy over him. It hurt, slicing a deep river of pain from his heart to his soul.

He slammed his hands down. What did he expect? She never looked at him the way she looked at Ford. She never would. Memories were all he'd ever have with her now. A sad ache throbbed through him with every beat of his heart.

He needed to preserve the tenuous friendship they shared before she ended up hating him. Time to cut his losses before things got worse.

He rounded the sofa and picked up his cell again and shot off a text.

TOBIN: Come home we need to talk I'm leaving

He curbed the intense urge to leave right now before everything went south.

He wanted to say goodbye.

He needed to see her one last time, despite the risk of triggering her memory.

His fingers wrapped tightly around the phone and ached as he fought his frustration and impotence when it came to fixing this and making it all go away.

He'd thought her memory gone forever, that he'd come here and in their shared grief they'd lean on each other and finally be together. But it wasn't meant to be. Despite his best efforts to keep Ford busy and out of the way, Ford's support had allowed Jamie to recover far too many fragments from a day Tobin wished he could forget, too.

He felt sorry for Jamie. He wanted to help her.

But helping her meant disaster for him.

Growing up he'd never had anyone to watch his back. He'd had to look out for himself—and that's exactly what he planned to do now, before it was too late.

CHAPTER 31

Jamie set the jug of sun tea back in the fridge. She downed half a glass and set it on the counter when her phone buzzed. She read Tobin's text. Her stomach tied into an aching knot. She couldn't put him off forever. Not when he was staying in her house. Guilt tightened the knot in her gut for leaving him there alone instead of facing him and the problem head-on.

Neither of them was in a good place. They'd fed each other's emotional turmoil. No wonder things had ended badly.

Except Tobin had intentionally pushed her buttons and tried to break up her and Ford. She didn't know exactly why, but he was an asshole and no friend for doing it.

If he was responsible for the mishaps and fire here at the ranch, he was dangerous, too. She could never prove he did it, but just the suspicion was enough to make her never want to see him again.

She needed to get her stuff and him out of her house.

Well, not her house anymore. Her body heated with the memories of how Ford brought her home the other night and showered her with love. In the midst of him helping ease her physical pain and making love to her like she was the most precious thing in his life, he'd asked her to move in. Not after they'd made love and in the heat of passion, but in a very calm and intimate moment they'd shared. She still couldn't believe it.

The hope she discovered still existed inside of her when Ford came back into her life welled up, tightening her chest.

"Where'd you go, Firefly?"

Ford stood ten feet away just inside the front door staring at her. The look on his face made her smile. He wasn't quite sure about approaching her. She hated that he still had reason to be cautious.

She picked up her glass to show him she was in the here and now. "Back to bed with you."

That made him smile and move into the room. "Oh yeah? Any one moment you're replaying in that dirty mind of yours?"

"Your sexy ass in my hands comes to mind. There are so many more good things to remember."

"Yes there are, like this morning when I had your legs wrapped around my head and my face buried in your—"

"Ford." The blush scorched its way up her breasts and rose up to her hairline, making her hot. Or maybe she was just hot for him.

He wrapped his arms around her middle and picked her up, nuzzling his nose in between her breasts. She wrapped her arms around his head, tried to laugh despite his hold on her ribs, and hugged him close.

"You're suffocating me."

"I've only been here for a day and half and already I'm suffocating you," she teased, giving him a playful smack on the shoulder.

He slid his hands to her sides and tickled her to let him go. "I meant that literally."

She wrapped her legs around his waist and took his face in her hands. His arms banded around her again to hold her in place. "Did you really ask me to move in and mean it?"

"Yes."

"Okay, then we need to go to my place and pick up some things because I'm out of clean clothes."

Ford tilted his head and narrowed his eyes, though they filled with mischief. "Silly girl, you don't need clothes if I keep you naked and happy in my bed."

"But who will feed the horses?"

"Good point. Zoey's looking for some chow, too." He set Jamie back on her feet and nudged her toward Zoey's bowl with a swat on the ass.

She filled Zoey's bowl, gave her a butt rub, then turned back to Ford just as he downed the last of her glass of iced tea.

"Hey, that was mine."

"I thought we shared everything now." The grin sent a wave of tingling heat through her belly.

"You're really enjoying this, aren't you?"

"I love having you here. Means I can do this anytime I want." He leaned down and kissed her softly, rubbing his big hand over her hip and down to cup her ass and pull her close. He nuzzled his nose against hers and smiled down at her. "Don't forget we're going to dinner tonight at Rory's. Granddad wants to see you again."

"I'm so glad he's home."

"He's probably not. He loves Bell and flirting with the nurses. Rory said he found Granddad asking for one of the volunteers' numbers. A sweet lady named Ruth, I think he said."

"In a couple of months he can flirt with the nurses

again when his grandbaby arrives. I can't believe you're going to be an uncle."

Ford smiled. "Me neither, but I can't wait."

"Are you looking forward to having a baby of your own?"

His gaze turned to the sprawling land out the window. "Someday."

She needed to know if he didn't want one now because he didn't think her mentally capable of taking care of a baby, or if he didn't trust her. "When do you want to have a baby?"

"I don't have an exact date, Jamie. When we're settled in here and you're better."

"What if I don't get any better than I am right now?"

Ford reached out and cupped her face in his big, rough palm. "Jamie, honey, you know that's not what will happen. You will get better and stronger."

"What if I don't?"

"You've made so much progress these last weeks. You work at it, it will happen. I know you want it. You don't quit."

"I don't want to hurt anyone again, most especially you."

"Keep working with Dr. Porter. Do your physical therapy. Give it time. And give yourself a break when things don't go the way you want."

She pressed her forehead to his chest.

"Maybe it feels like you have to have everything right now because you're afraid it will all disappear again." He tilted her head back so she looked up at him. The sincerity in his eyes touched and warmed her heart. "I'm not going anywhere. You are moving in here. We are going to be together always."

He sounded so sure. So reassuring. She set aside her worries and tried to do what he and Dr. Porter kept telling her to do, stay in the moment. In the here and now.

Where things were really good between her and Ford.

She leaned up and kissed him softly. "You better get cleaned up if we're going to dinner at your brother's place. I've got my appointment with Dr. Porter."

"You sure you're okay?"

"Yes. I'm glad we can talk about these things."

"You can talk to me about anything."

"I know. I'm unsettled because I need to resolve things with Tobin when we go to my place. Once he's gone, I can focus on me and my future with you."

"Then let's get it done." He rubbed his thumbs over her cheeks, bent, and kissed her forehead. "I'll take a shower while you have your session. I really am proud of you for sticking with it and working so hard to be well."

She leaned into his hand. "I'm excited about living here with you." She gave him a mocking frown. "Though you may not be when we bring my stuff from storage here."

Ford rolled his eyes. "I guess it was too much to hope all you had was your clothes."

"I had my own apartment off base. Don't worry, I don't have more than the basics."

"Do the basics include fifty pairs of shoes?"

"Maybe." She gave him a thoughtful look. "Maybe more," she teased.

"God help me."

"You asked me to move in. You can't take it back now."

Ford's computer chimed with the call from Dr. Porter.

"That's for you, honey." He gave her a quick kiss and a pat on the ass to move her along to the living room sofa where his laptop sat on the coffee table.

She flopped on the sofa, clicked to accept her call, but kept her eyes trained on Ford.

"Don't think I don't know you're staring at my ass," he called over his shoulder with a chuckle in his voice.

"I like the view," she called back.

"Hello to you, too," Dr. Porter chimed in, drawing her attention to him. "You're smiling again."

"I can't help it when I'm with him."

"Where are you?" he asked, looking past her at the different furnishings.

"Ford's place. I'm moving in here."

"Well, that was fast."

"Too fast?" she asked.

"Does it feel that way?"

She didn't even have to think about it. "Actually, it feels long overdue."

"There's your answer. You have a history. You trust him. He's supportive of your needs."

"He knows I still have a long way to go, but he loves who I am now and encourages me to keep working to get to the person he knows I can be. The person I want to be again."

"PTSD is tricky. Sometimes it's one step forward, two steps back."

"Sometimes it feels like three steps forward, ten back," she complained.

"You experienced that with Tobin's return into your life. You weren't ready to face him."

"He didn't make it easy. In fact, he purposefully made it hard."

"Do you believe his actions were motivated by jealousy?"

"Partly . . ."

"Maybe once he's back on base, back in the routine, absorbed in managing the cargo and people under him, he'll settle back into a normal life. Unless he's assigned overseas again."

Jamie's body jerked with surprise. "What? No." She leaned forward and gripped the edge of the sofa in her hands. Her fingers ached, but she didn't care. Something pushed against her mind, but she fought it back.

"Jamie, what is it?"

"Why would he want to go back?" She rocked back and forth, her stomach aching with the fear and anger she couldn't explain. "He can't go back. It's too dangerous."

"Is that what it is? You're afraid for him?"

"No." She shook her head violently. "He can't go back. Not after what he did."

"Jamie, calm down."

"He can't go back," she shouted.

"Why? What did he do?"

The question stopped her cold. A shiver raced up her spine. "What?"

"You said he can't go back after what he did."

"I meant after what happened. I don't know why he'd want to go back after what happened." The confusion in her mind filtered into her voice.

"That's not what you said, Jamie. What do you think he did?"

"Nothing." She stared at the wall, trying to slow the images racing through her mind. "I don't know."

Dr. Porter frowned, tapping his finger to a folder in front of him. "I received word from command today about the investigation." Dr. Porter leaned in. "Jamie, the bullet recovered from your chest came from an American rifle."

That something in the back of her mind pushed at her again. "So? You know that doesn't mean anything.

One of the militants could have taken it from one of our soldiers. In the heat of battle, they grabbed the nearest weapon."

"That's possible, but I'm more concerned and so is command that they matched the bullet to Tobin's rifle."

"No." She shook her head, tears filling her eyes. A sharp pain pounded in her forehead. "No. It just proves that someone took his rifle from him."

"He didn't say that in his debriefing."

"They probably didn't ask him."

"They did. He said he used his weapon to fight off the militants."

Her stomach pitched and rolled. "He made a mistake."

"Jamie, do something for me." She didn't like the urgent tone in his voice. "Close your eyes." She did. "Take a deep, calming breath." It took several to actually calm her racing heart. "After the explosion, after Tobin put out the fire on your back, what did he do?"

"He carried me to the side of one of the other vehicles and set me down away from the line of fire."

"What did he do then?"

"He fired, covering me, and called in a medivac and backup from the radio in the vehicle." She tilted her head.

"In his debriefing he said he called for help after everyone went down."

Jamie shook her head. "No, that's not right. He called right after the explosion."

"He's next to you. He's firing his weapon. What does he do next?"

Her heart raced again as she fell back into that time. "There are men closing in. Some of our men rush forward to head them off and protect the cargo and each other. Tobin tells me to stay put and runs to join them. I don't want him to go. I don't want him to leave me. My back, it hurts so much."

"How do you get shot if the team is between you and the militants?"

She didn't know. "I'm scared for Catalina. I search for her in the group. I have my rifle and a sidearm. I can help if I have to. My back hurts so bad, but I lie on my stomach under the truck and crawl forward to see if I can pick off some of the gunmen."

"Do you do that?"

Tears flood her eyes. She hadn't frozen. She did what she had to do to protect her friends. "Yes. Yes, I do. I have no choice. I have to save them."

"Yes, Jamie, you have to save them."

"He's there." She reaches out like she can touch him. "The man. He jumps up on the top of the lead vehicle and he's shooting. People are yelling and screaming, they're falling dead. The blood. It's everywhere."

"What do you do?"

I act. "I crawl out from cover and run toward him. I'm screaming for him to stop, but he won't stop."

"Jamie, why do you run from out of cover? Why would you risk your life like that when you need to cover your men?"

"He's killing them," she wails, lost in the scene in her head.

"Jamie, who shoots you?"

She runs to the vehicle and climbs up the side, trying to get to him and stop this madness. The dark man turns to her and for the first time the bright sun catches his face, the maniacal look in his dark eyes sends a bolt of terror through her whole body the second before he fires and the bullets rip through her body. She's falling, and he screams, "Keller!"

For a second she sees the regret and shock in his eyes before her back slams into the ground.

"Jamie, who shot you?" Dr. Porter's urgent voice called her out of the past as she fell into the back of the sofa.

"He yelled my name," she whispered.

Fury roared through her. She stood and went to the gun cabinet Ford placed her gun in when they got back to the house the other day. He'd ordered her to leave it there. When he was out checking cattle, she'd found the key, the clip he'd hidden in the office, the bullets, and put them all together at the bottom of the cabinet. Just in case. Now she put all the pieces together, jammed the fully loaded clip in the gun, grabbed her keys off the hook in the kitchen, and headed out the door with Dr. Porter's raised voice calling her back, barely a whisper above the rage screaming in her mind.

Ford ran out of the bedroom still dripping wet with his jeans on and nothing else when he heard the front door slam and Dr. Porter yelling for Jamie to come back. He picked up the laptop and stared at Dr. Porter on the screen.

"What the hell is going on?"

"Go after her. Tobin lost it during the firefight. He went blind to who he was shooting and killed his own men. He shot Jamie. She remembered what happened. She went after him."

Jamie's truck roared to life outside, the tires tearing up the driveway. Zoey barked and scratched at the door to go after her. He turned to see her out the window and spotted the gun cabinet's open door.

"Shit. She took her gun. I'll just bet she found the clip and bullets I hid from her. I gotta go."

"Call the cops. Get them over there. There's no telling what Tobin will do to keep her quiet. The military has evidence, but without her testimony it's all speculation."

"What do I do if she shoots the bastard and the cops arrest her?"

"I'll do everything I can to help her. She's not in her right mind right now."

"Fuck."

"Go, Ford. Hurry, before she does something she truly can't live with."

Ford tossed the laptop on the couch, ran back to his room, pulled on his boots, grabbed a shirt out of the dresser drawer, and ran for the door, pulling the shirt on over his head as he went. He barely remembered to snatch his keys off the kitchen table before he left, feeling bad for shooing Zoey back in the house and not taking her with him.

He needed to get to Jamie. She'd been through so much. He couldn't imagine how she felt remembering what happened and knowing that a man she called friend had not only killed the people she cared about the most, people who had become her family, but he'd shot her, too.

She'd kill Tobin. Ford needed to stop her before she pulled the trigger.

She'd never be able to live with herself if she murdered her friend.

Whether he deserved it or not.

CHAPTER 32

Tobin's hand shook as he picked up his ringing cell phone and saw the Georgia number. Command calling to give him his orders for when he returned. He hoped. He swiped his finger across the screen to accept the call and tried to clear his anxiety-clogged throat.

"Report to base immediately," Lieutenant Gedetti ordered without even a hello. "Command received new information regarding Sergeant Keller's shooting and they have some questions for you. You are ordered to report for debriefing tomorrow at ten hundred."

The news turned Tobin's stomach and made his thrashing heart pound in his ears. "I'm in Montana, sir. At Sergeant Keller's place, in fact." The last place he should have come, but he loved Jamie and had to take his shot at making her his despite the risk.

"Get on a plane and get back here immediately."

"If I can't make it in time?" He tried to think and plan what he'd say. He could bullshit his way out of this just like he did the first time they debriefed him.

He could still salvage this mess and keep his freedom.

The Army would want to sweep this under the rug. God forbid they admit one of their own was responsible for the deaths of US soldiers. The press would eat them alive and plaster the story all over the news, talking about battle fatigue, PTSD, and the legitimacy of the war. The military had enough bad press. He'd use that to his advantage, because it wasn't his fault. Those bastards attacked them. He'd had no choice but to kill those assholes. He'd gotten caught up in the melee and confusion and need to survive. None of it would have happened if not for those damn insurgents coming after them.

If that didn't save his ass, he'd convince them Jamie's spotty memory and volatile mental state made her an unreliable witness.

"You don't show, you'll be in violation of Article 86. Do not go AWOL. Report to the command office as ordered."

"I'll be there, sir."

"You better be." The lieutenant hung up.

Tobin wanted to chuck his phone against the wall. Instead, he pressed the back of his hand to his forehead, hit himself several times in the head, then swore. He might just be royally fucked.

Only one person could ruin everything. And she just pulled into the driveway.

He refused to go down like this.

Either she took his side, or he took her out.

CHAPTER 33

Jamie ran up the porch steps, the familiar gun heavy in her hand at her side, the gruesome images fresh in her mind along with the unbearable grief and betrayal ripping through her heart. She stopped short when the door opened and Tobin stood in front of her, tall, menacing, and knowing exactly why she'd come armed.

"Your watchdog let you out of the house with that gun?" Tobin sneered and shook his head. "Did he let you keep the bullets this time?"

She narrowed her angry gaze. "You don't want to find out."

His lips tilted in a lopsided grin that held no humor. "We both know you're not going to shoot me."

Jamie pulled down the front of her T-shirt. "We both know you shot me. Not once. Not twice. Three times," she screamed. "How could you even think about going back after what you did?"

"I can't change that or make it right, but if you keep quiet, I can make a difference over there."

"A difference? You killed people."

His eyes narrowed with accusation. "You killed people."

"To save our friends," she shot back. "The very

people you shot and killed in your fever to take down our enemies."

"I didn't know what I was doing," he shouted back at her. "Do you really think I wanted to kill them? Hell no. I couldn't see anything but an enemy that needed to be taken down. I wanted to save you, everyone. Then I saw the bullets ripping through you. You fell away, this look of betrayal and anger in your eyes. You were bleeding on the ground and everything around me came alive as you lay there dying." He put his hands to his head and gripped his hair, frustration and anger ripping a growl from his throat.

"You saved me from that explosion and then you tried to kill me not five minutes later?"

"I didn't mean to do it," he bellowed. "You have to believe that." His eyes pleaded with her to understand. "Those were our friends. They were family. You're the last person I would ever hurt."

"But you did."

His hands fisted at his sides and his mouth drew back in frustration. "Don't you think I've agonized over it since it happened?"

"And still you came here, knowing I wasn't in a good place, lost in the past and the pain. Did you cause all that trouble at Ford's place? Did you try to kill him?"

"I wanted to keep him busy and away from you. If he was out of the way, you'd come back to me, but the fire, I panicked when I saw how close you were getting to the truth with Ford's help, and I wanted to scare him off. I thought he'd walk in, flick the switch, and run out at the first sign of flames. He'd have another problem to deal with and lose the building and equipment. Nothing more. I didn't set up the shovel falling across the door, or anticipate the flames getting so hot so fast." Nothing but a calculated accident that nearly turned deadly.

"If I hadn't saved him, you would have killed him."

Tobin raked his hand over his head. "He made it out." The relief in Tobin's voice didn't soften her any toward him.

"You tried to take him away from me." She didn't understand how he'd shut off his heart and still claimed to want her. "All because you didn't want me to remember."

"No. I didn't want the woman I've loved for five long years to know what I'd done and look at me the way you're looking at me now. I see the hate and the anger and the pain I've caused you and it tears me apart."

"Then do the right thing and turn yourself in. Tell them what you did. If it tears me up this bad grieving for our friends, I can't imagine how you get through the day knowing what you did."

He shrugged. That dismissive jerk of his shoulders sent a bolt of rage through her system. Despite everything he'd said, Tobin was looking out for himself. Nothing and no one else mattered.

"I didn't mean for it to happen, but people do terrible things in the name of war, and we have to live with it."

"Are you seriously justifying what you did?"

"I did my job," he barked.

"Your job was to watch our backs, not shoot us."

"Yeah, well, you got yours." He rubbed the scar on the side of his head. "You nearly bashed my skull in."

"What the hell do you think I want to do right now?"

Yes, bleeding out and breathing what she'd thought were her last breaths, gun in hand, she'd fired, hitting him in the chest and his bulletproof vest. Unable to breathe from the impacts, he'd fallen close to her and tried to grab her but, out of bullets, she'd bashed him in the head with the gun butt and knocked him out. She'd fallen back and waited to die, gasping for air, dying from the burns, bullet wounds, and grief eating her alive.

"What are you going to do?" He took a menacing step toward her.

She gripped the gun tighter in her hand, her index finger pressed to the side but itching to squeeze the trigger.

"I won't let you go back. I won't put others in harm's way. You have to pay for what you've done."

He stood towering over her, trying to intimidate her, and ordered, "Tell them you don't remember. Tell them it was one of the militants. I swear to you, I won't do anything like that again. Hell, ninety-nine percent of the time I'm on base ordering others what to do. That you and I were in that truck, that you were driving and not organizing things back at base, too . . . total fluke."

"A one percent chance that you'll be called on to watch someone's six is too great a risk for me."

"Keller, come on," Tobin pleaded. "Don't do this to me. Don't break my heart again. If I don't have you, the Army is all I have left. Everything I've worked for for the last twelve years will be wasted." The hurt in his words didn't deter her.

"You threw it all away the minute you shot one of your own. And then you tried to burn Ford to death."

"What about you? You shot lover boy. What happens when I tell them you did that? Your future with him goes up in smoke. You keep my secret, I'll keep yours." Desperation tinged his words.

She shook her head, hating that she'd put herself in this position, that what she'd done to Ford might cost her the man she loved and the life she wanted. In the end, she couldn't live with herself if she kept quiet about what Tobin had done and what he might do again if she didn't stop him.

"I won't allow you to go back."

"You'll give up everything?" He bit out the words, not believing she'd really do it.

"For the ones you killed, yes. I owe them that. They descrve that."

Distracted by Ford's truck racing into the drive behind them, she didn't see Tobin come after her until a split second before his hands grabbed the sides of her shoulders, he picked her up, and threw her off the porch steps. She flew through the air just like in her nightmare and landed on her back with a thwack on the hard packed dirt and slid to a stop. The air rushed out of her lungs. She tried to suck in a breath, but Tobin leaped down the steps and landed on her middle, making it impossible to breathe. One hand at her throat choking her, the other making a grab for the gun she tried to raise up and shoot him with. He wrapped his fingers around her wrist, squeezing hard. Pain shot up her arm. He slammed her hand against the ground once, then twice, and the gun fell from her tingling fingers.

She couldn't breathe for the punishing grip he kept at her throat.

"Why couldn't you just forget?" Tears shined in his eyes, highlighting the desperation and betrayal he focused on her.

She kicked her knees into his back and tried to throw him off, twisting her hips, but he was too big and heavy.

"Why couldn't you choose me this once?"

He gripped her hair, picked up her head, and

slammed it back into the ground. Her head bounced. Lights flashed in her eyes. She gagged and scratched the hand at her throat, desperately trying to pry it free.

Ford slammed into Tobin, knocking him off Jamie's stomach and making him release her. The two men fell beside her in a tangle of legs and swinging arms, fists connecting with solid thuds.

Jamie rolled to her side and coughed, sucking in huge gasps of air. She pressed her hand to her throbbing neck, trying to breathe and not puke up her guts.

Ford sent a punishing fist into Tobin's side, making him gasp and bend sideways to defend himself. That only opened up his head for Ford to sink his fist straight into Tobin's jaw. His head snapped sideways and blood spurted out of Tobin's mouth as his teeth gnashed his lip.

Tobin grabbed Ford around the waist, rose up with an insane amount of strength, and slammed Ford into the ground, landing on top of him. Tobin got in a few good punches, but Ford used his legs to shove Tobin back and away and came up swinging, catching Tobin in the eye. Tobin stumbled back on unsteady legs, shaking his head to ward off the dizziness clouding his eyes.

Ford raised his fists, ready and poised to go after Tobin again.

Jamie fired one shot into the ground at Tobin's feet, making him jump back. "Don't move, asshole." Jamie held the gun in front of her pointed right at Tobin's chest.

"Jamie, no!" Ford ordered. "Don't do it."

She didn't look at Ford, but kept her steady gaze on the man who'd betrayed her, their friends, and their country. "You are going to pay for what you've done!"

"Jamie, please, baby, don't do this," Ford pleaded.

Sirens sounded in the distance, closing fast.

Tobin held his hands out to his side. Blood ran down his lip and chin. One eye was nearly swollen shut. His cheek puffed out in a dark red lump. "You either pull that trigger, or I'm out of here. Either way, there is no way in hell I'm letting them put me in a cage for the rest of my life." Tobin kept his hands open, arms wide, and slowly sidestepped toward his car.

She followed his progress keeping the gun trained on him. "I will never forgive you for what you've done."

"I know." His eyes filled with regret and a deep sadness she recognized because she'd seen the same look in the mirror. "I did love you." The words held the goodbye he couldn't bring himself to say, but she heard it anyway because he'd said he "did" love her. Not, *I do love you*.

Tobin ran for his car and jumped inside. He started the engine and tore out of the driveway and sped away. The sirens grew louder. Closer. He didn't have a chance in hell of getting away now. He had to know it.

Ford's big body pressed against her back. He wrapped one arm around her middle, and reached over her and put his hand over hers on the gun she still held in front of her. "Let it go, Jamie."

She wished she could let it all go.

She opened her hand. Ford took the gun from her. Spent, she sagged against him.

Ford tossed the gun in one of the daisy bushes he'd bought her and planted next to the stairs a second before a police cruiser pulled into her driveway. Several others sped by, chasing down Tobin.

"You called the cops." Was that her raspy voice?

"Yes."

"You thought I'd kill him."

"I hoped you wouldn't and they could arrest him for what he did overseas."

"He set the fire. To scare you, get you to back off. He never meant to kill you. But he almost did," she choked out.

Ford swore.

She stared down the road, seeing Tobin even though he was long gone. "Did you see his eyes? He won't be taken alive."

"They'll get him, Jamie."

"I couldn't do it. He knew I couldn't do it."

"You are not the terrible thing." He gave her the words his grandfather had said to her.

The sirens rang out in the distance but didn't soften as if they were getting further away. They had him.

Her phone rang in her pocket. She pulled it out, answering without looking at the screen, knowing exactly who it was.

"Tobin, please, don't do this."

"I'm sorry, Jamie. I wish things could have been different for us. I always knew you loved him, but I thought maybe you'd grow to love me, too. I can't stop thinking about what I did. It plays in my head and all I see is the blood pouring out of you, knowing I'm the one who hurt you. I thought I killed you."

"Show your hands. Get down on the ground." Cops yelled the order over and over.

"Tobin, please," she cried. "Don't do this."

"Goodbye, Keller."

The shots rang out over the phone and in the distance. She flinched as if she'd been struck. Ford held her up as her legs collapsed beneath her and a scream ripped from her aching throat. She dropped her phone. Ford gently lowered her to the ground on her knees. She buried her face in her hands and cried out all her grief and anger and pain. For the friends she'd lost. The pain she'd endured. And yes, for Tobin, the friend who'd betrayed her and others, who hadn't had the strength to face his past.

But she did.

Now she knew the truth. She'd stood up to him. She'd tried to save her friends. She'd given them justice, though she'd never wanted Tobin's death. As many times as she'd killed that dark figure in her nightmares, she'd never wanted this.

CHAPTER 34

Ford held Jamie close. Her wracking sobs tore his heart to pieces. He didn't know exactly what happened, but he knew enough to know she'd never grieved her fallen friends, because she'd needed to know what happened to them so she could let them go with a clear heart. Tobin's betrayal cut deep into her soul. A man she'd trusted, who had saved her life, had also nearly taken it. Her mind had been unable to believe the unbelievable, so the dark man in her nightmares had become a monster she couldn't face. Until she stood before him and called him a murderer and refused to let him get away with it.

"Mr. Kendrick, are you both okay?" the officer asked, approaching slowly.

"What happened to Tobin?" he asked instead of answering because he didn't know if Jamie would ever be okay after this.

"Uh, Michael Tobin refused officers' orders to drop the phone and put his hands up and get on the ground. He reached for something behind his back and officers fired, killing him."

Suicide by cop.

Jamie had been right. Tobin never intended to be

caught. He couldn't face what he'd done, knowing she'd never forgive him and he'd spend the rest of his life behind bars.

Ford crouched behind Jamie. Her tears faded and she sat quietly staring at the ground. He tried to comfort her with soft strokes of his hand over her head and down her neck. She didn't move or acknowledge him, or any of the officers who crowded the yard.

"Mr. Kendrick, we need to ask you some questions. When you called in, you said Mr. Tobin posed a threat to your girlfriend because she remembered that he'd murdered several members of her team. Is that correct?"

"Jamie is ex-military. She returned several months ago after a brutal attack left her severely injured. The military medically discharged her. Tobin shot her and is responsible for the deaths of several of their fellow soldiers. She came here to confront him and let him know that she would not stand by and let him return to the military."

"What happened when she confronted him?"

Ford touched his forehead to the top of Jamie's head and asked, "Did you argue?"

She nodded but didn't say anything.

"When I arrived, Tobin attacked her. He shoved her off the porch and went after her. He choked her." Ford brushed his fingertips lightly over the dark red marks around her neck. Clear evidence that corroborated his story for the cops. "She tried to fight him off. I tackled him and got in a few good shots. We all heard the sirens. He made a run for it. He didn't want to face up to a fire he set at my place, nearly killing me, or what he did here and in the military, which is why he gave your officers no choice but to shoot him."

"There's an ambulance en route. You should take

her to the hospital to get checked out. You, too." The officer pointed with the pen he'd used to take notes to Ford's bruised jaw and the ribs Ford kept his arm braced against to ward off the stinging pain. "Looks like he got a few shots in, too."

Ford pulled up his shirt and stared at the bruising already starting to bloom down his aching side. "I'm fine." He worried more about Jamie, who had gone so still and quiet it unsettled him. He barely felt her breathe beneath his hand.

"I'll take her over to the clinic myself." He didn't know what else to do for her. "Mind getting the truck door?"

Ford scooped Jamie into his arms and picked her right up, hissing out a gasp as his ribs screamed at him. She squirmed in pain, but settled against his chest. "Your back must hurt after that fall you took."

No answer. Nothing. Her eyes remained blank and unfocused on some spot in front of her that she really didn't see. He needed to reach her, but didn't know how.

He set her in the front seat of his truck, grabbed the flannel shirt he'd hung over the seat at some point, and draped it over her to keep her warm, despite the low eighties summer temps. He hoped the trembling in her body would stop once the shock wore off. He hoped she recovered and this quiet distance didn't linger.

She'd endured so much in the last months.

How much could she take and not break?

"We may need to talk to you and her again," the officer said.

Ford closed the passenger door and spoke at a whisper. "She's in no shape to answer questions. She's suffering from PTSD. I don't know if she'll ever be able to talk about this."

He wished Tobin had never come here. He wished she'd never remembered what happened.

He wished he'd never sent her away all those years ago and saved her this pain and trauma.

This was his fault.

Unable to fix the past, he'd be there for her now.

He needed to make some calls, but didn't want Jamie to overhear him. He gave her the space and quiet she needed as he slipped behind the wheel, started the truck, shut off the radio, and drove out past three cop cars. He turned right out of the driveway and didn't have to pass the scene back the other way where officers had stopped Tobin's vehicle and ended his life.

Jamie sat beside him, her face devoid of all expression, her eyes blank as she stared at the road ahead. He wanted to say something, but didn't know what, or even if she'd hear him.

Her hand lay by her thigh on the seat between them. He covered it with his, trying to give her comfort in some small measure. He jolted when she turned her hand and linked her fingers with his, holding tight. He squeezed her hand back and drove with a glint of hope in his heart that in time she would be okay.

CHAPTER 35

Ford waited outside the room he'd walked Jamie into and Bell ordered him out of ten minutes ago. It felt like a lifetime waiting to find out what she thought of Jamie's neck and the state of shock she'd fallen into, with a silence that disturbed him more and more the longer she didn't speak to him.

The door opened next to him and Bell stepped out.

"How is she?"

Bell bit her bottom lip and rubbed her hand over her pregnant belly. "I'm concerned."

"Is she hurt badly? She seems stiff. Sore. But she didn't complain on the way over."

"Did she say anything about what happened?"

"No. She needs time to let it settle and work it out in her mind. She's been through so much, Bell."

"Too much, I'm afraid. I checked out her shoulder. I'd like to get an MRI. She may need surgery. Not right away, but soon. I think I can help her regain some mobility."

"Really, Bell? That would be so great. I know you're an amazing orthopedic surgeon. You fixed Dane's leg after that bull crushed it."

"Don't remind me. I asked her a few questions to see how stable she is after what happened this afternoon."

"And?" Afraid to know, he had to ask, because he needed to understand how badly Jamie's mental state had deteriorated.

"She spoke very little. She's suffered yet another trauma. From what you told me, her friend committed suicide while she listened, knowing exactly what he intended. The violence she's suffered . . . She's in a very fragile state. But she showed signs of hope and a good outlook for the future."

Surprised, he narrowed his eyes on Bell, wondering if she was giving him an overly optimistic answer to bolster his spirits. "What exactly did she say?"

"That she had a really shitty day, but it'll be fine because she gets to go home to the house she shares with you. I take it you two are moving in together."

"Uh, yeah. She said that?"

"Yes. Which leads me to believe that even though she's not really with it at the moment, being with you will make her feel better. So you should go in, hold her hand, keep her calm. Don't push too hard for her to talk or do anything right now. She seems to be in a place where just breathing is enough. I gave her a sedative to help her relax and some pain meds for her back and neck. I'll keep her overnight and we'll reassess in the morning. Because of her background, I'm suggesting we don't leave her alone at all until I see a marked improvement in her mental state."

He didn't like that, but understood Bell's concern. "Give her time. I know she'll pull through this."

"If I really thought she'd hurt herself, I'd call in a psychiatrist. Right now, I'll try to contact her doctor and update him. I'll ask his recommendation."

"Thanks, Bell. Colt and Zac will be here soon."

"Sent for reinforcements, huh?"

"Colt's bringing her a change of clothes and Zoey."

Bell smirked. "Her emotional support dog."

"If anyone needs one, it's her."

"I'll let the front desk know it's okay to let the dog in."

"Thanks, Bell. For everything."

"I'll check back with you both soon. By the way, how are the ribs?"

He couldn't hide the pain or the tilted way he stood to ease the ache. He pulled up his shirt to show off his colorful side. "They hurt like hell, but you should see the other guy." He'd gotten off easy compared to Tobin.

"Broken?"

"I'll get an X-ray later. Right now, I need to be with her."

"I'll send the nurse in with some pain meds and an ice pack."

"Thanks. For everything."

"You said that already. And you're welcome."

He pointed to her belly. "When's the baby due?"

She rubbed her hand over the baby. "Any minute."

His eyes went wide on her huge belly, thinking she meant that she was in labor. "Really?"

She laughed it off. "I've got a couple weeks to go."

"Sadie's not too far behind you then."

"Maybe we'll be attending your wedding soon and you'll get one of these, too." She rubbed the baby bump.

He hoped so. Someday. "First, I need to take care of my girl."

Ford walked into the room, around the bed, sat in the chair next to Jamie, and took her hand. She stared right through him, but her fingers clasped his in a tight grip.

"Hey, Firefly, are you okay?"

"Dr. Bowden drugged me," she whispered, her voice rough and raw.

He hadn't actually expected an answer from her, but he took it as a positive step in the right direction. "She's going to do the same to me in a few minutes."

Jamie leaned up on her arm and looked him up and down. "Why? What's wrong? Are you okay? Are you hurt?"

"Woah, honey, I'm fine. Calm down." He cupped her face as she fell back onto the pillow, tears rolling over her cheeks.

"Why did he do it? Why?" she whispered.

"Aw, honey, he didn't want to hurt you. He wasn't in his right mind."

"Am I ever going to be?"

"You already are. You are so strong. You handled yourself so well today."

One eyebrow shot up. "You mean, I didn't kill him."

"You lost it when you remembered what he did, but by the time you got there and confronted him, you had your head. You saw him as your friend, someone who needed help, not the enemy you needed to destroy."

"I wanted him to pay, but not that way. I never wanted that."

"Of course you didn't. Because you care, honey. I have a feeling that now that you know exactly what happened, you'll find it easier to grieve and heal and put it behind you."

She reached out, grabbed his shirt, pulled him close, and held him tight. "I just want to go home."

"I will take you home as soon as you've had some rest and Bell says you're good to go."

"I'm okay, Ford. I swear it. I can't explain it, but I feel different."

"That heavy pain you've been carrying is finally gone," he guessed.

"Now there's a new one. Everything aches." She buried her face in his neck and sobbed her heart out. For her past. What happened today. The friends she lost, including Tobin.

He shifted up to sit beside her on the bed, lifted her, despite the pain it caused his ribs, and laid her across his lap, wrapped in his arms. He held her through all the tears and the wracking shudders. He held her close when the nurse came in. Jamie flinched and trembled in his arms, but that didn't stop the nurse from strapping the ice pack around his middle. She handed him the pain tabs, which he promptly popped in his mouth, crushed with his teeth to make them dissolve and work faster, then drank the glass of water the nurse handed him.

"Better?" Jamie asked as the nurse left them alone again.

He hugged her close. "Yes."

He didn't let her go until Colt walked in with a bag of clothes for Jamie and Zoey tucked against his chest.

"You okay?" Colt asked him.

"I'm good. Jamie needs some love."

"I've got a bundle of it right here." Colt approached slowly as Jamie looked up from his chest for the first time.

She sat up and held her arms out for Zoey. Colt handed over the pup, but hooked his hand behind Jamie's head and pulled her in for a kiss on her forehead. To Ford's utter surprise, she leaned into Colt's kiss without hesitation.

Colt stared down at Jamie, his hand still at the back of her head. "I don't even want to think how miserable that one," Colt nodded toward Ford, "would be without you again. You okay?"

"I'm getting there. The drugs help."

"Bell's a friend and an outstanding doctor. She'll keep you comfortably numb if that's what you need."

The door opened and Jamie's brother, Zac, walked in with Corey in his arms.

"You guys are what I need," Jamie said, holding her hand out to Zac.

Colt stepped aside and Zac moved in close, taking Jamie's hand and holding it tight. "I seriously think you've taken ten years off my life, sis."

"It's all going to be okay now," she promised.

"I hope so, because this one wants to get to know his aunt."

Jamie leaned in and kissed her nephew's chubby cheek. "I want to get to know him, too. There's a long overdue talk we need to have about where he came from."

A lopsided grin tilted Zac's lips. "You mean Ford hasn't given you the whole birds and bees instructional demonstration?"

Jamie actually laughed and the sound lightened Ford's heart and undid the knots in his stomach.

"He's an expert in the field."

Colt groaned loud and long.

Zac pinched his lips into a sour pout. "Yuck. You're my sister."

"You started it." She rubbed Zoey's belly and patted the bed beside her so Zac would sit Corey next to her and the pup. "Pet nice." Jamie took Corey's hand and showed him how to pet Zoey nice and soft. Corey squealed and smiled, trying to grab fistfuls of Zoey's deep brown fur. "He likes her."

"Maybe I'll get him a puppy. They can grow up together." Zac smiled at his son. "We'll have that talk soon about his mother. Maybe if I can make it make sense to you, one day I can make it make sense to him." Zac brushed his hand over his son's wispy hair.

"You can tell me when I come by to pick up all the stuff I have stored in your shed. I'm moving in with Ford."

"You are?" Zac and Colt said in unison.

"Yes. We're going to be together forever."

Ford clamped his hand on her thigh and smiled down at her. "Yes, we are."

CHAPTER 36

The Fourth of July, one year later . . .

Independence Day. A year ago, Jamie had been fighting day in and day out to survive every second of the day. Now, months after her past and present collided, she barely thought about her time overseas.

She'd had the surgery Dr. Bowden recommended and performed after her maternity leave. It cut the pain considerably and gave Jamie back her full range of motion in her shoulder.

She and Ford had gone to Georgia for her final debriefing with the military about the event that had changed her life and taken all her friends. Including the man responsible. She tried not to think about what Tobin had become. Instead, she thought about the good times they'd shared—Tobin, Catalina, Jo, Pedro, all of them.

Her life had become filled with family. Hers and Ford's.

She and Zac had that talk about Corey and his mother a couple of weeks after she moved in with Ford.

Her heart ached every time she thought about what happened. Poor Zac. She really felt for him. She understood his loss and how much he'd wanted to make it right for his son, for himself, and yes, for Corey's mom, but couldn't.

Pride swelled in her chest even now at how he'd stepped up to be the very best father he could be for Corey.

"I lost you." Dr. Porter drew her back to their conversation.

"Sorry. Just thinking about this time last year and all the changes that have happened."

"You've come a long way. You're happy living on the ranch with Ford."

Not a question. A statement of fact. "It's so much more than that."

"You're in love." Dr. Porter smiled at her.

"Yes. That, too." Her and Ford's relationship had grown stronger every day over the last months. She'd thrown herself into the endless work on the ranch as a means to heal and also to help make Ford's dreams come true. The ranch was thriving. So were they in the home they'd made their own with pictures of them together and with family and friends, things from their past, and other items they'd bought together.

Ford had been right. She needed something more. Focus and a purpose that was bigger than herself. She joined Luna at Rambling Range and helped her with the equine therapy program Luna had set up after inheriting the ranch. She loved working with the children. Helping them heal helped her heal.

She and Ford agreed not to talk about the future, but to live each day knowing that, no matter what, they would always be together. She kind of liked things that way, but hoped to one day marry the man she loved more each day.

"Are you ready to meet Drake?"

"I met his sister, Trinity, yesterday for lunch. She filled me in on what's going on at home. Add that to what you've told me about his PTSD and physical injuries and I'd say he's ten times worse than I was when I got here."

Dr. Porter gave her a cocky smile. "You could have given him a run for his money."

"I will today when I see him at Rambling Range."

"You're sure you're up to this?"

She cocked her head, confused. He'd asked her to do this, so why the question? "You don't think so?"

"I wouldn't have asked for your help if I didn't think you could handle him. He needs someone who's been there."

"Been there, done that, got the scars to go with it."

"Be careful, Jamie. His anger is a simmering volcano just waiting to erupt."

"That's why I'm taking the big guns with me."

"Ford," Dr. Porter guessed.

"And his brothers will be there. Fourth of July family barbeque. A nice ruse to get Drake there, plus it's time with the family. I can't wait to see Sadie and Rory's little boy, John, again." Rory named his son after their father. Ford and Colt teared up when they found out. Another good day, rushing down to the hospital to be with the family to welcome the next generation of Kendricks.

"Luna's pregnant, too, you said."

"She is. Colt is over the moon about being a dad."

"What about Ford? Is he looking forward to being a dad one day?"

"He is. Man, you should see him with his nephew." She smiled so wide her cheeks ached. "And with my nephew, Corey. He's so great with them, but we haven't talked about kids in a long time. We're taking our time, enjoying where we are right now."

"You really do look radiant, Jamie. I'm happy for you."

"Thanks. It feels like it was really hard to get here, but I'm so glad I did."

"Maybe you can tell Drake that and get him to believe it."

"I'll try. I have to go, or I'll be late. I've got to rein in Ford from whatever project he's working on now."

"Go get him," Dr. Porter said with a wink.

She signed off and smiled to herself. She enjoyed her every other week chats with Dr. Porter. She didn't really need the therapy anymore, but checking in with him forced her to look at her life in that moment and take stock of all the good she had in her life. Their sessions used to be all about the terrible things that happened in her life. Now here she was, about to embark on a whole new chapter. Helping a fellow soldier through a difficult time. She knew it wouldn't be easy. She hadn't been easy. But she looked forward to the challenge and connecting with someone who was in the same dark place she'd clawed her way out of this last year to true happiness.

She wished Tobin had given her a chance to share with him how she felt about what he'd done. She wished he'd given her a chance to forgive him. And she had, because she made up her mind crying in Ford's arms in the hospital that she wouldn't spend another day carrying around that kind of guilt, grief, and anger.

Jamie closed the laptop on the wide plank coffee table she'd brought back with her from her apartment

in Georgia. It complemented Ford's dark brown leather
sofa and chair. She smiled up at the photo on the mantel
Luna had taken of them horseback riding. She loved
seeing Ford atop a horse with his dark brown cowboy
hat drawn low over his brow. Sexy. Dangerous looking,
but really he was just her tough guy with a huge heart.

And a lot of love for her.

She went looking for him, walking out the front
door with Zoey on her trail, pulling it closed behind
her, and stopping in her tracks on the front porch when
she spotted the single red rose and a sticky note on the
floor. She picked both up and read the note.

*Firefly, come to our spot at the river. I'm waiting
for you. Love, Ford*

Ford had left her horse, Dusty, tied to the gate. Her
stomach fluttered with a thousand butterflies.

What are you up to?

She couldn't wait to find out and flew down the
steps, down the path, and to the pasture gate. She
untied Dusty and mounted, clasping the rose between
her teeth as she rode across the field, laughing with
excitement. Zoey ran after them.

He'd had an odd expression the last few days when
he looked at her. Like he had a secret. She even caught
glimpses of anticipation, like he couldn't wait to share
something with her. She didn't know exactly what he
had planned, but she hoped it was what she'd thought
and hoped for since she fell in love with him all those
years ago.

Ford's horse stood tied to a tree ahead. She reined
in and tied Dusty next to his buddy and followed the

path through the trees, picking up the red roses strewn along the way, guiding her to their favorite spot and Ford. By the time she cleared the trees at the river's edge she held a dozen red roses, and she smiled at the man who'd left them for her. Zoey rushed to him to say hello, then ran after a squirrel. Ford stood with his back to the water, his shoulder propped against a huge tree that overhung the rippling river, with a blanket and picnic basket in front of him.

She stopped on the other side of the blanket facing him and buried her nose in the fragrant blooms. She looked back up at him, smiling and sighing out her pleasure.

"A year ago today you came back into my life. The haunted look in your eyes is gone. The smile that seemed so hard for you to make comes so easy now."

"I'm happy."

"You shine, Firefly. You light up my life. I am so glad we found our way back to each other. I fell in love with you so long ago, I don't remember a time I didn't love you. I will love you for the rest of my life." Ford dropped down on one knee and held his hand out to her.

She covered her mouth with her fingertips, and gasped, "Ford." Tears flooded her eyes, but she managed to blink them back and walk to him and take his hand.

"You are the strongest, bravest, toughest person I've ever met. But what I love most about you is that you never give up on yourself, on me, on the love we share. I will spend the rest of my life making sure you never have a reason to give up on us. We may not have much yet . . ."

"We have everything," she choked out past the tears clogging her throat.

"I do, if I have you. Be my wife. We'll make babies and a life together on our ranch." He pulled a ring from his pocket and held it up to her. She didn't even look at it, completely lost in the love in his eyes. "Marry me, Jamie."

Of course he didn't ask, but pushed for her to give him the answer he wanted.

"Yes," she gasped out and fell into his arms.

He crushed her to his chest, kissed her again and again, the roses smashed between them, their sweet scent filling the air.

She fell to her back, bringing him down with her. He shoved the roses out from between them without breaking the searing kiss they shared. His hand slipped beneath her shirt and skimmed up her side, cupping her breast. He swept his thumb over the peaked tip and she sighed into his mouth, then swept her tongue along his.

In a frenzy to be skin to skin, their clothes went flying in all directions. They lost themselves in each other and the deep kisses and soft caresses that started off sweet and turned urgent and demanding.

Ford lay in her arms, broke their kiss, and stared down at her, infinite love in his eyes. "Did you mean it? Yes . . . to everything?"

She knew exactly what he asked. "Yes."

He thrust into her, filling her, no barrier between them. Heat and need rushed through her in a wave. She gripped Ford's shoulder and pulled him in for another deep kiss. They made love, next to the singing river, with the birds chirping in the trees among the wind-swept rustling leaves. She lost herself in him and the love they shared. It was magical. It was perfect. Like their life had become.

Jamie lay content at Ford's side, her head resting

on his shoulder and her hand over his racing heart. A soft smile touched her lips. He played with her shoulder length golden-red hair, letting the silky strands slip through his fingers. She'd grown it out over the last many months. She'd changed again on him. She wasn't the girl he fell in love with long ago. She wasn't the Jamie who'd come back from the war. The woman beside him was a combination of them, plus a whole lot of who he'd always thought she'd be. He'd waited to ask her to marry him even after she moved in, because he was waiting for that light he'd seen in her to come back to life. It hadn't been easy, but it had been worth the wait to see her this happy again.

He kissed her forehead and she nuzzled her cheek into his chest and hugged him with her body wrapped up close to his.

He pulled the diamond ring from his pinky. He'd shoved it on there when he couldn't wait to make love to her after she agreed to be his wife. He couldn't wait. For all of it, including the baby they might have just made.

He slipped the diamond ring on her finger and laid her hand back on his chest. Her head came up and her eyes went wide at the brilliantly sparkling diamond solitaire.

"You already have my heart, Firefly, but I thought you might like this, too."

"Ford, it's beautiful. It's too much."

"It's far less than how much I love you."

Her gaze held his. "I love you, too. Without you . . ." She shook her head, unable to put into words all she felt.

"You already said it, Firefly. We have everything." He leaned up, hooked his hand behind her neck, and kissed her softly.

His phone alarm went off. He kissed her one last time and pressed his forehead to hers and stared into her vibrant green eyes. "Time to go. You've got someone who needs your help, then we'll barbeque and celebrate the Fourth under the stars and share our engagement with the family."

"You planned the barbeque so we could tell them."

"Busted. Plus, it'll give you a chance to show Drake that you can find real and true happiness after you find your way out of the dark."

The easy smile spread across her lips. "I did."

CHAPTER 37

Ford drove into Rambling Range just behind another truck and trailer. Jamie sat beside him, her face turned to the window and the sunlight.

"Did I do okay on your surprise proposal?"

She turned her gaze and pretty smile to him. "It was beautiful. Perfect. Though most of the roses didn't survive getting crushed between us, or under us when we made love." A blush rose up from her neck to her sun-kissed cheeks.

"You loved it."

Her wicked grin made him smile, too. "I always do."

"We never opened the champagne I brought."

"I liked the way we celebrated better."

Ford parked the truck near the house. "Grandpa looks cozy." He cocked his chin toward Grandpa Sammy sitting in one of the porch rockers with Ruth beside him, holding his hand, and Chip, the golden retriever Ford had gotten him, at his feet. The old coot hadn't left the hospital without getting the volunteer's number. They'd been dating for quite some time. According to Sadie and Rory, Ruth spent more nights at the ranch than not. His grandfather might be old, but the old man wasn't dead.

"What are you smiling about?" Jamie touched her fingertips to his jaw.

"He looks happy."

"Wait until he finds out we're getting married. He'll finally have all his grandsons living in wedded bliss."

"He'll be happy, but he won't be satisfied until he gets a grandbaby from me."

Jamie put her hand over her belly. "We'll have to wait and see."

Ford rubbed his hand over hers. "I was nervous about asking you for so much all at once, but I'm really excited about getting married and having a baby of our own."

"Me, too. It'll be nice to give Corey and John and Luna's baby a cousin to play with, and of course a new addition to your growing family."

"Speaking of, you better get a move on. Luna's waddling over to greet the McGraths."

Jamie smacked his shoulder for teasing his sister-in-law. "I'm telling her you said that and Colt is going to kick your ass."

"He can try."

They laughed together as they got out of the truck. Ford waved to Grandpa Sammy and Ruth and headed for the group standing by the arena with Luna. Before they got too close, Jamie pulled him to a stop and handed him back her ring.

"Tuck that in your pocket again. I don't want to lose it. Plus, I want to keep it a surprise for tonight when we tell everyone."

Jamie gave him a quick kiss then rushed over to meet Trinity McGrath. Trinity gave her a quick hug. They'd become fast friends at their lunch yesterday, where they'd discussed the somber man leaning against the big black Ford truck with his arms crossed over his wide chest, his cane propped against his thigh.

"Thank you for doing this. He's pissed we made him come today. He thinks we're selling his favorite horse. He's got no idea why we're really here."

"Got it. Step back and give us some space when I come back. I need to get something." Jamie ran over to Colt, who waited for her next to the arena holding the ten-week-old Australian shepherd. Like her, Drake had forsaken all his friends and barely tolerated his siblings. He needed a friend. She had one that required his constant attention and would give him the unconditional love he desperately needed. It had worked for her. Zoey had helped save her life. She hoped the puppy helped Drake, too.

She took the pup and kissed Colt's cheek hello. "Thanks."

"You've got this," Colt encouraged.

When Dr. Porter had asked for her help, she hadn't known what she could offer, but as she thought about the things that got through all the haze in her mind, she formed a plan to help Drake. She could add the one thing that might have helped her: talking to someone who'd been there, done that, and had the scars to prove it.

Declan and Tate McGrath unloaded Drake's favorite horse and saddled him. He stood waiting, tied to the fence. Drake eyed her coming his way, then turned so she only saw the side of his face that hadn't been sliced open by shrapnel and stitched back together. Yeah, she got that. She'd tried to hide her scars for a long time. They still bothered her sometimes when people stared, but mostly because she didn't want to talk about where they'd come from. Drake didn't want to talk at all. In fact, he spent most of his sessions with Dr. Porter in complete silence. But he kept every appointment. Like Ford had once told her, she'd gotten lost in that dark place, but she hadn't lost all hope because she'd kept all those appointments.

All she could do was hand Drake a lifeline and hope he grabbed on. She had the strength to hold on and pull him out, thanks to the hard work she'd put in to save herself. Thanks to Ford's love and support.

She walked up to Drake and shoved the puppy into his chest. "Here. Hold this." She didn't wait for a reply. He instinctively grabbed the dog, so she let go and walked over to Luna and gave her a hug. "Are we all set?"

"Everything you requested." Luna leaned in to Jamie's ear. "Good luck."

Jamie turned back to Drake. "You need to think of a name for him."

"Why?"

"Because he doesn't have one." She turned away again and held her hand out to Declan. "It's nice to meet you. Your sister talks about you guys like you're a pack of wolves."

Declan shook her hand and nodded. "That's about right. Wild and fiercely loyal to the pack." Declan's gaze darted to Drake and back to her.

"I'm Tate." He shook her hand. "You sure you're up for this?"

"There's no way you're selling Thor to her," Drake snapped. "She can't handle him."

Jamie hid a smile. "Did you think of a name for your dog yet?"

"He's not my dog."

"Yes, he is, and he needs a name."

"Who the hell are you to tell me what's mine and what I need to do?"

Jamie walked up to him and stood two feet away, her gaze locked with his menacing one. She held out her hand. "Sergeant Jamie Keller. US Army, recently medically discharged. Dr. Porter asked me to meet you. I'm your new best friend."

He did not take her hand. "The hell you are. I'm out of here." He brushed past her, using his cane to support his injured leg, and headed back to the truck his family now blocked. All three of them stood with their arms crossed, their backs against the side, blocking the doors. "You've got to be fucking kidding me. You guys set this up?"

Trinity closed the distance to Drake and put her hand on his arm. He jerked away, upsetting the puppy in his arms. He settled the pup with a scratch to the belly and held him closer without even thinking about it.

Jamie wanted to smile in triumph.

"Please, Drake. Talk to her. She was a soldier. She knows what you're going through."

"No one knows what I'm going through," he barked. The puppy yapped at Trinity in his defense. Drake glanced down at the dog and frowned.

"You and I are going to go for a ride and talk about it," Jamie ordered, hoping he responded to something familiar.

He turned to her and shoved the dog against her chest. Unlike him, she didn't make a grab for the dog and kept her hands at her sides.

"Take it back."

"If you drop that puppy, I will deck you. If you don't get your hand off my breasts, he," she cocked her head toward Ford, who moved in beside her, "is going to fuck you up. Now, you may want a good fight, but you're in no condition to take him on. I know it. He knows it, but doesn't care because you're touching me. And you know it."

Drake pulled the dog back and glared at her even harder, but didn't once acknowledge Ford, who moved to stand with Drake's brothers.

"Listen, Drake, I'm not here to make your life harder than it already is. I'm here because Dr. Porter knows my story. He knows yours. He thought maybe I could help you because I know what it feels like to hold a gun and think, 'I can make it all go away.' I have been there. And now I'm here. I can help you get here. All I'm asking is that you go for a ride with me and give me a chance. What do you have to lose? If nothing else, do it for your family."

Jamie wasn't intimidated by the feral look on Drake's face. She'd been that angry and disillusioned once. Twice. A lot.

"Look, you're here."

"I didn't have a choice." He cocked his head toward his sister and two brothers.

One of Luna's best students ran up to her side. "This is Billy. He's my helper."

Drake stared down with ominous eyes at Billy's wide grin and excited eyes.

"You're really big." Billy's eyes filled with awe.

At six-two and about two-twenty, the guy rippled with muscles. The scars on his face and neck made him look dangerous and mean, but they didn't intimidate Billy.

"You're a runt," Drake snapped, obviously aggravated he'd been dragged here.

"I'll get bigger." Billy's positive attitude made Drake glare even harder at the little boy.

"What the hell am I doing here with a kid and you and a puppy?"

"Therapy," Billy answered. "It sounds bad, but it's not. Jamie is really good at it."

Drake eyed her. "Really? You're a shrink, too?"

"No. This is an equine therapy program."

"I don't want to talk and I can't ride." The bitterness in his words tore at Jamie's heart, but she got it.

"I admit it won't be easy, but you can do it."

"No, I can't."

"I couldn't do lots of things after I got hurt, but now I can. It takes time. And a lot of hard work that hurts sometimes." Billy smiled up at Drake, trying so hard to get Drake to like him.

"How would you know, kid?"

Billy looked up at her. "He thinks I'm normal."

"Well, he can't see your scars."

"His are all over his face." Billy pointed out the obvious.

"They don't bother me, kid."

Jamie wanted to cry foul, because they bothered Drake a lot. He did everything but turn his back to keep them from seeing the healing gashes.

"It's the ones on my leg and back that have left me broken."

"Damaged isn't broken. Damage can be fixed." Billy repeated the phrase she lived by and taught the people who came here. It was a lesson that took time to learn when you were in a bad place. Drake was in a very bad place.

"You don't know anything, kid."

"Can I show him?" Billy asked her.

"He does seem to think he's the only one with scars."

"That tiny thing on your face," he nodded to the

slash mark across her chin and jaw, "is nothing compared to what happened to me." Drake traced the wide gash down the left side of his face.

Billy pulled his arm out of his sleeve and showed Drake the scars over his shoulder and down the back of his upper arm. "See? I got some, too. I couldn't use my arm at all when I started coming here. But I did my physical therapy and now I can raise my arm and close my hand into a fist." Billy showed Drake with a triumphant smile on his face.

"That's really great, kid." Drake softened his voice to match the words, reluctantly praising the boy.

"Billy got that in the car crash that killed his parents."

Drake swore under his breath and sighed heavily. "Tough break, buddy."

"Yeah. I was sad for a long time."

Drake nodded, most likely knowing exactly how Billy felt during that dark time in his life.

"Billy, give me a minute."

Billy scurried off to join Luna with another little boy petting one of the horses.

"I got this," she traced the scar along her jaw, "from flying shrapnel after an RPG hit my truck and exploded. My friend saved me from nearly burning to death." She turned and pulled her shirt up to show the scars all over her back and neck. She pulled her shirt down, then turned back to him. "Then that same man I called friend, shot me here." She pulled the front of her shirt up to show him the scar on her side. "And here." She showed him the one on her chest. "And here." She pointed to her jean-covered thigh.

"Someone should shoot his ass dead."

"Someone did."

Drake nodded. "Your friend got what he deserved."

He had, but it didn't make it any easier.

"What is the point of all this show-and-tell?"

"You are not the only one bad things happened to over there. Bad things happen here, too."

"You have no idea what happened to me over there."

"You're right. But I'm a soldier just like you, and I can relate. I'm willing to listen."

"I told you I don't want to talk about it."

"I didn't want to talk about what happened to me either. I wanted to forget. The harder I tried to forget, the worse things got for me. But you know what? I'm a fighter. You're a fighter, too."

"Is this where you tell me that everything is going to be all right?" The cynicism in his voice grated, but she kept her patience.

She pointed to Grandpa Sammy rocking on the porch with Ruth. "Do you see that man, there?"

"I'm not blind."

"He's a vet. Like you. Like me. When I was in a very dark place, he said something to me that I think you need to hear. You have seen terrible things. You have done terrible things. Terrible things have been done to you. But you are not the terrible thing." She gave him a moment to absorb her words. "So get your ass up on that horse. We're going for a ride, and we are going to talk."

"That's what you think."

"That's what I know, because I was in the exact same place a year ago that you're in right now. I know how dark those bad days are and how fleeting the good ones seem if they even happen at all. I also know what it feels like to wake up one day and realize I have so much to live for, and I want to live." She cocked her head toward his siblings. "That's a lot to live for, a hell of a lot more than I had when I came home. They want you to be well. Deep down, you want to be better. So let's go. Unless you want to be shown up by a nine-year-old."

Billy was up on his horse, riding around the corral next to them.

Drake didn't move to mount the huge horse beside him. He stared off into the distance, anger and regret and fear in his eyes.

"It takes a hell of a lot of strength to ask for help," she coaxed.

"Can I get a leg up?" He bit the words out through the teeth he grinded. Asking for help was obviously not in his repertoire.

Without a word, she waved Trinity over to take the puppy. Jamie dropped into a lunge, letting him put his foot on her thigh, much lower than the stirrup he couldn't reach with his foot with the injuries to his hip and leg. She grabbed hold of his ankle and calf to stabilize him. He dropped his cane, grabbed the pommel and the saddle, and hoisted himself up, swinging his other leg over the saddle as she lifted him by his leg. The grimace on his face and a muffled curse and groan of pain told her how much it hurt him to move.

He settled into the saddle and stuffed his feet into the stirrups.

"How's it feel?"

It took a second for him to answer through the pain he had to fight to control. "Like visiting an old friend."

"Get used to it. You and I are going to spend a lot of time together."

"You're very sure of yourself."

"For a while I wasn't, but I had a tough-lovin' cowboy to set me straight. You have me." She gave him a sugary sweet smile to annoy him.

"Really?" His eyebrow shot up.

"You really want to take him on?" She nodded toward Ford, who touched his hat and smiled at her.

"He's definitely the possessive kind."

"No, he's the 'don't touch my future wife' kind."

Despite the sadness, hurt, anger, and regret in his eyes, he mumbled, "Congrats."

"Thanks, you're the first to know." She smiled up at him again. "See? We're sharing already."

Drake grunted and shook his head. "You got lucky." He was referring to her finding Ford.

"Yes, I did. Grandpa Sammy got lucky and found someone special while he was in the hospital. If you stopped snarling at all the pretty nurses and physical therapists your sister told me flirt with you at the rehab center, you might get lucky, too."

"Look at me. That's never going to happen."

"I thought the same thing. But that cowboy over there doesn't see my scars. He sees me. Sounds like you've got a lot of people who see past the scars to who you really are, and the guy they remember you used to be."

"He's dead."

"He's still a part of who you are now. You can get back to being the best of him and the best of the you, you are now."

"Still won't change the fact that when she sees what happened to me, she'll run screaming for the hills."

"She?"

Drake raised his gaze to the sky. "Fuck me. Don't go there."

Ford led a horse over to her. She took the reins and mounted. "That's not love, Drake."

"That's not in the cards. I just want to be left alone."

"Oh God, how many times did I hear that?" Ford complained.

"I know. He sounds just like me, doesn't he?" Jamie leaned down from her horse and kissed Ford.

"He's seen your back. Keep your clothes on now," Ford ordered.

"I will. You can take them off me again later."

Ford winked. "Yes, ma'am."

"We're out of here." Jamie kicked her mount to walk down the lane.

Drake followed her, mostly because his horse wanted to follow her mare. Billy waved from inside the arena where he worked with Luna and her brother, Trent.

"I'm not taking that dog home," Drake called to her.

"Yes you are."

Jamie stood beside Ford on the steps at the back of the house overlooking the patio and all the tables that had been set up for the barbeque. Ford whistled over the crowd to get everyone's attention. They all turned to him expectantly. "A year ago today, my one and only wish came true and Jamie came back into my life. We got a rare second chance. Today, Jamie agreed to marry me and be my wife."

Ford kissed Jamie as their family and friends cheered them on.

He turned to his grandfather. "You got what you wanted. All three of your grandsons will be happily married. I'm working on your third great-grandbaby, but it may take some practice before we get it done."

Everyone cheered again. Several rude comments came from his brothers. Jamie blushed beside him.

Grandpa Sammy stood and held Ruth's hand in his.

"You're going to have to wait your turn, Ford. I'm old and not inclined to wait for the things I want, so Ruth and I have decided to get married next month in a small ceremony at the ranch. Love is too precious to waste, too good to let go, and too wonderful not to enjoy."

"Hear, hear," Ford said, lifting his glass in a toast with everyone else. He clinked his glass with Jamie's and hugged her close. He had her. They had each other. They had love. They'd never let go and would spend the rest of their lives enjoying it.

EPILOGUE

Ford hooked his finger in his shirt collar and tugged, uncomfortable in the monkey suit, but happy to wear the black tux for Jamie on their big day. He'd thought she'd take months to plan the wedding, despite her many assurances that all she wanted was a simple ceremony and luncheon with their family and friends. He should have taken her at her word. Between her, Sadie, Luna, and Grandpa Sammy's new bride, Ruth, they'd put everything together in just short of two months.

He didn't care about the details. He just wanted his bride. But he had to admit the red and white flower arrangements and dark-blue-covered tables stacked with white dishes and crystal glasses looked amazing. Colt and Luna's backyard garden shaded by huge trees and blooming with flowers in every color turned out to be the perfect spot to tie the knot.

This reminded him so much of Colt and Luna's wedding last year. They were happy, living their lives on the ranch and expecting a baby. Ford wanted the same for himself and Jamie. In a few minutes, she'd be his wife. Someday, he hoped sooner rather than later, their child would play with his two older cousins. He really couldn't wait.

He tugged his collar again.

Rory stood behind him and knocked Ford in the ribs with his elbow. "She's here."

Ford stared, transfixed by the vision in white standing too damn far away. He wanted her here, next to him, with him for the rest of his life.

Hurry up, his heart called out. *God, I love her.*

Beautiful in the sleeveless gown with the wide satin ribbon bow tied just beneath her breasts, the long streamers dangling down to her feet. She wore her hair in soft waves with a crystal headband sparkling in the dappled sunlight. Her face glowed with happiness.

He took her all in, his beautiful bride, but nothing made her more appealing to him than her core of strength and perseverance. She truly was a remarkable woman. And she was his.

Jamie stood at the end of the aisle with her arm tucked through Zac's, staring at the man she loved. Ford stood next to his brothers. Colt and Rory's wives, and her best friends, Sadie and Luna, stood opposite the men as her matrons of honor. She couldn't believe this day had finally come. She'd waited so long, been through so much, and in the end, the fight to get here had been tough, but she'd made it.

"Ready?" Zac asked, patting her hand on his arm.

She looked up at him with a smile that came so easy now. "I can't believe it's finally here."

The indulgent smile he gave her went right to her heart. "If anyone deserves to be happy, sis, it's you."

"Let's do this." Jamie took the first step toward her bright future with Ford with a clear mind and heart. She had a purpose in her life that filled her up and made her happy each and every day. She loved Ford, the ranch they were building together, and the work she did with Luna and the children at the equine therapy program. Working with Drake allowed her to give back to a fellow vet. Helping him heal helped her heal, too. But nothing helped her more than Ford's love.

Jamie stopped in front of Ford.

Zac leaned down and kissed her on the forehead. He took her hand and placed it in Ford's outstretched one. "Take care of her."

"Always," Ford said with a promise in the word that touched Jamie's heart.

Zac went to sit next to her mother and stepdad. Although Sadie and Luna had helped her get ready for today, she'd still invited her mother because she didn't want to look back on this day and feel like something was missing. She and her mother would never be close, not even friends, but Jamie still held hope that one day things would be different. Today, she hoped to get through the ceremony and reception without wanting to kill her mother. She had high hopes, because Ford had assigned Rory to keep her mother away from her for the day.

"We are gathered here today to join these two in matrimony," the minister began.

Ford squeezed her hand. She glanced over at him and caught the intense look of love in his eyes. She turned from the minister as he spoke of love and second chances and stepped closer to Ford and held his gaze, lost in the emotion she saw in the hazel depths.

She repeated the vows and held back tears when Ford gave them back to her, their gazes still locked, anticipation fluttering in her heart. Her hand shook when he slipped the gorgeous gold band with daisies stamped side by side around the ring, tiny diamonds at their center, on her finger.

"Ford, it's beautiful."

"You said they're happy flowers. Every time you look at it, I want you to be happy."

"Every day I'm with you, I'm happy."

Ford brought her hand to his lips and kissed the ring in place.

"Hey now, son, you just wait for the 'I do's' to be done," Grandpa Sammy teased, bouncing his great-grandson, John, on his lap.

Jamie winked at the man who never ceased to show her what it felt like to have a real father. If possible, he'd become even happier and more boisterous after marrying Ruth last month. They suited each other perfectly. Sammy had been looking out for his grandsons alone a long time. The whole family was so glad he had someone special to look after him now.

Jamie took the ring from Luna and turned back to Ford. She slipped the ring on his big hand, repeated the minister's words, then brought his hand to her lips and kissed the ring in place like he'd done for her. Everyone laughed, including Ford.

This was how life should be, filled with joy and laughter and friends and family and love.

The moment finally came.

"I pronounce you husband and wife. You may *now* kiss your bride."

Jamie didn't wait for the minister to finish the words. She grabbed Ford's tie and pulled him down and in for a searing kiss. A cheer went up from their gathered family and friends.

Ford wrapped her in his arms and held her close, taking over the kiss and pouring all his love into the simple moment. His hand came up to cup her face. He broke the soft kiss and stared into her eyes. "I love you, Mrs. Kendrick."

"I've been waiting a long time to hear you call me that."

"I've been waiting a long time for you to be my wife."

The minister patted Ford and her on the back. "I present Mr. and Mrs. Kendrick."

Another round of cheers went up. Ford got swallowed in bear hugs from both Rory and Colt. Sadie and Luna hugged her in turn.

Her mother came to her and smiled. "You make a beautiful bride, Jamie. I hope you'll be happy."

Words she never thought she'd hear from her mother. Jamie gave in and hugged her mother close. "I am happy, Mom. And I'm happy with Ford." It had taken a while, but she'd found her footing and hiked her way up to the point where she was truly happy with who she was and the life she'd made for herself and with Ford.

She released her mother and walked into Zac's open arm. The other held her nephew Corey. "Proud of you, sis. Be happy."

"I want you to be happy, too." She leaned back, then gave Corey a tickle, smiling even as she held back her secret.

"You're glowing," Grandpa Sammy said, taking her into his arms.

She hugged him, then stepped back and right into Ford's chest. He wrapped his arm around her middle. "Like Luna?" she asked Sammy, hinting to the secret ready to burst from her lips.

The wide smile on his face dimmed. Ruth tapped his chest and stared up at him with a bright smile on her face. Sammy finally got it.

So did Ford. "Are you saying . . ."

She directed her answer to Sammy. "You're three for three on all fronts. Your grandsons are all happily married. You'll have your three great-grandbabies sometime in the next seven months."

Sammy let out a loud whoop.

Ford spun her around and kissed her again. He pressed his forehead to hers and stared into her eyes, his glassed over with sheer happiness. "You mean it?"

"You asked me to marry you and gave me a baby all at the same time. When you set your mind to something, you really get it done."

That made him laugh. "I love you."

"I love you, too."

Ford kissed her softly one more time. "Now we really do have everything."

ACKNOWLEDGMENTS

I can't believe this is the sixth book in the Montana Men series and the last of the Kendrick brothers. There is so much more to come, but I wanted to take a moment to thank some of the people who work so hard behind the scenes for me.

Thank you to my amazingly talented and kind editor, Amanda Bergeron. Without your hard work, insights, fantastic suggestions, and the way you stick with me through *every* round of edits this book and all the others would never be the grand stories I imagine in my mind and try so hard to put on paper. I love that, like me, you're never satisfied until it's just right. None of this is possible without you, my friend.

Thank you to the Avon team, including Caroline Perny, Shawn Nicholls, Elle Keck, the sales team, marketing, art, and all the amazing talent I'm lucky enough to have in my corner.

My outstanding agent, Suzie Townsend, thank you for always having my back, listening to all my concerns and gripes, giving me perspective, a pat on the back, a nudge in the right direction, what I need when I need it. Most of all thanks for your constant support, eye on the future, and being excited about all the many projects and ideas I have and want to do *right now*. I'm working on patience. You are the best!

Keep reading for a sneak peek at the first in an amazing new series, Montana Heat, from Jennifer Ryan

ESCAPE TO HOPE RANCH

on sale August 29, 2017 . . .

And don't miss the Montana Heat prequel novella

HER DANGEROUS PROTECTOR

on sale June 20, 2017.

CHAPTER 1

Welcome to Celebrity Centerfold. I'm your host Sharon Waters. Tonight, we delve into the life, career, and mysterious disappearance of Oscar-winning actress Ashley Swan.

Trigger sat in his recliner, drinking a beer, staring at the striking photo of Ashley on the TV screen and didn't care one bit about why some spoiled, rich, self-important movie star ditched her extravagant life. He rubbed his hand over his aching shoulder and the scar on his chest where he'd been shot. What did he care about some overpaid actress when two months ago he'd killed an innocent woman and last month he'd narrowly avoided killing his brother's girlfriend by a mere inch, then killed the man who tried to kill his brother?

Next week marks the one-year anniversary of the last confirmed sighting of the mega movie star when she appeared on the After Midnight Show *with Brice Mooney. The two shared an evident affection for each other that drew fans and jacked up ratings whenever she appeared on Mooney's show, but nothing compared to her appearance on his final show before he retired. Audience members, show producers, and Mooney himself said she was happy that night and enjoyed Mooney's celebration before he took his final bow and retired to his secluded ranch in Montana.*

Clips of Ashley Swan and Brice Mooney laughing together as she sat in the chair next to his desk during her appearances on the shows played on the screen. Ashley Swan flirted with coy smiles and sultry looks as Brice Mooney's adoration spilled out in his flirtatious comments and suggestive jokes. Ashley played along with the much older man, striking the perfect balance between shy modesty at his praise over one performance or another, and joking away Brice's obvious infatuation and comments about her exceptional beauty with outrageous flirtations she overplayed for the live and TV audience.

Ashley Swan has not been seen since she left the after-party that night. Rumors have circulated from inside sources who claim Ashley complained for months leading up to her disappearance about her nonstop work schedule, the pressure to get the next Oscar, the paparazzi dogging her heels everywhere she went, and tabloid stories about the many men she dated.

With an open missing persons case with no evidence of foul play or her death, no ransom demands, and all reports claiming she was unhappy living her life in the public eye, many believe she simply walked away from it all. What would make her turn her back on fame and give up her lucrative career? The pressure? Drugs? A secret lover who swept her off her feet and took her away from the bright lights of sin city to live a quieter, peaceful life in seclusion?

Where has she been hiding this past year?

The bigger question remains: Why hasn't anyone seen her?

Did she really walk away from it all without a word to her publicist, agent, manager, the studio, or even her hairdresser? Or did something darker claim her and we'll never know?

Trigger shut off the TV and stared out the windows to the darkening evening sky, trying not to think of all the horrors that could have befallen her. Lost in his suffocating guilt, heavy grief, and living with his nightmares, old and new, every second of the day, he'd locked himself away on his secluded property, hoping to find some peace. God, he hoped he didn't have to shoot anyone this month.

CHAPTER 2

Ashley's arms ached, her fingers tingled as the silk straps tied around her wrists and the carved bedpost cut off her circulation. Arms over her head, her naked body stretched with her back pressed to the cold, hard wood. She didn't feel the crisp winter chill in the room from the open window anymore. Another small but effective means to torment and degrade her. Numb from the inside out, she stood before her captor, indifferent to whatever he did next.

What did it matter now after all this time?

Every escape attempt futile and foiled.

Every plea for mercy unheeded.

Every day another day of torture to endure.

She didn't know how long she'd been here. The days and nights blurred into one big never-ending nightmare. She stopped wondering if anyone was looking for her, or even cared that she disappeared. She didn't think about the life she'd lost back in L.A. She didn't dream of her future, or regret all the might-have-beens that would probably never be.

She endured each and every day with only one thought in mind: Survive.

Some days, like today, she didn't know why she bothered. Last night, she'd made a mistake. Miscalculated her captor's tenuous hold on sanity. Or maybe more accurately, his need to inflict pain and have his fantasy play out just so. It had to be flawless, the illusion only he saw in his mind but expected her to play to perfection.

Illusion was her stock in trade.

She'd earned three back-to-back Oscar nominations, winning the third, for making people believe the characters she portrayed.

Until now, she'd refused to become the character her captor demanded, wanted, craved.

And she'd paid dearly for it the last many months she'd been here, but most especially last night. Her ribs and back still ached from the beating. Every breath felt like sucking in fire. Her cracked ribs would heal in time. She wasn't so sure about her fractured mind.

It had finally come to the point where she understood, believed she was his—to do with as he pleased.

She would never escape this hell.

"I hope tonight will be different." Brice pulled the ice blue gown from the closet. The elegant dress swished as he draped it over his arm to show it off. She'd worn such beautiful things on dozens of red carpets. But the thought of putting that on *for him* filled her gut with dread and pushed bile up her throat, choking her with fear.

Not that one. Not Aurora from *Flame in the Night.*

Any other character. Any other movie she could play out for him again and again, but this one only ended badly.

Last night's beating would seem like a trip to an amusement park. He wanted to punish her for holding out, holding back day after day, night after night. She'd reached the end of his patience and endurance.

He wanted what he wanted.

And he meant to get it from her, even by force, despite the fact that he knew the only way it would ever be perfect was if she gave in, gave up, and committed to giving him the dream: Her wholly and completely immersed in character and in love with him.

Before tonight, her mind screamed never. Now, that voice whispered its last breath in defeat.

Until tonight, she could not pretend to be the woman he wanted, a made-up character on screen, a woman who adored him with undying love. She could not pretend that she'd find a way out of there. She could not pretend that this was all a terrible nightmare.

She could not do this anymore.

She won the Oscar with her portrayal of Aurora, a woman who falls for a rich and powerful businessman disillusioned with people and the world until he meets her. Aurora reignites his passion for life. The love they share is something neither of them expected.

The movie instantly became a classic romance, one that would probably stand the test of time, and be adored by one generation after the next.

Brice wanted that love story to be his. He wanted Aurora to be his real-life lover. He wanted to have a love like no other. He wanted her to bring that fantasy to life.

But he didn't know how to love. He'd never felt that in his life. Within himself. Or from another.

She didn't think he felt anything at all. Not really. Which is why he tried so hard to feel something.

"You brought on what happened last night. If only you'd stop holding back, we could have the life we both want. We would be the envy of all of Hollywood. The world."

Yes, fans all over the world clamored for every scrap of information about her personal life. They devoured every picture and video of her on TV, the internet, and splashed across tabloid magazines. Didn't matter if the stories were true or not. Didn't matter if the man she was with was just a friend. People imagined an epic love story because that's what she'd given them on screen.

Just like everyone else fantasizing about being a movie star and living the perfect life, Brice wanted to live the dream that she knew was nothing more than illusion.

The backhanded slap across the mouth brought her out of her head and made her present in the moment.

"I'd hoped last night taught you to respond when I talk to you."

Unsure if he asked her a question, or said something that even required comment, she stared at him, hoping for some kind of hint.

None forthcoming, her continued silence, Brice's face contorted with anger at her perceived insolence. He tossed the beautiful gown across the bed and punched her in the ribs to get her attention. Her body bucked and contorted with the force of the smacking blow. Reflex made her try to pull her arms down for protection, but the silken straps held her arms above her head, her body unprotected. Flesh pounded into flesh as another fist socked her in the side, connecting with her already screaming ribs. She didn't cry out at the sickening crack or the excruciating pain that followed. She focused on trying to get her breath, her back pressed to the post behind her, and the feel of the wood against her skin.

Instead of focusing on the roar of pain, she lost herself in her mind and the dream she'd created by the rippling river: the cool water flowing over her bare feet, the sun warm on her hair and shoulders, the sound of the wind whispering through the pretty green trees all around her. Peace.

A trick she'd taught herself weeks into her captivity because she couldn't escape her gilded torture chamber, but her mind could take her anywhere she wanted to go.

Lately, a man joined her there at the river, his dark hair and narrowed eyes filled with pain and regret she recognized. Every time she reached out to him, he got further away, but still she held her hand out and ran toward him, hoping to catch him and feel his strong, protective arms around her.

If only she could reach him.

"You will scream for me."

And with those words, her sweet illusion vanished.

Yes, she would scream. The beating wouldn't stop until she did. If she screamed too soon, he'd beat her for being weak. Too late, she might not be able to scream at all. The game had to be played. She knew the rules and the fine line she walked every second of the day.

She'd play her part, or he'd bring on the pain.

He liked to hurt her.

One day, she'd find a way to hurt him.

She'd find a way to escape.

She'd save herself.

And the boy he called son, but treated like an unruly dog that needed to be beaten into submission.

If only he'd make one mistake. Give her one small opening. She'd find a way to overcome the crippling fear of more pain and certain death and take it.

But that day would never come. She knew that now.

The riding crop lashed across her bare thighs, once, twice, again and again as her body absorbed the punishment like a sponge does water, taking it in like memory. Bruises faded, cracked and broken bones mended, but every beating remained a part of her, darkening her mind and heart, leaving an indelible mark on her soul, never evaporating like water from the sponge.

Who would have ever guessed the guy everyone thought funny, charming, and warm was actually a cold-hearted bastard with a sick fascination with torture and pain.

His hand clamped onto her jaw, holding her face in his tight grip. She tried to stay in that place by the river in her mind, fighting to get to that dark-haired man with the reluctant grin he sometimes gave her, but Brice got in her face, demanding her undivided attention. With him this close, his body pressed to her naked one, she could only focus on him and the overwhelming fear twisting her gut. The anticipation vibrating through him rocked through both of them, dilating his eyes with a passion he couldn't fulfill no matter how hard he tried.

She paid dearly for his inability to fuck her. As much as he wanted her, without her devoted performance to his fantasy, he couldn't get what he needed to get it up and find satisfaction. So he found it in the excitement inflicting pain gave him.

She knew exactly what would happen if she finally gave in, gave him what he wanted and he still couldn't take her to bed and finish his fantasy. He'd kill her for giving him everything he wanted and blame her for not being able to be the man, the lover, who fulfilled her every erotic need.

"The sacrifices I've made for you. The things I've done to please you."

He'd cut his thinning, graying brown hair short and styled it like the young actors and rock stars did these days. That messy bed-head look with an edge. He kept his beard trimmed short, though it didn't grow in evenly. Across his cheeks and jaw, the patches were varying shades of brown, gray, and white. It didn't make him look distinguished or youthful. He looked ridiculous. Especially now, when he was dressed in a black skinny leg suit, white shirt, and gray tie. He tried to attain the slim, ripped physique of the men she played opposite in the movies, but with his penchant for fine wine, decadently rich foods, and advanced age, he'd never have the physical perfection of some twenty-something man again. Thirty-six years her senior, he deluded himself into believing a young woman like herself would see a sexy, distinguished, worldly man. All she saw was a delusional old man, trying to be something he'd never been even in his youth.

"You have everything you need here."

A beautiful room filled with antique furniture, thick carpets over gleaming hardwood floors. Priceless floral art on the walls. A plush bed with silk sheets. An all too inviting Jacuzzi tub in the marble bathroom. Velvet drapes over embroidered sheers.

Bars on the windows. Locks on the door. And the converted walk-in closet that served as her cell with its hardwood floor and heavy metal doors with the wood veneer to hide what lay behind from this side of them. No light. No window. An empty, dark box. A place to hold her until she gave him what he wanted.

The rest of the room a temptation she didn't dare want.

But she did, especially when she lay on that cold, hard floor aching from yet another lesson in pain and endurance.

His hand clamped over her breast in a punishing squeeze. She hissed out a pain-filled breath, but he took it for excited passion. "This is what you want."

She wanted it to be over. She didn't want to spend another minute in that black box. She didn't want to hurt anymore. She didn't want to feel anything anymore.

All she had to do was become his living fantasy and it would all be over.

What started as psychological torture and rare outbursts of physical abuse had turned into increasingly dire beatings. The gnawing ache of hunger her constant companion. Every breath hurt. Every bone and muscle ached. Every second she spent alone and lonely and desperate and sad in her cell had become one too many. She couldn't do this anymore. She wanted out. She needed out. One way, or another.

Living in hell, she decided to walk right into the fire and end this once and for all.

"You know what I want."

He took her weary acceptance of the inevitable as breathless anticipation. "What, my darling?"

"To begin our special evening." She had his attention. She normally didn't speak unless spoken to first, or in reaction to Brice reciting lines to her movies and the part he expected her to play.

She cast her gaze toward the pretty, torturous dress on the bed. Despite the weight she'd lost since being held here, he had the dress altered time and again to always be one size too small.

He held it in front of her, down low. She stepped into the gown, spun on her toes to face the bed post, twisting her bindings painfully around her wrists. She blew out all the breath from her lungs. Brice muscled the zipper up her back, taking his time and prolonging her pain as the too-tight dress closed over her bruised back and battered ribs.

His hands rested on her bare shoulders. She sucked in a shallow breath, needing the air, but hating the pain it caused as her lungs filled and constricted against the confines of the heavy dress that pushed her breasts up until they nearly spilled out the top. Just the way he liked it.

His fingers combed through her tangled mass of oily hair. He hadn't allowed her the luxury of a shower in three days. He mussed it more, letting it spill down her back and shoulders. His body pressed against her back, pushing her chest into the bedpost as he reached above her and lifted the strap off the metal hook, stretching her arms so high it felt like her arms might pop right out of the sockets. She endured the painful prickles and tingling as blood rushed down her arms and into her hands. She didn't move. Couldn't with his body smashing hers into the post.

He dipped his head to her ear. "Don't disappoint me tonight."

She leaned back into him. Despite the layers of satin and chiffon of the full skirt keeping her skin from touching him, the creepy crawlies danced over her nerves. His arm wrapped around her middle, squeezing her already aching ribs until they screamed with pain. She held it together, even as his thin lips pressed to her cheek.

"Has the scene been set?"

He vibrated with anticipation. "Yes. Oh, yes."

"Then let's begin." A single tear slipped past her lashes and rolled down her cheek. She hadn't cried in a long time, having spent her many tears long ago. But something about reaching the end, knowing all was lost and that she just couldn't take it one more second, sent a wave of grief deep into her soul and shattered it.

Brice took her hand and raised it to his lips, kissing the back of it like some gallant knight in shining armor. He didn't mean to save her. The devil in him wanted to destroy her. She feared he already had, but tonight would be the end.

Finally.

Like the prince in Cinderella, Brice dropped to one knee, picked up the crystal encrusted heels, and slid them onto her feet. He stared up at her with such worship. If she didn't know the monster behind those adoring eyes, she might actually believe he loved her.

She walked with him out of her beautiful cell and down the hallway, knowing she walked to her death like an inmate leaving death row for the last time.

At the top of the stairs, she stared past the living room to the beautiful dining room table laden with expensive white china and sparkling crystal glasses. Covered dishes held the fragrant food he'd never actually allow her to eat. The incessant gnawing hunger in her gut made her mouth water. She wanted to run to that table and gorge, but fear and painful memories froze her in place.

"Look at the beautiful garden, Aurora."

Without a window in her cell, she craved the outdoors, the pretty landscape. Even at night, she longed to be out there and smell the flowers, the wind, any sense of freedom. But he wouldn't let her out there and tortured her with the gorgeous view.

At least that's what she originally thought, but over time she realized he had some strange fascination with the garden. A look came into his eyes when he stared at it, like he saw more than anyone else.

His eyes were filled with that overexcited look right now. "I'll go down first. Then you can have your moment and sweep down the stairs to me."

She glanced at him, his eyes sparkling with anticipation. "Of course."

Brice rushed down the stairs. She prayed he stumbled and fell to his death. He hit the landing in the wide foyer and turned to stare up at her. Dressed in the elegant suit, he appeared the picture of an eager gentleman waiting for his lady love.

I am Aurora.

She embraced the numbness, swept her tangled mass of hair over her shoulder, put her trembling hand on the banister, and forced herself to take the first step to her death. She made her way down each tread with her head held high, the dress swept out behind her, her gaze locked on Brice just like in the film. She showed him the regal woman while on the inside the pain and anguishing inevitability crushed her heart and soul.

Brice took her hand at the end of the stairs again. The triumphant smile made her stomach sour. He led her to the table, held her chair out, and pushed it in as she sat, ignoring the piercing pain radiating from the backs of her bruised thighs.

Just like in the movie, she held her wine glass out to him. "Let's celebrate." The words stuck in her throat, but she pushed them out with a breathy tone that had the anticipation in Brice's gaze flaring with passion that turned her stomach.

Brice filled her glass with red wine just like Duncan had for Aurora.

He held his glass up. "A love meant to be will find a way." The line from Duncan was meant to convey the love he and Aurora found when after months of living in the same building, probably passing each other dozens of times but never seeing each other, Duncan discovered her struggling in the pool when a leg cramp made it difficult for her to get to the edge. He rescued her. Coming from Brice to her under these circumstance, the words made her skin crawl.

She held her glass out to toast her demise.

The doorbell rang behind her, halting her shaking hand and sending a bolt of fear quaking through her body. She trembled, not knowing what to do or what this meant. Although people came and went from the house, Brice always ensured that when he let her out no one saw her. But Brice let her see them, the influential people who could help her if only they knew she was there. If only they weren't in Brice's pocket. He tormented her with their presence by making her watch them through the two-way mirrors in the secret passages he'd had built into the house. While they enjoyed themselves at the lavish parties Brice threw, she stood behind the glass and watched how Brice ensnared them in a trap they didn't see.

Just like he did to her.

Brice grabbed her by the throat, his fingers biting into her skin and cutting off her breath, and pulled her close. She dropped the wineglass, spilling red wine over the pristine white table cloth.

He growled his frustration at her clumsiness.

She clawed at his hand at her throat, desperate for air.

"I don't know who would dare come here uninvited, but it must be important to drive way the hell out here at this hour. Be good. Don't make me punish you, my sweet Aurora. I'll find out what they want and send them away. Nothing will ruin our night."

He rose and drew her up with him, pushing her back

and releasing her neck at the same time. She coughed and sucked in a much needed breath, her chest constricting against the confining dress, her throat sore from Brice's grip. He took her by the arm and dragged her to the stairs and up. The frosted panes of glass concealed her and whoever was at the door.

"On my way. Be there in a minute," Brice called from the top of the stairs. He rushed her down the hall and into her room, past the luxurious bed, and shoved her into the converted closet turned cell. Weak from being unable to breathe with the constricting dress and the meager food Brice allowed her, she stumbled and fell to her hands and knees. Knowing better than to turn her back on a wild animal, she scrambled away and turned to face him.

"Don't worry, darling, I'll get rid of whoever dared disturb us and be back for you. We will have the perfect night, Aurora."

The doorbell rang downstairs three times. Brice lost the lover's look in his eyes and gave her one last fierce frown, turned, and shoved the heavy metal door closed, rushing off.

She hung her head and breathed a sigh of relief for this short reprieve. When she raised her head again, the sliver of gray light slicing across the dark floor didn't register at first. Then it hit her.

He made a mistake.

He left her an opening.

Literally.

He didn't push the door all the way closed, so the thick automatic bolts hadn't sprung home, locking her in.

No telling how long she had before he came back. She fought the instinctive fear that told her to stay put or face dire consequences that only meant more pain if caught trying to escape. Again.

Nightmares of her earlier attempts swamped her mind, but out of those gruesome images glowed a glimmer of hope that *this time* luck was on her side. She conquered her fear and moved to the heavy metal door, pushing it open an inch at a time, the muscles in her arms quivering with the effort. She listened intently for any sound of Brice's return. Not a floor board squeak or footstep sounded.

Her heartbeat thundered in her ears as she struggled to push the heavy door closed until she heard the familiar thunk of the bolts sliding into position. If Brice didn't open the door again tonight, distracted by his visitor too long to want to play with her again, she'd gain precious time to get away undetected. She didn't know where she was going, only that she needed to get away. Fast.

She crept out the bedroom door. Instead of going left toward the main staircase, she turned right and padded down the hallway past several closed bedroom doors to the back stairs. She tried not to think about what she'd seen people do in those rooms while Brice held her by the neck and forced her to watch through the two-way mirrors. At the end of the hall, she stood in front of the large window staring at the rolling gray clouds darkening the sky and closing in fast. The last thing she needed was to get caught in a storm, but wet and cold was better than locked up or dead any day.

She opened the door next to her, knowing exactly what she had to do even if it was dangerous and would slow her down.

"Do you want to stay here or go with me?"

Adam deserved a chance to make his own decision

after his life had been decided for him, and she held part of the blame.

He nodded. Lucky for her, he was dressed with his shoes on. "We have to run. Get your coat and hat."

Adam disappeared into his closet and came back with a blue knit cap on his head and one arm stuffed into his red coat. She took his hand and pulled him with her down the back stairs. At the bottom, she unlocked the French door and opened it slowly, hoping it didn't creak and give her away. Taking the four-year-old might be the right thing to do, but it added a level of danger and consequence that might be her downfall.

After the way she'd been treated, knowing how the boy suffered, she had to do everything in her power to keep him safe.

She quietly closed the door, fighting every urge in her brain and body to bolt. No lights shown on this side of the house, but she couldn't take a chance Brice or his guest spotted them through the massive windows facing the beautiful garden and rolling land. She couldn't go around the front and to the road and risk being caught if they were out on the porch, driveway, or still standing in the entry. The only way to go would be the hardest path, but she'd take it and hope that she got them both away from this house of horrors.

Her heels clicked on the flagstone path along the veranda leading to the garden. She pulled them off and ran barefoot over the gravel to a huge tree. She ducked behind it, keeping Adam close. He didn't make a sound, but pressed to her side, his body trembling as even he understood the danger they faced.

She glanced back at the house. The only lights were from the dining room and kitchen. Another light went on in Brice's study. If she ran to the left, across the horse pasture, she'd hit the road in about a mile, but Brice could certainly see her scaling over the wood split rail fence in her bright light blue gown. Her only option was to go right across the back of the property. She didn't know what lay that way, but anything was better than the punishment waiting for her if Brice caught them.

She leaned down close to Adam's ear. "We have to run. Really fast."

Adam nodded, squeezed her hand, and ran beside her all the way across the garden until they crossed the manicured lawn and hit the dirt beltway that separated the ranch property from the vast landscape that made up the acres and acres of land Brice owned, giving him the privacy he craved and needed to keep his dirty secrets.

*G*ive in to your Impulses!

These unforgettable stories only take a second to buy and give you hours of reading pleasure!

Go to *www.AvonImpulse.com* and see what we have to offer.

Available wherever e-books are sold.

AVONIMPULSE